Devil's Laughter
*The Devil Laughs When You
Make Plans*

BY

Barbara Stewart

Published by New Generation Publishing in 2013
Copyright © Barbara Stewart 2013
First Edition

www.newgeneration-publishing.com

New Generation **Publishing**

Prologue

'Looks like they've finished, Vi. That's Zet, the daughter. She's let 'erself go, no mistake, used to be so smart, too. Looks pale as death, don't she?'

'On 'er own, too. Where's he, then? You'd 'ave thought at a time like this...Odd if you ask me, Audrey.'
'They was always odd, that family, Vi.

Like somethin' out of the *News Of the World*, it was. I could tell you a thing or two about the goings on in that 'ouse, which reminds me....' 'What?'

'Tell y' later. Fancy a cuppa?' 'Wouldn't say no.'

***

Standing at the open door, you know that those windows are not as empty as they look. In this street of whispers there is nowhere to hide. There are no front gardens here; no wall, fence or bush. Walk out of the front door on to the pavement and you face an audience of windows, reflecting, today, a slate grey sky.

Crow Street, the eyes and ears of London's East End, will be missing nothing, neither the black vehicle parked in the road, nor the man waiting to close the rear doors when the job is done.

'That the lot then, luv?' he calls cheerfully, and your stomach gives a sickening lurch because you know what will happen next. You know that everything you once knew will be taken away from you.

'Yes.' You nervously clear your throat. 'Yes, that's it.'

'Bye then, luv.' He is powerfully built - they always are - dressed, despite the weather, just in denims and navy-blue sweater. Watching him crash the black doors together, quite irreverently, is a shock; you hadn't expected it to be so undignified.

Doors fixed, he turns back, giving you an admiring dark wink and an unshaven grin. They all flirt, don't they?

3

Even with a thin, hollow-cheeked woman who has done nothing to her pale hair and pale face this morning.

Embarrassed, you feel a flush warm your cheeks and glance down as if you don't recognise yourself; long legs, icy cold in stiff denim that matches your eyes but doesn't fit where it touches any more; boots still muddy where you had earlier walked in the park beside the river.

Watching him walk away, you feel a stirring of shame. You weren't very nice to him; he's only doing his job. A rough diamond if there ever was one, yet the pugnacious face has a kind look. Maybe he understands.

You swallow hard, wondering why, when you have often said how much you hate this street and certainly have few happy memories of the house, you are feeling weepy? A stranger's kindness perhaps. Doesn't help. And it isn't his fault, the hair, the way it is; long and tied back in a ponytail, reminding you of someone you once knew and have, you could say – you could almost say – forgotten.

You slip your cold hands into the pockets of your leather jacket, automatically checking that the wedding ring hasn't slipped off. It's loose now; you'll lose it, Zet, if you're not careful.

He is pulling open the cab door now and you call an apologetic, 'thank you,' as if he and his scruffy, gum-chewing mate have done you a favour. Your voice sounds thin, perhaps he didn't hear, but he waves before he climbs into the cab, slamming the door behind him. Somehow you find it necessary to watch, the way you are drawn to watch a coffin disappear into the ground, knowing that this lump of anguish called a heart will, almost unbearably, sink with it.

With a tormented grinding of engine parts, the van heaves itself away as if the weight inside is too much. The sides of the van, with the words House Clearance just visible because rain has washed off some of the grime, almost touches the houses each side of Crow Street as it rumbles off, taking with it your childhood and the remains of a life, leaving behind just the sickly stink of diesel fumes.

Inside, you lean back against the door, closing your eyes. Hearing the familiar click of the catch as the door closes, you wonder how an atmosphere from years ago can linger. This dim passage somehow reminds you of sadness, of goodbyes rather than hello's.

Opening your eyes, you remind yourself that you had not intended to stay. A quick - in, do the job and out - was what you had, sensibly, planned. Those who know you - or think they do - often say, "There's no sentiment in Zet. Zet's the practical, unemotional sort. Steel bends easier than Zet does."

You had hoped that this would be the case today but it seems that the unexpected surge of memory in this house where you grew up has shaken you. Bracing yourself, you move away from the door, imagining with dread the bareboned rooms, as unfamiliar as another planet and just as lifeless. Like my life, you can't help thinking, not so much sorry for yourself as hurt and bewildered by the tragedy of it all when you had planned it to be so different. You feel a spine chilling dread of change and a dread of things staying the same. God, what a mess. And there's nothing here to help you, if that's what you're hoping. Not in the aching loneliness of this empty house.

High-heeled boots beating on unfamiliar floorboards like drums at a military funeral, you pass from the passage into the unfamiliar emptiness of the tiny front room, and it leaps for your throat...the message... *gone*. I can't bear this, you think. But you have to bear it; the practical side of you knows that. This is one thing you can't run away from, even though the urge to run from the rest of your life is making you feel, lately, like a pressure cooker about to explode.

The front room smells damp with that unlived in cavelike odour of old houses. The chill sinks like teeth through

5

your jacket to your bones, you're shivering, and that is all you feel - bones in a bag of skin.

You can't just go, it seems. You have to say goodbye. You are riveted to the chugging of the van...it's at the pub on the corner now...it's turning into the main road and ... that's it.

Alone. Even the word sounds like a hole. This morning, clearing out the house had felt terribly like another bereavement. You hadn't expected that this would be the last, the real goodbye.

Beyond this room, there are sounds that seem sordid, out of place. The joyful rush of rain flowing into drains, gurgling in gutters; the steely whine of a train; a plane groaning overhead like a bellyache; the harsh busy clanking of cranes towering beside the Thames; impatient vehicles swishing past on the main road. But inside ...inside there is unnatural silence, into which your breath flies like loud whispers. The whispers become words, past conversations, a ripple of laughter, footsteps on stairs. It seems as if the room comes alive with dancing sunlight and moves into you; you can smell roses, hear the Spanish singer and the click of castanets. Imagination, Zet. Don't be silly. Nevertheless, you turn your head, listening.

As you do, something catches your eye, over in the corner, where the sofa once stood. On the bare brown floorboards, you see a scream of red. Once there was music, always music. Now there are only your footsteps drumming on the floorboards, as you cross the room to check.

Just a shrivelled burst balloon, clinging to old dust... and a howl begins deep inside you. There was a night once, a family night, especially happy for some reason; something good had happened and then it went wrong. It was to do with a secret, a secret told and the party was over.

The smell and taste of years gone by – laughter and tears, familiar voices, a sexy tango - rush back like a slap in the face, taking your breath away and hurting so much that all you can do is wrap your thin arms around yourself as if keeping broken bits together.

Leaving the room, you start to climb the disturbingly loud stairs. Near the top there's a bend and here, in your imagination, you can see a little girl in pyjamas sitting unobserved, listening to secrets, not understanding, not then, about love, passion, violence and grief. Grief at the loss of a child. The wrong child.

Reaching the landing, going into the front bedroom, you see that the removal of heavy furniture has revealed, like flotsam left by a receding tide, a dusty powder puff, a Spanish fan, a wine-bottle cork, an empty scent bottle - and yourself, left behind.

Honestly, Zet, furniture in bare rooms, smelling invisible perfume, hearing voices from long ago, you think, crossing the room. Get real.

You are standing at the window now, staring out with unseeing eyes. It isn't only this, the loss, the empty rooms, you think, clenching your hands until your nails scratch your palms. it's...where do I go from here? When I leave this house where do I go; what shall I do?

Rain taps against the glass and suddenly it's as if the teeth of a dog sink into the back of your neck, holding you there. And when it starts… the sudden leakage of clinging sweat, your heart pounding and that twist of fear in your stomach… you know how close you are to the edge.

Zet is the most controlled person on earth, people say.

Over the next few weeks, you will be explaining to those same people, who cannot believe that you could do such a thing...'I left the house feeling as empty as a paper bag; I had no way of resisting it.'

Now, pressing your forehead against the ache of cold glass, it's uncanny the way you feel that you have been like this before, just like this...at the window, alone and afraid. Even more uncanny is the presence you feel beside you.

7

I'm not alone, you suddenly realise. I have company.

You feel no fear, realising, almost straight away, that the ghost is yourself as a child, waiting to take you back, waiting to find out how and why; why it all went wrong. 'Help me,' you whisper.

The ghost holds out a hand.

Part One

Chapter One

The hands of the white faced wall clock came together like a prayer. It was time for the old year to go and Zet wasn't sorry. Apart from the fact that the year had brought no changes for the better, an East End nightclub, panting with hot blooded hysteria, was hardly her idea of a good time.

As Old Lang Syne was drowned by squeakers, poppers and screams of 'happy new year,' and balloons floated down, she wondered, like most people there, what the new year would bring. She knew what she wanted, how she wanted her life to be. She always had. She had written the script years ago.

With balloons bursting all around and rainbow coloured streamers landing on her neat blonde hair and black jacket, she politely returned the kiss from a brown-haired man she felt she knew and then lost sight of him as she was hugged by over-excited friends and tugged into the circle. She didn't feel part of it all, the tears, laughter, loud boisterous singing and kissing strangers.

She was only here because her mother had suddenly decided to hold one of her awful parties. Years later, when her life had gone wrong, Zet would look back and think how destiny plays tricks. If her mother had received a more exciting offer, up West, say, or if one of her chesty coughs had come on, Zet would have stayed at home and her life might have gone as she had for so long planned.

Her friends, in the taxi coming here, had been excitedly chatting about their own plans. Their desires seemed to go no further than tonight as they giggled about meeting the man of their dreams and falling in love.

Here? No chance. Zet had kept quiet. Her imagined man would not be seen dead in a place like this. These girls she had known at school, with whom she had nothing in common except familiarity, fell in love – if there was such a thing – so carelessly and lived without direction,

11

neither of which was Zet's way of life at all. She was different, always had been, she knew it and they knew it too, which in their eyes gave her a spurious kind of glamour. She had attitude, an envious amount of freedom and a mother people gossiped about.

Colliding with hot, jigging bodies, she was nearly pulled off her feet, losing one of her shoes and her dignity. She had to hobble around until someone – it was the brown-haired stranger- retrieved it and held it out to her. He helped her balance as she slipped the shoe on, he untangled her from bodies and streamers, ignored hands trying to pull them back into the circle, and led her from the dance floor. She went with him. Why did she do that? What else was there?

There was relief. Relief at being off the floor, away from the scrum! There was a chance to smooth her hair, catch her breath and remember that she hadn't thanked him. She turned to do so with one of her full strength smiles, her first real smile of the evening. The rare, brilliant smile, wide and face transforming, that caught people unawares.

The stranger - for she soon realised they had never met before – looking stunned, quickly recovered and found a vacant table and two red plastic seats before he went to the bar. He returned with his face, above the Campari soda and glass of beer, looking anxious, as if he expected her to have disappeared. They raised their glasses to welcome nineteen seventy-nine; after which, he tried, above the beat of the roof-raising rock group and things that squeaked and popped, to introduce himself.

'Jonathan Bestwellen.'

Waving a dismissive hand, she shook her head. Trying to talk over the music and noisy celebrations was too much effort and what was the point anyway? While he had been helpful, and she was grateful, she really couldn't care less who he was.

While she sipped her drink, wishing the night was over, violently coloured lights moved around the room; some, like Smarties, fell across his face, and she turned away from the deep-set brown eyes that were observing her with interest. Don't encourage him. She never dated local men; she had other plans. She also had determination.

As the lights swept away across a room tipsy with Christmas decorations, she half heartedly returned the waves of friends still jigging on the dance floor. Mandy gave a thumbs up sign, Cathy indicated for Zet to join them, which she answered with a firm shake of her head.

'Wild horses wouldn't drag me back there,' Zet told him, with a brief glance over her shoulder, as if confiding a secret. He was encouraged enough to drag his chair closer and speak into her ear.

'I could tell you weren't enjoying it.'

She turned on him with a raised chin and one of her affronted looks, 'How do you know what I was feeling?' Finding his face so close, she moved back a bit.

Not seeming to notice the coldness in her voice, he smiled knowingly. 'You don't fit in.'

He was right, of course, but this stranger's mental probing made her uncomfortable; she would go to the cloakroom, wait for her friends there.

She would have done, in fact she was about to stand up, if he had not said, indicating the packed dance floor, 'You're classy, too good for this lot.'

So she remained there. 'You don't know me.' she said, with a shrug.

'I have eyes, I can see. But you're right. I don't even know your name.'

He had a pleasant smile, and her shoulders rose and fell as she gave a resigned sigh.

'Rosetta Swanne, called Zet.'

'My friends call me Jonty.' His hot breath puffed into her ear and she moved sideways, away from him. The

13

faint smell of beer was not unpleasant. He was just too close.

***

The music had lowered to smoochy; he could actually hear the clink of glasses as bar staff, tired and indifferent, began snatching up endless empties. Draining his glass, he set it down on the table. 'I think they're trying to tell us something,' he said, with a wink, as a passing waiter grabbed it. Then he gave her a long assessing look, intrigued *...lovely smile ...doesn't flirt...not up for grabs...too beautiful to be available...so different.* And yet something, maybe the mood of the night, or the beer that had loosened his tongue, made him take a chance.

'What about meeting for an Indian one evening?' he asked, knowing he wasn't the strutting, outgoing sort girls went for and expecting to be turned down. He wasn't wrong.

He inwardly cringed at the cool, doubtful expression in the blue gaze she turned on him. In the end, she shrugged and he knew it was no good. Flicking paper strands from the black dress and jacket that he thought suited her smooth blonde looks well, she turned away, scanning the room.

Trying not to sound desperate, he offered, 'Another drink before they close the bar?'

'I'm all right, thank you.' Without turning, she indicated her glass, still half full. 'I hate cloakroom queues; I'll hang on a bit.'

She sounded dismissive. It was useless, he could tell. She had her back to him, he noticed how straight her back was, how upright she sat, yet in a graceful way. She was watching the crowd unsteadily pushing and shoving their way towards the cloakroom. He was obviously nothing, in her eyes. But something in him didn't want to give up.

14

Something about her was pulling him towards her, but she was pulling away and he was so longing to see that smile.

'The night's not over yet, Zet. And no work tomorrow.'

She stifled a yawn, 'What do you do, anyway?'

'I'm with the London office of Cullen International,' he told the back of her smooth head. 'Used to be Adam Cullen but the Company expanded.' Not a hair out of place, he thought, when other women around them were looking the worse for wear. And despite her slim, graceful figure, she had an air of competence and strength; she wasn't fluffy or giggly. She seemed very self assured, there was something controlled about her; she was not the sort to be moved by pleading.

He didn't want to appear desperate. It was just that he wasn't usually so drawn to a woman at a first meeting. Sad, but nothing he could do about it. He pushed back his chair with an irritated scrape on the wooden floor. suddenly anxious to go. 'I'd better....'

She twisted round to face him. He was about to stand up when she set her glass down on the table and studied him as if seeing him for the first time. 'I remember reading a newspaper report about your Company.'

He answered her questions politely but reluctantly. Why was she pretending to be interested? He knew he sounded sulky and dull, but as he described the Company's activities and the new thrusting and ambitious chairman, he sensed a change come over her; the chill had left her voice; her eyes were alert and curious and she even looked impressed.

'So you are Product Marketing Executive.'

'That's right.' Settling back in his seat, he teased, 'Do you want a reference?'

'Just interested,' she said, cool again, as the music and flashing lights died, sallow, disconsolate main lights came on, the musicians started to pack up equipment, and her friends bore down upon them on waves of alcohol induced love.

He stood up. His good mood had burst like the balloons around them. He knew he sounded sulky when he said goodnight and turned away towards a group of his friends. How odd that despite not knowing her, leaving her gave him a sense of loss. *You could fall in love with a smile.*

Without finishing her drink, she stood up. Flicking streamers from the shoulders of her black Biba jacket on to the debris strewn floor, she told her unsteady friends who were sharing her taxi that she would be with them in a minute, and they got the message and so did Jonty's friends, who went away with the sort of nudge, nudge, wink, wink that happens on these occasions. She ignored them.

'Make it Chinese,' she said coolly, before heading for the cloakroom, 'And I'll come.'

Chapter Two

An icy wind swirled the long black coat around her straight-backed, slender figure as she dodged the high street's Friday night crowds, high heeled leather boots pounding the pavement with the resolute stride of someone who knew where she was going.

She could see him ahead, a friendly looking, sturdy man, a couple of inches taller than her five foot six. It wasn't just the warm glow spread by the newly-opened restaurant that felt welcoming and inviting, it was also his relieved grin when he spotted her. It was oddly like seeing someone she had known for a long time.

Inside was warm and spicy; there was a dignified, orderly atmosphere, crisp royal blue tablecloths, napkins stiff as beaten egg whites, gleaming cutlery and glassware and attentive waiters, all of which suited Zet admirably, for she liked order in her life, not having had much of it.

After the usual settling in seats and ordering from the menu, they talked and unexpectedly, she found herself liking him. He wasn't loud and overpowering, there were no innuendos, he didn't make silly jokes or act as if he expected her to go to bed with him. He was natural and easy to be with. So at first, the talking was easy. And then, her heart sank.

'You live with your parents?' he asked.

There was a pause. 'My mother. I live with Her. He lives somewhere else. What about you?' she asked, changing the subject.

'My parents are o.k. Still together,' he grinned. 'Can't imagine them being anything else; they're closer than this,' he said, crossing his fingers.

Haunted by memory flashes of her childhood, Zet could find nothing to say. Looking at him, dark head bent, concentrating upon extracting prawns from his rice, it crossed her mind that there had been an edge to his voice.

17

'I'm mad on sea food,' he smiled, looking up, catching her watching him, and she, with inner warmth beneath her cool surface, decided she was mistaken.

As they ate, she learned about his 'A' level passes, that he liked playing cricket and that West Ham was the greatest football team on earth. To a background of low music, tinkling glasses and hum of conversation, she encouraged him to talk about his job, and wasn't surprised when he casually told her, 'I've been told I'm in line for my Manager's job when he retires.'

He'll go far, went through her mind. As she ate, she felt an inner flush of excitement and recognition. She valued achievement, especially when confirmed by financial awards, and admired people who got on.

He had stopped talking and was watching her with eyes softly lit, as if - and the idea made her insides flush again - she was wonderful. 'I've gone on a bit, what about you?' he asked with his generous smile.

What could she say? For a moment she played with her chopsticks before answering. If only she had a career that was brilliant and interesting. 'I'm a dental receptionist,' she admitted at last. 'Oh, just to fill a gap until I find something more interesting. You know how it is,' she added with a bright smile, picking up food with the chopsticks.

Anyway, so what? She had been lucky. 'The dentist is my Gran's brother's son-in-law,' she explained as she ate. After a sip of wine, she added, with what she hoped was a fond smile, 'He was desperate for a receptionist so I offered to help.'

'You'll be good at it too, you seem the cool, calm type.' He gave up on the chopsticks and picked up a fork. Before he ate, he gave her one of his assessing looks. 'But you don't like it,' he guessed.

He was right but she frowned, irritated by his assumptions about her. He laid down his fork and looked at her intently as she remained silent, slowly chewing her food. She rinsed her mouth with wine, hoping he wouldn't ask how many exams she had passed. Her fear of job interviews amounted to a phobia; in fact, any form of exam or test was an insurmountable obstacle. Rejection made her break up inside. Fortunately, she had taught herself to act with confidence and self-assurance. She could appear bold to those who didn't know her, and no one did. She allowed no one close enough.

'What would you like to do, then, Zet?'

His voice was warm, his eyes interested, but she hesitated. If he knew what her real ambition was he would run a mile. She pretended to concentrate upon choosing from a dish. The truth is, she had long ago decided what she wanted from life. It wasn't a career she was after. She thought about her lack of experience, not to mention exam passes. She reminded herself that her salary was good, enabling her to dress well, and there was another advantage, one that would help to attain her objective.

The surgery being a private practice meant that she met successful businessmen, men with drive, ambition, and a good salary. Somewhere in the wings waited her imagined man. The man who would tick all the boxes.

Suddenly aware that Jonty was watching her from across the table, waiting for an answer to his question, she moved uncomfortably in her chair. Why not tell him about her only talent? At least it was some sort of achievement she could brag about. 'My friends think I'm mad,' she began. 'I like housekeeping.'

His brow furrowed. 'Really?'

She nodded. 'I run everything at home.' My mother, she had been going to say, is hopeless, but she stopped herself just in time, for she didn't want to tell him about Iris. She didn't want to tell *anyone* about Iris.

Instead, Zet told him, 'I have a diploma in Cookery,' watching his reaction. She didn't mention that her father had paid for the Course she attended in London; she didn't want to talk about him, either. Neither did she explain that she only took the Course to avoid working where most of her neighbours did, in one of the surrounding factories, and had been surprised to find that she had a talent for cooking. To her relief, Jonty looked impressed.

'So you are planning a catering career?' he asked, helping himself from dishes on the table. 'Maybe open your own restaurant one day.'

'Well...er...' She really had no ambition like that. 'I would need to gain a lot more experience first and it's not that easy.' She broke off, pretending to concentrate upon choosing from a dish before she went on.

'The dentist needed someone, so I stepped in to do him a favour and, well,' she sighed, 'I stayed.'

'Where did you get your lovely name from?' he asked, as the waiter removed plates and brought coffee. Zet answered with little enthusiasm.

'I was named after a film star my mother once knew; she was Irish, I think, killed in a car crash in America before I was born.' There was more to it than that but...mustn't bore him. 'My mother,' she said, as if she hated the word, 'is mad on the cinema.' A pause, and...'I never go. I prefer live theatre.'

'I prefer the theatre myself,' he agreed, a lazy smile showing – she noted - perfect teeth. 'Your mother sounds interesting... knowing a film star, I mean.'

Zet stirred her coffee into a muddy whirlpool, breathing the fragrant steam. She loved freshly ground coffee. 'A mother with her head in the clouds isn't much fun,' she pointed out, clicking the silver spoon down in the delicate china saucer.

He lit a cigarette and inhaled. He had looked at her admiringly when she said she didn't smoke. 'You don't take after her then,' he said, studying her curiously. 'You obviously have your feet firmly on the ground, Zet.'

'One of us had to,' she said, a steely note in her light, somehow controlled, voice. He looked puzzled, and on the verge of asking questions. Quickly, she finished her coffee, replaced the cup in the saucer, smiled widely and thanked him for the meal. Looking dazzled, he called for the bill.

While he paid, Zet took up her crumpled napkin and folded it into a neat square, and then into a triangle. After which, she ran her fingers over the napkin, thoughtfully ironing out the creases, and mentally ticking boxes.

As their dates became regular, she wasn't at all surprised to find that Jonty, with his earnest eyes, friendly smile and untidy hair, was exactly as he appeared to the world; nice, genuine, the sort of man you warm to and trust. Most importantly, he was intelligent and ambitious.

She learned that he lived with his parents in Dagenham, his only sister had recently married, he always had a cheerful remark for children and he was patient with old people, even her sharp-eyed, outspoken Gran who, to Zet's annoyance, they bumped into in East Ham one Saturday afternoon after Zet had been with Jonty to her first and, she silently vowed, her last, football match.

'Thank you, darling,' Gran fluttered and flirted when he politely took her overloaded shopping bags and offered to drive her home. On the way, Gran drew him out about his family, tutting and calling him, "poor lad," when she learned that his father had been very strict, especially about his son's education.

There was no playing truant for him, Zet thought, mind going back to her own childhood as she watched the listless, once busy docks silently pass by the car window.

Sitting in the back, along with Gran's lumpy bags, settled comfortably on the leather seat, she thought about herself…twenty and going nowhere. She wasn't keen on her job and the atmosphere at home was uncomfortable.

As a child, she had so wanted to be clever but to her intense disappointment and frustration, she couldn't keep up. The reason, an overheard conversation between two teachers suggested, was the tragedy and her home life. A child of a sad, broken home, they called her, as if she had a terminal illness. School was a place of no hope. The teachers had labelled her and let her fall. Where she landed, however, was up to her; and it wouldn't be in this muck heap!

Wrinkling her nose, she glanced from the window and gave Jonty directions. He turned the car into one of the ugly streets of terraced houses almost bowing at the feet of the towering factories. Catching his eye in the mirror, she smiled, calm on the surface, but arriving at the house, helping to cleave Gran from the car, her mind was busy.

Had she at last met her imagined man? If so, it would be true to say that she wanted him, and the life she could have with him, more than anything in the world. Her stomach churned, excited because in her mind's eye she could see her future exactly as she had planned it to be. Was she on her way? Could she make this dream come true?

There was just one hurdle to jump. Well, two actually. Families.

Chapter Three

Restless, unable to relax, Zet was looking for something to distract her. No good worrying about what the afternoon would bring. She could handle it.

Glancing at one of her mother's magazines, one article caught her eye. *Want to change your life? Want something better? Don't just wait for it to happen. Paint the house, take up a new hobby, travel, or make a garden. You'll be surprised how even one small change can bring about others.*

Morning sunshine fell across the page, drawing her attention to the window through which she could see everything she wanted to escape from. Past her own back yard and square of dirt, fences and the backs of squashed together houses seemed to be closing in on her. There was no sky. One day she would have sky. In the meantime…if and when Jonty came here,…she glanced around the room and out through the window. What would he think? An idea formed.

The clink of the fork hitting stones set her teeth on edge, but she didn't like being beaten. Flowers. She would have flowers here; she had made up her mind about it.

Rows of back windows peered at her like malicious eyes, watching her battle with thistles, thorns, nettles and long, tough grass. People around here had heard Iris say often, 'Once she makes up her mind, that's it. Stubborn, that's Zet.'

Pulling off the old leather gloves that had once belonged to her mother, she rubbed the sweat from her brow. Despite the gloves, her hands were stinging. Sitting back on her heels, she stretched to ease the ache in her shoulders and took a moment to think about Jonty.

Nice, the way he smiled with his eyes, the way he talked without clever or flirtatious innuendos, the way lines appeared on his brow when he was being earnest.

23

And amusing, the way he enjoyed his food. He would be interesting to cook for. They were compatible in other ways, too. She felt her insides move with excitement when she thought how perfect it was.

Going inside for a cold drink, she saw they were up. Tony the Tan, as she called him, and Iris, dark hair in masses of creamy-tipped curls, petite in the flowing rose-sprigged negligee she had triumphantly bought at Petticoat Lane in which, she boasted, she felt like Elizabeth. Elizabeth Taylor, she meant.

The milk slipped down Zet's throat like cool silk but she frowned. It would take a miracle to turn the ugly back yard into a garden. She voiced her frustration aloud and Iris, humming with the radio, looked up from painting her nails purple. 'You want perfection,' she said, blowing on her nails. 'You can't get it in this life, pet.' Zet was drawn, as usual, to snap.

'You can talk. What about all that dolling yourself up and dieting?'

'That's different,' Iris shrugged, coughing and flicking her lighter at the cigarette dangling in her mouth. 'Can't be too careful with your health.'

Tony lowered his head over the newspaper, isolated by shaggy sun-streaked hair and a cloud of smoke; a cigarette was burning in an ashtray. Zet couldn't keep the dislike from her voice.

'It would help if you got rid of those Spanish plonk bottles and the rubbish in the yard. Like that paint you "found." He looked up, narrowing his eyes.

'I can get a good price for that.'

'I'm fed up with this tip,' she said coldly, and he pointed a finger at her.

'Don't move in on my space. I don't like it. And if you think you're too good for this house, get out. All right Miss Snooty?' With a malicious grin, he reached for his cigarette, flicked off the ash, missing the ashtray, and put the cigarette to his mouth, inhaling deeply, leaving Zet feeling as if she had been punched in the stomach.

'You always spoil things, Zet,' Iris accused.

Raising her chin, Zet walked out, followed by her mother's voice singing to the radio… '*I never promised you a rose garden.*'

Zet saw her mother as a child, an infuriating, and sometimes naïve child, with an insatiable need to be amused. In fact, it was almost as if their positions were reversed. It was Zet who preferred a quiet life and took responsibility for the home.

Zet sighed, forcing the spade into hard grey soil. There was something about Iris, something about the expression in her seal brown eyes that looked surprised to find herself where she was; as if she expected to be, or thought she should be, somewhere far better. Sometimes her face was lit up, at other times the light went out, followed by a small-voiced, 'Oh, well, never mind.'

Tony had moved in just over a year ago. He was larger than life, a bear against Iris; charming, jolly, with a short fuse and a habit of patting the starry-eyed Iris's bottom and letting his hand linger. With his mane of fair hair, tanned skin, and blue, faraway eyes, he put you in mind of a sailor but he was in fact a long distance lorry driver. When he was away, Iris wasn't fit to live with and in no time had, as usual, turned things to her advantage. When she could arrange time off from her typing job at the factory, or feign illness, she travelled with him either to France or Spain.

Bashing clods of earth with a rake, Zet gazed around contemptuously at the fenced-in back yards. You can't blame Iris for wanting to get away from here. 'Life is for living,' was one of Iris's sayings. 'It isn't a rehearsal, you only live once.' Hearing a burst of girlish laughter inside the house, Zet raised her eyes to the scrap of sky.

Running the rake across tamed, subdued earth, though, her spirits rose. Beneath her hands something resembling a garden was appearing. She did like her plans to work. Yet, glancing around at the soot-stained house, and up at the window of her little room, her pleasure died. She felt that she didn't belong any more. Strangely, although she hated it here, she was conscious of a sense of loss but more disturbing was that her spat with Tony had left her with the stomach clenching sensation of having been catapulted into the air and left to fall.

Glancing at her watch, she dismissed her morbid thoughts, brushed clinging soil from her hands and hurried indoors, leaving sparrows to swoop down and pounce on displaced worms.

Time to wash and change, Jonty was fetching her at three to take her to meet his parents. And hurrying up the narrow stairs to her back bedroom, she made up her mind that they would like her.

Chapter Four

'Been married twenty-five years, Min and me,' bragged Albert Bestwellen. Min, short plump body, slim ankles, dyed auburn hair and a pale pink smile, forty- five or thereabouts, nodded. Her eyes adored him often and he could obviously do no wrong, of which he was fully aware.

Balancing a bone china cup and saucer on electrified knees, Zet was wishing she were somewhere else. Jonty, brow furrowed, watched her. They all watched her. She sipped weak tea that Gran had a rude name for and in the silent room that smelled of polish, clicked the cup down into the saucer.

'More tea, Jonathan?' 'No, thanks, mum.' 'Albert?'

He nodded, watching Min pour tea into his cup and add milk and sugar. He picked up a spoon and stirred in a slow, precise way. Albert, small and neat with a tough little moustache, thin mouth, watchful dark eyes, thinning dark hair carefully parted at the side, was the sort of man you knew would have shining shoes and clean fingernails, write letters to newspapers, keep files and study his bowel movements.

Catching sight of a nineteen fifties wedding group photograph standing on a solid, polished sideboard, Zet cleared her throat and asked, 'How did you meet?'

Setting his cup down, Albert leaned forward and rubbed his hands: 'Min's home at Plaistow was bombed in the war and her family were re-housed next door to me. She was eleven and I was fourteen.'

Min smiled and nodded. Jonty sighed and inspected the room as if he had never seen it before and Zet forced wonder into her voice.

'So you've known each other since you were children, then?'

'That's right.' He looked pleased and Zet awarded herself a Brownie point.

27

'We have a good marriage,' he went on, 'and I'll tell you why. We put each other first. Children come second. Remember that. Eh, mother?'

Min bobbed her devoted head and inspected her red, swollen-knuckled hands as if they were medals, while Zet felt uneasy. It's as if Jonty's on the outside, almost as if he isn't here. 'Do you have a job, Mrs. Bestwellen?' she asked brightly.

'Oh, goodness...no, dear,' she answered, and Albert's brows shot up.

'She had Jonathan and Susan to raise and a house to run.'

'I read,' Min said uneasily.

'Not while I'm around, she doesn't,' Albert bragged. Min flushed and Zet pulled in a breath but before she could speak, Jonty broke in.

'Zet's got an uncle lives in Dagenham.'

'And an aunt in Southend,' Zet added, helping him out. 'Another uncle lives in Ilford and one at Basildon, Gran's only got one child at home now, my aunt Sophie, but I've aunts and uncles and cousins scattered all over the place....'

Silence. I hope they don't ask about Iris. Her stomach rumbled and her face felt a lick of warmth. Otherwise, she was cold. An unlit coal effect gas fire stood in front of a boxed in fireplace. Central heating had been put in, but Albert bragged that he worked out the heating units meticulously. In this silent, chilly room in which you just sit and don't eat, clocks, Albert's obsession, ticked like racing pulses.

Zet jumped when Albert spoke, looking at her with narrowed eyes.

'Your parents are divorced, then?' 'That's right,' she said, raising her chin. 'So there's just you and your mother?' Zet hesitated. 'Yes.'

'You must be very close, then, dear,' Min said tentatively.

28

Zet, whose worship of her mother had died a long time before, who found her mother's affairs distasteful and felt, really, as if she had grown up parentless, forced a weak smile and nodded.

'Zet's a dental receptionist, dad. And she's a cook. And she, er....'

Zet's fixed smile was making her cheeks ache. Feeling a twinge from her smarting hands, she said desperately, 'I like gardening.'

To her surprise, Albert's face lit up...well, almost. He began barking questions at her that she couldn't answer; it was like a school exam, she couldn't cope and in the end, red faced, she panicked, admitting she was stuck. 'I don't know where to start,' she blurted and then could have kicked herself but Albert looked pleased.

'You've come to the right place, love. Come outside, I'll show you my garden, and then we'll walk down to my allotment. Poor girl. No man around the house...tch.'

Zet nearly laughed. No man around the house? Those awful night-time sounds from her mother's room, forcing Zet to buy a bedside radio, even though she wasn't particularly a music lover.

'Min, sort out that gardening book I got for Christmas, Zet can borrow it.' Albert became quite animated and throwing Jonty a bright smile, Zet followed him out.

Min's voice drifted after them, 'isn't she elegant, Jonathan? Classy, and clean looking. What a lovely smile.'

'Manure.' Albert's bossy voice moved down the hall. 'I know where you can get some. Dig it well in. I'll let you have some begonias.'

Zet admired people who knew more than she did.

The trouble was.... Now she had met Jonty's family it was time she asked him back to her house, or they would think she had something to hide. *Didn't she just.*

Chapter Five

Jonty looked dazed, as well he might. 'With love from dad,' he said, handing Iris a bunch of daffodils, which she received with a queenly gesture. Almost as an afterthought, he gave Zet a dozen tough green shoots wrapped in yesterday's Telegraph. 'Dad said plant them today.'

Gardening was the last thing Zet felt like doing and even Jonty, still reeling from Iris's smacking thank you kiss, looked reluctant as he followed Zet outside.

'Do you like gardening?' she asked, placing a plant into the hole he had made.

'Sure,' he answered, kneeling beside her, pushing a trowel into the earth.

The soil felt warm beneath her hands as she firmed the plant in. He likes my things...gardening, good food, theatre, keeping fit and he wants to get on in life. These things slipped around in her head as she planted and planned, hearing the soft thud of his trowel beside her, breathing the scent of earth and roasting Sunday lunches. And somebody, somewhere, she sniffed, was using creosote.

Loud music and the resonant tones of a radio announcer drifted from open windows and back doors, along with kitchen clatters and voices, car engines, and shrill voiced children playing football in the street. She thought to herself...you can never get away from it, the noise and the smells.

Her own house was unnaturally silent. Her shoulders felt warm from the sun, the plants looked strong and resting back on his haunches, he told her, 'You've made a hit with dad. Mum likes you, too.'

She smiled. Handling the plants, his hands were squat, square-fingered, strong looking, yet she remembered how they felt when he touched her, surprisingly soft and warm, and careful in a way, as if afraid she might break. They

30

hadn't gone all the way yet; she liked him for not trying persuasive tactics the way others did. It really got her back up when they acted as if they had the right.

When friends taunted her for still being a virgin - sex by numbers apparently being the contemporary art - she took the smirks from their faces by informing them that they had thrown away their power. To her, it seemed commonsense to hold back. How do you know, though, when the time is right?

'Must wash and check lunch,' she said, and saw his eyes light up. He loves his food, she thought, getting to her feet and brushing her hands down her tight-fitting jeans.

'I am a bit peckish,' he admitted with a grin that she thought was really quite lovable. She also noticed him eyeing her body greedily. He had big appetites, this man, she realised. The time isn't right yet.

Indoors, she cast a critical look round. Apart from a lava lamp, an airbrushed picture of a pair of huge red lips eating a spoonful of syrup, and an Elvis photo print mirror, every spare space was filled with Spanish dolls, fans, a stuffed donkey and the like, because as well as Tony's business trips, they took package holidays to Spain.

Over the years, Zet had taken over the cooking, fed up with the mush that Iris served up – if she had time. Gradually, Zet had added to this the housework in a house always in turmoil with unmade beds, clothes waiting to be washed or ironed and a messy kitchen.

Iris hadn't minded Zet sometimes playing truant from school for the purpose of house cleaning, in fact she was exuberantly grateful. Zet began to study cook books as if she was taking a degree. Feeding her mother, receiving her approval, became a strangely satisfying experience. She fed and nurtured the mother who seemingly had little interest in doing the same for her daughter.

This morning, Zet had *suggested* that Iris shouldn't play her music too loud. 'You won't drink too much, will you?' she asked now, glancing at the glass in her mother's hand. 'And please don't you and Tony start horsing around.'

Her mother gaped at her, and Zet, suddenly self-conscious, hid her flushed face by peering into the oven. Then she hurried to wash and change, followed upstairs by delicious cooking smells and the sound of the front door slamming as Tony arrived home from the pub where he had arranged to meet a man "on business."

She had already decided to change after working in the garden and pulled from the wardrobe a mini dress in oatmeal, which fitted her perfect figure like a glove; she slipped on matching strappy sandals, leaving her long legs bare. Iris was all in white... hot pants, sequinned boob tube and platform boots.

Returning downstairs, Zet found Jonty looking at photographs on the mantelpiece; he was holding one in his hand, gazing down at it. It was a black and white photograph of an angelic, bubble-haired child, and Iris gave a pleased laugh.

'That's me,' she said, in a breathy voice. Bright brown eyes fringed by false lashes were watching his reaction. 'I was in pictures.'

'Right,' Jonty joked, winking at Zet. Iris looked deflated.

Anyone would think, Zet thought, pulling the cork from the wine, that Jonty was interested in Iris's silly chatter. He also seemed comfortable with Tony, and was asking about his foreign trips when Zet called everyone to the table.

'Don't you go abroad for holidays, then, mate?' Tony asked, as they took their places. Looking down at his plate, he asked, 'what's this?' which he always did and which annoyed Zet intensely.

'Beef Wellington.'

He shrugged, declined Zet's offer of wine and poured himself a sizzling beer. If he burps, Zet thought coldly, I'll kill him. She glanced around. The room seemed crowded with the four of them around the table, what with the sofa, armchairs, the new wall unit and the television. One day, she promised herself, I'll have a house with a separate dining room, like Jonty's parents, and a room just to sit in.

Jonty was shaking his head. 'Dad doesn't believe in foreign holidays; he's British, he says. So it was Yarmouth for us. I go away with my mates now, we usually go to the Broads, hire a boat, you know.'

'I've been to Yarmouth,' Iris said in a comforting voice, 'its nice there.'

Jonty smiled at her.

'I'd like to go abroad,' Zet remarked, passing round a vegetable dish. 'Not Spain, but somewhere nicer.'

'We could go together.' Jonty said hopefully, spoon poised over glazed carrots.

The vegetable dish paused, and then moved on as they helped themselves. Tasting the succulent beef and the sauce that went with it, Zet relaxed a bit; the meal was good. Then she anxiously realised that Jonty looked taken aback by a bombardment of foreign holiday suggestions from Tony and Iris. Hardly noticing the good food they were gobbling, they were more interested in showing off what experienced travellers they were. They sound pushy and bossy, Zet brooded, hating them.

Hurrying through a perfectly turned out ice cream bombe that they hardly noticed, they couldn't wait to bring out the photos. Worst of all, just what Zet had dreaded... Iris played a record she had brought back from Spain, rummaged in a drawer, brought out castanets and treated Jonty to her version of flamenco.

Cringing, Zet glimpsed something bemused on Jonty's face when Iris landed, laughing uproariously, in Tony's lap.

This couldn't happen in his house. Zet cleared the table with an irritated clatter, not knowing that Jonty was warming himself against her family like someone coming in from the cold and had, at that moment, begun to adore Iris.

Afterwards, Zet escaped with him to her favourite place.

Chapter Six

'That was a wonderful meal,' he told her. He sounded as if he meant it, and she inwardly glowed with pleasure.

Beds of early roses gave out a scent like talcum as they crossed the grass and climbed stone steps to walk beside the river. Behind them, factories were steaming like kettles as she told him, not of the hours she had spent in this park when she should have been at school, but of her childhood dream of crossing the Thames on the ferry to Woolwich, in South London, which was considered to be nicer than the East End.

'What did you find when you did go over to South London?' he asked with a teasing smile.

'No dirty old factories, for a start,' she retorted defensively, 'really good shops and...'

'We have those in East Ham and Romford.'

'Yes, but,' looking across the river, she pointed out, 'you can see from here, behind the town, green hills and woods; that's what I like, but I haven't seen much of it yet.'

'South London has Kent, we have Essex. Do you know, Zet, a crowd of us used to go cycling,' he smiled, 'and you'd be surprised how ordinary a distant beautiful view can be when you reach it.'

***

She looked irritated. When she thrust her chin in the air like that, and an icy gleam came into her blue eyes, you sensed that, despite her delicate look, there was steel there. He had a sinking feeling it was something he'd said.

She was feminine and strong, a fascinating mixture; different from any other woman he had known. He loved her paleness, her long legs, the slender outline of her thighs beneath her clothes. The pert firmness of her small breasts in his hands nearly sent him through the roof! He longed to make love to her but he sensed her holding back. Is she really as unresponsive as she seems? Or am I too careful? She isn't like other girls. But Zet's dignified, classy, he reminded himself. Maybe the back seat of a car isn't her sort of thing and she's right.

She was a queen to him, and that wonderful smile! He wondered if now she had invited him home, next time Iris and Tony were out, or away.... He imagined his hand slipping between those long legs.

He realised two things. He had an erection and she was talking while staring intently into his face like a child afraid someone will take its toys. He sighed heavily and shoved a hand into his warm pocket.

'I'm going to live in a house that breathes fresh air,' she was saying firmly, 'and doesn't jostle for space with the one next door. I want a proper garden, with flowers and my own tree. I want a view and space and sky. It would be lovely to live in the country…' She paused before adding insistently, 'don't you think?'

'Well, yes,' he shrugged, with a softening and yearning that he knew must show on his face. She looked pleased.

***

Hearing a throbbing engine, she turned her head to watch a rusty looking tanker pushing its way down river towards the open sea. A sudden surge from the tanker's wash sent tea-coloured water leaping, creamy headed, towards the park, depositing a piece of driftwood on a forlorn looking strip of shingle beach just below where they were standing. The water was clawing at the grey wood and sucking at mud the colour of pale, uncooked liver and smelled of dirty mops.

Wrinkling her nose, she turned away, walking towards a wooden bench. Jonty followed more slowly. Sitting down, gazing across the river, she felt the wooden bench,

36

smooth and warm beneath her thighs, shudder as he sat down beside her. She turned and saw his hair, as soft and easy as his nature, lift in a sudden breeze. 'You should use a spray, Jonty, to control it.' She put out her hand, smoothing it down.

The breeze carried the lonely squawking of gulls and had a chill in it that reminded her that summer wasn't here yet. But at least they were a long way from autumn. She shivered. Light shimmered through the branches of a chestnut tree; pale shadows stretched fingers towards the seat where they were sitting; sky like sour milk gleamed down eerily on to the shimmering mud.

'I can imagine tea clippers billowing up the Thames, can't you?' he said.

Not really, no. All she saw was decayed, slimy driftwood stranded on the beach and staring at it with dislike, she felt, illogically, that the park had let her down. This had been her special place, and she had so wanted to show it to him.

Turning back to him, she felt her insides flush. Her skin tingled, the way it did when she was anticipating, or organising, an important occasion, aiming for perfection, determined not to fail. Restless, she stood up.

Walking back, without speaking, through the park, he stopped beside some shrubs; nothing special, rather prickly looking things smelling like herbal shampoo. Looking at him questioningly, she met a dark, needy stare. He seemed to be turning over something in his mind. She waited.

At last he surprised her by saying, in his genuine way, voice deep and emotional... 'I like your family.'

You must be joking, she thought, with the taste of lemon ice cream still in her mouth. He was staring at her intently; it was a look that made her insides react as if she were in a fast descending lift; she felt she should say something.

She felt the soft, warm grip of his fingers on each of her upper arms, as if holding her there, she saw the movement in his throat as he swallowed, and she saw his forehead crinkle; he looked earnest and anxious and vulnerable.

'But when,' he asked, "can we be alone?'

A shock ran through her body. This is it then, decision time. She blew out her breath as if she had been running. Looking into his face she saw anxiety, need, and a safe place for her dream of the perfect future. She saw her imagined man.

Her body flushed, but she carefully kept her voice controlled. 'They're going up West on Saturday night.' She smiled brilliantly. 'If you want to come round…'

'Want to?' he echoed, bending his head. It was a long, sweet kiss they shared, different from their other kisses. It was scent on the breeze, a commitment, sunshine and the promise of a new life, better than she had ever known. It was a sublime moment, wrapped in his arms, feeling that nothing in the world could hurt her, even in autumn.

Zet's father gave them a splendid wedding. Zet had decided to have no bridesmaids. 'We'll put the money towards furniture,' she sensibly decided, although she asked Aunt Sophie to be her Maid of Honour.

What she refused to do, regardless of tradition, was ride to the church with her father. Instead, it was Aunt Sophie who rode with her, wearing a long dress in raspberry pink that she enthused would be perfect for the firm's dinner and dance.

Zet met her father at the church door. Maurice Swanne was a mild looking, sad-eyed man, no taller than Zet. He seemed thinner, and older, than she remembered. People once said they were alike but although they shared the same fair hair, Zet's eyes were a sharper blue, her square jaw stronger, her mouth set more stubbornly than her father's sensitive curve. He worked in the nearby sugar refinery, as his father had before him. He was a foreman now, apparently, not that he had ever shown interest in promotion; he was a plodder with few enthusiasms, fond of doing nothing.

Standing in the porch in heavy white satin brocade, wearing a tiara on a head buzzing with plans, Zet felt on her cheek, like a shock, the cool-lipped, cautious kiss of a father she had hardly known.

'Be happy, Rosie.'

Rosie! She hadn't heard that name for ages and something clutched her throat. As her harassed, pink-faced aunt fussed around her, arranging her train, there was triumph in the smile Zet threw her father across the roses and freesias.

'I intend to be,' she said in her best steely voice, chin raised, holding his gaze. 'A very happy family,' she stressed, her voice accusing.

The old scorn was there, the score had not been settled, not even by this fabulous wedding or the white Rolls Royce or the generous gift of money towards a deposit on one of those new houses near Epping Forest. She didn't hear his sharp intake of breath or see the swiftly concealed pain in his eyes, for the organ thundered into the wedding march. She only lightly rested a steady hand on the arm he offered and swished down the heavily scented, fidgeting aisle with him - a stranger - beside her.

Confident and unafraid, her head was already filled with plans of how she intended her future to be. Like a film she had watched many times before, she passed the turning faces of her friends, relatives, her boss, a watery-eyed Gran, Jonty's family and friends, her "Jackie Kennedy for the day" mother, Tony and his tan squeezed into a rented suit, and on towards Mr. Right. As planned.

And, as planned, the sun shone brilliantly, following her inside so that as Jonty turned, Zet appeared to be floating towards him through a tunnel of light... smiling, beautiful, serene, and his. He could hardly believe his luck.

The great doors silently swung together, dimming the church, shutting out the sunshine along with a raucous sound like screams of laughter. The gulls from the river, of course.

Or the sound of the devil laughing?

Chapter Seven

Through bursts of determined laughter, shrill voices and deep-voiced conversation, she only just caught what he said, and the thrill was almost sexual.

'Your husband's a lucky man.'

With a polite, careful smile on her face, she flushed with pleasure. 'I don't know about that, Mr. Wainwright.'

'Jack, please.'

He was probably the only guest here tonight whom she genuinely liked. She was full of admiration for the way he had started from the bottom and worked his way up to Northern Manager. Looking at him, she met astute granite eyes in a craggy face, topped by a head rather like a brown egg edged with wispy grey hair. His down-to-earth manner matched his tough physical appearance and what you saw was what you got; humour as dry as a stone wall, a big-hearted extrovert. His smile was kind.

'You're a grand lass to arrange this do.'

'Hotels can be lonely,' she said, checking the room with an eagle eye. 'This gives you a chance to socialise with your colleagues.'

'Tell you what,' he winked. 'Your dinners have done Jonty's reputation no harm, either. My wife would run a mile rather than organise one.'

Moving aside to let a woman squeeze past, he added, 'I rang through to Yorkshire tonight, told her about your dinners.'

Zet hid a smile. Bet she hates me. She remembered his wife at a Company dinner; a patronising, artificially gracious show off; acted like royalty. 'It's no trouble,' she said aloud. 'I love doing it.'

'She said to make sure and tell her what sort of house you've got.'

Surprised at his bluntness, Zet took a sip from her glass. His shrewd eyes missed nothing, and she felt proud as his glance swept the room, passing through immaculate

41

posing bodies and resting upon large framed photographs of snowy mountains. Glistening tiers and peaks sent out a glacial blue and white light, you could almost feel their tingling coldness. She followed his gaze.

'One of Jonty's friends is a photographer; he blew up our holiday photographs. I thought the stainless steel frames suited them.'

'Effective,' he nodded, going on to survey glass fronted cabinets, lamps, glass tables and great vases holding dried grasses and wheat. The patio doors that took up one wall were pulled back, making the garden seem to spill into the room, bringing with it the scent of fragrant climbers, tobacco plants and roses.

'Nice for you to be near the forest. And you've a bit of garden.'

She smiled. The garden seemed large to her. 'I wanted space around me. I like being near trees, too, so, yes, this is perfect. Would you like a refill?' she offered, seeing his glass was empty.

Handing over the glass, he pulled a fat cigar from his top pocket. 'Please,' he answered with a smile, 'then I must circulate.'

Weaving across the room, smiling into shrewd, moneymaking eyes, which never left the ball, Zet basked in the pleasure of it all. The house was perfect, especially this room which was great for entertaining. She loved the way her strappy shoes sank into the thick carpet, and how the warm red and royal blue Axminster complemented the cool blue ice shade of the leather sofa and armchairs. She loved the body-warmed air; loaded words blending with expensive perfume, whisky and brandy; the rumbling conversation laced with sudden laughter…

Polite voices, hand against heart… 'Believe me…'

Narrow eyes… 'I told him, old boy. I won't take no for an answer.'

Taut sympathy… 'Of course. Oh, I know….' 'Have you… you know… heard anything…?'

42

Measuring glances, ringing tones, gunshot exclamations, egos that, like dandruff, appear with dark suits. She came upon Jonty and stood beside him with a carefully amused smile while he finished a story. She was no good with jokes, and waited patiently until baying laughter burst from the listeners.

'Can you take Jack a whisky and soda?' she smiled, touching his arm, seeing from the corner of her eye that someone stood alone.

'Sure.' He reached for the empty glass.

Handing it to him, she made her way to Jonty's boss's wife, Brenda Gleeson of the rip-roaring laugh, horsy teeth and angular bones barely covered by an expensive black dress that did nothing for her sallow skin. She was sipping gin and tonic.

'Where did you get that super dress, Brenda?'

The woman beamed. 'Where else, Zet darling, but my little place in Bond Street? ' Shrewd eyes did a swift reccy, 'and how brave to wear that brilliant scarlet with your colouring. Now tell me,' her voice became hushed, 'do you really do all the food yourself for these dinners?' She spoke as if Zet had told her someone had died.

'I like cooking,' Zet told her, annoyed to hear the defensive note in her voice.

'In that case, you could make a career of it, darling!'

'I prefer to concentrate upon my home for the moment,' Zet said, with a polite smile. Then, fearing she sounded boring, added, 'until the children are older, then we'll see.' She knew that Brenda ran a craft shop.

'But what do you do,' Brenda cried, 'to keep your mind active?'

'Well…I'm studying porcelain doll-making and aromatherapy at the College.' Brenda looked as horrified as if Zet had said she was learning Chinese.

'But my dear, will those subjects get you anywhere?'

Zet's fingers tightened around the stem of her glass. 'I don't know about that, I just find it fascinating to make dolls from start to finish. Anyway, aromatherapy is fashionable,' she pointed out. 'It's just a hobby.'

She trembled slightly, nails digging into the palm of her free hand. Across the room, Jonty was talking and listening in his open, eager way, head slightly to one side. His hair was more neatly styled these days, but still became wayward at times. Pulling in a breath, she uncurled her hand and forced her body to relax.

Nothing meant more to him than being at home. Feeling calmer, she smiled to herself, remembering the slammed front door announcing his arrival, brief case thumping on the hall carpet, his boyish grin coming through the kitchen door. And right here, where she felt safe, was where she wanted to be at the moment, thank you very much.

'We have a lot of interests,' she was saying, as Brenda's husband, Lewis, came up, a Roman nosed raconteur with sculptured hair, portly, desk-bound pale and shrewd.

'What's this about interests?' he asked, looking at Zet with raised brows.

'I was telling Brenda,' Zet said carefully, 'I don't have time to get bored. We go to the theatre and gym, we belong to the tennis club and Jonty's started to play golf.' Golf is good, she had told Jonty. You meet the right people.

Sipping whisky and soda, he moved closer. She felt his hand, damp and plump, touch her bare back, fingers splayed, and she thought of the squid on the fishmonger's slab that morning. Sipping red wine did little to ease her dry mouth.

'Our Jonty's a lucky man,' he winked. 'And it hasn't escaped us that his wife is an asset to the Company too. Don't play yourself down, you're a talented girl.' He eyed her keenly. 'I get the impression that anything you attempt, you do well.'

44

Zet was surprised. 'Thank you.' She couldn't resist throwing a pleased smile in Brenda's direction, until she became uncomfortably aware that his searching, penetrating stare was still fixed on her. She felt a twinge of anxiety. What was he seeing?

He smiled. 'You're a good looker, too. You remind me of the film star, Grace Kelly.'

'That's irrelevant, Lewis,' Brenda snapped. 'Why are women only judged by their looks? The eighties woman....'

Lewis removed his hand from Zet's back, leaving a soggy imprint. He drained his glass. 'We're not going to start on about the woman thing, are we?'

Brenda opened her mouth but smiling carefully, Zet excused herself, placing her glass on a nearby table. 'I must go up and check on the children.'

Picking up a doll and a book from the floor and straightening Alyson's Little Pony quilt, she went over the evening. She wasn't keen on parties herself, particularly the ones Jonty's mates threw, but anything that was useful or connected with Jonty's job was another matter; mixing with successful people made her feel alive, pumped her with adrenalin. It was a nuisance, this inadequacy that reared its head from time to time, but she was sure no one noticed. Calming thoughts and deep breathing helped, and so, she hoped, would the aromatherapy course.

Remembering the praise she had received, her cheeks glowed. Is it possible, she found herself wondering, as she moved around the room, returning toys to the toy box, to be any happier than I am now? Everything has worked out. Just as planned.

Leaving the room, hearing conversation and laughter drifting from below, she slipped into Darren's neat, tidy room. His Star Wars quilt was smooth on the unruffled bed, his round face saintly, his breathing noisy. Touching his warm forehead, she went to open his window.

The moon was patrolling the clean indigo sky; she could see a star, here and there, unblinking and smug. The moon looked ethereal and magical from here, but she knew it was a mirage, not what it seemed and up close, television pictures showed nothing but ugly, barren rock.

A shadow crossed the patch of moonlight on the lawn below, pale smoke drifted up; she caught its rich aroma. Jack, she thought, seeing his shining head, and turned away, trapped in the cobweb of fear and breathing her way out of it.

No reason for it. Everything's perfect. I made a good choice, she told herself, pulling the curtains firmly together, going out and gently closing the door.

Returning downstairs, she picked up her glass and mingled, up to date on current affairs, a good listener, attentive to their needs - the verbose, the randy, the vacuous, the wingers, the toady, jocular, all as high as a fever.

'How was Norway?' someone asked.

She smiled. 'Wonderful clean air, incredibly beautiful. We usually go to France, but this year we felt like a change and Spain's not my sort of place....'

'Spain's had it,' someone said. 'Try Greece.'

'I'm not keen on heat,' she smiled. 'I prefer cooler climates.'

'Unemployment has hit three million,' she heard someone say in a deadly serious voice.

A moth flew into the room, and she heard it sizzle against the glass lampshade. Moving towards the doors, she gave them a gentle tug and they ran smoothly together, closing against other winged intruders who might get their wings burned.

Lying beside Jonty in bed, she was too aroused to go to sleep.

Leaning towards the bedside table, she picked up a pen and, by the glow from the Teasmade and moonlight,

46

scribbled on a pad.... anchovies, prawns, coffee, cheeses. That should satisfy the appetites of Jonty's friends tomorrow evening.

She felt it raging inside her, the skin-prickling demand that could never be assuaged until every job was completed. It wasn't that she couldn't relax, she could, as long as she was organised and once everything had been taken care of.

The bedsprings creaked; she felt the excited heat of his body as his warm hand snaked across her taut, well- exercised body, scrunching up her long, silk nightie. Electricity in her body made it cling to her skin, resisting him.

Smiling to herself, she turned on to her back, reached across and pulled his head towards her, feeling his lips, plump and damp against her neck. He smelled, familiarly, of mint toothpaste and Pears soap. Hiding his face in her shoulder, his body, a little plumper and softer than it had once been, clung as if he was trying to climb inside her.

Her mind drifted... along Safeway's lanes, reaching out for cottage cheese... fat free, heaven reduced, odourless. And rubber scented Dutch cheese. Folding her arms around him, welcoming his burning flesh, the skin on his back felt smooth yet tough, like cantaloupe melon, her hands, moving downwards, felt the rounded buttocks. He moved away to wriggle, breathless as a runner, out of his pyjama bottoms. She held up her arms and the fragrant silk nightdress, crackling cross- resistance, rose up and over her face and disappeared somewhere.

He was an exuberant lover. Pushing her legs apart, he thrust into her. The plumber, she remembered...must ring the plumber tomorrow ...the washing machine's on the blink. He came out dripping, triumphant and limp, like a baby fallen asleep over a bottle.

With a satisfied glow, she turned her face to kiss him goodnight. He was supporting himself by one elbow, eyes mooning, hungry looking.

'Do you love me?'

Her pale brows rose. 'Course I do, you silly thing, don't I show it?' She knew what his answer would be.

'You're wonderful.' He spoke as if he couldn't believe his luck. 'I love you.'

'Good.' That settled, she turned and leaned out of bed, scrabbling on the floor, finding her calm, white, lavender scented nightdress and slipping into it, enjoying its cool freshness, before snuggling down, secure in the knowledge that everything was as it should be. Sex with your husband gives you a safe, comfortable feeling, part of the familiar routine of home. She quite liked it.

Listening to his steady breathing, she drifted into contented sleep... Dear Jonty, hardworking, unselfish, easy to live with, we never argue.... so lucky. Perfect....

The following day, they came closer to arguing than they ever had before.

Chapter Eight

Jonty pulled open the mock oak front door. 'I'll walk to the car with you, Mr. Swanne.' He smiled kindly at the man standing a little awkwardly in the hall,

Zet blew out her lips with relief. She felt the way you do when you remove tight shoes. In contrast Alyson and Darren were jumping around Maurice, doing everything they could to keep him there. Zet pulled the children away, 'Your friend's upstairs waiting,' she said shortly. 'Off you go Darren. Alyson, tidy your room.'

'Oh, mum...'

'Never mind mum. Off you go. Bye, Maurice.'

Darren thumped upstairs, Jonty went to speak to a neighbour, Alyson tugged the sleeve of Maurice's grey suit jacket. 'Ask her, granddad.'

Suspicious, Zet looked from one to the other. 'Ask me what?'

Giving no sign that he had heard her impatient sigh, Maurice reached into his pocket and pulled out his pipe. Alyson, with a wary glance at her mother, ran upstairs, slim and daintily built, fair hair bouncing behind an Alice band.

Taking his time, Maurice drew a matchbox from his jacket pocket and fumbled for a match. 'I was telling Alyson about the dolls' house.' The match scraped, flamed.

'Dolls' house?' she asked sharply, the scent of his tobacco taking her back to a place she didn't want to visit.

After a moment puffing with obvious pleasure, he pulled the pipe from his mouth and said, 'The one I made for you when you were little.' His brow creased. 'I promised Alyson I'd ask you if you still have it, maybe in the loft, or at your mother's.'

There was suddenly silence in her head. Until she became aware of a car screeching past, driven by an angry young driver; someone starting up a lawnmower; Jonty talking to Geoff next door, who was cleaning his new Rover.

'It was broken,' she said curtly, digging her hands deep into the mauve tunic she wore over grey trousers. 'I threw it.'

He looked down at the pipe in his hand. He had been clever with his hands. Local children all used to come to him for their rabbit hutches and things. It seemed an age before he said, 'I could have mended it, love.'

She shook her head. 'You were never there,' she reminded him coldly. What was he trying to pretend he was, the doting father? Too late for that. 'Goodbye, then,' she said, about to turn away and go inside. Instead, something sprang between them, holding her in a vice. It was his silent, penetrating stare. It was a frozen moment, heavy with words, vital words, about to be spoken. Fear leapt inside her. She looked down at her nails. When she looked up the moment had passed and he was walking away with those defeated slanting shoulders that irritated her. The words remained unspoken.

Watching him go, she had a feeling in her bones that something was not quite right. There had been raw grief in his face; she only just realized it. But why should there be? He had done what he wanted to do. He had wrecked her childhood and didn't care. Furthermore, she reminded herself, he had never said sorry.

A curious black cat glanced her way and slunk across the open plan lawn, making for her neat flowerbeds; deep in thought, she turned and went inside and unable to believe his luck, the cat began to dig.

Standing at the window, she watched Jonty join her father, shake his hand and wave him away in his grey car. A dusty, lazy, ordinary sort of car, the sort that you somehow knew never went anywhere adventurous or exciting. Or fast.

All she needed was for Jonty to seek her out in the kitchen, saying, 'We should invite your dad to stay.'

'I don't particularly want him to, darling. We've never been close,' she reminded him, checking the items on the Formica work surface.

'The kids adore him,' Jonty argued, unfamiliarly awkward. 'And it's a long journey home.'

'Oh, come on! He's not elderly, he's capable of driving thirty miles.' Barely hiding her irritation, she mentally noted... rice, smoked haddock, cod, onions, celery, cream, mayonnaise, prawns, and mussels. Trust Maurice to stir things up, and why, after all these years, had he mentioned the dolls' house?

Envy of everyone in the street, it had been; beautifully made, they all said. She thought back to the day, soon after he left home, when she had struggled to throw the heavy dolls' house on the skip. There were always skips in the streets in those days, filled with lead fireplaces, yellow sinks, and rubble from knocking two rooms into one.

The following morning when she left to go to school, the skip was still there...the dolls' house had gone.

Strangely enough...why hadn't she realised it before? She glanced from the window at the houses well spaced out around them, Tudorbethan executive homes, a replica of their own and - it was really quite creepy - a replica of the dolls' house.

She heard Jonty's voice from a distance. 'Can I do anything?' he asked stiffly.

She blinked and shook her head and as he sat the kitchen table, rustling the sports pages of the newspaper, she took milk from the fridge and chopped up cod.

She was reaching into the cupboard for anchovy fillets, when Jonty said, 'He looked a bit strained today, I thought. Must be lonely going back to that flat after our lot.' Hearing bumps and bangs above their heads, he glanced up at the ceiling. From Alyson's room drifted the thin, lonely note of a recorder.

'Peaceful, you mean.' Zet forced a smile, more interested in pouring milk over the cod in a saucepan.

Jonty shuddered. 'I'd hate it.'

The smell of fish rose to her nose and clung to her hands. 'But you didn't walk out,' she reminded him, slamming the saucepan down on to the gas ring. Turning to face him, she said firmly, 'look, I've not said much about the past; maybe I haven't made my feelings clear. Maurice betrayed me, as well as my mother. Divorced couples conveniently forget that they are betraying the child as well as breaking up a home.'

She found herself breathing heavily. 'He didn't even say goodbye,' she finished. Her throat closed up. Her next words were strangled.

'It wasn't long after…you know…that nightmare autumn. Wouldn't you think a tragedy like that would…somehow…pull a family together, instead of….?'

His eyes softened as he watched her turn away and take a long time pouring water from the tap into a tumbler, drinking it down as if thirsty.

'I understand, Zet.'

He always did. She rinsed her hands under the tap and dried them on a towel. There was very little they disagreed about and what was she thinking of, anyway, allowing the past to disturb her so?

'Now let's forget it.' Managing a smile, she folded the towel, laid it down neatly and crossed the room. When she reached him she tickled his ear, pressing her slim body against the warmth of his back, enjoying her power. Even with two boisterous children around, Zet never neglected the fact that physical closeness was important in a marriage. She knew he admired her, knew that she was indispensable, as she intended to be. She had no intention of being left, as her mother had been.

Chapter Nine

'It's odd we haven't met before, Sarah,' Zet said, looking down at the small, round, dark-haired girl. 'Jonty said you've been away.'

Sarah smiled and a dimple appeared in each cheek. 'I was in Australia when you married.' Her eyes were round, brilliant, copper brown and curious. 'I've been working my way around the world for the last four years. Been most places,' she said, in a voice with a giggle in it.

'Sorry if I broke up the, er, gang.' Zet said to the girl who had lived almost next door to Jonty for most of their lives and was, Zet had been told, one of the boys. Sarah's eyes followed Jonty, who was serving food and chatting with a group around the up-to- date music centre, enthusing over Spandau Ballet and Wham.

'Jonty looks happy enough,' Sarah observed, turning her bright gaze back to Zet. 'Besides,' she added, 'most of the crowd are going steady now; once one goes, they all go.' Her eyes danced. 'Like lemmings.'

Zet was curious. 'What about you?'

'Me? You're kidding. Apart from the fact that I'm not a bit domesticated, I have things to do,' Sarah said in the confident, hearty voice of the Sports Mistress she had been for a while. 'I'm thinking of working in a ski resort this winter; I've all sorts of plans, I couldn't give up my independence, especially as I believe marriage has only a four year shelf life.'

'It's possible to be married without losing your independence,' Zet challenged.

Sarah's eyes widened. 'Of course, absolutely.'

'Jonty and I married for life,' Zet said tightly. 'We make decisions together. And,' she stressed, 'We like the same things.'

'That's all right then,' answered Sarah cheerfully, adding, 'dear old Jonty wouldn't be bossy anyway. I used to boss him about rotten,' she giggled. As Zet gritted her teeth, she went on, 'He was a good sort. Always lent me money when I was broke...that sort of thing.' Her tone became serious. Looking Zet straight in the eyes, she said, 'Jonty doesn't stand out in a crowd, he's a bit of a clown at times, but we all think the world of him.'

Zet, who had twice tried to speak, gave up.

A quick sip of rum and coke, and Sarah was talking about Jonty's parents. 'His mother's a dear, but we all hated *Him*.'

'Actually,' Zet broke in, 'I find the mother a bit of a doormat. I prefer his father.'

Sarah frowned. 'You weren't around to see the way he belted Jonty.'

'He was a naughty boy, eh?' said Zet, trying to sound amused.

'Rubbish. It was for nothing. Like - if Mr. Bestwellen came home from work and found Jonty not doing his homework, he'd use his leather belt on him.'

'He wanted Jonty to get on,' Zet said, almost as if she knew what to say to annoy this girl. She wasn't disappointed.

'My brother got on,' Sarah retorted, 'without any beating. Jonty called our place his second home. You've met my parents, haven't you? Mum wrote and told me all about you.' There was the slightest wrinkling of her pert little nose.

Jonty visited Sarah's parents more often than he did his own family, but Zet didn't bother to go often. Sarah's father was a loud, jolly man, who drank a bit too much; her mother, a nurse, was Scottish, a busy, practical woman and Zet rather liked her. She certainly treated Jonty more like a son than his own mother did.

Sarah's lively voice broke into Zet's thoughts. 'Didn't Jonty tell you about his father beating him? Maybe I shouldn't have said anything.' She didn't look sorry.

'Don't worry.' Zet faked a smile. 'I won't mention it unless he does. It takes time, in a marriage, for things to come out,' she said and Sarah nodded agreement.

'After all, I've known him longer.'

Turning the conversation over in her mind, Zet made her way through to the dining room; a pang of affection made her tuck her arm into Jonty's and he looked surprised. A grateful grin spread over his face and his eyes shone with a message; love you.

Sarah came up on his other side. Studying the ravaged table, she piled her plate with salad, adding bread and cheese... 'Brie.' She spoke in the ecstatic tone of one who loves, even food, with abandonment. She beamed at them both, speaking over the Rolling Stones, laughter and loud conversation.

'This is going to be a great party, I can always tell.' Addressing Jonty, Sarah added, 'we've had some fantastic parties, our crowd, haven't we, Laddie?'

And to Zet: 'He's mad on sea-food.'

Rolling his eyes, he answered, 'Yummy, yum...'

...'Yum, yum,' Sarah finished, rubbing her tummy, giggling at a private joke.

Zet pointed towards a large earthenware bowl surrounded by dishes of rice and saw Sarah's eyes pop. 'What's that?'

'Mixed fish mayonnaise.'

'Oh! La! La!' Sarah reached for another plate as Jonty, smiling fondly at her eagerness, teased her by holding the colourful bowl of fish out of reach above his head.

Sarah merely laughed and dug him in the ribs until he couldn't stand it and she was able to grab the bowl and serve herself. Turning a disapproving back from such childish behaviour, Zet reached for cottage cheese and crispbread. He's ticklish. I didn't know.

Sarah chewed and gave her verdict, 'Yummy. Different from bangers and mash over a camp fire, eh, or jellied eels at Southend?' she said, dimpling up at Jonty.

He bestowed a brotherly pat on the dark, cropped head way below him and Greg, who had been his best man, came up and started pulling the afternoon's cricket match to pieces while Zet and Sarah turned in opposite directions.

Chapter Ten

They were driving home from duty visits to North Woolwich that Sunday, the blue Ford, smelling of new leather, humming contentedly, the children absorbed in a colouring book their favourite grandmother, Iris, had given them.

Jonty waited until he had steered past a boy wobbling on a bike before saying, 'Your family thinks the sun shines out of your eyes.' Which made Zet laugh.

'You're blinded by prejudice. I was a bit of a cow, you know,' she admitted with an unconcerned shrug, confident that he wouldn't believe her.

'I don't believe you,' he said, driving faster now the road was clear. 'And you're really Sophie's pet, aren't you?'

'Aunt Sophie's special. I used to twist her around my little finger.'

'That, I believe,' he grinned, checking the mirror. 'Why did she never marry?'

A car swept past them. Zet thoughtfully watched it go. 'Don't know.' She wrinkled her brow. 'Sometimes I think....'

'What?' He steered the car into the tree-lined avenue, turning left and beginning to negotiate the twisting road and tee junctions between immaculate lawns, spindly shrubs, young poplars and self-conscious new houses that didn't touch each other.

'Oh, just that there's a mystery somewhere.'

Unloading children and the presents that Zet's shopaholic Gran always gave them, often unusable, she mentally went back over the day.

They had suffered paella from a packet and soggy chips washed down with Spanish wine and hilarity in the company of Iris and Tony and afterwards had taken the children round to see Sophie and Gran, whose birthday it was.

Trooping inside Gran's house with her family, the tiny terraced house always, to Zet, seemed overcrowded and depressing. Faded curtains, which had once been brown with an orange design, hung in the front room; dull green curtains hung lopsided in the back room overlooking a small grey yard where weeds pushed through concrete like whiskers on an old face, and stray cats that Gran insisted upon feeding, relieved themselves and fought their war while, inside, Gran relived her own.

In the cramped front room, kept for special occasions, a barley sugar twist standard lamp stood between brown armchairs, and an old walnut radiogram next to a hard, unyielding wooden-armed settee. Framed family photographs crowded a glass-fronted sideboard stuffed with trinkets. The inevitable studio portraits of Iris as a child hung or stood everywhere interspersed with the more amateur photographs of clear-eyed, gap-toothed unbelievably angelic children now grown-up into far from elegant adults. Zet couldn't say that she liked any of them.

Zet hated coming here. The minute she walked in she felt herself resisting the family chain and the past. Yet today, handing over presents, something unfamiliar looped around her heart and tugged. What must it have been like to be widowed at thirty something, with four children and one on the way? Zet hadn't considered this before. It seems that having children of your own deepens your sensitivity to the pain in the world. Mind you, she pondered, watching Gran's swollen hands gently accept the porcelain doll Zet had made, from all accounts widowhood hadn't condemned her to a life without fun. There was the pearl necklace.

Looking down at Gran, Zet saw tender watering eyes in a pink face crushed like a pressed rose. Looking at the doll on her lap, Gran sounded awed. 'I've never owned anything so beautiful, Zet.' And more sharply, 'How much is it worth?'

Smiling to herself, Zet told her and Gran shook her head.

'Eighty quid. Amazing. Bloomin' clever you are. You should open a shop. What made you go in for it...making dolls, I mean?'

Leaning forward, Zet reached out and straightened the blue crinoline dress the doll wore. Smelling Gran's lily-of-the-valley, she said thoughtfully, 'I don't know; maybe because it's my own creation; something appears out of nothing. I design the clothes, too, and I'm learning how to make the leather shoes.'

'And the hair?'   Patting the gold ringlets, Gran's swollen hands were the colour of the raw bacon she cooked every day in the café; Zet felt her heart contract. 'I buy wigs, but I've booked a course on wig making,' she explained and, awkward with her emotion, jumped up.

'Now, Sophie and I will get tea,' she said bossily, as Gran made a protesting movement. 'Go and talk to Jonty if you can drag him away from cricket on the telly.' Jonty and the children were in the back living room, another room crowded with table and chairs, sideboard, armchairs, television.

In the yellow Formica and brown linoleum kitchen, helping Sophie lay a tray, Zet casually asked, 'enjoying your weekend?' quite unprepared for Sophie to round on her.

'Sundays bloody Sundays. They seem a month long.' Pouring boiling water into the brown pot, Sophie loudly clinked the lid on, her face, not the plump, placid face Zet knew but one pinched by painful emotions. She was filling the room with her resentment. Zet could feel it. Embarrassed, she began arranging chocolate digestives on a plate. 'Well...I love Sundays,' she insisted, 'All my family together.'

59

Sophie looked away. In a flat voice, she said, 'I'm glad everything's worked out for you, Zet.' Avoiding Zet's puzzled eyes, she poured sugar into a bowl. Screwing the neck of the Tate & Lyle packet angrily, as if it was the cause of all her troubles, she placed it in the cupboard of the kitchen cabinet, slammed the door, it wouldn't shut and Sophie struggled with it, slammed it again. It was old. Sophie gave up.

Turning, she added with an edge to her voice, 'you wouldn't put up with anything that didn't work, anything imperfect. You're one of those people who has life all mapped out; I envy your sort. Emotions wouldn't get in the way of your plans.'

'No way,' Zet said, forcing her voice to sound normal, even cheerful, in an effort to change her aunt back into the woman she knew and loved. 'I leave the emotion to you and Gran.' As she spoke, Zet was busy piling cups, saucers and two plastic beakers on a tin tray, covering a picture of a perfect thatched cottage. She remembered this tin tray from years ago, which made the cottage look familiar, as if it was somewhere she had visited.

'But it's not luck,' she argued. 'You have to make a plan and stick to it.' Looking up, she saw Sophie smile sadly.

'You're okay, then, Zet, with your little family?' 'Blissful,' Zet said, picking up the tray and edging

from the cupboard sized room. 'You don't have to worry about me,' she insisted, over her shoulder. 'I've got it all worked out and just like those games we used to play, auntie dear, I'm winning.'

'Hope you're right,' was the moody answer.

'What do you mean?'

Sophie's voice came from behind Zet in the narrow, gloomy passage. 'I always think, when things are going too well something horrible will happen. Just warning you, Zet.'

Chapter Eleven

Early evening, usual time...the front door slams, the Evening Standard slaps down on the hall table, his briefcase thuds down on the floor. All normal.

In a grey marble and dark oak wood kitchen, steaming and sizzling contentment, smelling of steak, kidneys, wine, onions and gravy, Zet heard those familiar sounds above the sensual music of Ravel's Bolero. As she worked, she had been watching the portable television, admiring the skill and perfection of skaters, Torvill and Dean.

Removing a golden puff-pastry pie from the oven, she placed it on the kitchen surface. Perfect. She liked the familiarity of her world, no shocks, no changes.

And then the door opened.

Removing oven gloves, she checked the veg, slipped off her apron, smoothed her hair and walked to meet him smiling, anticipating the feel of his cold, slightly roughened outdoor cheek beneath her indoor warm lips, when his aftershave had worn off and he smelled of fresh air with a tang of office suit and an aura of the outside world about him.

He kissed her first. 'Good news or bad news first, Zet?'

She smiled. He was a bit of a joker. But he couldn't wait; it burst from him.

'I've been promoted.'

Zet's heart gave a leap of joy. Her hands came together as if to clap. 'Darling, that's great.' She opened her mouth to tell him how wonderful he was, for Jonty needed encouragement, but something stopped her. He was no longer smiling; concern crinkled the corners of his eyes and she felt a cold shiver, as he gently held her away from him. He bit his lip, frowning. 'Zet, listen.'

'I'm listening.'

'I'm to be Northern Manager, based at Leeds.' He watched her kindly and carefully, as a doctor might.

'But that's Jack's job.'' Hands locked together, as if frozen in the middle of clapping, she studied his concerned face. 'Isn't it?'

There was a burst of applause, the music ended; expertly controlled skates slithered to a stop on the glistening, deceiving ice. Suddenly aware that vegetables were bubbling nervously in their stainless steel pots, she turned away, crossed the room to turn down the gas and click off the television, returning with a previously prepared tray and a pot of coffee to join him at the breakfast bar where he was now sitting.

She slid on to a stool opposite him. He reached in his jacket pocket for cigarettes, remembered he wasn't supposed to smoke in the kitchen and flung the packet on the bar. His fingers toyed with a raffia tablemat. 'They've got rid of him.' He wouldn't look at her. Instead, he was staring at the cork notice board as if absorbed by sports gear Monday; birthday party Saturday; dentist Tuesday.

'Things haven't been good up there for a while. It's my job to pull it back up.'

Her pulse quickened, but she poured coffee and pushed a mug towards him as if she wasn't buzzing with relieved elation. So that's it; he's worried about the responsibility, that's all.

'You wouldn't be thinking of turning it down, would you?' she asked. suspiciously, watching him help himself to milk and sugar. 'Because if it's my advice you want….'

'They didn't give me the chance,' he interrupted. Looking across the bar, his expression was unusually cynical. 'I was told, not asked.'

Her voice cut sharply into the silence, 'They must have confidence in you.'

'So they said.' He wrapped both hands around the mug, studied his coffee but made no attempt to drink. 'I'll be based in Leeds.'

She had been worried for a moment, now she relaxed and beamed at him, feeling absurdly happy with the world. 'You'll have a long day, ' she said, sipping coffee, 'with the travelling.'

'Zet,' he began cautiously, 'don't you realize where Leeds is? It's a four hour train journey.' He ran fingers through his hair. 'Not possible, I'm afraid.'

The oven timer pinged. Zet felt a hard ball settle in her stomach. 'What are you trying to say?' Studying his wary expression, she experienced a sensation as if someone was running the cold blade of her sharpest kitchen knife down her spine.

'Zet, I'm going to have to get digs for the week and come home at weekends.' His voice said he was relieved to get it over with. 'That's the bad news.'

She put down her mug with a sharp click. 'No.' Her lower lip trembled, like a child's, her hands were gripped tightly in her lap; they were damp.

***

'I thought you'd be pleased about the promotion,' he said unhappily. 'More...' he hesitated... 'security... more money.' He tried to force enthusiasm into his voice, but who was he trying to kid? If Jack, with his record of thirty years hard work and loyalty, could be dismissed so quickly, so callously that he barely had time to clear his desk, how could anyone feel secure?

Stepping into poor Jack's shoes was like sliding on ice. He shivered. It occurred to him that real life meant climbing mountains. Zet, he knew, expected great things of him. For the first time he questioned, with a sinking feeling, whether he cared as much as she did. Am I, he wondered, the climbing mountains sort of bloke?

***

'I am pleased,' she cried, indignantly. 'Of course I am, but...' In her mind's eye she recalled the day her father went to work and didn't come home.

Swallowing hard, Zet added, 'But I'm not hilarious about you being away. Can't we move there?' She saw from his expression that he hadn't expected this; he knew she loved their house.

'Wherever you go,' she announced, firmly, 'I go.' The next minute she was reaching across the bar, curling her fingers around his, coolly insisting, 'That's final.'

He clutched her fingers. 'I might have known,' he said, envying her courage, 'What would I do without you?'

Reaching out, he pulled her head towards him, gazed into her eyes, kissed her mouth, and she felt a wave of pleasure as she moved back from his exuberance and patted his hand.

He slipped from his stool and picked up his mug. 'I'll have a quick wash.'

He looks happy now, she thought, hearing him whistling, "*If I ruled the world*," on his way upstairs. Breathing deeply, she crossed the gently steaming room and, mind whirling, automatically attended to the vegetables, removed plates from the heated drawer, and taking a knife to the pie, she cut into perfect, crisp pastry, releasing a fragrant scent of beef, onions, mushrooms and her special rich gravy.

'Make plans and the Devil laughs,' Gran said in her memory. 'Life doesn't always go the way we want it, Zet.'

Chapter Twelve

'Maybe we took the wrong turning,' he said, steering the car around bends in a dithering, uncertain sort of lane that seemed thin as a strand of spaghetti between a big sky and endless fields. Zet waved the Estate Agent's letter she held in her hand.

'I'm quite capable of following instructions,' she said, as they turned another bend.... Oh, look.' She leaned forward in her seat.

Ahead was a narrow humped bridge - Jonty had to slow the car to squeeze across and above the growling engine, Zet, with the window down, heard a rushing, chuckling sound. There was a river tumbling over boulders and leaping down into a succession of small, foaming waterfalls, full of life and joy and she felt a sharp, deep-down reaction. It was like a sound she had heard all her life that at last she had reached.

The next thing she saw, leaning forward expectantly as the bridge passed behind them, was a village green surrounded by twenty or so cramped and humble looking stone cottages, all flush to the path. Her heart sank. 'I wanted a front garden.'

He glanced at her. 'No point in looking inside the house, then.' He sounded grumpy. 'We've looked at a dozen places already, our buyers are getting impatient,' he ran fingers through his hair. 'I've got just a month left before I'm due at the Leeds office.'

'I know, I know. I just haven't taken to any of the houses we've seen.'

'We've got to go back down south tomorrow, Zet,' he warned as they drew up before a cottage at the end of a row.

She sighed and tried to be co-operative. 'Might as well look while we're here. We need to stretch our legs.'

The thick walled, two hundred year old cottage was the last house in the village, larger than the others, with a garage built on the side.

Zet hid her impatience while he struggled to turn the reluctant great key in the lock. Not quite the roomy cottage with character and roses around the door she had planned. Can't see myself living here. She wrinkled her nose.

'Stop fiddling with it, let's leave it, Jonty.' Pointedly, she spun round and retraced her steps to the car. She had no intention of lowering her standards, running out of time or not. She had her hand on the car door when she was stopped in her tracks by what sounded like a croaking voice. It was the key grating in the lock she saw as she turned round. The low, hefty wooden door, badly in need of painting, squeaked open.

She hesitated.

Inside was very different. The cottage, with mischievous delight, spread out and moved back. The cramped front hid a spacious, low-ceilinged, oak- beamed home.

'Mmm!' Standing in a dim, flag stoned hall, the chilly air smelled of dust and old wood and something else that brought her out in goose bumps. Atmosphere, she supposed.

'Mmm!' She pushed open the latched door to the kitchen. Blinking in sudden light, her heels tapped across the room. Warm beams of sunlight were pushing through cobwebbed panes of glass falling on to the stone floor and spreading across bulging white walls.

'Needs wall units, amongst other things,' Jonty mentioned, pulling a face.

'The windows are crooked,' she observed in a low voice, awestruck.

'So are the walls.' He spoke in the doom laden voice of one who does not like DIY, as he followed her out of the room and across the hall.

In the sitting room, which ran from front to back with a window each end, her eyes ran over a beamed ceiling she could reach up to and an open fireplace wide enough to fit a sofa in. Their glances met, slid away, and he followed her from this room into another.

'A separate dining room.' With a knowing, almost loving, smile, she walked from there into a conservatory.

In silence they watched a secretive spider scuttle away across the concrete floor. Playfully, Jonty went over to a window and wrote in the dust...Jonty loves Zet. Her withering look made him rub it out. Acting abashed, he put his hands behind his back.

But her mind was not on Jonty's play-acting. She was seeing ferns, hanging baskets, wicker furniture, and smelling scent, warm humid scent, even in winter.

Eventually their feet squeaked in amazement up narrow wooden stairs to inspect three bedrooms with sloping floors that sang as you crossed them and old lead fireplaces and wide-silled windows just a foot from the floor.

The front bedroom overlooked the village green and the two back bedrooms looked out across waves of land... green, gold, brown corduroy... circled by hills.

***

'Not what you're used to, Zet,' Jonty said in the low, shivery voice you use in churches and empty houses. 'Different from Epping,' he said, rubbing his cold hands.

'Obviously.' She stared at him with a look in her eyes he had never seen before. It was lust.

Her eyes swept away as if he was invisible. Chilled, he was gripped by the feeling that he wanted to leave this place. As if here, his fear of losing her would become a dreadful reality.

She was like someone in a trance. He touched her pale hand. 'Zet?' and she turned to look at him with unseeing eyes. 'I was just thinking,' she said in a thin unfamiliar voice. She turned away and walked sleepwalker fashion from the room. Awkward and hesitant, he followed.

Hearing the reassuring, everyday feminine clomp of her shoes on the stairs, he dismissed his misgivings. They were both tired, that's all, seen too many houses.

The bolts on the inside of the kitchen door were stiff, they had to practically force the door open, but once outside, pushing through brambles, disturbing intricate spiders' webs, Zet was back to her normal self. He laughed with relief.

All the houses in the terraced row had merely yards at the back, but "theirs", being at the end, had a garden that had once been a lawn and flower beds backed by swaying yew trees. That wasn't all....

As if something signalled, as if she *knew*, she looked at the side of the house, and a secretive looking brick wall. Roses spilled down the wall and over a wrought iron gate, pink, white and butter coloured roses, and she breathed in the scent of honey, musk, and fruit salad as if she never wanted to stop. The gate stood half open, like a beckoning hand. And that's where she went.

With an astonished glance at Jonty, she walked through the gate. He followed with an indulgent smile. The smile slid from his face...and moved to hers. She was enchanted. She saw an abandoned orchard and a garden, creaking and whispering mysteriously in the wind; old dying apple trees, rampaging, sour smelling nettles; rank grass and holly; stinging leaves and arched, branched evil looking thorns, wild flowers and an uneven path. And, secretly, he loathed gardening.

***

Thrilled, she advanced like an explorer...an explorer with a fast beating heart. The path she followed was hardly a path at all; it was a path, she thought, breathing earthy smells, that had forgotten where it was going.

His voice came, somewhat urgently, from behind her. 'Not what you're used to, Zet.'

She glanced down at her smart leather shoes, to which earth clung, and said nothing, dwelling instead on what the Estate Agent had told her. The efficient, dark-haired woman had not found much to say.

The previous owner of the cottage, a woman, had apparently died a few months ago. She had lived alone, suffered from ill health and that's why, Zet thought, the garden is rebelliously rampaging towards the walls as if trying to clamber over and escape to the moors on the other side of the wall.

Smaller, secretive paths disappeared between trees she didn't know the names of but which all looked old and creaked like ships, their untidy heads combed by a strong breeze and she felt a tug on her heart.

She glanced round at him, saw he was trying to read her face.... and laughed. It was a rare, loud clear laugh that made Jonty grin and shrug. She had obviously decided that living here was not on. He didn't fancy clearing a jungle and things needed doing in the house. He didn't do d.i.y. Fingers like thumbs. He watched her lovingly, with an air of patient acceptance.

A curlew scaled the heights and dived back down, its rough cry rippling like laughter. Cool air, musky from bonfires, heather, peat and log fires, touched her cheeks and there were those navy-blue hills and the running, jumping water that made her blood sing along with it. There was a quickening inside her, as if she wanted to fly.

She looked up as a circling bird called something that sounded like...there's more... there's more...there's more.

And indeed, a shiver in her bones told her there was. Oh, yes, there was more.

Chapter Thirteen

'Almost there,' Zet said. Since leaving the motorway, she had been staring through the windscreen, tension and anticipation fluttering in the pit of her stomach.

'This is a wriggly-worm road,' Darren giggled in the back of the car, making Jonty laugh.

'Certainly is.' And addressing Zet, 'Thank God the end's in sight. I don't want to move again in a hurry.'

'Your dad was a big help.'

'You, too,' he told her, manoeuvring the car around a bend. 'You left me nothing to do,' he said with satisfaction. There had been a lot to organise at the office and he found it all unsettling, quite disturbing in fact.

'When you move so far away, your life has to change,' Geoff had warned.

'She might not like it,' Sarah had said.

'It's a big step,' Gary had told him, shaking his head. 'We had to help,' complained Alyson from the back of the car.

'Only your own rooms,' Zet called, staring ahead. 'But I had to help Darren with his.'

'You didn't help me, so there...' 'Liar.'

'That's enough you two,' called their father in his good-natured way, and Zet came to a sudden decision.

'Can you let me out here, Jonty?' They were approaching the village and a little sheepishly, as the car slowed and stopped, she said, in answer to his surprised expression, 'I want to stretch my legs.' She smiled. 'I'll meet you at the cottage.'

He drove on, with two travel weary children wishing out loud, as they had done for most of the journey, that they were back home with their friends, grannies and aunts. 'Why does mummy want to walk, dad?'

Zet wondered too. At home she had seldom walked. But here, and now, on the edge of something – she didn't know what – it was like – suddenly – a leap too far.

71

Soon, she was standing on the bridge, leaning against the low stone wall, watching the river tumble away laughing between banks of overhanging trees. That was the beginning, when she felt her blood racing with the water.

To anyone watching, she looked, standing there alone on the bridge, like a woman waiting for someone.

When she walked alone, with the damp, wild moorland wind tugging her once neat hair, she felt newly washed, filled with peace. She was fascinated by aloneness, by being at one with a big sky, by feeling springy sheep-nibbled grass underfoot instead of pavements. She felt as if a longing locked up inside her had burst out into the open. Yet, she still felt a sense of waiting. It was for more, for wilder places she yearned.

The children settled in well. The old village school was now a converted house; as a result, village children were bussed to and from the new big school on the outskirts of the nearby market town.

If Zet felt the urge for town life, then Harrogate,

York and Leeds were less than an hour away. Everything was perfect. She was living in a bubble of happiness that even the shrieking winds leaning on the cottage walls and the bitter cold of winter wriggling beneath ill-fitting doors and shaking windows could not dispel. And snow – for the first time she enjoyed it. If she heard a warning in the wind...

'Is there a gym around here?' Zet asked, preening a bit in her smart mini dress. 'Too busy 'ere to bother wi' gym and the like,' Norah next door said bluntly.

'Mebbe one at Harrogate,' grandmotherly Lizzie from across the green offered.

Sheila, who ran the shop where they were all gathered, commented across the crusty loaves and stalwart yeasty buns on her counter, 'you need to put on a few pounds, not lose 'em, lass.'

Norah sniffed. 'Them gyms take more pounds from the purse than off the hips, I've 'eard.'

Neighbours were kind, gifts of fruit and vegetables often appeared on the doorstep, but Zet couldn't impress these women. It really annoyed her whenever she came up against a barrier she couldn't cross, so she set to work to change things.

She put a note through every cottage door, inviting the villagers to a housewarming buffet. Just casual, drop in, she said, scrubbing the cottage until it gleamed. She could have cried when no one turned up. Right, she thought grimly....

The following day she went around handing out leftovers. They preferred good home cooking, they told her, to all that posh muck but rather than see it go to waste....

She began to see that she didn't have to sell herself, these people accepted her for what she was, and secretly she felt as if a load had lifted from her shoulders.

'Don't look so down-in-the-mouth,' Jonty teased, coming out of the cottage carrying a suitcase and holdall. 'It's Christmas Eve.'

'As if I didn't know,' Zet answered shortly. She was already at the car, placing neatly wrapped parcels and a box containing a fresh turkey in the boot. A shopping basket filled with homemade chutney, mincemeat, jam and other gifts from the villagers, followed. A tractor was chugging backwards and forwards in a nearby field. The morning smelled of earth and frost and evergreens and wood smoke.

She stared longingly at the blue hills, ice capped like the frosting on the Xmas cake she had made to take with them. 'It would have been nice to spend our first Christmas here.'

73

Jonty looked anxious. 'But it's family.'

'I know.' She forced a smile for the children's sakes. There were so many people to see, and Gran couldn't - or wouldn't - travel here.

'We've always got together at Christmas, all of us,'

Gran said doggedly. 'Once it was every weekend,' she recalled tearfully. 'We used to sing around the piano.'

'I've heard it all before,' Zet had said over the phone, kindly.

Jonty had already given her his Christmas present, and it wasn't at all what she expected. He surprised her.

Guessing that she missed doll making, he had thoughtfully bought her a kiln, so that she would be able to fire her dolls. Funny Christmas present, she supposed, but she was pleased with it. She had all sorts of plans buzzing in her head as she slipped into the car.

I can't wait to get back home and make a start. As they drove away, she turned her head and watched the cottage move back. There was a waiting air about it, and she shivered. It was the same sensation she'd had before Jonty was transferred here.

It was the feeling that something was coming towards her.

Chapter Fourteen

'I hate sacking people, Zet.' Letting his briefcase thud down on to the kitchen floor, Jonty reached out and squashed her to him. His body felt damp, hot and smelled sweaty.

He was heavy, leaning on her and she wriggled away. 'It's your job,' she reminded him sharply, smoothing her hair. 'You know very well that Cullens needs to cut back on staff.'

'Have a heart, Zet.' Turning, he flung himself from the room leaving her staring after him. I thought he was strong.

Overhead, the ceiling groaned as he walked across the sloping bedroom floor, she heard the crash of hangers as he changed out of his business suit. She wished she knew why, when the figures for the northern depot were looking healthier, and Jonty had been congratulated at the last meeting, he seemed tense lately.

He had taken to drinking a whisky and soda after work and she carried his drink and her tea into the newly decorated sitting room. It looked exactly the way she had imagined it that first day they inspected the cottage. She had planned it then. The warm pink and petrol blue colour scheme looked good against dark oak beams; the fireplace was a focal point, with brass ornaments and an arrangement of dried flowers. No need to light a fire; the central heating they had installed was efficient enough and cleaner.

Newly installed French doors were open on to a patio, which always gave Zet a glow of achievement, remembering how she had struggled to lay the stone slabs because Jonty was busy at work and anyway, she had discovered he was no handyman.

She had sorted the garden, too, pushing the undergrowth away, savage with her scythe, finding a certain pleasure in pulling up choking weeds and exposing plants to light and air. She had no sentiment. Anything that opposed her came out. Gardening was gritty reality, a gutsy, physical affair. It was making a plan and sticking to it, letting nothing get in the way. It was, most definitely, writing the script. You have to choose the characters that will go your way and weed out those that won't.

This afternoon, she had enjoyed feeling her fingers spreading in the warm spring soil as she planted stocks behind the alyssum, pressing soil in firmly around them, birdsong shrill in her ears as they hopped around her, searching for worms.

But it was her hidden garden that gave her the most pleasure. This was what she called the wild patch between the dreamy old walls. This was the part of her that she didn't want tamed, and was almost a secret because others seldom went there.

As well as gardening, she spent happy hours making dolls and as a result, had been surprised to find that her cautious offer to give classes at the Women's Institute had been accepted with enthusiasm. So much so that she was planning classes at home once a week and had booked a stall at the Harrogate craft fair to sell her work.

A scream, mixing with shouts and laughter, came from the area beyond the garden shed where a swing had been fixed to the cherry tree. The children had friends in. She sighed contentedly. Then she frowned. It's just Jonty....

I think he's being weak, quite honestly. Everything has turned out so perfectly and he's spoiling it. It's my job to support him, I suppose. But how?

Suddenly restless, she wandered across the room to the front window and looked out. The jangle of the shop bell came faintly across the village green as Norah's big bottom disappeared into the shop, reminding Zet of a conversation there the other day.

The discussion had been about a pub in the next village where there was live music at weekends. Sniffing paraffin, soap and freshly baked bread, Zet had kept quiet

76

about London theatres, the tennis club, golf dinners, nightclubs and the dinners she used to give. She turned from the diamond paned window, an idea forming in her mind, not knowing then… how could she have known….

You walk into an ordinary room and life changes forever.

Chapter Fifteen

The room was not even attractive, just an extension to the old stone inn. Years later when she looked back, she would remember her thoughts when she went inside for the first time. *Nothing exciting is going to happen here, that's for sure.*

Leaving Jonty at the bar, she crossed the well-worn carpet, weaving past shabby tables and chairs, a small dance floor, merging bodies, moving mouths, kind eyes and warm, good-humoured voices, the scent of chips and beer.

A haze of cigarette smoke was drifting towards a low stage and curling up the beam of a spotlight, beneath which a portly, handsome, white-haired man, holding a microphone, was trying to make himself heard above the hum of conversation, through which laughter - kind laughter - was threading.

'Have you heard the one about...?'

A ruddy-faced man kindly indicated two chairs and coolly smiling her thanks, she sat down. Disappointed. We needn't stay long. Carefully crossing her legs, she studied expectant faces, met many a curious eye and when Jonty arrived carrying drinks, her raised brows said...not what we're used to, but a bit of light relief.

The compere's voice was a background to her thoughts. She really couldn't care less about a man rescued after being stranded on a desert island for ten years. Jokes never made her laugh. She was watching Jonty turn with a grateful smile when the man beside him spoke to him. His movable face, with its range of expressions, had lost the vulnerable, worried things. He was always drawn to people who showed him attention.

He glanced over at her, as if for reassurance and she pushed down a prickle of irritation. He's so devoted; he needs me behind him all the time. Which is all very well, but sometimes his total love makes me feel

78

uncomfortable. I can't be that absorbed back to him, and then he looks wounded and I could shake him.

The crowd had gone quiet enough for the Compere's voice to be heard clearly. *'"You can have anything you want," the woman told him, "Well," our rescued castaway said," there is something actually, for ten years I've thought of little else...."*

'"What's that?" the woman replied, moving closer.' The Compere paused before going on. *"I'd give anything," the castaway answered..." for an apple crumble."'*

Amid the jeers, chuckles and applause, Jonty burst into laughter and reached across the table for her hand. Pleased and relieved, she knew that her idea had been the right one. He had been working too hard, that's all. A bit of social life was what he needed; perhaps in the summer they could find a tennis club, too, and he should get back to golf. Returning his smile, it came to her...I've done it. I've achieved my goal. Everything is perfect. She looked down into her glass and found it empty.

He rose from the midst of a seated crowd, dark and rugged, an intensely masculine man with a hint of ruthlessness and inner drive, striking more than handsome. These facts hit Zet instantly and then everything slowed down and moved in slow motion.

'A hand for Brad,' called the Compere, Rita crashed a chord on the electronic keyboard and Zet jumped...the applause was thunderous. She felt the air stir.

Her eyes fell on the movement of his muscles as he plodded to the stage - in no hurry - received the mike from the Compere as casually as if he was accepting a cup of tea, nodded curtly at Rita, ran shrewd eyes over the audience, and began.

His voice was...oh, it had that tremor, the lilt, the spine-tingling emotion of the Welshman...although he was obviously Yorkshire through and through.

79

'*Welcome to my world*,' he sang, and Zet felt as if the breath left her body.

She couldn't take her eyes from him, discovering … his rock hard body; the thick tautness of his thighs beneath the black trousers; a black waistcoat and white shirt stretched across a broad chest that pulled notes from somewhere deep down and sent them into his throat to drizzle out like warm olive oil, unimportantly almost, but effective.

As he sang, she was conscious of the contradiction of such power-driven stillness, an untamed energy that promised exciting things. Just watching him the crowded room emptied. She might have been jerked up into outer space and left to slowly free-fall. As his voice blew fantasies through her mind, something inside her began an unstoppable slide and tumble. Dazed, she knew something.

She knew that if this man, this stranger, walked towards her, holding out his arms, she would, without hesitation, walk straight into them.

Glad of the dim, red shaded wall lights that hid her flush, she took a gulp of bitter lemon. Jonty was nodding approvingly in her direction, reaching for her hand. Her hand, sticky and damp and newly manicured, crawled away from him.

The song ended, she excused herself. The room felt emotional, shocked, her body might have been frying in hot oil; enthusiastic clapping fell against her ears and then, as she stepped outside the room and closed the heavy door, deadened.

She stood for a moment, breathing in cold, old stone and old wood, before she made for the Ladies' cloakroom along the endless, dank stone passage of the original part of the inn.

Inside, she met a stony, crypt-like silence. She stared at her face in the mirror – creamy skin unusually pink, eyes startled, a deeper, emotional blue. Turning on the cold tap, she rinsed her hands and dried them on a roller towel and turned to go... this wild creature isn't me, she thought, catching a last glimpse of her disturbed self in the mirror before she left the room. She stepped out and he was there.

He looked bold and domineering - not her type, she registered. Stopping in the passage to let her pass, his lips curled back, showing glistening teeth. He was broad, so broad she felt squashed by him in the narrow space. And strong. It was written into every line on his face, lips, nose, and jaw line, not to mention shoulders. His hair, the colour of oak tree bark, looked as if it had been swept with an impatient hand back from a high forehead. His eyes were...suddenly she felt mortified.

'Have we met?' he asked, returning her stare with an intrigued frown.

Her skin tingled as if she had been in the sun. The bulging stone wall, like the cold barrel of a gun, pressed against her backbone. Pull yourself together, Zet. She swallowed, raised her chin and answered as coolly as she could manage. 'No. I'm...we're new here.'

'To the district or the club?' 'Both.'

'Shall we see you again?'

He was obviously a man of few words. She nodded. 'Good.'

And that was it. He turned away, leaving her staring after him, registering that his hair was unusually long, drawn back in a ponytail, and that he left a slipstream of aftershave that drew her senses with it.

Anguished as a lovesick teenager, she longed to remain there until he came out of the Gents' cloakroom. How silly! But as a teenager you never felt like this, Zet. Even then, you had your dream of happy families.

The man of my dreams, she reminded herself, is waiting for me in the clubroom.

She had married him. And so, because she must, she pushed open the door of the clubroom as if she hated it.

The Compere was telling another joke. Her feet dragged. She had felt safe here, in Yorkshire. Safe from city violence and safe from the knowledge she had somehow always carried inside. Passion means danger.

She walked like a sleepwalker, filled with a baffling sense of loss, into the clubroom. Laughter came to meet her. It had been an ordinary room.

***

He loved the way she walked around naked in front of him. But tonight, she quickly pulled her nightdress over her head. He could smell lavender.

'You were right,' he said gratefully, as he undressed. 'Did us good to get out socially. You worked hard on the house and garden, darling, it should have occurred to me you needed a break. You look tired.' Shrugging on pyjamas, he slipped into bed.

'Why am I the one who always has to come up with the ideas anyway?' She punched the pillow.

'Because I love you, darling. I want you to have everything you want, do the things you want to do.'

Into the expectant silence came the click of her bedside lamp going off. His followed and he settled down. She was tired. Been doing too much.

An owl hooted gently outside. She had learned to love the unthreatening silent nights here where only the animal kingdom hunted. Turning on her side, away from him, she could smell the lavender she had sprinkled on her pillow because she wanted to go quickly to sleep. In sleep, she was roaming the wild moors somewhere, and unexpectedly bumping into him, or strolling along the lane when he passed in his car; he would stop, say, 'I've been thinking of you' and she would say....

The following day she went to Leeds. It was an odd day.

Chapter Sixteen

She and a butterfly stomach, hating the city; a day of blinking traffic lights, the surging power of vehicles defying commonsense, a flute-playing beggar and his rippling soulful music; stern stone buildings.

The day trudged on, a blur of preening mirrors, strip lighting white as caustic soda, foraging in shops, dresses for flirting in, a head full of folly and fantasy, a howling inside like a baby cry. Less a wife, more a woman, a woman with a hunger, choosing clothes to please a man who wasn't her husband.

In the end, she chose a plain dress the colour of clotted cream, in the longer knee-length, with shoulder pads; a wide wine red belt showed off her narrow waist. The skirt was straight and just showed the outline of her long, low hips and lean thighs. The salesgirl smiled enviously.

'He'll love you in this, whoever he is.'

The new heated rollers in her hair felt hot, tight…she wasn't used to them, she usually wore her hair smooth. Will he be there tonight? she wondered, slipping into the new dress…reaching for a blue velvet box…taking out the pearls her mother had given her for her eighteenth birthday, resting them against her throat.

As her hands went up to fasten the clip, she felt an inner shiver; there was a disturbing sensation of sadness. Fingering the cool, creamy pearls, she remembered Iris had worn them often. They still held her mother's perfume bringing chilling memories with it...the house smelling of L'aimant perfume...her mother's heightened tension as she prepared to go out. Her aunt arriving ready to spend the evening playing games. Zet standing at the front bedroom window, watching her mother go, afraid of being left, afraid maybe of the dreams in a mother's heart. The woman separating from the mother.

84

On impulse, Zet rose from the dressing table, padded in bare feet down the creaking stairs to the telephone in the hall. She was oddly relieved when she heard Iris's girlish, breathy voice answer.

'Everything all right, mum?'

'Course it is,' Iris answered, sounding forlorn. 'What are you up to, pet?'

Zet told her and Iris said, 'you should get out more. Life's for living, you know. I still think you made a mistake, burying yourself up there.'

Zet couldn't stand criticism. Trying to keep the irritation from her voice, she changed the subject. 'How's Tony?'

There was a pause and the reply...'Okay,' had very little conviction.

'We've had a bit of a row,' Iris readily admitted, when Zet pretended to push her.

'About what?' Hearing Jonty come out of the bathroom, she glanced at the hall clock and the breath left her body. With an effort, she concentrated upon what her mother was saying.

'I wanted to go to a tea dance. They've started doing them on Saturday afternoons at the South Woolwich town hall over the river.' Enthusiasm threaded Iris's voice. 'Just like the old days.' Zet could imagine the eager look on Iris's face. Then she heard her say, 'Tony said he wouldn't be seen dead at a tea dance.'

Zet could believe that. 'It's not really his thing, is it, mum?'

'I suppose not.' She sounded wistful. 'Oh, well, never mind.'

After replacing the receiver, Zet returned to the bedroom and removed the rollers. Jonty, who had finished dressing, was waiting downstairs, poring over a report he had brought home from the office. She sat at the dressing table and brushed her newly trimmed hair into its well-behaved bob but with more body than usual.

Zet had sensitive skin, so she sprayed herself with essential oil she made up herself, choosing tonight a blend of rosewood and ylang ylang, the most sensuous oil of all. A few drops in a phial of spring water smelled gorgeous.

'Wow!' was Jonty's reaction when she came downstairs. 'You look terrific,' he grinned, aiming a kiss.

Expecting it, Zet moved away. Calling out goodbye to Norah, who was baby-sitting, she paused a moment. Glancing back up the stairs, she was chilled by a frightening sensation that she wasn't coming back. She had read the children a bedtime story, hadn't she? They couldn't be in better hands, Norah being a district nurse. Nevertheless, Zet felt uneasy, but she was being ridiculous, she decided, leading the way out to the car.

Jonty opened the car door and settled in the driver's seat and Zet paused a moment, looking up at the night sky. Before they moved north she had never realized the great, silent bowl of sky could be so dark and so studded with stars.

Trying to get into the car, seeing Jonty's teasing grin inside, she realized he was holding the door so that she couldn't pull it open. Attention seeking again, she thought, gritting her teeth. One look at her face, though, and he gave in. She slipped carefully into the car, snapping the door closed.

The short journey seemed to Zet to wind through long, dark petrified corridors. Dark shapes leapt out like devils either side of the car, until the headlamps pushed away what were merely hedges and trees. There was silence in the car. Zet's head resembled a colander; every thought ran straight through it and drained away, except one. A great, thumping, pulsing thought that felt raw and ready to bleed.... Will Brad be there tonight?

A rabbit, caught in the headlamps, froze, stared mesmerized and bounded away. He knew his teasing annoyed her but he couldn't stop himself from doing it. When her eyes glistened, you knew she was annoyed. He

86

remembered her eyes the night they met, a cool, calm gaze that checked him out.

As he drove, with a silent Zet merely the scent of gorgeous perfume beside him, but not part of him - a long way from that - he thought about her. The rare smile, a smile that was choosey, a not-given-for- nothing type smile. The way she spoke, choosing her words carefully, her voice precise, bell-like, or steely, depending on mood and occasionally a withering hail of bullets. She looked fragile, yet she could paint houses, hang wallpaper, lay paving stones, dig gardens, chop down branches. She would even have made a successful businesswoman with her analytical mind.

From the time he met Zet, he had been in awe of her, but had imagined himself melting her aloofness with all the warmth of which he knew he was capable. Yet too much affection, he was aware, irritated her. There was only one vulnerable side to her; she had nightmares that made her wake up trembling. To be honest, he enjoyed comforting her. She never talked about the nightmares, though, as if to admit to them diminished her in some way.

He pushed away a pang of loneliness. They were different, that's all, and hadn't he first been attracted by the aloof dignified look that set her apart from others? If he could only melt her with his love, but he took comfort from her delight in her home and the care she gave him, which surely proved she loved him. She made his home somewhere he was always glad to return to; she drew him back as if he were on a piece of string because there was nowhere else he would rather be.

His trip to London last week had been enjoyable, though. He had taken the opportunity to meet up with his old friends at the local pub. Afterwards, he walked Sarah home, intending to call in and say hello to her parents. They were passing a street lamp when she asked, 'How's your wife?'

87

'She's perfect,' he answered, glancing down into her face. Her eyes looked luminous and full of sympathy.

'You're not the one who loves the most, are you, laddie?'

'Don't be silly.' Then, awkwardly, 'You haven't taken to Zet, have you?'

Reaching her front door, they paused. He sensed a struggle going on inside her, but ever outspoken, she said, 'I can resist her charm. She's...a super housewife, though; so competent she could have come out of a spray. I just think you're in danger of giving up your identity.' He smiled and shook his head. Going into the house, he was made a great fuss of and until now, he had forgotten Sarah's comments.

Circling the village green, he steered the car into the gravel-crunching car park, cut the engine and silently told the absent Sarah that he was a lucky man. He and Zet might love in different ways, but they didn't fight, they co-operated with each other, they had a happy marriage, lovely kids, and beautiful home. He had sensed what Sarah left unspoken, that Zet had a cutting tongue and like his father, she was behind him, urging him on. But in Zet he somehow found it exciting and reassuring.

Zet stepped from the car, cool, elegant and untouchable, wearing a long, white knitted jacket over a cream dress. Her face looked solemn as she stared at the brightly lit inn, its windows glowing like the ravenous red embers of a fire.

Shoes crunching gravel, he walked around the car. 'Turning chilly, he said on joining her. His smile held apology. 'Let's hurry up in out of the cold.' He reached for her hand. She shivered. Her eyes were fixed on the door of the inn as someone came out, leaving the door ajar. The red glow reached outside like fingers of flame, and from inside came a roar of laughter.

Chapter Seventeen

He sang '*Feelings...feeling that I want to hold you..*' His narrowed gaze ranged the audience and lighting upon Zet, paused. A nod of acknowledgement, the briefest of smiles, and something pulsed inside her. She was fascinated by him. The way he was standing with tree-trunk legs firmly astride; the way his tongue slipped around and caressed words.

The song ended. She felt bereft. She watched him hand the mike to the Compere, step down from the stage and rejoin his friends.

There was just one woman with his party, a small, neat woman with a dark choirboy haircut, about thirty, the sort you would barely remember, the sort who wore cardigans and sensible shoes and read a lot and didn't look as if she laughed often. Zet had a feeling she had seen the woman before, but couldn't remember where.

Rita began playing a session of disco beat, and, too agitated to sit still, Zet pulled a surprised Jonty on to the shaking floor. Whether or not Brad was watching her, she didn't know, but she told herself he was, which lent impetus to her gyrations and had Jonty - clumsy but always ready to have a go on the floor – smiling. He looked happy, elbows flapping, body bouncing, singing *Rivers of Babylon*, adoration in his eyes. But Zet danced, as always, alone, and, her expression said, far away. Except that a glance showed her Brad reclined back in his seat, one arm across the chair back, feet stretched beneath the table. Fingering a brandy glass, he sipped now and again or sometimes just looked thoughtfully into it, twirling the stem in his fingers. The dark woman had to touch his arm to get his attention.

They met again in the corridor that reeked of chips, roasting meat and gravy. His downward, piercing stare poked into her insides, made them heaving and happy.

'Must be fate.' he murmured, reaching out one arm, so that her breathing stopped, her eyes widened. He rested his hand on the wall behind her, looking searchingly down into her upturned face.

'Nice to see you again.' Somehow he made the word *you* sound special.

Her hot, damp hands were pressing on the cold wall behind her and, searching in vain for something intelligent to say, 'You have quite a fan club,' was all she came up with. He smiled and shook his head.

'We don't take it seriously 'ere.' His voice was like gravel, words clipped and spare, with a strong northern accent. Flattery, she felt, wouldn't move him; it would drip off him like rain on rock.

She admired talent and told him truthfully, 'You have a splendid voice.' Inhaling a deep breath of him, she took it inside, tasting it in her throat, wanting the rest. His slow half smile was extremely attractive, she thought, somehow knowing that this man had hidden depths, dark experiences and would take what he wanted.

He removed his hand from the wall and stood erect. 'You enjoyed the song?'

'Very much.' His was the sort of mouth-watering scent you smell when blackberrying. Sunshine on green leaves, tree bark, undergrowth. Hidden delights.

'It seems such a waste,' she said, mildly cross. 'You're very talented.'

Another brief smile dismissed his talent; his brows came together in a slight frown, as if he had questions he could not voice. Her skin felt airbrushed, and then with an abrupt, 'Thank you,' he was gone. Deflated, she returned to the room where couples were dancing to something slow called *When I Fall In Love*.

'Do you mind if I dance with your wife?'

Zet writhed. How old fashioned. And Jonty, she thought crossly, was very bad mannered the way he barely

90

turned to Brad and shook his head, before returning to football talk with a man at the next table.

Brad, of course, she had seen coming. He was holding out his hand. And she, with an annoyed flounce and high-held head, was stepping out into space and tipping off the edge of her safe world.

She had never before wanted to be anything but safe, until she found herself caught in those hard, dry hands, held near his chest, her hot cheek brushing an expensively clad shoulder. For the sake of company banquets she had once persuaded Jonty to go to ballroom dancing lessons. They had learned just the basics, enough to move around the floor efficiently. Dancing, to Brad, however, meant plodding around the floor with a movement neither graceful nor rhythmic, but purposeful and somehow sensual. It was the slowest of slow dances.

His dancing said that he would go his own way, do his own thing and everyone else could move around him, thank you very much. Self assured, this older man.

Sometimes their thighs touched. His fingers played, accidentally, of course, up and down her spine and her dress hung from her hot body like an impatient scream. The hand he held was not the cool, dry one she wished it to be.

Her heart was pounding the way hearts do in dentists' waiting rooms - the terror, yet the inevitability of it. If you run, you take your pain with you, so you might as well stay and the hurt might just be worth it.

'And the moment that I feel that, you feel that way, too...'

He sang to her in a low voice. She saw a pulse flicker in his throat, level with her eyes. His skin looked tender there; beneath his shirt his chest would be.... against her lips would feel....

'What do you think of Yorkshire, Rosetta?' He liked her name, he had said.

'Mm?' She thought for a moment, so important to find the right words, make an impression. But in the end she could only say, with feeling, 'I've fallen in love with it.' Her hand in his trembled. 'Quite honestly, this place,' she added, 'has given me my breath back.'

He had to bend his head to hear, then drew back and studied her with interest as she raised her chin to say to him, with complete candour, 'I didn't know I needed so much, the...the space, the air, the freedom to be myself.' Embarrassed, she looked away, adding, over his shoulder, 'I feel close to heaven, or at least,' she tried to joke, 'knocking on heaven's door up there on the moors.'

'Rosetta,' he said solemnly, tightening his grip around her waist, guiding her through other dancers, 'I've been searching for heaven all my life, but they keep moving the sign posts.' She pulled in a deep breath and let it out slowly, still looking up at his tight- lipped smile, the devilish glint that came into his eyes.

'Maybe you can show me the way,' he said. And they moved slowly, studying each other.

'I've been too busy with the move to explore much....'

'I'll have to show you around, then, Rosetta.'

When? There is no when. This is only casual talk, flirting talk. When...can never come. Be sensible, Zet.

Chapter Eighteen

The school bus clattered across the bridge, heading for town, and then the village, abandoned, fell into an unnatural silence.

So silent that Zet, stepping over short, wet grass, heard the hissing sound her sandals made. The chill damp seeped through to her feet. Glancing up at the low, threatening sky, she shivered, wrapping her arms around her body. She felt none of her usual joy, but a fierce need, impatient to be at one with her garden.

It was late coming, summer. She had waited forever, it seemed, for the bursting out of her garden. But the days were wet and blustery or pale as skimmed milk, and flowers remained stubbornly budded, as if tucked up against the cold.

Walking the lanes between high hedges, she imagined him passing in his car; he would stop, ask if she wanted a lift; she would act surprised, not letting him know that wherever she walked, her eyes searched for him.

There is something erotic about a stranger, the space around him where everyday life, possessions, moods and characteristics, are absent. Instead, he is sensation; anticipation; a plan. He is larger than life, extraordinary, and perfect, the pull of his masculinity primitive and instinctive like a time before guilt was invented.

Brad filled her head like a motion of air. He was making love to her up on the moors as well. And they were dancing.

Daydreams more real than life at home, which ran on oiled wheels because she planned it that way. Except for her garden, that refused to bloom. Working out there, she was conscious of a warning in the wind.

'We get a lot of wind here, y'know. 'Norah, built like a rock, was admiring the garden, and warning dolefully, 'It can be right vicious at times.'

Zet smiled. Norah, eyeing the stubborn lips, shrugged a silent...wait and see.

Something told her - it will happen. She had planned it so. She had searched out tough roots, heaved stones, bedded plants, sprinkled Growmore, laid paths leaving gaps for thyme. She understood that thyme, like all herbs, had to be crushed before it released its pleasure-giving scent.

A rambling rose, Albertine, clawed at the house wall; Zet had discovered it beneath old vines and ivy, freed it and it had rewarded her efforts by scrambling happily, trailing buds, not only up the house wall but escaping over the adjoining wall into the hidden garden. The buds looked ready to burst; she could feel it in herself, the tense, tight covering.

Pushing the old gate open, hearing its familiar squeal, she stepped inside the crumbling walls where tangled undergrowth coiled around her and trees closed overhead, dimming the world. She breathed deep breaths of wet earth, leaves, bark and sweet bluebells, and sensed a pulse beneath her feet, as if the garden was raring to go.

The winding path, studded with wild daisies, led her unevenly between shrubs, trees and flowers that she didn't know the names of. Zet didn't care that her feet grew colder and wetter as she trudged through damp grass to her favourite place beneath a cherry tree. Sitting on a tree stump, she let herself blend into her surroundings.

She listened to the breathing expectation, the garden's rustle and murmur, drips from rain-soaked leaves. This place was never still. Trees swayed; finches, robins and sparrows hopped and flitted in and out of the dancing shadows, chattering like happy children; thrushes and blackbirds perched overhead, the most thrilling sounds bursting from their throats. Moments flew, too, losing themselves in serenity. Once. Not now.

'The world's a different place.' Wrapping her arms around her knees, she thought how he filled every waking moment; she couldn't eat, sleep, and she could hardly breathe as if, without him, breathing was unimportant. She felt that if she couldn't know him, life would be unbearable. He was a mystery waiting to be solved.

The rhubarb leaves, big as elephant's ears, flopped at her feet with a cross, sour expression and seemed to say...pull yourself together. The wind, creeping like a cold conscience into the twittering garden, carried the scent of the moors from the wild, uncharted places she had yet to explore.

'Your eyes tell me how much you care...my endless love.'

As they danced, Brad broke off from singing to say, 'You're a lovely looking woman.' He sounded matter of fact, not flirtatious, but genuine.

'Last week,' he continued, 'you looked like a glass of milk straight from the fridge.'

'Really?' Above the music, Zet's crystal clear voice sounded surprised. So nothing of her inner turmoil had shown.

His fingers brushed the sleeve of the scarlet off the shoulder top that she wore with a mini skirt in the same shade. 'And then,' he complained, 'you turn up in this vibrant red thing. Very confusing. Hot or cold? Fire or ice?'

Glancing up with what she hoped was an enigmatic look she saw his grey eyes narrow. She was very aware of his dark lashes, the flicker of wall lights on his saturnine face. His breath touched her as he leaned closer. 'Which are you, Rosetta?'

'Which do you want me to be?' she asked, as the music stopped. Their delighted bodies jerked together for a split second and reluctantly separated.

Jonty's good-natured grin met her as she reached the table, sat down and picked up her glass, inspecting it as if she didn't know what to do with it.

'He must like you,' Jonty teased. 'He dances with you every week.'

Zet pulled a face. 'He dances with everyone.' Her eyes narrowed, watching Brad take the floor with the dark-haired woman. 'He's a rotten dancer, anyway.' She kept her face averted from Jonty.

She felt cross tonight. Nothing seemed in harmony. Singers were out of tune. Jokes fell flat. Through the windows across the room she saw the moon hanging bloated, enormous, sending a river of silver flowing across the dark village green towards the inn, and with a sense of unreality, she felt herself slipping over the edge of the world, a long, unstoppable drift towards the darkness beyond the horizon.

Somehow she found herself talking and smiling charmingly at Jonty's new friend, John, his sister and brother-in-law, while her slim fingers played with a beer mat, and their new friends brought more wine, which slopped down into the emptiness that Zet hadn't known existed. I have everything I need. I'm so lucky.

A plump, red-faced farmer mounted the stage and sang, "*If I said you had a beautiful body would you hold it against me?*" and Zet suggested sharply to Jonty that if the farmer sang at work it would curdle the cows' milk.

Hearing her, John's sister - Margaret Cartwright her name was, and her husband was David – laughed.

'Eeh, it's all a bit of fun, love,' she said, thinking Zet was joking.

She had thin red hair you could see the scalp through, invisible lashes and pale green eyes which were fixed on Brad, who was returning to his seat. The dance had finished and her voice sounded loud as she said, through her small, pouting, discontented mouth, 'That Brad's a lady's man, never sticks to one; he has wandering ways. That Mary, the one with the dark hair, is out to get him, though, she...'

Her words were drowned by music. He wasn't married then. But miserably, Zet wondered...is he playing with me? She was only half listening to Margaret. 'We own the land next to your cottage,' she was saying, voice raised against the music.

'I didn't realise.'

A cautious expression crossed Margaret's face. 'Happy there, are you?'

'Of course. It's perfect for us.' Perfect marriage. Perfect kids. Happy.

Margaret nodded doubtfully, sipped her drink, seemed to be thinking. Placing her glass down, she stared Zet directly in the face and reached out. Zet felt the touch of fingers like frozen chips on her arm. With excitement threading through her voice, Margaret said, 'the farmer we bought the land from lived at your place. He....'

A deep voice interrupted. It was David, Margaret's husband. 'Dance, love?' He jerked his head at the floor, winking at Zet. Standing up, she smiled at him, relieved, and followed him on to the floor.

She felt awkward in the arms of this burly, weathered man in a tweed jacket. He took her hand and looked down at her with kind eyes. 'Maggie bin giving you the latest gossip, then?' When Zet nodded, he laughed, and with a firm, podgy grip on her waist, inexpertly whirled her around.

Afterwards, she had just sat down breathlessly at the table, when she saw Margaret stare behind her. Turning her head, Brad was holding out his hand and with a pulse of happiness, she rose, excused herself and went with him, trying not to smile. Jonty gave her a sympathetic wink and returned to sport talk. Whatever this is, she shivered, slipping into Brad's arms, it has a grip like death.

Brad was steering her through the dancers when he said, 'I haven't forgotten my promise.'

It was stuffy tonight, in the clubhouse; he had removed his jacket. Moving backwards, she was conscious of the

97

hot skin of his shoulder burning her fingers through his white shirt. 'What promise?'

'To show you around,' he said, reaching a corner and turning her with a sudden reckless movement. Getting her breath back, her smile was cool.

'I'd forgotten about that.' As the music stopped, his answering half smile said he didn't believe her.

'I'll take you on a tour,' he said.

Chapter Nineteen

And he did. As far as the wild moors that rippled endlessly like the sea. As far as a sheltered spot within the sound of running water, where the ground was soft springy sheep nibbled moss. There was in-and-out type sunshine. Rocks hid them from the distant road, which ran off laughing, like trailing white ribbons, leaving them alone.

Moorland raced the scorching wind towards distant stonewalled, hill-climbing fields, the peat scented wind was flapping like fire and as he stood there, back resting against a great rock. she saw that he looked at one with this wild place. He appeared to be turning things over in his mind, a sight that was surprisingly erotic.

He turned his head. The naked desire in his eyes burned through any armour of caution she might have left, setting her pulse racing. The blood leapt in her veins as he came towards her. And something in her began to tick joyously. This was meant to be; the moors, the wildness inside her, had been waiting all her life.

Her hair whipped across her face. Reaching her, he lifted the strands from her eyes, tucked them behind her ears, his fingers brushed her lobes and she shivered, looked at him, startled, lost. He fleetingly touched her hand, she felt one small doubt whimper inside her and then a rebellious happiness, knowing there was no way she could stop this.

He took her in his arms, not very close, but very gently, and they danced, there on the moors; without taking their eyes from each other, they danced to the music of the wind and water and his humming. *Feelings*. She felt his chin rest for a moment on the top of her head and then a soft touch that could have been a kiss and her scalp felt stung. And then there was no space between them; instead of wind it was his fingers, warm against her scalp, his face between her and the wide, wild, scudding sky. Cupping her head in his hands, he searched deep into her eyes.

'I want you, Rosetta.' Hard voice, but deep and urgent and as penetrating as a depth charge. Her insides leapt with a wild, fierce joy. She knew by his intake of breath, that he saw it all in her eyes, and could feel her wonderful trembling.

She raised her hands, ran her fingers, as if she couldn't see, against his face because she had been longing to touch him, and then she pulled his head towards her. A magnetic force drew their lips close, hovered, made contact, and the world exploded.

His mouth felt hard and hot. A long, breath-held kiss began, as if they had been waiting forever. Mouths working, she wanted to stay there always. Bodies blended, time blended, the hills, sky and wild moors slipped into timelessness.

Her body felt liquid as he spilled her on to the soft moss. The music of the moors... birds, water, wind... moved around them, through them. She felt his firm hands undress her and she was back to raw, the journey seemed ancient, as if she swept down a passage to time's beginning.

Her clothes fell on to the heather...his hands cupped her breasts...her skin tingled then his scalding lips sought her body and she moaned, floating somewhere, free, lost.

He raised himself and knelt...don't stop, she wanted to scream, don't stop. But he was only undressing, and she sat up, holding him there, kissing his mouth, his stern face, his pale, dark-haired chest, the tanned muscles on his arms, his hands. As his clothes fell away, she stroked the flesh of that big, healthy, granite body; he removed the band from his hair and let it wave to his shoulders. It was like making love with a Greek statue. Or almost, for she felt the hot blood raging in his veins, the pounding of his heart. She felt moss like velvet move beneath her, and smelled the essence of him, as his hands, lips and the

100

wind, brushed her bare flesh, eased her, freed her, kissed her until she moaned. There was the gravity pull, the coming together, the unstoppable, powerful force and suddenly... fusing, clinging and he was raising her hips, pushing himself into her, she was holding him, feeling his hardness thrusting inside her, wanting more. He absorbed her until she felt her flesh run into him.

A savage man took over; a moan left his lips, followed by a surprised gasp. He felt he was racing towards something new, unexplored. She was enthusiastic yet cool and shy at first; it turned him on in the most unexpected way. 'I can't wait,' he gasped. But she was with him now, filled up with him, pushing against him to take more. The moors heaved as if about to quake open. He felt pleasure ripping through her, again and again. Climbing into each other they were shooting for the highest hills.

Afterwards, as they rested, he asked how she felt, and she shook her head. Blew out a breath. Ran fingers through her messed up hair. Laughed. 'Bewitched, bothered and bewildered, I think, as the song goes.'

Me too, he thought. What happened? It was as if he had lost something of himself inside her. Unsettling, but completely and utterly satisfying. With his head resting against her heart, one arm across her body, his eyes closed. Her fingers began to play with his hair.

Then there was just the flying wind, a birdcall... *more...more...more...* and water chuckling to itself as it ran away. That, too, faded; she was asleep before the wind lulled and seemed to sigh... at last, but what next?

Chapter Twenty

Summer came.

The sun burned the sky white and warmed the wind and her garden burst into life. Buds flung themselves into an ecstasy of plump, sweet-smelling roses overnight, there was a frenzy of undressing, an orgy of galloping togetherness as the alyssum spread out, cool white and green, at the borders; just like children joining hands and singing with bright faces, she thought, shocked by happiness into a greater awareness of things.

Early mornings found her wandering on to the lawn, cool dew squelching between bare toes. She was intimate with her garden, drawing in breaths of pleasure, touching furry, soft or abrasive things, brushing soft petals against her cheek. The tulips were late arriving, she drew her finger tips up the tapering scarlet flower, feeling its tough, satiny surface and thought of the new underwear she had bought which felt slippery beneath denim.

In her saner moments Zet could not believe it had happened. But the sane moments were few. Lit from within, it was extraordinary the way she automatically, and without guilt, compartmentalized her life. She didn't neglect Jonty, the children or the house; too long she had trained herself for that job. Her off duty moments were spent with Brad, pulsating with such happiness that she wondered – was I alive before?

Nothing must spoil this. 'It's not a forever thing,' she said, knowing his free spirit. 'Just until it's time to go.' She wanted to reassure him. He looked at her with an expression impossible to fathom.

'When will that be?'

She told him about her happy family. He looked as if he was turning things over in his mind.

'What you're saying,' he said slowly, in his gravel voice, 'is that I have no future place in this life that you've planned. You've made a space, for a while, but our affair is only until....' His tough brows rose, his look was quizzical.

'Only *until*,' she said happily, wanting to press herself to him.

'I'll accept that.' He looked mocking. 'A moment - we'll have a moment - *until*. I won't stand in your way; I won't ask anything of you. It's for now...to walk on the moors, drive with you, make love to you. I won't spoil your life, I promise.'

She felt a chill. He sounded so intense. 'Permanence,' he added with a deep sigh, 'is not something I'm after, Rosetta. I love women, but I love them my way. I don't pander to them. There are things more important than women.' A pause and...'so you don't have to worry.'

She said nothing. A strong man's love, she realised, arouses both passion and uncertainty.

They were sitting with their big stone warm against their backs when he said, with feeling, 'I grew up 'ere.' He was looking around the wind-combed moors, his face stern. 'This were my playground when I were a lad.'

She heard satisfaction in his voice and realised the truth of something she had read somewhere. You are as the earth around you is. There was an innate masculinity, a ruggedness, about men here; even those dressed smartly and smelling expensive exuded this sense of rock and earth.

There were hidden parts in her that he reached, parts that had been buried deep, tangled emotions that he drew from her, when once she had been so calm and controlled. For the first time, a man's skin drew her to touch him, to enjoy feeling his body throb and stir beneath her lips. She understood at last, the rage of sex.

Not only that, gestures of friendship and concern contrasted with his hardness. He might be autocratic and difficult, but he listened. She didn't have to concern herself with his life and problems. Though she was interested, it was none of her business; she rested on him.

103

His voice was hard and could sound intimidating as he spoke his mind, without sentiment. 'You're an enigma,' he told her once. 'Cool and ladylike, perfectly formed, like a doll. But every now and then your eyes flicker with fun, your voice holds excitement, you laugh as if you think you shouldn't. Makes people feel they don't know you. Makes you seem unreachable I imagine, to some people,' he added gruffly.

Brad lived alone. 'Surrounded,' he said with a pretend leer, 'by four foot thick stone walls.' He told her that he had been born at Dale View; he talked about his business selling and renting out farm and building machinery...'from my concrete bunker,' he joked, 'in a new business park just outside York. But I have a good manager; I don't spend long there. I have time to walk the moors and lose myself there; and I travel around, singing at clubs, going abroad, whatever I fancy.'

'Farming has had it,' he added, eyeing the land with apology.

Zet followed his gaze across the moors to the hills. That's where his heart is, but he had the good business sense to tear himself away. She admired that.

This was the first thing she learned about him... his love of the land, and his strength. To her he was a wide clearing. She felt, sometimes, like a child with him, the fatherly, older man dominance and protectiveness new to her and appealing in a way she would never have dreamed of, coupled as it was with intense passion as her own sexuality was revealed to her so unexpectedly and so thrillingly.

Physically she had never been so moved, never reached a point where she was out of control; now, she was fascinated by what would once have repelled her.

Passion spent, Brad was good company. They could discuss and even argue in a way she couldn't do at home, for Jonty, so easily wounded, shared her views and objectives and liked the same things. He had no enthusiasm, no curiosity or sense of adventure. He took on the identity of who he was with as if he thought he himself wasn't worth much.

Brad was himself, whoever he was with. She loved his enthusiasms and curiosity, his longing to explore life and the world. To Brad, life was an adventure, a part of him, she discovered, which was obviously inherited.

'In the eighteen hundreds my forebears sailed to America,' he told her. 'A lot from this area did, in the rush for gold. It was a tough old life. One family returned because of outlaws and Indians, afraid for their children, but scarlet fever swept the ship on the way back; two children died, a girl and a boy. I was named after the boy.'

She loved the child he was named after and mourned the brave family, shuddering to think what it must have cost, physically and mentally, to emigrate in those days.

He never said, "I love you". She sensed he never would. She looked at him sometimes and thought...God, you're so brilliant to look at, to be with, to make love with...I love your round cheekbones that make you look as if you should be smiling, but you seldom do...the gentle touch of your hard hands...the sexy way you move...the fragrance of you that makes me want to kiss you all over...the way the atmosphere in a room changes when you come in...I love you Brad. But she didn't tell him out loud. She wasn't sure whether it was just so obvious that nothing need be said, or whether the words conveyed too much permanence. Or whether affairs had certain rules. An affair stands alone; love seems to need a future.

But what now? Have I put myself in too vulnerable a position? Am I not becoming a little too eager to please Brad? He could leave me any time.

So she edged her way under Brad's skin, became everything she thought a man wanted in a mistress. She wanted him to love her, need her, become her. She wanted all of him. *Until.*

'Something about you, Rosetta, is unreal.' With his little finger he was tracing the curve of her cheeks and her perfect nose.

She closed her eyes. Tingling….

'Makes a man want to get beneath the surface,' he said, unusually soft and thoughtful, brushing to a shiver the soft skin inside her elbows. 'You're a mystery parcel.'

His face too, looked softer, the hard lines less prominent, as he laid her down, spread her on the heather and before he entered her, said, as if the words were forced out of him, 'I've never met anyone like you. You fascinate me.'

Her heart made a wild fierce leap. Her smile was brilliant. She smelled the tang of heather on his skin, the incensed sweat of love. His face, as he kneeled above her, looked washed, like someone who had made a confession. Don't ever let me have to live without him shivered through her mind, before sensible thought swam off into the blue and the moss moved beneath her and her body split open and took him inside and closed around him and she carried him with her wherever she went.

They drove and walked, explored villages, shadowed valleys and "top of the world" hills; he showed her great thrilling waterfalls and she felt small as a mouse looking up at them.

One hot day, coming across a small waterfall, they were tempted to strip off their clothes. Standing naked, with icy water cascading dizzily down upon her, she laughed out loud with the joy of it.

Afterwards he wrapped her in a tartan car rug, warmed her shivering body against his hot flesh and they made love.

Warm and relaxed in the back seat of the car, smelling leather, sex and petrol, with the rug itchy against her soft, damp flesh, she laughed up at him, saying, 'Don't we do mad things?'

Looking down at her, his face was dark and intent. 'Passion and madness,' he growled, 'go together.'

For an instant, a long ago scene caught in her memory like a fly struggling in a web. She recalled the terror she had felt, and shivered.

'Be damned to sane, safe, dull normality,' he added, pressing her closer, and feeling the fire in him, the pounding heart, she heaved a contented sigh.

When the exploring was done, he took her home.

Chapter Twenty-One

The house, with crumbly biscuit coloured walls, stood on the edge of a moorland village, about twenty minutes' drive from Zet's home. A housing estate, with billiard-table lawns and sputnik hanging baskets, sparkled across the lane behind a high wall.

The estate was built on farmland he had sold to a building firm years before. 'No need to work, the money I got from that,' he said, opening the front door, 'but a man needs work. Good job the old man didn't live to see that lot, though.'

She slipped from bright sunshine into the shadows of his stone house. As he led her in and out of rooms, he changed, took on another dimension, other people became attached to him and he was no longer just the man she loved.

He was not just hers and she found herself yearning to know more about him. She had heard talk at the club about tragedy in his life and while her heart had ached for him, she had not asked him about it, feeling that if he wanted to tell her, he would.

The house was detached, square, the way a child would draw, with four windows and a door in the middle; she could imagine that on chilly days smoke would be waving from the chimney like a question mark.

The dining room, with its chill seldom-used atmosphere, smelled of leather, polished wood and old books. Sunlight struggled inside through small windows, forming dancing patterns upon a heavy carved oak table and matching sideboard. Two walls were lined with bookshelves and there were two leather armchairs, giving a restful, if gloomy, library type atmosphere.

Moving across the hall, they lingered in the low-beamed sitting room, much cosier, she thought, liking its faded chintz, well-trodden green carpet, oak bureau, a piano that had belonged to his mother, and up to date stereo equipment.

Next, he led her along a stone flagged passage into a cheerful terracotta tiled kitchen. Along with modern units and an electric oven, there was an Aga, pine dresser and a solid pine table that would seat a dozen people. From here, she unlatched the back door, anxious to see the garden. When she stepped outside, she couldn't believe her eyes.

A patch of untidy grass stretched between the house and a low stone wall. 'There's no garden,' she exclaimed, turning to Brad, who was standing behind her.

'Look again.' He pointed. 'That's my garden.' Turning back, she followed his pointing finger.

Beyond the wall, wild moorland swept like an ocean towards distant navy-blue hills. She nodded.

Upstairs, she could see the same view of the moors through the open window of his bedroom; the wind that suddenly blew the curtains into the room brushed her face with the scent of peat. She privately thought the bulky old furniture hideous; the dark oak wardrobe would have hidden a football team, the brass bed was family size, high and wide and nest-like. She wondered....

Switching her mind away, she studied photographs on a chest of drawers: elderly stern looking people whose faces complained that stopping for a photograph was wasting time; there was a small shy boy and a plump little girl, and just one of a jolly, practical looking woman with soft, curly moth coloured hair, a wide amenable mouth and bright eyes, who obviously made jam and scones and chutney and belonged to the Women's Institute and the church, not the sort of person to die the way she had. Her life had been cut short and Zet felt sad, which he recognised.

'Margaret, my wife.' There was sudden pain in his eyes. 'There are more photographs, in an album somewhere,' he added in a sombre voice. 'I put them

109

away.' He ran a hand across his mouth and she shivered, as if a ghost had come into the room. 'After the accident,' he said.

'Brad.' She fixed her eyes on him. 'I heard about the accident, people talk. You have two children, too, I believe.'

He looked surly. 'There's obviously nothing I can tell you about myself that you haven't heard. Did they tell you the accident was my fault?'

'No,' she said carefully and getting to know his moods, she let it rest. This was one of his taciturn, withdrawn days, when the shadows beneath his eyes seemed more prominent.

They roamed the moors near his home and walking back through the squeaking wooden gate in the wall, it seemed to Zet as if the future walked with them like a dark hand on her shoulder. The sound of that gate, she thought, with a lurching stomach; I'll always remember it.

In the garden, he admitted to "black dog" moments… 'Part of my Welshness.' He closed his arms around her from behind and bent his head to rub his cheek against hers. A way he had. As if he said…I've hurt you, but we're still close.

'Half Welsh,' he added, with a crooked smile, 'on my mother's side.'

Turning in his arms, she said, 'Tell me about your parents.'

This seemed easier for him. 'My father died of a heart attack, then mother fell off a tractor and damaged her hip, couldn't walk again. Without the outdoor life she loved, she faded away. She used to sit here a lot,' he patted the wooden seat outside the back door where they were by then sitting. 'I'm grateful to them,' he said sharply. 'Gave me a good start in life.'

Sounds came from the estate, a baby crying, a barking dog, a groaning lawn mower. She stared at the grass

110

where only dandelions grew. 'Do you miss your children?' She felt the itch she had felt with her garden; she wanted to dig and find out who this man was.

He shook his head. 'My daughter, Gill, was the one I was closest to, and I have to say,' his voice held pride and a trace of regret, 'that she has blossomed out there in America. Here, she had no confidence. Took after her mother for being plump,' he added. 'Maybe she was teased at school.'

She nodded. She, herself, had been teased, even bullied, for the opposite reason, being skinny. Staying home from school to do the housework had made her feel safe. She tucked her hand into his arm to show she understood.

She had known about his daughter going to America, but gossip suggesting she had escaped a father she didn't get on with, made him seem cruel and hard. As if he knew what she was thinking, he patted her hand.

'Gill had no boyfriends, no social life here. She went over to stay with relatives for a holiday and, to use her expression, she couldn't find her way back. She's engaged now, works in a bar, has loads of mates, she says.'

Zet pressed, 'But don't you go and see her, or your son in London?' Gossip said his son had left after a row, gone to London to find fame and fortune. Found neither and ended up in a hostel for the homeless, living with drug addicts and drunks.

'No,' he snapped. 'I'll wait until I'm asked.'

They looked away from each other, across the moors. His dark moods affected her deeply. Something was wrong between him and his son and she yearned to put it right. She didn't like families split up but Brad brushed away the sympathy he sensed she felt. 'They know where I am if they need me, and the way my son is going, that day won't be long coming.' He stirred his legs restlessly as he added, 'I like my own company but I have friends, I enjoy horse riding and singing around the clubs,

111

travelling, and there were my afternoons of shooting and golf until I met you.' He looked down at her, apologising for his taciturnity with a leering smile. 'I like working with wood, too.'

She looked at him questioningly and he pointed to something at the side of the house partly hidden by a lopsided, overgrown bush. She had not noticed it before, but walking over, edging around the bush, she saw a beautifully made wooden structure, not unlike a very special kind of beach hut, with a view across the moors, which she thought would be even better with the bush cut down a bit.

'I made it for mother as a summerhouse,' he explained, 'so she could sit outside on the little veranda even when the wind blew. She loved it.'

'You really made it?' Returning to the seat, Zet looked at him in amazement. 'But it's so perfect.'

He nodded. 'I'll show you some of the furniture I've made.'

She shook her head in wonder. 'With your business, singing, everything, you still have time to make things like that.'

'I love doing it,' he told her. 'Working with wood, you know.' He looked down at his hands, spreading out the fingers. 'It's good to use these.'

Sitting down beside him, she probed a bit more. 'Were you upset when your son went to London instead of staying and helping you with the farm?'

'Whether I was or not,' he said grimly, 'they don't do what parents say today.'

She said nothing. While her own childhood had been free and easy and Iris had more or less let Zet do as she liked, for her own children Zet wanted a disciplined home; she believed in being fair, but strict.

Looking into the distance, he said, 'After Meg died, I moved back into this house, leaving our new bungalow for holiday lets. Mother looked after the children; dad and

I worked the farm. Dad was a stubborn old devil, wouldn't modernise, but I sold the bungalow and bought the land across the lane from him. Turned out to be a goldmine,' he said, proudly.

Curiously, she asked, 'Why didn't you take up singing professionally?'

'Why? There were a lot of us in the sixties, you know, thought we could sing. Besides, I'd been brought up to work on the farm.'

'With that voice,' she sighed, 'you could have gone far.'

'I had a wife and babies.' He shrugged. 'Making it in show business is an enormous risk for a family man, plus the fact that you have to be away from home a lot. Didn't want that.'

She could have felt so envious of that family.

Then there was the day they had been walking on the moors when the heavens opened. Indoors, he kissed the rain from her face and put a light to the fire. They drank coffee and ate while drying off in a room dancing with flames. Tangerine flames flickered against the black grate…shadows swayed on white walls…and as firelight played upon their naked bodies, he drew her - damp and eager - into his arms.

She felt his face burning against hers. Someone was singing, "*Lying here with you, I'm born again.*" She could smell the toast they had made, still hear their laughter. 'Some cook,' he had teased as she was trying to impale bread on a brass fork and toast it in front of the fire while summer rain eased and patted the windows gently. 'Do you want to go upstairs,' he asked.

'No,' she murmured against his mouth, licking away toast crumbs, smelling butter on his skin. She didn't like his bedroom. With buttery fingers she stroked the part of him that throbbed for her - velvet and rose-red as tulip petals. He pulled in a breath as if she had hurt him,

113

reached for her and moved into her and the logs sent up sparks, the fire roared and the room smelled of apple wood and sex.

She, who had always liked to plan ahead, never knew for certain what they would do when they met. He was a spur-of-the-moment sort of person. She found herself on horseback for the first time, not knowing whether to laugh or cry. They flew kites, visited castles, joined a jousting tournament, and even went down a coal mine.

She drew the line at shooting. His guns hanging on a rack in the hall sent a shiver through her. He saw it, and asked and she mentioned the nightmares she had suffered since childhood. With Brad, she could talk about herself, her thoughts and feelings, as she had seldom done to anyone else.

'It's always autumn. I can smell dead leaves and blood. There's a man pointing a rifle at me; I'm in a cage...there's nowhere to go...I know he's going to press the trigger, I can't move, then I wake up.'

Brad was sympathetic and after that, they entered the house by the back door and she didn't have to pass the guns in the hall.

But fears and nightmares had no chance against the fun and happiness she knew with Brad, the newly discovered madness and laughter. He drove wherever the mood took him, through narrow, steep-sided dales, past rushing rivers, stone barns and abandoned mines, waving to passing back-packers in sturdy boots and shorts.

One day they reached the Tan Hill Inn, 'the highest pub in England,' he told her. They walked hand in hand, with wind gusting in their faces, across the wild, deserted backbone of England, with ten thousand acres of moorland to themselves. The wind shrieked with grouse and curlew calls, tugged fingers through her hair, smacking her face until her skin was pink. It was the wildest place she had ever known and she excelled in it.

114

'This is a breathing place all right,' she puzzled him by shouting, leaping on to a rock, throwing out her arms and her chest as if about to sing something from the *Sound of Music*. She was delirious with happiness, freedom, air, and he threw back his head with a rare laugh. She was unique. A wave of tenderness caught at his heart.

'I sometimes wonder,' he teased, smelling the freshness of her in his arms as she jumped down, 'what you breathed before you met me.'

She pulled back from him, suddenly still. 'Nothing,' she answered with a direct look.

He drew in a sharp breath; his eyes filled with the soft glow that started off quivers inside her and they remained like that, eyes locked, until his arms came around her, her own went around his waist, and she rested her head on his chest. Home. It was a moving, gentle, timeless moment. I'll always remember this.

Afterwards, inside the four hundred year old inn, bulging walls and low beams and wide fireplaces reminded her of an old film her mother had liked. 'I think it was called *Wuthering Heights*.'

She was sitting on a bench beside him, tucking into a giant gravy-filled Yorkshire pudding, while around them walkers stripped off outdoor clothes and boots and stuck their thickly socked feet in front of the fire and the warm air was thick with the scent of chips, gravy and damp wool.

'Have you never read *Wuthering Heights*?' he asked. She shook her head, a little deflated when he tutted, and said, 'It's a classic. What sort of an education did you have?' She laughed it off.

Zet had never laughed so much. She was manically happy, with dramatic mood swings.

When she was away from him, she wasn't away. He was there, larger than life. Shopping, cooking, doll-making, weeding, watching the children play or just

115

sitting in her hidden garden, she painted mind pictures of him. He was pools of sunlight and sex. He was skin and hands and in charge. He was abrupt, outspoken, dour, quiet, he was resentments running as deep as Yorkshire rivers and like the rivers he could be forceful, determined to run his own way. He was stony silences, he was sudden ideas, he was her danger, her edge of the world. It was as if, beyond him, lay something deep, dark and unspoken. The widest of all, the deepest of all, nothings.

She wouldn't let herself think beyond the edge.

Zet had taught herself well, to mould into a man, fit into the pattern of his desires. She now found herself doing the same with Brad. She intended to become the perfect mistress. She could have it all.

She was soon to find, though, that an affair, however glorious, is not just a river of honey but a rough, sometimes icy sea, and that as much thought – and planning - needs to be given to an affair, as to marriage.

Chapter Twenty-Two

It hurts, to think that you lied to me...

'Do we have to listen to that, Jonty? ' Zet let the doll's dress she was stitching fall into her lap and looking surprised, he reached out and switch off the cassette.

'I didn't think it was particularly disturbing,' he said, turning back with a puzzled frown. 'You seem to like music lately; more than you used to, I mean.' His aggrieved tone implied that he could do nothing right. 'Do you prefer something else?'

She shook her head and bent over her work. 'I'm trying to work, and you,' she pointed out, 'have that report to finish tonight.'

It was then, glancing up again, seeing his anguished brow and boyish indecision, that she felt a pang of compunction. She knew what it was like now, didn't she – to be the one who loves the most? This sudden awareness swept her with panic. But it's not the same, she cried to herself. I've the sense to keep cool, not let Brad see. Oh, Brad. Her throat clotted. She was so afraid of doing something to push him away.

Was this how it was, then, to love too much, this throat catching fear, the silent screams, the ache for reassurance? A fine sweat broke out on her legs, her underarms, her brow. Her busy fingers stilled. Yet at the same time, she realised that she would never feel the same about Jonty again. When you've been unfaithful, your husband alters, becomes a stranger again. Jonty had become insubstantial. She spoke to him gently. 'How's the report coming along, then?'

He sounded hurt. 'Just about finished.'

'Ready for me to read?' Anxious to please, she put down her work on a side table next to a naked doll on a stand that looked a bit, Zet reflected, like Sarah.

He rose. 'Coffee?' he asked, sounding resentful, and handed her a brown folder.

'Not for me, thanks.' She settled back, uneasy in the chintz covered deep armchair. She didn't seem to fit her own home lately.

Returning from the kitchen, he drank his coffee standing by the open French doors with his back to her. Purple air drifted inside, sweet with flowers, grass and damp earth from the recently hosed garden. The nagging voice of a hedge trimmer died away leaving the room silent with concentration, apart from the rustle of turning pages, bird whistles, a panic stricken flutter of wings in the cherry tree. Obliterating darkness was not far off and Jonty sighed, returning to his chair.

By the time he clicked his empty mug down on a small table, she reached the end of the report. 'It's fine, I think,' she said thoughtfully, crossing the room to place the folder beside his mug.

Returning to her chair she felt an urgent need to help him. 'That supplier you complained to me about, the one whose deliveries are always late....'

'The chap's had problems.'

'Haven't we all? But you're not putting it in the report? Why?'

Shoulders hunched, he leaned down to open the briefcase at his feet. 'No need now, he said he would sort it out,' he answered, looking up, face set and stubborn.

'Rubbish,' she said sharply, watching him slip the file inside the briefcase. 'Being kind gets you nowhere.' She heard two loud clicks as Jonty snapped the briefcase closed. Jumping up, she crossed the room to close the doors against the chill she felt creeping inside.

As she shot the bolt, something made her pause with a start. Among the shadows pressing on the glass hovered a pale, sad face with haunted eyes. With an intake of breath, she whisked the heavy floral curtains closed on her own reflection outside in the dark, looking in, as if she didn't belong. That was frightening.

118

When we met, she thought impatiently, as she crossed the room, he had seemed ambitious. Well there's little sign of ambition lately, she thought, and reaching her chair, she sat down with a long drawn out sigh. Cullens was cutting down on staff so much that he had more chance of getting his work typed if he handed it into the shrinking typing pool first thing in the morning. In fact, Zet had long ago taught herself to type so that in an emergency she could type his reports.

Picking up the doll, she settled herself with another sigh that said...I've done all I can. Can't do any more. Her face settled into lines of displeasure. Two gunshot reports re-opened the briefcase.

'Who is the woman you go to the club with?' she asked Brad, keeping her voice casual. 'She looks...very pleasant.'

'She is. I've known her all my life.' 'Is she married?'

'Not Mary. Dead set on being a career girl is our Mary. She's manager at the Estate Agents now. We're old friends, nothing more...really.'

So that's where I met her before. Zet looked around the kitchen where they were drinking coffee. She noticed a prepared casserole standing on a kitchen unit and following her glance, he half-smiled.

'Old Bertha's my cleaner, but she often makes me something. We single men get spoilt.' A teasing smile made him look boyish, and there was a knowing gleam in his eyes as if he knew what her next question would be.

'Does Mary spoil you?' She pictured the woman.... tightly controlled dark hair, a disappearing mouth and a sudden liking for smarter clothes.

'Sometimes she asks me round for dinner; or she comes here, so I can return her hospitality, you know.'

'I know', Zet smiled. 'Does she cook here?' she asked too brightly.

'I can manage,' he said, looking amused. 'But sometimes she insists.'

'I have a cookery diploma,' she told him, showing off.

'There are a lot of good cooks around 'ere.' Seeing something injured in her face, his voice deepened. 'You have a husband...I have Mary and....'

She smiled, forcing a teasing note in her voice, 'and all the other women who spoil you.' She was watching him over the rim of the cup.

'It's a terrible, terrible, life,' he joked, pushing his empty cup aside. His expression darkened. He moved restlessly, watching her across the table. 'But at least I'm free, Rosetta. Wasn't for your marriage, we could do a lot more.'

Her cup clicked down into the saucer. He was talking as if they were a couple, as if they belonged and she felt a spurt of pleasure, followed by a savage inner thrust of despair that made her look at him, eyes wide with shock. 'Like what?'

With a grim, taunting smile, he said, 'A holiday for instance.'

Her heart turned over. He doesn't mean it, surely. 'Where?'

'I like Greece.' He paused, holding her eyes. 'I like the Lake District, too, but I'm a wanderer. I can't go for too long without flying off somewhere.'

Was there a warning in his voice? Zet could think of nothing to say. Does Mary like Greece? And the word holiday took on a darker meaning. The thought of them both going off in opposite directions, with other people, not seeing each other for two weeks was quite unpalatable. She recognized challenge in his stare.

Behind him, on the wall, the hands on the clock stood at three o'clock. It ticked, as old clocks do, racing against her pulse. She heard car engines starting up as parents prepared to collect children from schools. It began then. The splitting in two.

120

Zet began to loathe weekends and evenings. Sundays were a month long, and she wondered who else had said that once.

'*For always, you will be my lover*,' Brad sang into the mike.

Glancing across the room, Zet saw Mary watching him intently; smoke weaving around her from the forgotten cigarette she held.

'I hate this,' Brad grimaced down at her as they danced one of the two dances they allowed themselves. Zet didn't answer, uneasily aware that there were times, as now, when his face could look cruel, with a savage message that he would strike all irritations from his path.

She took comfort from the pressure of his hand just above her waist; his spread fingers almost touched one breast. His grip tightened, her insides slipped, and he went on, eyes blackly glittering down at her. 'I want to throw you down, make love to you and if those blue eyes of yours don't stop telling me you fancy me too, I might just do that.' His voice was huskier than usual. 'You're beautiful, Rosetta.'

Flushed with pleasure and misery, she made herself smile coolly and grimace at Jonty as they shuffled by and tell herself there were no curious faces watching them. Except for Mary, whose square, unvarnished fingers were strangling a wine glass.

Jonty smiled at her when she returned to the table and Margaret leaned across, saying, 'Heard the latest gossip? Well....'

Zet hardly listened. Something about the butcher running off with someone's wife. It was suddenly difficult to breathe. I can't do this any more. Her head was beginning to ache. It all beat at her. The loud music, Margaret's monotonous voice...her own inner voice saying it must stop. The room swung around her, as she fought for breath and thought she might faint.

'Course,' Margaret was saying. 'You've heard about Mary's new rival, I suppose.'

Zet felt sick; she shook her head, Margaret looked triumphant. 'That new barmaid.' Her voice went on, and on, while Zet, with an aching heart, knew this was the last time.

Chapter Twenty-Three

'I'm bored with the club, Jonty. Let's not go any more.'

Anxious and tense, she met his face across the breakfast table. He held her eyes, as if trying to read her and, stomach twisting with nerves, she forced herself not to look away. He looked surprised, but shrugged.

'If that's what you want,' he said easily, picking up his "World's Best Dad" mug.

'Yes, yes I do.' She felt the prick of tears. He always fits into my likes and dislikes as he fitted into my life and tried to become me. Her heart contracted. Jonty...you're a good man, how can I do this to you?

With a pang, she remembered how she had once loved their lazy Saturday mornings. The kitchen smelled of toast and coffee, marmalade and malted shreddies. The children were out somewhere helping to organise a fete.

Cakes! She had promised to make cakes. If only she hadn't broadcast her cookery skills; the villagers' original lack of interest had turned to...Our Zet will do it. She gritted her teeth at the crunching sound coming from behind Jonty's newspaper. And she couldn't stand the way he slurped coffee...stop it, Zet. Make an effort. Be kinder. 'Hope it stays fine,' she said, brightly, glancing at the window.

Finishing his toast, he threw the paper down, 'You're different.' He was watching her carefully and she went cold.

'In what way?'

'I didn't know you were a nature girl,' he said sulkily.

She let out her breath and stood up. 'We don't know anyone until we live with them, do we? I mean, you told me once that you liked gardening. There's no evidence. You were once keen on tennis but you're not interested now.' She glanced with distaste at the newspaper stuck to a buttery knife. And why does he always gulp drink loudly, as if he's dying of thirst.

He watched her over his mug. 'I must start the cakes,' she said, turning away, and he felt dismissed, thinking miserably that he had never felt close to her, even in the early days; now, it was worse. She was pre-occupied, less interested in his job, tired at bedtime and undressed and dressed as if she was on a beach. 'You help people too much, maybe,' was all he could think of saying.

'What's wrong with that?' she asked, taking a mixing bowl from the cupboard.

He loved her straight back, the curve of her waist, her neat bottom. I could go over there now, he thought longingly, run my hands all over her and... But no, it's like smoking. Not in the kitchen. Putting down the mug, he reached for more toast. Eating filled a hole.

'You make yourself part of people, so they want more of you,' he said, pulling the butter dish towards him, digging the knife into the butter.

She glanced over her shoulder, looking annoyed. 'What is this? Therapy?'

'No,' he answered, with a full mouth. 'Just sussing you out.'

Resenting it as if he had raped her, she pulled the scales and flour container towards her, just as the front door slammed. Voices raged in the hall, Alyson shrill, Darren defensive. The door burst open and they rushed in with the anguished look children have when they are hot and thirsty. 'We're not staying,' Alyson cried, slim and straight-backed, with a confident air. 'The image of you at her age,' Iris had told Zet.

Alyson had the same wide apart blue eyes, heavy brows, even hairline. She had Zet's elegant nose and graceful movements but showed her affection exuberantly, and loved with abandon, as Zet had never

124

done. She watched her daughter tugging the fridge door open.

'Got an ice lolly, mum, or Ribena or something?'

'I want squash,' Darren announced, always sure of himself. He's got your ways, Gran had told Zet, as if Darren had picked up a germ.

Studying him, Zet's insides shifted and she felt a splinter of pain; it was as if she hadn't looked at this chubby little boy for a long time. He had his father's dark, floppy hair, the tortured brow, sturdy body and bowed shoulders. In ways, he was gentle yet determined, stubborn, tidy and self sufficient, even at eight, and mad on animals. I love you two, she thought, with a painful tug on her heart that made her speechless.

'I'll never forgive you,' Darren was telling his sister coldly.

Zet found her voice was unsteady. 'What's wrong, Darren?'

'He just has to have his own way,' Alyson burst out scornfully. 'He wants to lead the donkeys in the rides but I'm doing it; I'm older.'

He slammed the fridge door, 'I asked first. And the donkeys like me.'

'Before you rush out,' Zet said firmly, 'did you do Friday's homework, Alyson?'

'Oh, mum,' Alyson whined, flicking back her hair. 'That's all you think about.'

'I did,' Darren offered, round face saintly, and Alyson turned on him.

'You're too young for homework, you silly yo-yo.'

Darren looked mulish. He liked to keep up with his sister, which annoyed her intensely. He stretched towards the tap, running water into his glass, watching the deep orange drink turn yellow. 'I had to do an exp'riment with bath water, so there. Dad helped me.'

Zet glanced at Jonty. 'I didn't know.' Something gripped her chest and squeezed it. And then she felt cross.

125

He had time for things like that, while she always had to be the one to discipline and push the children because he was soft with them.

Alyson, sucking her lolly, looked jealous and flung herself on to her father's lap and he immediately hugged her. 'He's my daddy.' She was very possessive with those she loved, whether people or toys.

Jonty rested his chin on Alyson's neat head, a sublime smile on his face and Darren was gulping his drink, pretending not to care when, suddenly, the glass slipped from his hands, smashing down on to the stone floor.

'Oh, for goodness sake....' Zet grabbed a dustpan, brush and floor cloth and Darren cried great strangled sobs. Jonty reached out an arm and pulled him close and Darren's sobs became the hiccupping, gratified, pleased with the attention type. Yelling, Alyson clung to her father, pushing Darren away.

An orange pool spread across the floor and kneeling down, Zet could have wept herself. This wasn't how she had planned things.

Wandering in a vacuum around the crowded fete, she was unable to push aside the sense of loss, the approaching lonely void of Saturday evening without the bitter sweet anticipation of seeing Brad. She closed her eyes against the ache that was constantly with her, along with something she had no right to feel.

What does he do after the club? Does he take Mary home with him? You have no claim on him, Zet. I know. And I know that if I don't keep my anguish to myself I'll lose him. He won't tolerate possessiveness. So why torture yourself by imagining driving over to his house early one Sunday morning, surprising him... them...oh, God?

She found a vacant picnic table and sat down. The sun stayed away but the air was warm and humid, the sky a hot stainless steel lid cooking them gently. A plane from

126

the nearby airfield droned overhead, a brass band was playing but every tune sounded the same. She felt unreal, as if she wasn't there, even though she spoke to the handsome young vicar, bought things she didn't want at the stalls, watched Jonty at the games that had been rigged up.

Then there was the cake stall...she was just thanking God that her turn serving had finished, when Jonty crunched over dry grass towards her, carrying a bottle of cheap wine and a coconut the colour of his untidy hair, face beaming, asking for praise.

She felt miles away from the sickly smell of diesel oil and crushed grass, old cowpats, sausages and fried onions. Children screeched from one of those bouncy castle things, a tractor groaned around giving rides, a miniature train hooted, tongues licked ice cream and mouths wrapped around hot dogs and tangled with queasy pink cotton wool candy floss. It was all friendly, innocent and sticky.

Only I've lost my sticky, Zet realised, with a thump of her heart; she was sliding off the picture, there was no absorbency, she was unattached to this long, boring day, which was only just beginning.

She wondered, with the turbulence inside her, how she could sit so calmly, eating strawberries and cream, on a wobbly chair in farmer Braithwaite's field.

What was Brad doing? She saw the strawberries, deep rose-red, glistening and swollen with juice, and her loins twanged a fierce need.

A shadow fell over the table. Jonty had dumped his prizes on the table and gone off. He was now back, carrying thick white cups of tea from an urn manned by Big Brenda, who also ran the scouts. Brenda's plump arms lifted, poured, wobbled, face contented, motherly, and Zet was moved by a different need. She scalded her throat with the strong tea that was just as Gran made and longed for the old lady. Longed, surprisingly, to be in that

127

"boring" house, being tucked up in old-fashioned white cotton sheets by someone motherly.

'There's a flower-arranging display in the big tent,' Jonty announced cheerfully, sitting down.

When she didn't answer, he sounded urgent. 'You like flowers.'

Sex, she was thinking. Since knowing Brad, her loins lived on the edge of exploding, yet when Jonty reached for her the fire died; it was absent-bodied lovemaking. How odd.

Ripples of longing ebbed and flowed. The last strawberry lay in her bowl, sure of itself and the desire it aroused. She sliced her spoon into it and placed half in her mouth, biting into its swollen softness until the jammy juice flowed over her tongue. The cream, ejaculated from a can, had dissolved into nothing. Jonty, with a teasing grin, reached out and flicked the last piece of strawberry into his mouth, leering at her as he chewed. She felt her eyes widen with surprise.

She clicked down her spoon. Her pants were wet. 'You don't have to come and look at flowers,' she snapped. 'You said you wanted to watch the sheep dogs. We're not joined at the hip you know.'

***

Where once he had hated being away from home, lately the monthly meeting in London had become a respite.

'Hope your wife doesn't mind,' Sarah said with her endearing giggle as they tucked into their meal in the fish restaurant overlooking the river Thames.

'Why should she mind?' he said, to which she answered curtly.

'I'm surprised that a townie like her should be happy in Yorkshire.'

'You have the wrong idea about Zet; living in the

country was a dream of hers. I'm glad I was in a position to give poor Zet what she wanted. You should see her...I feel as if I've given her the moon.'

Sarah, smoking a cigarette, wore an expression like the television adverts for indigestion tablets. 'You rode in on your charger and took poor Zet away from all that.'

He studied her uncertainly. 'Can I have a cig?' 'Thought you gave up.' She pushed the packet over. 'I tried,' he answered, clicking her lighter until it flamed. 'Zet doesn't like the smell. I go in the garden sometimes, for a quick one.'

'Are you happy?' Sarah questioned in her blunt way, looking unusually serious.

He dragged deeply on the cigarette. 'Why not? Nice home, good kids, my job's okay and I have a lovely wife, in fact, perfect.'

There was a hint of satisfaction in Sarah's reply. 'Mum said her mother's a bit of a weirdo. They met at the wedding.'

He smiled. 'Iris is great.'

Sarah's eyes widened. 'You don't find her silly and artificial then? Mum said....'

He shook his head. 'I see someone who wants to be happy,' he said quietly, stubbing out his cigarette in an ashtray. 'Her determination sometimes turns me over.'

Sarah's voice was dry. 'She told mum she was film star once. Mind you, she'd apparently had a few.'

'I did hear something about it.' 'Do you mean she was?'

'So I've heard. It was when she was a kid.' He pushed the ashtray towards her and she stabbed her cigarette into it, looking disappointed.

'Seems odd no one remembers her.'

'It was years ago. I asked Sophie about it once and she said, "ask Gran." So I did. Gran just grumbled something about war and turned funny.'

Sarah shrugged, as if to say...they're all funny if you ask me. 'Sounds like this Iris is living in a dream world. No wonder your wife is, er, different.'

Jonty changed the subject then, and they talked of other things. He called a taxi to take them back to her home, her parents welcomed him warmly, and before he went two doors along, where he was staying overnight with his parents, he thanked Sarah for coming. Standing at her front door, she looked surprised at such formality but smiled and said nothing.

She looked up at the old, cold light of stars barely discernable through the orange haze of street lamps and watching her, he found himself saying, 'You make me feel better, Sarah,' and she turned to him with widened eyes.

'Better than what?' she asked. 'What's better than perfect?'

'I don't know,' he said, confused, but she laughed in the old jolly way. 'I'll walk you to your gate, Laddie,' she said, tucking her arm into his. 'And remember I'm your mate. If you ever fancy sausages over a camp fire or jellied eels at Southend instead of...' she hesitated... 'Cordon Bleu, then I'm your girl.' There was hidden meaning in her words and she hoped he heard. She had been halfway around the world, slept with many men on the way and now she was back for a while. What would it be like to sleep with the boy next door?

'I'll remember,' he answered, looking up, searching for stars.

Chapter Twenty-Four

Hearing her name called as she hurried from the cottage, Zet jumped, going hot and cold. Not now. Heart sinking, she saw Norah, laden with shopping, squelching towards her across the soggy green. Zet tried a casual wave. Her long legs, in stiff new jeans, carried on walking hoping to get past before Norah reached her. No chance.

Norah's voice reined Zet in. 'Aah, God knows when school holidays are coming; down comes the rain.'

Zet's heart did an icy triple spin. *Summer holidays?*

Innocently, Norah added, 'that will nip your walks in the bud, can't see youngsters walking these days.' Seeing Zet's expression, she added cheerfully, 'I'm always here, m'dear, if you want to drop the bairns in with me for an hour or two; in the afternoons mind, I work mornings.'

Zet could have hugged her as she went on, 'They're well brought up bairns,' she said approvingly. 'No trouble. You're a nice couple, really fitted in 'ere, for incomers.'

She hesitated, glancing behind Zet at the cottage. Lowering her voice, she said, 'that's why we all 'ope things'll work out for you, like.'

Zet smiled. 'Norah, you're a wonderful help.'

'That's what neighbours are for. Want a cuppa? We can have a bit of gossip.'

'Don't tempt me,' Zet said, satin underwear sliding beneath rough denim. 'I'm off before you mention your delicious scones.'

Norah looked pleased, but scoffed, 'Go on with you.

Rather sit by the fire meself, on a day like this. Off you trot then.'

Off Zet trotted. Her trainers made heart-thudding beats on the ground as she hurried out of the village, crossed the bridge, turned left into a private field and walked along a public footpath beside the hurrying river.

The water leaped beneath overhanging branches, slithered over stones, slurped around obstacles and she worried over her own obstacles, the school holidays and the looming threat of the annual holiday.

Jonty had brought the subject up last week. She had been sitting at the newspaper-covered table beside the window, painting eyebrows on a doll's face. Watching a repeat of Jaws on television, the sight of sand and sea had set him off. 'Holidays?' She felt as if shark's jaws had her around the throat. 'What with the move and everything, we'd better leave it this year.' She laid down her brush with shaking hands, afraid of making a mistake.

He sounded disappointed. 'We could go down south instead, I suppose,' he suggested without enthusiasm, 'and visit the family.' She felt trapped.

Screams burst from the television, she saw the foaming sea, red with blood, felt a fierce need of Brad. Staring at the screen she saw the thrashing fin, the great open mouth. 'Let the family come here.'

'Lot of work for you,' he answered, eyes on the screen. 'And Gran won't come, nor Sophie.'

'That's up to Gran,' Zet snapped. 'She's been invited; if she wants to be funny, tough. Sophie, well,' Zet didn't let the hurt show in her voice, 'she's never been here; anyone would think she'd be glad to get away. And work's no problem...I'm organised.'

Fond grandparents, she was thinking, as she trudged across the field recalling that conversation, take children out for the day. So do aunties. Why does Sophie avoid holidays? Anyway, the children will be happier roaming this wonderful place than being stuck in airports and coaches.

Walking between scrawny hedges necklaced with diamante drops from the morning's rain, the air smelled of aniseed-scented tansy that grew wild in the tangled flower banks. 'I'd love to take you to Greece,' Brad had said the day he had given her a glass of ouzo to try.

'Too hot for me,' she had replied, sipping but not liking the aniseed taste very much. 'White hot beaches and burnt skin are not my style.'

'What about long, cool siestas,' he had smiled - that tantalizing half smile - and pulled her close to him murmuring, as his hand caressed her responding breast, about sizzling skin spread against cool white sheets and isolated tamarisk trees sheltering beaches the colour of melted butter. She became quite carried away, until something niggled...who did he experience this with usually... before me?

And a further little niggle added, if he loves Greece so much he'll go with you or without you. There was always Mary, who had tough brown skin like a walnut.

Her footsteps quickened until, above her head, surly looking boughs fell back, exposing a sky gone dark again. Ahead stood Fiveways, where five lanes met and where, according to the locals, you sometimes heard the echo of a woman's laughter. The story went that one windy night a young woman had arranged to meet here and run away with her lover; her farmer husband followed her and shot her in the back as she fell laughing into her lover's arms.

But that was long ago, if it had happened at all. Today, a car stood waiting on the grass verge; it would smell inside of nicotine and leather and it looked glum because it was never polished. But Brad's arm appeared through the open window. A wave, and everything was all right.

Home. Smiling, she spread a towel on the sheepskin rug in front of the log fire. Brad slipped off his navy-blue towelling robe and threw it on to the sofa. Tangerine flames flickered on glistening brown skin, moist from the bath they had taken together. He stretched on the rug at her feet. Her eyes ran lovingly over the curve of his waist, spread of his shoulders, tight, pale buttocks, rigid muscles in legs well used to walking and riding. Dropping to her knees beside him, she began.

Placing her hands near the base of his spine, she left them there, feeling his flesh quiver beneath her palms, making contact. She could hear wind rattling doors and windows, a softly playing cassette and the flames of the fire flapping and hissing its own special music. Apart from the fire's glow, the room was dim, daylight partly excluded by the small window.

On the floor beside her stood three small brown glass bottles containing ylang ylang, jasmine and almond oil. She spilled almond oil on to her palms, followed by drops of the scented oils and moved so that she was astride his buttocks.

Starting at his spine, she moved her hands firmly up his tense body. Beneath her fingers she felt the pleasured response of his flesh and heard his contented sigh as her fingers became more and more sensitive, playing him like an instrument until his flesh sang. She firmly slid her hands up towards the bulge of his strong shoulders and swept out to the outer edges. More gently, she stroked down the sides of his body returning, with a rhythmic movement, to the tense buttocks. She went back up his body, kneading knotted areas with the heel of her hand, reaching his neck, with its tougher outdoor skin, where she squeezed and kneaded again.

Next she used gentle effleurage down from his neck to the more relaxed buttocks, stroked upwards with feathery strokes and, leaning forward, stretched herself on his back, skin against skin, stroking his arms, hands and fingers and she might have been swimming; she felt liquid with contentment, felt herself drain into him. Flat on him, his body's throbbing pulses beneath her, strong muscles bearing her light weight, she wanted to stay there forever.

Moving away, she asked him to turn over which he did with a groan, exposing a blissful, un Brad-like smile, eyes closed. She began again, oiled hands slipping, sliding, stroking, breathing the deliciously oils. She finished by running her fingertips down his furry torso and suddenly paused. She felt odd. Her hands were tingling and she felt her energy draining away.

I must be too hot from the fire, she told herself and, shaking off her peculiar lethargy, she began again, running her fingers down his inner thighs to massage the soles of his feet, gently, taking her time, until she felt that he was tension free and relaxed.

'Aah....'

She smiled. That this powerful, dominant man, who physically, and in many other ways, took her and put her where he wanted her, should be lying here, passive, saying...do what you like with me...was extraordinarily exciting and arousing.

She ran her fingers around his coarse-skinned face, massaging lines, down the slightly hooked nose to his taut mouth, up the bulge of his cheeks, around his closed, heavy-lidded eyes, to his forehead, through his wiry black hair, moving the scalp, noting a glint of silver in the waves. A last few downward strokes and she reached his groin, feeling his passion rising beneath her oiled hands; his skin was smooth, satiny, his erection was hot, hard, searching, and she felt her own body's urgent need.

She lay along the length of his body, long legs against his, her breasts squashed on his beating chest, feeling his hard hands come around to hold her buttocks against him. Stretching, she slithered up his body until she could press her lips against his in a long, slow kiss. He moved her, slippery skinned, against him, and while the curtains shivered and firelight danced with shadows, he slipped like a velvet flame inside her, rising, reaching up, arousing an exquisite trembling in her bones.

They were warm from the fire, slipping, sliding, mouths working. His eyes were closed, his face young and vulnerable as if he were sleeping and having wonderful dreams, and laying her head down, face lost in his strong dark hair, she moved with him until he awoke with a cry.

They pulled the sofa close to the fire. The contented, sleepy, shadowy afternoon room smelled of his favourite toasted teacakes, butter and wine and scented oils. They were stretched out on the sofa, Zet half lying back on him feeling relaxed and contented; she was wearing one of his old white shirts; his robe hung open, she could feel his skin warming her through the shirt and his torso pressing against her spine.

On the carpet stood empty wine glasses, a plate holding crumbs, currants, and a used tissue glistening with butter.

'You should take this up professionally,' he said, and she glanced round, catching sight of his relaxed smile.

'I've got certificates,' she boasted, turning back. 'Certificates for what?' he teased, one arm pulling her closer.

'Aromatherapy, cooking, doll-making.'

His nose was pressed against her messed up hair, breathing in because he said he loved the wet violet scent of her hair. His voice was muffled, 'Clever girl.' Surprised, she turned again, and found his face very close, looking down at her with loving in it and there was that softer glow in his eyes, the different gentleness of his hard hands when they touched her lately. The shadows in the room were still, thoughtful, probed with tangerine streaks and an idea flared.... but fled away. She tried to catch it, but, sleepy, couldn't.

'You should have a certificate for love-making,' he murmured against her momentary distraction. 'You're wonderful at it.'

She answered without thinking. 'Only with you.'

They stared, shocked, into each other's eyes, seeing questions that mustn't be voiced. There was a way of playing this game.

'He's a nice man, my husband,' she said uncertainly, not wanting Brad to think she was uncaring.

'Yes.'

'He doesn't touch me, somehow. I mean, there's nothing....' Her head rested on his shoulder, her face was tilted, looking up at him. A line appeared on her forehead.

His eyes were slits of murky water. A muscle moved in his jaw. 'No,' he said.

She felt disloyal and oddly affectionate towards Jonty. 'We sleep together,' she said awkwardly, 'and, somehow, we move apart for sex.'

The fire spat out sparks. 'I shouldn't need to know,' he said abruptly.

'And I shouldn't need to tell you.'

In the pause that followed, she watched flames eating spitefully into a log and felt it in her stomach, almost as if she had a premonition of what he was going to say.

'Do you think, my darling, that we've had the best of it?'

'What?' She drew in a panic stricken breath. His hand gripped one of hers, and she looked down at their clasped fingers. 'It? Us, you mean?' She was accusing, cold, as if he was belittling what she felt, what she thought they had and she wondered how you knew...when an affair ended and love began and then, like the stroke of a whip, she discovered something else...that there is a point of no return.

When he spoke, he sounded knowing and kind. She wondered if he had done this before when a woman became too serious. He said, 'It's hard for me to say this, but I wonder whether we should stop seeing each other.'

She felt sick. To hell with his kindness, he'd had enough. He wasn't the sort to settle for one, so they say. Her throat tightened. Through stiff lips she said, 'You don't love me?' As soon as the words were out, she wished them back, for love had never been mentioned. Love was the hidden part of it. She hadn't wanted to frighten him away by anything too intense. His reply was unexpected.

137

'That's just it; I do. And I'm jealous. And what I feel could kill the love.' There was a violent note in his voice. 'I could sometimes even...' he paused before going on in a voice that sent shivers up her spine...'kill that nice husband of yours.'

Shocked silence. The intensity in his face as he turned to check her reaction, was frightening. His arm pressed her too hard against him and he murmured the words she would, until this moment, have been thrilled to hear, 'I want you, all of you, for myself, all the time. I never thought I could feel like this, but I do and it can only lead to pain. I believe,' he ended roughly, 'that there's safety in numbers.'

'You knew I was married, ' she reminded him, hearing her voice crack.

He nodded. 'I couldn't resist you. But I didn't – couldn't – know that things would go so deep.' He hesitated. 'Sometimes, after a tragedy, you start running, and don't stop until someone special comes along and forces you to face up to yourself. I don't know that I'm ready for that.'

Was he saying goodbye? She was half turned, still lying on him but curled in the foetal position. Don't leave me, she was inwardly crying. Please don't leave me. I can't bear it. She turned her face into the old- smelling arm of the sofa, feeling the warm, tough closeness of him, feeling her essential need of him, sickened by the knowledge that if he left he would take with him everything of her that functioned, leaving a shell.

The heat of the fire suddenly rounded on her, the flesh might have been peeling from her bones. With a roar, the log collapsed, sending sparks up the chimney, the curtains billowed into the room and outside, a curlew was shrieking with laughter.

The fire began to die, the room grew darker, and storm clouds covered the windows as if the world was ending and his voice made her shiver with premonition,

'Whatever happens, my darling, never think I don't love you, and always will.'

'There's no such thing as *always*,' she said in a hard voice, feeling the old belligerence because things were not going her way. Into her mind came her nightmare of the man pointing the rifle at her, as if to remind her that life could be wiped out at any time and being abandoned was always on the cards.

Oh, Brad. What can we do? She would think of something. She had to find a way. She was good with obstacles, people said. And she began to plan even as they drove to the crossroads where he always dropped her. They said a stilted goodbye, and she walked the rest of the way home.

'Jonty.' He turned from the television screen immediately. 'I've something to tell you,' she said, trying to keep her voice from shaking.

'I'm all yours,' he said affably, reaching out and turning the sound down.

Chapter Twenty-Five

She hesitated. I don't know why the hell I'm feeling so nervous. She swallowed hard before she told him. 'I've decided to start my own business.'

Jonty looked startled. Zet had always said she couldn't understand mothers who preferred to work than be at home and she didn't care how old-fashioned that was.

'Cooking?' he asked carefully, as if expecting to have his head snapped off. She didn't disappoint him.

She raised her eyes to the ceiling. 'There's more to life than a kitchen.'

'Dolls then?' He looked aggrieved.

Her voice was cutting. 'Aromatherapy.' 'Aromatherapy?'

I wish he wouldn't keep repeating everything. 'I'm qualified.'

'I know you are, but....' He ran fingers through his hair, such a familiar gesture her heart smote her. How do you leave someone who is so good to you? How do you hurt him when you know he only lives and works for his family? Her skin burst out in cold, clammy sweat. There are the children. She couldn't bear them to be hurt, as she had been hurt and her childhood ruined. Hands squeezed her insides and the screw began to turn.

Brad hasn't asked you to leave Jonty, she reminded herself. Why? Obvious, isn't it? He prefers his freedom. Leaving home and going to the wayward, freedom-loving Brad was obviously not on the cards. Yet, she lived with the fear that for Brad, there were available women. He had said recently...'you only see me when you want to, not when I want to. Don't I matter, then?' he had asked. That had hurt for of course he mattered. But she still left him.

'I've placed an advertisement in the local newspaper,' she told a puzzled Jonty, hiding her feelings with a crisp and businesslike voice. 'I intend to run a mobile service, treating people at home. This is the ideal area; so many people live far from the town, in fact some houses are extremely isolated.'

'I know. Yes, I see.'

'I'll travel to them,' she explained and his brow furrowed.

'In what?'.

'A car, of course. What did you think, a broomstick?' After a hurt silence she went on hurriedly, 'We can afford a second-hand car and I can buy stock with the money I've earned from my dolls.' She wouldn't feel guilty if she used her own money.

'You look guilty, Zet.'

Her head shot up. 'What?' She reached for the doll beside her and, for something to do, tried one of the shoes to check the fit. The doll felt smooth and cold beneath her trembling hands. The shoe fitted perfectly. The silence was heavy and she felt terror inside her, fear of the unknown, of change, of her husband pointing his finger, showing up her guilt and herself with no defence. Steeling herself, she glanced up, dreading what must come and found him looking at her steadily, kindly. Beneath his unbearable scrutiny she felt her cheeks grow warm. He had always had a knack of reading her.

'Surely you knew I would understand, Zet.' 'Well, I....' Her voice faltered, she felt lost.

'You don't have to look at me as if you've done me a terrible injury.' He suddenly smiled his nice smile that had something relieved in it. 'I think it's a brilliant idea. You haven't been yourself lately. I'm an idiot. You're not used to country life, it's too quiet for you; do you good to get out and meet people apart from the villagers.'

'Yes, well....' She couldn't trust herself to speak. He was looking at her so kindly and he didn't know how sick she felt. The standard lamp was beating down at her with unbearable warmth. Yet deep inside, enthusiasm stirred. She had lost interest in the home lately; oh, it ran like clockwork, but she felt little pleasure in it. Aromatherapy

141

was not only gaining in popularity but was something she enjoyed. I can make a success of it, she thought, feeling some of the strain leave her.

'It won't interfere with the home, Jonty; I can control the amount of business I take on. Norah would meet the children from the bus, but I'm hoping I can organise things so that it won't be necessary. Not often, anyway.'

Saturdays, her mind ran on; even, on the odd occasion, Sundays; she felt a jolt of guilty joy. A reason to be out. It was awful the way the word *escape* came to mind. But keeping Brad happy was her desire. *And keeping him away from anyone else.*

Jonty's voice sounded far away. 'I'm not worried about being neglected, Zet, not by you. You've never neglected the home yet.'

She swallowed the lump that suddenly blocked her throat. 'Thanks.' 'No; thank *you*.'

She bowed her head. Her lashes were wet, the shoes in her lap blurred.

Chapter Twenty-Six

Who would have thought it? Glancing from the kitchen window as she filled the kettle from the tap, Sophie saw Zet, of all people, on her knees beside a flowerbed. It wasn't just that. Sophie frowned. There was something else different about her niece, something beneath the surface that Sophie, who knew her niece better than anyone, sensed. Absentmindedly, she plugged in and switched on the kettle just as the telephone rang. Going into the hall, she picked up the receiver.

'I'll get her for you.' Clicking the receiver down on the table she went to call Zet. Leaning wearily against the back door, Sophie heard shrieks of childish laughter coming from the bottom of the garden. The children were playing in the Wendy House Maurice had built, and taking turns on the swing. On the patio, Jonty and Maurice looked relaxed on sun beds - if things had been different it would have been a comforting scene.

'It's an enquiry about aromatherapy,' she said, as Zet hurried in, wiping dirt-stained hands on her jeans.

'I can fit you in at one tomorrow,' she heard Zet say. 'That's the third this week,' she told Sophie, hanging up and tearing a note from the pad with a satisfied rip.

'Good,' Sophie said flatly. 'We're taking Alyson and Darren to Filey tomorrow, so they'll be off your hands all day.'

A shadow crossed Zet's face. Not meeting her aunt's eyes, she looked down at a bowl of pot pourre, running her fingers through it as she said, 'the children will enjoy it. We'll all go somewhere together the day after.'

Watching her, Sophie thought Zet appeared ill at ease as she replaced the pen in its round hole beside the pad, saying, 'Things have really taken off, Sophie. I mean, people in the villages have had to drive to Leeds or Harrogate for treatment. And many of the houses around here are miles from anywhere. I can't fail.' She sounded defensive, as if Sophie had accused her of something and Sophie answered curtly.

'You wouldn't, would you? Once you've set your mind on something, that's it'.

Zet returned her stare as if trying to read a mind. After an awkward silence, she offered, 'I could give you a treatment.'

'Don't waste your time on me.'

Footsteps tapped across the stone kitchen floor. Jonty called, 'aren't you the lucky one, Sophie. That's more than I've been offered,' he said over the clink of beer cans. The fridge door slammed and he threw Zet a petulant glance before he returned to the garden. Ignoring him, Zet moved towards the stairs, face closed and mulish.

'You only have to say, Sophie.'

'Thanks,' Sophie said. Watching Zet hurry upstairs, the wide white sleeves of her blouse flapping, Sophie had the impression of a bird in flight. Before she turned away she heard Zet pick up the bedroom telephone, tap buttons and speak in a low urgent voice.

The kettle clicked off but Sophie no longer fancied coffee. She felt cold and wanted the sun. It's the sort of cold, she thought, that seeps right inside you. Funny, with the weather so warm, but old stone cottages, I suppose, are always like this. God knows what it must be like in winter.

Outside, Sophie hesitated. The garden was hot and rainbow coloured; sunlight warmed her shoulders and hit her eyes like a laser and she breathed in a warm spicy scent from the roses that rambled everywhere; as her eyes adjusted she saw different colours and textures of silk and velvet creating a tapestry effect. The skirt of her beige shirtwaist dress brushed against mint that grew beside the door. Reassuringly normal, somehow, the scent of roses and mint. A giant terracotta pot of white marguerites dazzled against blood red geraniums growing in small pots around it.

She reached into the pocket of her beige cardigan, taking out sunglasses. She wore them a lot lately, even when the sun wasn't shining. Even in the house.

Small, ordinary things bring comfort was what went through her mind as she crossed the patio.... half empty beer glasses on a white wrought iron table; children's chatter; a creaking swing; bees mumbling; a whistling blackbird; a plane groaning overhead; a distant tractor; clanking lawn mower. And Zet talking secretly upstairs.

As her shadow moved towards him, Maurice looked up and patted the squashy sun bed beside him. Jonty asked if she wanted a drink and sinking down on warm cushions with a troubled frown between her eyes, she said she didn't. Nice men, these two. Maybe she was imagining Zet's strange behaviour and the shivery atmosphere in the cottage. Maybe the cold is inside me, she thought, eyes behind dark glasses suddenly moist.

Because he understood, Maurice looked away from her self-absorbed face, watching the garden and the noisy, playful birds he loved. 'It will soon start fading,' Zet heard him say as she arrived, smiling, on the patio carrying a tray. The smile died; she looked daggers at Maurice, who would kill off her garden.

But he had turned back to Sophie, saying, kindly, 'Nothing lasts forever.' She nodded and looked down at her ragged nails.

Zet thumped the tray down on the table. The tall glasses rattled and Jonty nodded at a glass jug containing a red drink floating with slices of orange. 'What's that?

'Sangria,' she said, picking up the jug. 'It's mother's and Tony's favourite Spanish drink.' Her eyes fell on Maurice. 'Nothing dull about their lives, is there? Tony gives mum a brilliant time.'

'What's it made of?' Jonty asked quickly. 'Lemonade, red wine and brandy,' Zet answered, stirring the drink, making ice cubes clang like stones against glass.

'Not for me.' Watching her pour the drink into glasses, Maurice lazily stretched and lay back on the sun bed. 'I prefer beer.'

Zet's chilling glance said...you would, no sense of adventure. She handed the others a glass. 'We're going Spanish tonight,' she told them, chin in the air, sounding hostile. She sipped her drink and with her throat tingling like ice and fire, added, 'It's paella for dinner.' Her voice was brittle. 'I assume you eat paella, Maurice?'

He had been lying with eyes closed. 'Can't I'm afraid,' he said, opening his eyes and raising his head. 'My stomach's playing up a bit.'

'What a pity. I have some boil-in-the-bag cod. That do?'

'Anything that's easy, Rosie.'

Zet turned away.

It had appeared overnight. She saw it as she padded barefoot out into the garden with her first cup of coffee. Somehow, it turned her over. She stopped dead, dew, like tears, seeping between her toes.

It was a birdhouse, complete with little rush roof. Excitable yellow finches and mild brown sparrows already surrounded a feeder piled with nuts. The card was attached to one of the rustic poles of the base. "To Rosie, Happy birthday. Dad."

At breakfast, she opened cards and presents. There were the usual aprons, tea towels, soap and bath oils. Silk French knickers from Sophie looked up at her from the wrapping, pink with shame and she felt her cheeks grow warm to be looking at them in front of her husband.

Alyson presented her with a hideous plastic garden gnome. Zet took it into the garden and placed it in the centre of the lawn. Fancying she saw something anxious and vulnerable in her daughter's eyes, Zet said, hiding emotion with a smile, 'I really like my gnome,' and Alyson looked relieved.

Jonty had to act the fool, making a mystery of it, saying her present was hidden and she had to guess where and she honestly didn't have the patience to try very hard. In the end, he led her, with the others following, into her hidden garden. Taut as a spring, she did try, pretending to wonder what Jonty's present could be. And then she saw it, beneath the cherry tree, next to the rhubarb.

It was a carved stone seat, cold and cement grey, awkward and unlikely to offer comfort. She forced a 'thank you,' smiled at Jonty, the children made her sit down, the cold struck her legs, Jonty, looking anxious, sat down on the rigid seat beside her and she kissed his cheek and Alyson took a photo with her new camera.

'Perfect,' Zet said. It was a game of Happy Families. He kissed her back.

'Knew you'd like it.' He looked pleased with himself. 'It's so you.'

Chapter Twenty-Seven

On Monday afternoon, Brad kissed her until she felt she had climbed inside him, handed her a book bound in red leather, a sprig of heather and a heart-shaped stone he had found at their place on the moors and had polished. The book was called *Wuthering Heights*.

He cooked a special fresh salmon lunch, served in style in a dining room that seemed dismayed by the unexpected extravagance of jugs of shop bought flowers and her laughter. The room smelled of moorland breezes, clotted cream, strawberries and champagne and hot candle wax and intimacy.

Afterwards, in the sitting room, he pulled heavy curtains across. 'That's right, keep the world out,' she laughed and he smiled his dark reluctant, closed mouth smile, and the screeching curlews couldn't be heard above the sound of music.

Stretched out on the sofa in front of the fire, with Brad playing the piano just for her, she felt spoilt, loved and very much a woman. He felt very much like a man who was spoiling the woman he loved. They both felt very much like making love, which they did. And then they ate exotic cheeses and biscuits with seeds, which meant she went home with no appetite. Sometimes anything that happened at home interrupted her mental journey back to Brad. She felt sad because it seemed as if she was losing part of her children's childhood.

Despite having her little red Fiat, she still enjoyed walking with the breeze and its scents washing her face. Now she had her car she could drive and then walk. 'You can get fed up walking the same old lanes,' she told everyone loudly.

Sophie gave her a searching look. Do you mean marriage? the look seemed to say. The same old lanes. What do you find out there on the wild moors?

'I'll walk with you one day,' Maurice offered, finding her in the hidden garden.

'I walk too fast for you,' she told him brusquely. As if he hadn't heard, he sat down beside her with his hands on knees, looking around at the garden as if searching for something he had lost. Zet felt his presence but kept her face averted.

'If you like,' he offered tentatively, 'I'll cut some of this down for you, love.'

She turned, giving him a look of sheer dislike. 'Destroy what I love, you mean?'

He shifted on his hard seat. 'Sorry.'

'So you're having a fling with Sophie now.'

He turned his head. Both his inspection of her and his voice was sad. 'Your tongue can be deadly, Rosetta, do you know that?' When she looked away, he added wearily, 'You're like a beautiful snake.'

Icily, she said, 'Strike before I get hurt, eh?'

He watched birds hopping in and out of sieved sunlight. 'People need people,' he said, after a moment, 'at least, some of us do.'

Something in his tone made her flush and she kept her face averted, her chin up.

'There's just one space inside people that's never filled,' she heard him say gravely. 'No-one can grow into it; it remains a gap. That's where a lost child lies.'

She shrugged. 'Your choice, Maurice. Why did you leave us, anyway?' she asked, as if she didn't care. She turned to look at him. 'Who was it? An office slut? I've heard about office affairs.'

He didn't flinch. 'Nothing like that. There are two sides to marriage you know.'

'I suppose it was mum's fault,' she said scathingly. 'Whoever was to blame,' he said sadly, 'I let you

down, Rosie. I should have stayed and tried harder, but

I left, causing you great pain. Blame me if it makes you feel better.'

She wrapped her arms around herself. 'I've done all right. Aren't you proud of what I've achieved?'

'Yes,' he said uncertainly. 'You've done well. A wife, mother, and daughter anyone would be proud of. You reach for the sky; you're strong-willed, a planner, rigid with a good framework.'

She looked at him coldly. 'You could be describing the Eiffel Tower.'

'A good analogy.' He forced a smile. 'It dominates; if you kick it you get hurt; it rises above problems. I'd love your strength,' he told her, after a short silence. 'My mother was strong.'

'She had to be with all those kids,' Zet snapped, jumping to her feet. 'Thank God for the Pill.' She strode away. Hurting.

Jonty had to go to London for a three-day seminar. Zet wished him luck and couldn't believe her own.

'Just my luck,' she sighed to Sophie. 'I need to go and see this new supplier in the Lake District, but with Jonty away....'

'No problem,' Sophie answered in a flat voice. 'Your dad and I will be here.'

'If you don't mind....'

Sophie shook her head. Being with children took her mind off things. 'On the other hand....' she said innocently, 'Couldn't we all go to the Lakes with you?' Her wide blue eyes looked up into Zet's horrified ones.

'I can't really...I mean, there will be meetings and where would we all stay? The hotels get packed this time of year.' She picked up a cloth and cleaned an already clean kitchen top, face averted, mind wandering. Brad all night...not having to leave him. Oh, wow! She tingled at the thought of it.

Sophie shrugged. 'Maybe another time,' she said moodily, and walked out.

From the kitchen window, Zet saw Maurice, stretched on a sun bed, put down his book as Sophie approached, she saw his face crease into one of his smiles that crinkled his forehead and made him look worried at the same time.

When Sophie perched on her bed beside him, Maurice reached out and patted her hand. Their hands remained clasped and Sophie lay back against the puffy cushion and closed her eyes as if life was too much.

Zet watched, horrified. What's going on? She had questioned her aunt when she arrived, but had received an evasive reply about having been off colour, she had needed a break and Maurice offered. I must get the truth from Sophie when I get back from the Lakes. The Lakes. She was so excited she could hardly breathe. It was madness. Madness.

Chapter Twenty-Eight

The minute she climbed out of her car at the station car park and he was there, waiting, she felt not only weak with relief but also blissfully possessed. Kissing, hugging, smiling into each other's eyes, for once they cared not a damn who might be watching.

'It's allowed at railway stations,' she laughed, when their clinging lips and arms reluctantly disengaged.

'Thank God we're not saying goodbye.' He spoke with the relaxed, released air of the freedom loving traveller, taking her weekend case from her car and carrying it towards his own. They were different, both of them, she sensed, locking her car and following him. Seeing another side of each other almost made them strangers again.

She was close to exploding with excitement; climbing into his car, she slammed the door closed. Is this really happening? Yes, this is me. sitting beside him. We're leaving the car park, waiting to join the traffic in the high street. Her hand went anxiously to her mouth. Nothing can go wrong now, can it? There's a gap. We're off. Two days. The car moved faster; she felt as if she had received a long desired gift.

It showed...of course it did. In her shining eyes, her bubbling chatter, her need to keep touching his thigh, his arm, his hair, his neck. The A66 across the Pennines stretched behind like a ribbon she had been cut loose from; her spirit flew like hair blowing in the wind; the car sped with abandon on and on, engine throbbing its familiar song in her ears; she could have choked with happiness.

It was like those magic painting books she had loved as a child. Touch black and white pictures with a wet brush and colours appear. Touch life with love, and isn't the world coloured? Isn't it just?

Unexpectedly, the day splintered with pain.

Slowing to pass through a village, hearing shrill young voices and shrieks of laughter from a children's playground, her heart seemed to crack open. She glimpsed little bodies flying on swings, climbing frames, spinning, sliding. Pain, so intense it was almost physical, sliced Zet in half. Her throat closed up.

Through the village, speeding up, back on a straight road…pushing aside the part of her heart that missed her children…leaving it crying.

Frothing cappuccino at a roadside café; crunchy French bread and cheese at an inn; tea and laughter at a restaurant where a Pianola played happy ragtime by itself. Her love for Brad was like blotting paper; pain, guilt and responsibility were absorbed like spilled ink.

There were so many thrills to experience. His thigh moving beneath the palm of her hand as he drove; stopping in a lay-by to admire stick-in-the throat scenery; William Wordsworth's cottage; lakeside villages with skeins of tourists circling craft shops; ducks waddling across beaches; great, flat silver reflecting lakes. A certain lakeside, mountain-backed hotel. A bedroom. Their first night together. Love through the night; a moon, pale as clotted cream, watching through the window and sliding away across the black-skinned lake leaving silver trails of dawn behind.

They were strangers to the night, daytime lovers. He had never seen her without make-up, with her head on the pillow watching him undress, waiting for him. He removed her new sexy red nightdress and threw it across the bedside table, hiding the face of the staring clock on the Teasmaid.

He looked at her as if she was new. Her heart thumped noisily against the quiet white sheets. He bent his head and feeling his hot mouth and warm breath against her skin, damp and oiled from her bath, she grasped his long, thick damp hair, flowing to his shoulders, and sighed with pleasure.

153

Emotion stuck in her throat when she looked up at him after the climax. It was love. It was his skin, hot and familiar against her hands, the rock-hewn profile, his dark snapping eyes, the way his hair grew thick and wavy and sprang from his scalp like tough heather sprang from the earth, his arousing lips, his tough- skinned hands on her body, his gritty voice... all reached the core of her.

She slept, and was aroused by the pressure of arms around her; she curled into him and they loved again. With his breath warm on the back of her neck, she went to sleep cradled in his lap with his arms around her. The world can end now.

She lay on him when morning tore too soon into the blessed seclusion of their room, teasing, not letting him go, linking her arms around his neck and snuggling her naked body close to his. He slid his hand between her thighs. 'I'm mad about you,' he said, brusquely, like a confession. 'You're beautiful.' He kissed her unpainted mouth.

Remember this, whispered the stolen blue-green hours...

...Her hand caught in his strong one as they crunched across a stony beach, laughing at ducks, laughing at breakfast, floating across Windermere in a shower of rain and laughter on a thudding steamer; the lake reflecting their happy faces, a rainbow arching across the sky.

...The perfume factory, where she filled in an order for a stock of oils; the narrow winding streets of a lakeside village awash with tourists; wandering hand in hand in and out of fascinating shops; feeding each other fudge;

...Brad, looking young and carefree, inspecting paintings in an art shop. His touchingly soft smile when he presented her with a watercolour of Windermere, called Reflections, because white sails and mountains, a rainbow reflected in the lake, caught the perfection of their day.

The grey road home.

Smiling over coffee, forcing smiles over lunch, miserable over afternoon tea and stick-in-the-throat teacakes. Her red car waiting in the car park. Transferring from his warm car to her cold one the gifts and souvenirs that had the smell and the colour of the moments she had lived through. Moments gone, and seen ever after as reflections.

'Have you got the hump?' she asked.

'Yes,' he said shortly. 'Thank you for a lovely weekend, as the saying goes.'

She said nothing, but the bleak look in his eyes went right through her. Guilty. Guilty with him, guilty at home.

The stern back of his car as he drove away with the empty space beside him.

If you put too much water on the brush, the colours in the magic painting book run into each other until the picture is just a blur, like a rainbow crying.

Chapter Twenty-Nine

"It's impossible, tell the sun to leave the sky..."

Zet sighed. If only Sophie would not keep playing that Perry Como tape.

The evening was heavily scented with tobacco plants, honeysuckle, stocks, lavender and roses. Yet the garden was beginning to die. Red-hot pokers caught her eye, shooting up from the border, raging against reason and commitments. Like love.

As Perry Como drooled on, Zet rose restlessly from her seat and walked away. Moments later, she was sitting beneath the cherry tree in the hidden garden, reflecting how her need for Brad filled her life, when she heard Sophie's voice.

'Something about this place frightens me, it's so secretive,' she said, trudging along the path towards Zet. 'I prefer the real garden.'

Zet scoffed....'flowers that stand in a row; no secrets.'

'What have you got to hide then?' Without looking at her, Sophie walked over and inspected the lopsided, patched up shed as if it was a work of art.

Zet didn't know what made her say it. 'What do you do, Sophie, when you're married to a good man and in love with another?'

Silence. Wild sweet peas climbed the dry, worn wood on the shed, their little feelers so fragile that one wondered how they climbed. Their petals, pink and mauve, fluttered like tissue paper hearts; Sophie seemed fascinated by them. Then, 'so that's it. I wondered.' Turning, she slowly walked over to the seat and sat down, staring into Zet's face.

'I'm disappointed.'

Holding back tears, Zet said, 'Why should you be disappointed?'

Sophie sighed. 'Because you made a perfect life for yourself, you did everything right, not made a bloody mess of it....' She broke off and looked away.

'Do you want the cushion, Sophie?' 'No. I'm well padded in that region.'

Zet didn't hesitate for long. She could talk to Sophie. Sophie had always been on her side. By the time she finished talking, some of the tension had left her. Shadows were creeping like violet ink around them, and sunlight slunk away like worms as the sun took back what it had generously given for the last two weeks.

'Love,' Sophie exclaimed bitterly, studying her bitten nails. Looking up, she hesitated before saying, 'When you love, you give your power away.' With an oddly shamed expression, reading Zet's disbelieving eyes, she nodded, 'He was married to someone else and I loved him so much I gave him the power to hurt. And he did.'

'How long did you know him?' Zet asked, intrigued. Sophie, of all people....

'Eight years.' Avoiding Zet's shocked expression, Sophie stared at her hands, twisting in her lap. 'His wife was the helpless, dependent sort, not in the best of health. She needed him.' Swallowing, she admitted, 'He wasn't the first.'

Zet shook her head slowly, aware of a sinking sensation. 'So what hope is there for us?' she asked. She felt angry, as she added, 'I feel I'm too compliant, in fact I know I am. I was independent once, for God's sake.'

'It happens,' Sophie said, shifting uncomfortably. 'Look at me. I don't have relationships - I have emotionships. The break-my-heart-and-hope-to-die type.'

Zet felt as if she had received a blow. 'Sophie... you wouldn't?'

Staring up through darkening branches, Sophie shrugged. 'I've thought of it, but you know what pulled me through?' For a moment, Zet saw the old, familiar, loving smile as her aunt looked round. 'You. And to think your mother would have aborted you if I hadn't persuaded her not to. I promised her I'd help look after you and yet it was you who gave me a reason to live.'

Watching the loving, hurting face before her, Zet felt full up. On impulse she tucked her hand through her aunt's plump arm and received a grateful squeeze.

'I'd never have believed this,' she told her aunt after a long pause when both were reliving moments of the past. 'I thought you were...well, I mean I never thought of you being involved with men.'

'Because I'm not glamorous?'

Zet liked the comforting warmth coming from Sophie's sturdy body. 'I don't mean that. You were modern, independent, today's woman, you know? Women don't need men, you used to say.'

Sophie gave a hard, cynical laugh. 'Today's woman with yesterday's dreams. Which is what we all are,' she said bitterly, 'don't kid yourself otherwise.'

'I used to think you'd look lovely wearing make-up.'

Sophie grimaced. 'A mistress doesn't. It comes off on the shirts.'

'Tell me about it.'

Sophie talked to Zet as she had done to no one else. Ever. For it had been her secret life, a twilight life, the life of the Other Woman.

She had worked in the same office as Matthew. Pious Matthew, who didn't like dishonesty, told her right from the start that he wouldn't leave his wife because she needed him. Sophie had therefore decided that she would be the perfect mistress.

As she talked, she re-lived it all. The "violet hour", the time men spend with their mistresses between the office and going home to their wives. Secluded car parks are full of them on dark winter afternoons... rocking cars, steamed up windows, John Dunne playing love songs on the car radio, drinks from a thermos, Christmas a week early; and

158

in summer, picnics, walks, and sex among the bluebells, desperate for the return of hiding winter darkness. The car is Home, Monday to Friday. Weekends are lost, holidays torture, afraid to go out in case he phones. An unexpected visit is a treat, a phone call received like a gift.

She had been careful never to nag him to leave his wife, careful not to criticize his wife, careful to fit in with his plans, careful not to cry when they parted, careful not to be possessive, careful to be there when he needed her. Seeing Zet's horrified face, Sophie looked shamefaced. 'Sounds dreadful, doesn't it?'

'But surely you had some respect for yourself?' Zet asked in a low hurt voice.

Biting her lip, Sophie admitted, 'I was terrified of losing him. Besides, it's not all sex, you know. An affair can include companionship as well. In fact we first got together because his wife suffers from agoraphobia, she would never go out. He needed company. He was considerate, though, he never lost an opportunity to phone, or take a day off work now and then for a trip out somewhere. If he had an excuse to stay out a bit later he'd take me to dinner, if we could find a restaurant that opened early.' She blinked away tears; 'I've never been in a restaurant after eight.'

'And now?' Zet asked gently. 'I assume it's over. What happened?'

'What happened?' Sophie asked with a hard laugh. 'What happened, pet, was that Mat's wife died. Something I'd hoped for, and I know that sounds awful but her health, you know....'

Zet felt awful too, the way her heart leapt. 'So?' 'Last month he married someone else.'

'You're kidding!'

Sophie rested her head back against the seat and closed her eyes. 'He married a secretary he met when he was transferred to Head Office, in the City.'

159

Sophie opened her eyes and checked Zet's reaction. 'Wind-tossed vessels, people like me are. Others look at life, plot a course to their goal and set sail, cutting through the dross. I could have sworn you were the latter. I admired that.'

'I haven't lost my steering wheel,' Zet insisted, 'just my anchor. I don't know what's going to happen.'

'You know what mum always said?' Without waiting for an answer, Sophie went on in a small voice....'the women in our family have always fallen for vagabond lovers. They marry the quiet ones but fall for the vagabond lovers.' With something wistful in her voice, she said, 'my first love was a quiet man. He preferred someone else.'

In the sad violet evening, Zet saw the shadowy garden quiver, as if someone had walked through it, brushing against undergrowth. Something touched her face. The scented air was filled with whirring wings and Zet, brushing a hand against her face, told herself it was nothing more than that.

'Come on,' she said out loud, 'it's getting dark.'

As they rose, Zet, trying to sound normal, asked, 'what's it like...afterwards?'

Sophie thought a minute. 'Imagine' she finally said, 'a brillo pad rubbing across an open sore...all it takes is a clock face, between five and seven; a word, a song....'

Zet's skin tingled like ice. As they walked back arm in arm, she could faintly hear voices from beyond the wall, and the sound of Sophie's tape coming to an end.

For to live without your love is just impossible.

Chapter Thirty

'When the moors turn purple,' Norah was fond of saying, 'the wind will come and that,' nodding at Zet's garden, 'will be torn to shreds.'

'Thanks a lot,' Zet said dryly, using newspaper to clean a trowel and hand fork before putting them away.

'Just warning you.' Norah's voice changed. 'Zet?' 'Yes?''

'Er...everything all right with you?'

'In what way?' Zet closed the shed door. Hiding her impatience, she turned to look at Norah's concerned face.

'I mean with the family and... the cottage. You're all well?'

'You can see we are. Why?'

Norah stared towards the cottage, lost in thought until she pulled herself together with a shrug. 'Just wondered.'

'There's something bothering you,' Zet said, following her gaze. 'Something about the cottage. You might as well tell me.' Norah looked shame-faced.

Zet sighed. 'You're not going to tell me it's haunted, Norah. Honestly....'

Norah sniffed. 'Folks say....' 'Say what?'

'Just that folks who lived in the cottage have always been struck by tragedy.'

Zet smiled stiffly to show she wasn't bothered. 'You'll have to tell me its story one day, Norah, but I haven't time now.'

Norah looked relieved. 'Some more of your folks arrived yesterday, then?'

Everyone in the village knows that, thought Zet, nodding and smiling like the sunflowers, which towered over them, the children's only contribution to the garden.

Norah went off to work, she had a bedridden patient to see to, she explained, matter-of-fact again, capable, solid as a rock.

Zet felt alone in the garden, although she wasn't. The cottage drew her eyes - nothing about it to cause the uneasy curling in the pit of her stomach. On the contrary, its mellow walls and glistening windows gazed back at her like a smile.

She felt reassured by the sounds of ongoing village life. Voices inside houses floated outside. Horses clopped lazily by. Norah's front door slammed. Her car coughed, burped, chugged away.

Warm shadows were creeping towards the patio and...what could be more normal... there was Min, coming out of the cottage carrying a tray of tea. Albert had sent her into the kitchen to make it while he joined Zet in the garden. Like Zet, he worked silently.

The garden was quiet; Jonty had taken the children along the lane to see some horses. She could feel the remains of the day still warm on her cheeks....

'Your eyes,' Brad had told her, as they trudged, limbs perfectly synchronised, on the moors, ' are navy blue coloured when you're aroused.' Reaching their rock, he leaned back and pulled her against him, 'I've figured out what makes you so irresistible.' Feeling the curves of her body against him he pulled in a hiss of pleasure.

'You have?' She was busy placing light, teasing kisses on the corner of his mouth. It was such a hard, stern mouth, it amused her to make it soften and curve.

'The fascination of wanting to know you gets under a man's skin. It's fun trying. And in the trying, you find yourself, unexpectedly, in caring hands. You find yourself trapped, quite comfortably, in those hands and you want to lie there....' His voice broke off and she wondered why he turned his face away and why her heart was racing.

Turning, she leaned back against him, pulled his arms around her and calmed herself, head against his chest; with his body behind her hard, warm and pulsing, she

162

wished, for forever. But only *until*. There was no such thing as always.

Zet dropped onto a chair and accepted her tea. She was suddenly curious about Min, who was gazing, as she drank, at a terracotta container.

'One of my failures,' Zet told her between sips of tea, trying to be kind. 'I fancied a hydrangea there, but it hasn't flowered.'

'Perhaps it doesn't like being stuck in a container.' Min clicked her cup and saucer down on the table. 'Perhaps it would prefer to be free in the garden,' she added in the "unimportant little me" voice that grated on Zet.

Zet raised her brows. 'It's a thought.' She saw Min glance at the open book next to her cup and her guarded expression as she looked across the garden at Albert. Gently, Zet asked: 'What's the book, Min?'

'It's about this bored housewife who gets into her car one day to go shopping and just carries on driving.'

Zet tried to joke. 'Has it given you ideas?'

Min reached out and snapped the book closed. 'I can't drive.'

Her mother came. Afterwards Zet was to wish the visit hadn't passed in a blur.

Not my sort of place, too quiet,' Iris said, big eyes anguished. 'Nothing happens here, does it? I mean, don't you ever long for some excitement, pet?'

They were drinking sangria on the patio, discussing their day at York and the shops, watching Zet, barefoot and bare legged in shorts, hosing the flowerbeds down.

Lost in hot and sexy daydreams, Zet made no response, vaguely aware of laughter, and her mother's voice.

'I was naughty today; we went into Betty's and had scones with cream and jam.'

The lawn was in shadow from the house, the hosepipe spray flung dazzling drops across flowerbeds into the evening sunshine, the sound of dripping leaves was soporific.

Suddenly a rainbow appeared through the spray and Iris pointed, her brown elfin face breaking into a smile.

From beneath Zet's soaked feet rose the rich scent of grass and wet earth and Brad was aching in her mind. 'Turn off the water someone,' she called sharply.

Tony detached himself from the soft cushions and padded in raw leather sandals across to the tap just outside the back door. The water slowed to a dribble, the rainbow shivered and disappeared, Tony returned to his sun bed and Zet plodded on to the patio, leaving wet footprints, hearing Iris speak in an annoyed tone.

'It's an autumn sun now.' She sounded as if she had been wronged. 'It's like an impotent man.' Faces turned towards her, startled, and she grinned.

Waving her glass at the sun, she added, 'It still hangs there, but it doesn't do anything. Just little arousals now and again with no life in them.'

Tony studied his ringed hands. They were in his lap. He quickly moved them and looked away.

The sun slipped behind tossing trees. To Iris, the sun worshipper, it was a gesture of defiance, the last straw. Her wide, lovely eyes became tragic.

'There must be something to do here. Isn't there a musical on the telly, even?'

'Life isn't a gold staircase and dancing girls,' Zet was drawn to reply sharply

'For some, it is,' was the moody answer. 'For those whose mothers didn't ruin it for them.'

Jonty, who until then had been immersed in the sports pages of the newspaper, looked up. 'There's the Club,' he suggested, and Zet could have hit him. Iris lit up.

'I'll go and get ready,' she grinned, jumping up, doing a little dance, strappy sandals tapping on the flagstones. 'I

164

love dancing,' she said to no one in particular. 'Musical notes are like shoes, to me. I slip my feet into them and off I go.'

Watching her mother dance into the house, happy again, Zet was dismally certain that this would be an evening she would prefer to forget. She wasn't wrong.

There was Iris up on the stage singing - belting out, in fact - her favourite song, *Over the Rainbow*, thoroughly enjoying herself; Zet cringing with embarrassment; Zet watching Iris dance with Brad, looking like a doll in his arms; he didn't ask me to dance; Zet trying not to watch Brad's table, and leaving early because of sheer, blind jealousy; Iris complaining, all the way home in the car, that the night was still young.

'We country bumpkins go to bed early,' Zet snapped. Watching headlights pierce the dark lane, fists clenched in her lap, her body was filled, it seemed, with deadly vipers....

'What was that Margaret saying to you, pet? You didn't look very pleased.'

'She's harmless,' Zet sullenly told her mother. 'Just a gossip, that's all.'

'Have you heard the story about the ghosts at the crossroads?' Margaret had asked.

Zet, feeling nervy, hadn't been interested. 'Yes.' 'Did you know that the farmer who shot his wife lived at your cottage?'

Zet's brows rose. 'No,' she said slowly. 'I didn't know that.'

Margaret looked satisfied. 'He shot himself, afterwards, in his bedroom.'

Zet went cold. 'I thought the story was just a legend.'

'Oh, no. True as I'm sitting here.' Her small eyes gleamed with pleasure. 'And those who came after had sad endings, too,' she said with relish.

165

Got any foreign trips coming up, Tony?' Jonty asked, steering the car around the now familiar bends.

Tony cleared his throat, but before he could speak, Iris answered for him.

'He goes on long trips now. Bucharest is next.' 'Lucky devil.' Jonty slowed to cross the bridge.

Above the purring engine, Zet could hear the lashing, invisible water.

'Will you go with him?' she asked.

'You're joking,' Iris answered from the back seat. 'These trips, he keeps to himself. I'd like to know why, too.'

Oh, thought Zet as they entered the sleeping village. I see.

Illuminated by the moon, the village looked ghostly. Drifting smoke rose from chimneys, pale grey against navy blue, for all the world, Zet thought, contemptuously, like gossips with their heads together.

The children returned to school. Family visits ended. The air smelled of heather, and burning leaves; incensed smoke rose mournfully into the paler sky; morning mist and cobwebs clung to hedges and plants. The hollyhocks died.

Zet was living on the edge of two separate lives.

There was her life with Brad. Beyond him lay nothing but a full stop. Her brown autumn world was like a balloon, she was blowing all her life with Brad into it and it became bigger and bigger with the chances she took, and surely more transparent. She was afraid that one day it would burst and 'they' would no longer exist. 'You can bear the unbearable,' Sophie had said.

At home it was a strain to act and sound normal; she felt like a puppet with no life in her. Does anyone notice? she wondered. If only she didn't feel so frozen when away from Brad, observing life as if it moved behind glass, as if she wasn't part of it.

But she was, as a telephone call from Sophie reminded her, and shocked her to the core.

Chapter Thirty-One

It was a new sounding Sophie with a lilt in her voice. 'I've got the chance of early retirement, with a lump sum and a pension. So has your father,' she quickly added as Zet went to speak, 'We're planning to put our money together and buy a house.'

Zet was struck dumb. What about the broken heart, the lost love?

More seriously, Sophie added, 'I know what you're thinking. Not long ago I was breaking my heart over losing Matthew. But something strange has happened. The pain doesn't last, Zet. I found myself living without being tied to clocks and phones and longing and hurt. It feels,' she said, almost apologetically, 'good to be free.'

Zet felt her throat clot. Did Brad feel this way with her? He had mentioned recently - had that been a trapped look in his eyes? - that he had never before spent the whole summer here without going off abroad somewhere. Not package tours, he would just get on a plane, arrive, find digs and wander. Like a vagabond. Brad needs to wander. And I need the security and safety of my home.

From a distance, she heard Sophie ask softly, 'You don't mind, do you? About your father, I mean.'

'I don't know what to think, actually.' 'Well...think that your father was my first love.' 'What?'

'The one I told you about. He met your mother and,' Sophie sighed, 'that was it.'

'You're welcome to him.' Zet replaced the receiver.

Going out into the garden to fetch in washing, she looked up at the darkening clouds, felt the peat-scented wind on her face and shivered. What next?

She watched a butterfly land on a leaf and her heart missed a beat, having read somewhere that they only live for one summer. Shadows followed her back to the house, seeping like bruises across the lawn and reaching her, touched her with cool knowing fingers, while the trees

168

moved restless branches as if wringing their hands. Summer's not over yet, she told herself, frightened suddenly by loud, panic stricken squawks and flapping wings.

Glancing up, she saw black shiny bodies, like witches in wet suits, rising into the sky. Something had startled them maybe, but they always made her shiver and feel unsettled, as if they foretold disaster.

It was just sometimes.... when she was driving to meet Brad, or when they were out together and she saw mothers with their children.... that she wished she was whole again and not split into two halves. Mother versus woman.

'You're what?' Zet cried. 'But Brad....'

Somehow, when they met that day – a sixth sense told her that he had something to say that she wouldn't like.

They were sitting inside the summerhouse, out of the wind, looking out over the dales. Her head was slanting on to his shoulder, he had his arm across her shoulders and her insides were frothy with the sheer pleasure of it.

He was watching the movement of a plane making circles and buzzing like a dentist's drill in the echoing sky. He was very still, absorbed, gone from her. Without looking round, he told her.

It wasn't something a man tells you every day, and, incredulous, she thought she had misheard.

'You're what? But Brad....'

'I'm taking up flying again,' he repeated with dogged determination.

He looked so dour, as if he was announcing he had a fatal illness. She wondered how he could even think of flying, after what had happened. Eyes following the plane, he said, as if admitting a crime. 'I used to think I never would fly again. Once.'

She nodded, and the stern lines of his face softened. 'Knowing you has somehow given me back my wings,

169

Rosetta. I haven't flown since.... well, not for years. But I had a trial run on Saturday, and it went well.'

'What do you think about when you're up there all on your own?' she asked to hide the hurt because he hadn't told her about Saturday.

With the teasing, boyish half smile that made her weak, he said, 'the same thing I'm thinking when I'm making love to you, my darling. How to stay up.'

Instead of being reassured, she had to go and ask herself why he was taking up a new interest. Was it the beginning of him breaking away? She had to spoil things by digging, even while she warned herself not to. 'I thought you were going to say you were going away.' She kept her voice light. It didn't help that he said nothing. Up in the sky, the plane groaned into the strained silence like someone in pain.

There was a plane moaning around the sky the morning another card came.

She had filled the washing machine with P.E. kit, switched on, picked up the mail from the doormat and carried it into the garden with her coffee.

Dropping the mail on to the patio table, she stood for a moment gazing up at the plane prowling overhead. She always imagined it was Brad. She shivered.

'I'll be watching over you, darling,' he had teased. The plane's engine spluttered and seemed to cut out,

which always turned her icy. This time, it wasn't the plane that sent shivers down her spine…

Lakes, mountains, reflections…a copy of her painting stared up at her. There had been three postcards before this. Thank God the postman called into Lizzie's for coffee before delivering the mail. Jonty left before eight to drive to Leeds.

Birds in the bird house were squabbling over stale bread, she heard Norah's car start up. The steady hum of the washing machine and the moan of that plane began to drill into her skull.

Lake Windermere, read the description. *Reflections*. Heart pounding, fingers shaking, she turned the card over. This time it was addressed to Jonty. The blood drained from her face as she read the message.

"Saw your wife and mystery companion at the Lakes."

The handwritten message was as cryptic as the others. The first had read, *"Saw you at the Lakes."* The second had read, *"A great place to escape to, isn't it?"* The third had read, *"You weren't wandering lonely as a cloud, were you?"*

Back indoors, Zet moved with a sense of unreality into the conservatory. Sinking down into one of the cushioned wicker chairs, she studied the painting.

Brad and me, she remembered...we saw no one but each other, really, during those two days. Who could have seen us? Moreover, who would be spiteful enough to send these postcards? And for what purpose?

She felt sick that she had been spied upon and her wonderful weekend with Brad sullied. With tears horribly close, she tried to work it out. The first postcard had been posted from the Lakes, the others were postmarked Leeds. Was it Mary? Brad, when she told him, denied that Mary could have been at the Lakes; she was apparently saving up her holiday quota for a winter in the sun. How did he know that? What about these other women he knew? Was it even Brad himself?

The wicker chair creaked as she made an irritated movement. What a thing to think! Really, she was becoming paranoid. It had been the school holidays, anyone I know could have been at the Lakes, and there are gossips a-plenty here.

Rain began to claw at the windows and patter on the roof; the garden was tossing angrily, stirred by wind. You're silly, Zet, to be so upset. It's just, she sniffed, pushing tears back, the shock, the frustration of being

171

unable to do anything, the uncertainty of what will happen next. And it had all been so perfect.

Through the blurred window she noticed the rest of the mail had been blown from the table and hurried out to retrieve soggy bills and junk mail from the ground. Her mug was still on the table, coffee not drunk. Rose petals, like bloodstained rags, were scuttling about on the patio.

Back in the kitchen she switched on the kettle to make fresh coffee, heard a zip scraping against the glass door of the washing machine as if trying to escape and, reaching into the cupboard for the Nescafe jar, glanced from the window.

She brought the jar slowly down to the counter.

Beneath ominous black clouds, the moors were sweeping towards the hills like a sea of purple.

The next day, Jonty came in from work, stared at her dumbly for a moment, bit his lip, and finally told her the news that made her push the white-knuckled back of her hand into her mouth to stop a scream.

Chapter Thirty-Two

Zet felt the blood drain from her face. She stared across the kitchen at Jonty, not caring that her voice betrayed all the horror and shock she felt.

'Move? But we can't.'

Her shattered reaction stunned him, left him helpless. He looked down at the table beside which he was uncomfortably standing. Two empty orange juice glasses stood there with plates containing cake crumbs. The children had rushed in from the school bus, eaten and hurried out again.

'It's not my fault.' He sounded mulish. 'They want me at the London office.'

'But we've only been here a year, it's ridiculous.' Forcing back tears she heard herself rage at him, 'I've got the house, the garden, my business, everything, just how I want it...'

'They pay me,' he suddenly said, voice unfamiliar, as crisp as a sour apple. 'Industry today is hard and cruel. Where the Board says you go, you go. Even if it's Timbuktu, or....' He threw his hands in the air and shrugged his shoulders.

Anyone would think he didn't care. Looking at him with dislike, she felt sick as her life crumbled around her like a pack of cards and there was Jonty with his usual helpless expression, watching her with a crinkled forehead.

'I didn't realise you liked it here so much.' There was something raw in his voice as he added, 'we have no social life; you lost interest in the club. Your business is all you care about.'

She felt her face grow warm as if he had slapped her. 'I didn't know you felt neglected,' she said stiffly.

'I don't, Zet.' His voice sounded tired. 'I could never feel that with you.'

He turned away. Tears suddenly filled her eyes and she blinked them back. She gripped the edge of the sink with both hands, suddenly hating, not him any more, but everything else. The deceit, his job, the loss of his perfect wife, herself and the triangle that suddenly strangled her. But most of all, life without Brad.

No, she panicked. Life without Brad...please God, no. She wondered how it was possible to scream and scream with no one hearing you.

Instead, she automatically filled the kettle, plugged it in, switched on and waited in a dreadfully silent room until the water bubbled and raged and the kettle clicked off. She made coffee. Minutes later, she watched Jonty through the window. He was sitting on a chair on a lonely, leaf spattered patio, smoking a rare cigarette, and she felt a wrench of pain. It was as if her heart split and sadness poured in, swamping her.

It wasn't just the children...it was the goodness of Jonty. What am I going to do?

Through tears, she saw him finish his cigarette, shiver, and stand up. He needed the warmth of his home. She watched him wipe his feet carefully as he came through the back door and this hurt, too. He always tries to please me. She was standing cuddling herself and something about her made him pause, as if struck. He stood watching her, his usual open, honest, expressive face closed.

Without looking away, he leaned back, letting his weight close the door with a snap like the lid of a coffin going down. He spoke quietly and with sudden dignity.

'This north wind blows hell out of you, doesn't it?'

It was the next day. Glancing through the sitting room window, her heart sank. That's all I need. She had heard the car pull up and laying down the doll she was trying to concentrate upon dressing, she went out to the front door and waited there for her father, who made a great fuss locking up his new black Ford.

174

He'll only make the situation worse was the thought uppermost in her tired mind, muzzy from a sleepless night. She was due to meet Brad that afternoon. As usual, the need to be with him outweighed everything else and the agonized night had only made her need for him more intense and served to bring her to a decision. She could not be without Brad. There was one problem

…how to spare Jonty and the children from too much hurt. Just one problem. Surely she could find a way.

'Maurice.' She let his dry kiss land on her cheek and hurried him into the kitchen, where she tugged at the tap until water drummed angrily into the kettle. Pounding the plug into the socket, she switched on. 'What brings you all this way so soon?' How was she going to get out to meet Brad with him here? You'd think people would phone first…

'Sit down, love, I've something to say.'

'Sorry,' she said crisply, glancing at the pine wall clock and shaking her head, 'but I have an appointment. You should have phoned. Business, you know.'

Sitting up straight, white cold-looking hands flat on the table in front of him, he studied her shrewdly. 'You've grown into a nice looking woman, talented, efficient, honest, but one thing you lack is a forgiving heart.' The kettle clicked off.

In the shocked kitchen she felt her throat constrict. 'I think that's an awful thing to say.'

'Strange as it may seem, the world doesn't revolve around what you think,' he said in a tight voice. 'And I'm here for someone else's sake. Sit down.'

With a startled glance at his stern, lined face, and another at the clock, she drew out a chair and sat at the table opposite him. She had never seen him in this mood before. Was it anything to do with Sophie?

She hid her sudden anxiety with a cold, 'I'm sitting. So?'

175

He made no attempt to soften the blow. 'It's your mother. She's ill.'

'Ill? She didn't say anything when I phoned last week.' Zet caught her breath. 'You've seen her, then?'

He nodded. 'How come?' 'She needed me.'

Not trusting herself to speak, Zet stared at his grey face and hollow cheeks - she had only just noticed. Reaching across the table, he touched her hand.

'I've never stopped loving her, you know.'

Her hand slid away from him. 'No? Then why did you leave her?'

The lines deepened around his eyes and across his forehead. 'I didn't, love. She met someone else and wanted her freedom. I've never been able to deny her anything.'

'That's not true, how can you...?'

'It's true,' he said, looking at her steadily with honest and unflinching eyes.

She was shaking her head from side to side. 'Why? Why didn't you say?'

'It was done. Why should I?'

She brought her hands up on to the table, curled like a cry of pain, nails cutting spitefully into her palms. Leaning towards him, her voice was a wail. 'It turned me against you, dad.'

She heard his indrawn breath; pain filled his eyes as he said quietly, 'don't you think I know that? But...it wasn't her fault and she's been unhappy for a long time, even before Tony left.'

Zet didn't recognise her agitated voice. 'She didn't say Tony had left. Why didn't she tell anyone Tony had left?'

'Why? Because she left me in a flare of trumpets, running after happiness.' His face twisted and Zet felt a knife turn inside her as he said, with such compassion, 'and who can blame her for that?'

'I do,' Zet's chin went in the air. 'It seems so unfair. You let her have the house and went into a flat for her sake?'

He nodded. 'Seemed right. It was your home, too.'

He reached out again. This time her fist remained still and he squeezed it. 'Don't turn against her, she's lonely, frightened and ill.' He swallowed. 'She puts on a good act, you know your mum. The show must go on.' His voice faltered, 'But when the audience has gone....'

His eyes were pleading with her. Zet felt her heart begin to thud. 'She's going to get better, though?'

His words were almost inaudible. 'The doctor said it's going to be a fight, but there is hope....'

There was no hope in his voice and Zet stared at his drawn face as if he had struck her. His grip on her hand tightened.

'We'll have to see, won't we, Rosie? We'll be fighting it together. His mouth drew in until it was a white streak of pain and after a while he repeated heavily, 'We'll have to see.'

She swallowed hard. 'You'll be together?'

'Yes. I'll look after her.'

Zet slumped on the chair, head swimming. She thought she had known so much. She had known nothing about these people.

'I promised, Rosie, you see. Years ago...in sickness and in health.'

Zet looked at him piteously, went to speak, couldn't, and suddenly she was weeping. Her head went down and she wept as she hadn't wept since she was eight years old. And there was the man who had been hurt - so hurt by the two women in his life - holding her and stroking her hair with a hand that was gentle and loving, the father's touch she had once yearned for.

She thought of Jonty, working hard for them and loving them. She thought of him living alone, missing them. She thought of her children without their father.

177

Watching her father fumble about making coffee, she pictured her mother, falling in love with unsuitable men, searching for glamour and happiness. She remembered her mother's visit in the summer, how sometimes she had looked wistful. She had been thinner, too.

Ironically, her parents would be together again, just as she....

With great concentration, her father carried the mugs over to the table and sat down, his unguarded expression showing stark fear. Staring down into the coffee, a wad of soaked kitchen towel in her hand, her eyes ached, everything ached. A band of iron began to tighten around her chest. She never knew where the strength came from as, raising her head, she croaked like a stranger.

'I'll help you, dad. We'll all look after her.' Every word she spoke was screwing up her insides as she told him about the move back down south.

He listened and nodded. With a weary smile, he

said, 'Odd, the mysterious coincidences of life. But you mustn't neglect your family. They're worth loving, a family,' he said, which made tears once more pour down her face.

'Forgive me, dad?'

His eyes were watery. 'No question,' he said. 'No question. I'll take you to see your mother and - love - no tears, eh? Be happy. She...we both...want to be a happy family. That's all she wants. Now.' There was a faint note of satisfaction in his voice.

The curtains fluttered. The tang of peat and heather came inside as wind rushed around the room and swept back out to the moors. From somewhere came the wild cry of the curlew...its sharp beak might have been tearing her to pieces.

'Yes,' she forced from an aching throat. 'A happy family, dad.' She closed her eyes, but the pain wouldn't go away. She knew it never would.

178

Chapter Thirty-Three

Two car doors slammed. Panic-stricken grouse flew away, click... click... clicking; sheep raised black faces, stared inquisitively, thick coated against raw wind which would soon be combing the moors with steel grey fingers.

'I won't come to your place today,' she had told him over the phone in a voice that shook...'Can we meet at the rock?'

There had been no welcoming kiss, as if they were strangers already and that in itself was a kind of death. There were no sideway glances as their feet crunched over heather. Even eyes must not meet, it seemed. Except once, when she told him.

The look in her eyes was anguished, pleading ..don't ask me to stay. He didn't, of course, he had promised. *Always*, he reminded himself, wasn't something he had wanted either. Except.... There was a burning in his chest as he forced back a groan. He loved this woman as he had never expected, or wanted, to love any woman again.

Drawing in a deep breath, he saw her face, pinched with cold and desperately sad. He saw the dear familiarity of her and his heart ached. The helplessness of it all, the dread of life without her, made him angry with himself and with her.

The wind took a vicious grip on her hair and tossed it around her face; she could feel the dry, deep lines of anguish as if old age, also, had come too soon. She thrust the hair back with icy cold fingers. The silent space between them grew, although they sat quite close, he with one leg raised, an elbow resting on his knee, leaning back against the rock. It gripped her heart, seeing him like that, as he had been so many times before.

A bereft and frightened figure, she was cowering against the rock, turned away from him. How could two who had been so close separate like flesh ripped from flesh; like peeling off a plaster, taking pieces of skin with it? She hadn't really expected him to be gentle but what he said made her turn a tearstained face to him in disbelief.

'I'm not going to be like your bloody wimp of a husband,' he told her, eyes cold and hard and black. His grey eyes had always turned black when he was emotional, moved, upset, or hating. 'I'm not going to squeeze you to death. If you want me, you'll come to me,' he said in such a cold, autocratic way, she could have screamed.

Tearfully, she said, 'It's not as easy as that.' 'Isn't it?'

'Damn you. You know it isn't.' I love you so much, she wanted to cry, but how can I hurt them? The search for happiness, for the perfect partner...for this, you destroy a child's world? My husband, who has done nothing wrong, and my mother, what about her?

He said nothing. He wanted to take that look from her face, carry her off and make her happy. He was powerless. He hated himself for that, too. He lit a cigarette. Inhaled. Threw the smoke from his mouth. 'So it seems to be me versus your family.'

'No, you don't understand,' she insisted, wrapping her arms around her raised knees, dropping her head so that her voice was muffled. 'It's me versus me.'

'Life's like a fairground,' he said roughly. 'You start something for fun and it becomes a ghost train ride. You become scared.'

He might have been discussing a shopping list, yet his admission of weakness touched her. She raised her head. 'What do you mean by fun?' Her voice shook.

'I told myself it was for fun,' he said bleakly, 'at the beginning. But I was lying to myself. Yes, I knew you were married, but something happened between us, you wanted me, too, you looked like a woman waiting, not married at all.' He shook his head. 'I don't, can't, blame

180

myself for letting nature take its course, I might just as well blame the wind for blowing. Remember when I first asked you to dance?'

She closed her eyes tight. 'Yes.'

'You looked at me,' he said with a cold half-smile, 'A long, cool lady with mystery in her eyes, and I felt as if I'd been shot through the head.' Stabbing out the cigarette on a stone, he went on, 'I told myself...it's nothing, just a scratch.'

'And?' She longed to touch him.

He had been gazing at the land around him all this time, now he turned his head and her breath caught in her throat; his hating eyes...she swallowed...it was like staring into the cold barrel of a rifle. 'I couldn't stop the bleeding. That's why,' he insisted, 'If you go, you go. A complete break.'

She felt crushed, only now admitting to herself that deep down there had been a vain hope that they could work something out. It was the ending she was scared of. Like in her dream when, with the rifle aimed at her, she dreaded oblivion.

'But we could telephone,' she heard herself plead, 'just now and then.' And silently added... Maybe I could come up for a weekend.

'No.' His jaw locked. 'I might go to the States, after all. See my daughter.'

She stared at him, beaten. Things couldn't have gone on like this anyway. He obviously had the States already planned. At least I'm the one leaving. I always planned it that way. No man was going to leave me, I said.

She felt as empty as anyone could get. He had taken her to Whitby one wonderful stolen day, and they had gone into an old, smoke-blackened kipper shed and she recalled the kippers hanging up, shrivelled, dry, empty. That's how she felt now. She wondered, fingers picking at heather blurred by tears, whether it's true that you have to pay for every happy stolen moment. It seemed so.

181

'When my wife died,' Brad suddenly said, 'I made up my mind I was going to live, not with grief, but with pleasure. Life can be wiped out in seconds, just trying to please somebody.'

What the hell has this to do with anything? She forced back tears. 'It was a plane crash, wasn't it?'

He ran a hand over his mouth. 'She was learning to fly to please me,' he said in a harsh voice. 'Flying? She no more wanted to fly, than I wanted to make jam tarts.' After a pause, he went on, 'Now I please myself, and

I don't want someone to kill themselves for my sake. You do what you want to do.' The mouth she had loved to kiss was a cruel, straight line. His voice was as final as the switch on an electric chair.

Zet looked away. The moors were water-coloured and moved mistily. Keeping her face averted, she said painfully, 'your wife did what she wanted to do for herself, not for you. What I feel is different. Can't you get it into your head that leaving you is not what I want to do, but what I have to do? Maybe, if you had asked, I would have gone up in a plane for you. I would even burn on Greek beaches for you.' She struggled to speak. 'I love you that much.'

'But not enough to stay here with me.'

How cruel, if he was asking her now. 'I can't,' she cried, on a wail of pain, as he rose to his feet. She scrambled up, too, legs stiff from tension, heart thumping. He stared down at her, a last tight-lipped stare.

'I'll always love you....'

'Nothing is for always,' she interrupted, feeling the old belligerence that used to be there when things were not going her way.

'I was going on to say,' he said grimly, 'that I'll love you until I die, but I won't die of loving you. I've known two good women. One I destroyed, then there's you.'

He looked away from the desolation in her eyes and held out a clenched fist. Slowly he opened his hand,

182

saying, 'You, I let go. I could win you, but obviously the cost to you would be great.'

Such a look of pain crossed his face that she reached out to him. He turned away. Her hand dropped to her side. Frozen with shock, she watched him stride across the heather towards the waiting black car and she thought her heart was going to burst with the pain of it.

The wind caught his goodbye words and tossed them away across the moors; wild fingers tugged his hair and the heather raged before her eyes, a feverish purple. If he cried, only the moors saw.

His car door slammed, jolting her like an electric shock. His engine spluttered and the car began to move and with a stunned whimper, she wanted to run after it, reach out, scream...don't go. She closed her eyes. Such pain.

She opened her eyes to a desolate wilderness of wind and aching air. The empty moors seemed to heave. They watched her... grouse, curlews and sheep... spinning around her in some sort of dizzy dance.

She drove the red car off the moor. The car jerked up on to the proper road, a familiar movement that so often had pronounced the end of their preoccupation with each other, the beginning of the real world. Today, it was the beginning of dying.

At the crossroads where five lanes met, she stopped the car, weeping too much to see. Pulling down the flap of the glove compartment, she pulled out a packet of tissues, mopped her eyes. A pheasant strolled across the lane, scuttled into a hedge and then she heard a sound that turned her cold. It was gunfire. She drove on, over the humped back bridge. The river ran away and turned the corner without looking back. A lonely figure stood there, hunched over the parapet. Her father, waiting for the school bus. He didn't see her.

183

The cottage felt like a tomb; she made for the garden. Norah had a bonfire, a pall of smoke, smelling like old, dusty curtains, hung across the garden, whipped into phantom shapes, shifting memories in her head.

From a distance, she heard more snapping gunfire. It was the shooting season. She thought of the farmer's wife who had once lived here, who used to meet her lover in the orchard, now Zet's hidden garden, while her husband was out in the fields. Her husband shot her at the crossroads and then shot himself.

After that, a woman had bought the cottage without the farmland. Her husband died within a year. Taken ill two years later with a stroke, her elder sister came to look after her. Upon her death, the spinster sister had, according to the locals, gone crazy. She had lived a whirlwind life in her middle age, bought a car, travelled abroad, went out with married men, gossip said. One day, out on the moors, her car crashed. She had lain next to her dead lover for two days up on the moors before they were found. The resulting injuries had left her crippled and she took a year to die.

And then, Zet thought, feeling sick...I came. I want to die. But I can't. I can't hurt my children, my family.

The wind had bent, snapped, stripped, devastated her flowers and she didn't feel anything much. Hearing the sky howling with thunder, she looked up at fat, black clouds; they seemed to be rolling about laughing. And then the rain began, hissing down, pounding on her scalp, soaking her hair, and running coldly down her face.

This was how her father, children, and the local police officer found her.

Jonty had been shot.

Part Two

Chapter Thirty-Four

Inside, she was an empty cave, full of echoes.

First, a spiteful sea, driven by emotion and rage and sexual desire, then it settled down to the empty cave...the heartbeat boom of distant passions, the receding grasp of power. She was a married woman who felt like a widow.

The only thing in life, Zet sometimes thought, is grief. It wasn't, of course. There were her children, her rediscovered relationship with her father and, more than anything, her mother.

Furthermore, there was her work. She found herself feverishly determined to make her mark in life, courting personal success as she never had before, as if success was a form of revenge. It was no longer enough to be the wind beneath a man's sails. She was time filling, flying, non-stop busy.

'Sorry. Can't stop,' became her theme tune.

Zelter skelter, her father fondly called her, looking proud, in a distracted way.

She was working as an aromatherapist at a clinic started by Frankie, a counsellor; a reflexologist, an osteopath, and a homeopath soon joined the staff and it was no problem for Zet to organize her hours to fit in with caring for her mother.

To Zet's surprise, the dolls, which had started as a hobby, were also turning into a lucrative business. Then there was Jonty.

Physically he had recovered. He had been shot in the arm, neck and shoulder, dangerously close to his chest and according to doctors he had been extremely lucky. Everyone called it an accident. But Zet knew different.

He had been driving home across the moors when, not far from Fiveways, someone had shot at the car.

Person or persons unknown, was the verdict, but Zet had no doubts. Her lover was capable of killing.

187

To add to her mental turmoil, Jonty had changed, in his resentful stares, the failure in his eyes and a new cynicism that didn't suit him. He even treated the clinic as a joke.

'What are you trying to cure people of, Zet, being human beings?'

Zet felt puzzled and hurt. He was being unfair. After all, she had been behind him all the way in his own work. He had said himself that no wife could have been more encouraging or helpful; it wasn't her fault that he had not made a success of things.

She couldn't help thinking how strange it was that the two things should have come down on her like a two-edged sword. Jonty's move and her mother's illness.

Iris's home was different, as it is when you have guests. Indeed, Zet found that illness moves in like an uninvited visitor, an invisible, pus-coloured presence.

She had difficulty coming to terms with what she found in the house: a mixture of death and light heartedness. Iris had an absorbed and heightened passion for everything. It was as if she was playing a part, with death the antihero.

This matter-of-fact, joking attitude was the way Iris wanted things to be, and everyone tried hard to go along with it because, after all, being positive was part of the cure. She was spoilt, fussed over, the centre of attention, which Iris took as her due in the manner of one intending to enjoy it to the end.

Although Maurice was there, running things, Zet helped look after the house, bossed doctors, scrutinized their treatment and with a new viciousness inside her, sought out all she knew about alternative medicine.

Iris's brothers and sister would have helped if they could, but they were so busy…. And Sophie took to her bed, wanting nothing to do with illness. Gran was a surprise; she was matter of fact and stalwart, and would have helped looked after Iris, but the gentle Maurice was surprisingly firm. Iris and her mother had never got along, and he didn't want Iris upset. Their relationship astounded Zet.

'What age do you expect to live to?' he asked Iris one day, when she had been teasing him.

Zet cringed, but Iris smiled happily and answered, 'Fifty-five.'

Maurice retorted, 'Well, you won't make fifty-four if you go on like that.'

'I'll say what I like,' Iris answered with her gamine grin, tossing her head.

'Lady, you'll be the death of me,' Maurice smiled, shaking his own, rapidly greying, head.

Iris spent a lot of time watching old films on television. Maurice, who called Iris by his old name for her, Lady, bought a video player so that when, on rare occasions, her own films appeared on television, he could video them. No one admitted that the singing, dancing, cheeky-faced moppet with the squeaky voice seemed unconnected with Iris. No one admitted to boredom, or smiled at the banality of the films, their bad quality, or the artificial scenery.

With Iris, Maurice and Gran coping by living in the past, Zet found herself fascinated by the revelations. Like most young people, she had been bored by the past. 'Here we go again,' she would say, raising her eyes skywards when anyone talked of the old days, or those who were dead.

It was obvious to her now, analysing her young self, that she had been angry and wanted nothing to do with the family she felt had let her down. Somehow now, the past was running with the present and she was part of it.

Sophie, up and about with Valium and a haggard expression, lost weight, and mourned that she always chose the wrong man. Zet realised that Sophie had no self-regard; she wasn't worth much, in her own opinion, or her mother's. Gran had no patience with her.

'Silly so and so,' she scoffed. 'Plenty more fish in the sea. It's always been Iris for him, everyone knew that.' Her tone implied... who would want Sophie when they could have Iris. 'You'd think she'd be thinking of her sister, selfish cow.'

One day, Zet lost her temper. 'Are you homeless, Sophie, are you starving, have you,' she snapped, 'got cancer?'

Sophie's eyes popped; she had been the only one to discipline Zet as a child, now the tables were turned. Zet hadn't finished. 'If you're none of those things,' she said coldly, 'then you've got a bloody lot to be thankful for and we all have too many worries on our shoulders to look at your long face for much longer.'

'It's easy for you,' Sophie retorted, flushing. 'You've always been a coper.'

Zet could have hit her. 'I'm not coping at all. Apart from mum, there's Brad. I know that there's no medicine I can take, nothing to drive him out of my mind, nothing to keep him from my dreams,' she said, unable to prevent her voice from cracking. 'I'm a walking sore. But other people need me, and your sister needs you.'

After a silence....'You're like a bloody snake,' Sophie complained, with a faint smile. 'Hissing and sliding around me...come here, do that.'

True. When she could, Zet fitted Sophie into her tight schedule... shopping sprees, relaxing and restoring aromatherapy treatments, a facial at the clinic by Jodie, a beautician who had recently joined the staff, and a massage by herself, although Sophie put her foot down about seeing Frankie.

'I've never been one to talk about myself. All this counselling. Load of rubbish.'

All in all, Zet had quite enough to keep her busy. There were the children, the house to run, the clinic, her mother, and there was Jonty. Jonty with new moods but still with the grateful-to-be-loved eyes.

Yet she was only human and there were days that unfolded with a groan and creaked to an end, when she wanted nothing to do with the paling dawns, which took away the company of Brad. Not Brad, the killer, but the Brad she had known.

Brad. Brad. His whispered name, his ghostly face, the remembered voice still sent a yearning flame through her. Her body still ached for him. But there were things in his nature she had known nothing about. His violent action had obliterated any path she could find back to him. And she would have done. She knew in her heart that missing him so fiercely she would have found reasons to see him again.

Sadness, she discovered, is like a grey furry cat that you nurse sometimes for company, and at other times its claws make you bleed and sometimes you have to put it out if it gets under your feet when you have other things to do.

One thing she didn't have to do was to throw parties, as she once had. There was just the usual firm's Christmas cocktail party at a London hotel, and she wondered if it was her imagination that Jonty's colleagues were cool towards her. Or maybe the worry of the job situation took away their Christmas spirit.

Jonty was Sales Executive now. 'That's a nothing title,' she told him, horrified to discover that he had taken a step down the ladder for reasons unclear to her. She quietly despised him for not minding demotion. She was shocked and angry when, to make matters worse, she discovered his drop in salary.

'How could you have done this to us? No wonder I have to work all the hours God sends.'

As soon as the words were out, she knew they were unfair, but she couldn't help herself, she was so disappointed. They could have had so much by now. If it weren't for what she earned they would be struggling, with the cost of buying and running a home these days.

His reaction, defensively belligerent, something about hating the rat race, didn't ring true; he had never been a good liar. To herself she decided he was a coward, he couldn't take the pace.

'I'm happier when he's away on business trips,' she admitted to Frankie.

Frankie was a small, neat, no-nonsense, dark-haired woman of about forty; the only softness about her was a full mouth that often twisted with wry humour.

They were talking over coffee in Zet's treatment room and Frankie said bossily, 'Relax. You look like Atlas carrying the weight of the world. What's wrong?' A woman of few words, she listened patiently, sipping coffee, while Zet spoke, reluctantly at first, of her marriage. Afterwards, Frankie put down her mug.

'Aren't you arguing, Zet, rather than talking about what's making you both miserable?'

Good point, but...'What's Jonty got to be miserable about?' Zet answered flatly, gripping the handle of her mug but forgetting to drink.

Frankie had been raised in a large, warm-hearted Jewish family in the East End where, she said, with eight people in three rooms, not even emotions and moods had had privacy. 'Why don't you ask him?' she suggested. 'And tell him what, apart from worrying about your mother, is making you unhappy.'

Zet was shocked into silence, which made Frankie suggest, 'Tell me, if you like.'

After a brief hesitation, Zet did; just a rough outline, leaving out the shooting. She ended up...'so you see. How can I tell Jonty that he isn't Brad?'

Quietly, Frankie said, 'Perhaps he knows.'

'Oh, no. He's still the same loving person - apart from the rows and a certain,' Zet hesitated, 'cynical attitude at times. In fact,' she sighed, 'he's even more loving.'

'Do you mind?'

'I've always minded. It's as if he wants me to himself, body and soul. I resent it. Sounds awful, but a man who loves you too much can demand more than it's possible to give.' With a furrowed forehead, she paused and went on, 'Sometimes it's as if I mentally feel his mind trying to worm into mine. I tend to shut down then, turn off, and deny him what he's asking.

'I used to tell him that I'm me and I don't intend to be owned by anyone. He didn't like it.' She picked up her mug and sipped cold coffee, pulling a face. 'It's the probing glance across the room in the evening,' she explained urgently, putting the mug down. 'Do you know what I mean?'

'I understand,' Frankie said, in her formal way. She hesitated a moment before adding, 'But some people would call this love and togetherness.'

Zet could have sworn she heard envy in her friend's voice and stared at her curiously. Maybe Frankie was thinking of her own marriage which, she had briefly explained to Zet, had been short-lived due to her husband's violence. Zet remembered her disbelief that this small, calm woman had been a battered wife. At the moment, it seemed to Zet that Frankie was saying that many would envy her, which made Zet feel very much alone.

'Where's Alyson?' he asked, coming into the kitchen and thumping his briefcase down on the table. He brought cold air in from outside and, without turning, carrying on chopping stalks from broccoli, Zet kept her voice pleasant.

'Can you move that, Jonty? I'm going to lay up in fifteen minutes.' It had annoyed her intensely that there was no dining room in the new house, just a dining area in the kitchen.

193

Hearing a chair scrape on the lino that she also hated, she said tartly, 'Alyson's in her room. I sent her there.'

Sitting down, he frowned. 'Why?'

Zet was busy at the oven. 'Because she lied.' 'That doesn't sound like Al.'

'You would say that. Twice this week she told me she had no homework to do.' She glanced round. 'Then I get a phone call from her teacher asking where it is.'

He was pulling off his tie. 'All children do that sort of thing at some time,' he sighed, undoing the top button of his shirt

She gritted her teeth. Lately he has to go against me in everything. 'Not in this house, they don't,' she snapped. 'You would have got a good hiding, wouldn't you?'

He was silent and she added, 'If my parents had been stricter, I'd have done better. I'm not letting my kids waste their lives.'

'Don't push them,' he frowned, fingers playing with his tie. 'I know what it's like.'

She changed the subject before another row started. 'How was work today?'

'All right,' he answered shortly. Sniffing the warm kitchen, he sounded awkward, as if he, too, was trying. 'What's for dinner?'

'Chicken Kiev.' She turned down under the broccoli, feeling taut and nasty. 'Made with chicken.' Remembering her talk with Frankie, she sighed, turned out under the carrots and went to sit down, facing him, hands gripped together, in prayer-mode. 'We used to discuss your work.'

His expression hardened. 'Discuss? Did we? I thought it was more in the line of you criticizing,' he said, making her sit back as if struck.

'That's not fair. You said I was a great help.' His childish shrug annoyed her. 'Don't you care,' she snapped, 'about being passed over for promotion?' Her hands dropped to her lap and twisted together, such were

194

the intensity of her feelings. 'What about the dream you had about going to the top, the plans we made? For chrissake, you were almost there and you lost it.'

***

He was conscious of lovely smells in the room, the whine of the spinning dryer, the atmosphere of competence. And tension stretching between them. Everything had changed, every word and gesture she made seemed charged with tense significance. But look at her. He felt an ache inside. Her eyes were brilliant with anger, her pale skin smooth, her hair silky. She looks, he thought, like perfect material, not flawed flesh and blood. Suddenly he jumped up, sending the chair flying. 'Not my plans. Yours.' Righting the chair he set it down with a thump. 'And who ruined everything?'

She felt the heat explode beneath her skin. 'Are you blaming me?' Her chin was raised as he stood over her; her eyes were wide with horror and in the steamy atmosphere, something between them threatened to explode.

The oven timer pinged.

He slumped. For a moment he remained standing, leaning on the chair back, head bent, then he turned and flung himself from the room.

Picking up the tie he had left on the table, she began to wind it neatly around her fingers.

Upstairs, the steamy bathroom still smelled like a wet garden where Zet had bathed and changed after work. Pulling off his shirt, Jonty opened the linen bin, dropped it inside and paused. Reaching into the bin, he pulled out the damp bath towel she had used and held it to his face.

Chapter Thirty-Five

'The garden seems to come right into the room, pet.' Iris's eyes, less brilliant now, looked gratefully at Zet, who had worked unceasingly, evenings and weekends, as if possessed, to get the garden just as she wanted it.

While she was busy in the garden, Maurice had been busy inside, turning the living room into a downstairs bedroom, because Iris's treatment left her too exhausted to climb stairs. He had installed patio doors and she could wander in and out of the garden or remain in bed with the doors wide open, whatever she felt like.

Today, Iris was resting on the bed, flicking through a magazine; dance music was playing softly on the radio; lively, young footsteps clicked on the pavement outside; a jet droned above the Thames on its way from Heathrow towards, maybe, all the places Iris had loved.

Hating the sounds of life, Zet turned away to stare into the garden. 'It's hot out there today.' She hadn't been sorry to come into the house out of the sun, for a break.

'You made me a paradise, pet,' Iris said, looking at Zet over the top of the magazine. 'Have a rest. Don't do any more.'

Hard to believe, Zet thought, staring outside, that this was once a sad little garden and concrete yard. Taking an idea from the many photographs of Spain Iris wistfully browsed through, Zet had planted cobbles into sand, coloured cobbles like eggs, to make a courtyard; she had painted the surrounding fences the blue of a Mediterranean sky and she had installed a fountain. There was also a small circular chamomile lawn.

She had packed in as many plants as possible, to give a dense effect and to hide the surrounding fences, using raised beds, and terracotta pots. There was a mingling of shrubs, leaves of all shapes and sizes and textures, a couple of miniature trees and even a fig. The scent, on a

196

humid day like this, was a stew of tobacco plants, herbs, roses, carnations, and the sweetness of sunlight on leaves.

The great fat mauve heads of buddleia suddenly jostled together, nudging each other in an unexpected breeze. Moments later there was a warning roll of thunder, lightning zipped open the sky and rain came hissing down, bouncing off the white garden table, making pinging noises on the wrought iron.

Zet felt the cooler, watery air rush against her face and tried not to think of autumn and death but she found it so hard to bear, the way Iris talked about death, as if.... well, as if it was only a film she was discussing.

The buddleia's mauve blossoms were like sodden sponges, heavy and still; the garden dripped steadily, and in the small yellow watery sky above the glistening slate roofs, a rainbow appeared.

'Look,' Zet cried, turning round.

But Iris's lovely eyes were closed. The magazine had slipped to the floor. On a table beside her, stood a tall glass half filled with Sangria - heavy on the brandy. Iris smiled in her sleep.

The perfume of wet petals and soaked earth washed inside, catching in Zet's throat. Placing a blanket over the thinner body of her mother, she watched Iris sleeping...a tiny bundle of helplessness and fortitude; she was laughter, she made the house sing, the dust dance and neighbours talk. She made balloons okay for grownups and men love her.

When Zet turned back to the garden, the rainbow was broken in half by cloud and one half just drifted away.

'My so-called career came to an end at seven.' 'Because of the war?' Zet asked her mother.

'War be damned. Someone told the studios mum had been a stripper. Studios were fussy in those days, twofaced lot.' Her pointed face darkened. 'They dropped

197

me. The telltale was someone from Crow Street, I bet. Bloody big mouths. Eyes and ears of the world, this lot.'

She shrugged. 'One minute I was everyone's pet, the next they wouldn't touch me with a bargepole. I'd been fussed over, dressed up, given elocution lessons, told to pretend and most probably,' she grinned endearingly, 'horribly spoiled.'

Doubtfully, Zet asked, 'How did you get in films?'

'I came first in a baby show when I was three.' Iris smiled, remembering …singing and dancing in front of the cameras, the lights of the West End blinking into a great black car; a room where she curled up like a mouse and slept to distant music amongst rich brown Chanel scented furs.

She told Zet how it was afterwards...the grey, cold, snarling school playground, feeling different, forced inside herself, playing games in her head. 'Your dad understood,' she told Zet. 'With him I felt like a leading lady. He courted me with cinema and theatre tickets. We used to meet on the steps of the Odeon.' She sighed. 'It was my world.' Her face lit up. 'Or we would go up West to a nightclub.'

Zet, watching animation play on her mother's face, seeing remembrance in the larger eyes, knew, with a thump of surprise, that it was all true. But Iris was sounding tired. When she stopped talking, Zet poured her a glass of water, watched her drink and suggested she slept for a while. But, her mind faraway from the room, Iris shook her head.

Instead, with a grateful smile, pausing for breath now and again, she told Zet, 'Your Gran got a lot of money from the studio. After the war, when I couldn't get any more parts, she used the money to open the cafe and buy her house. Mind you, she missed the rich men who took her to parties and that. It was from one of those she got those pearls I gave you. So it all stopped... for her as well.

198

'I could have gone to Hollywood,' she added. Zet was intrigued. 'How come?'

'Rosetta.' Misty eyed, Iris rested her head back on the pillow.

'The woman I was named after?'

Iris nodded. 'Rosetta was a well known film star in those days; but to me she was a princess.'

Hearing a wistful sigh, Zet searched her mother's face. 'What was she like?'

'She had long eyelashes and a beauty spot and black hair, and was probably flat chested and wore falsies, because when she cuddled me her boobs were hard as iron. She and her husband couldn't have children, they wanted to adopt me,' Iris bragged, 'and take me back to Hollywood,'

'How exciting.'

'Would've been,' Iris said glumly, 'except that mum said no. I was her way to riches, wasn't I?'

'Be fair, mum. What woman would give her baby away?'

Iris looked blank. It was one of those moments when you feel more questions, deeper ones, could be asked. Iris's eyes closed. Zet's heart felt like lead.

Maurice opened the front door. Instead of his usual brave smile, the lines on his face swept into a wide grin.

'It's good news, then, dad,' she said, going inside. He closed the door.

'The doctors believe she's in remission,' he said, after they had kissed carefully. 'They've cracked it...to use the Specialist's expression.'

Zet thought it an odd one, as if Iris had learned a new language. Although maybe dying was a different language, maybe death was a new way of living. Everything had changed.

Zet found Iris in the garden. She looked fragile and beautiful, gipsy like, in a colourful blouse, long flowered skirt trailing in chamomile, feet bare.

Zet stepped out through the patio doors. She didn't know what to say. She felt she should hug her mother, but couldn't. Instead, in a wobbly voice, she said, 'I used to like doing that, in Yorkshire.'

Iris turned, the evening sky livid behind her. 'What? What did you do in Yorkshire, pet?'

Zet's throat constricted. It was sudden, the pain; as if she was crawling naked through barbed wire, catching her flesh on remembered things...

.... lovemaking by the fire...the squeak of the garden gate...a plane buzzing in the sky. It only took a word, a scent, a song, the weather map in her daily paper, a mention of Yorkshire on the radio, and her mind would slip into the deep shadows of Brad's house and she would see and feel it again.

Iris was looking at her, waiting. 'I used to walk barefoot on the grass,' Zet said.

'You don't now? At home?'

Home? Home was a place where the wildness is.

Iris walked towards her, slender feet curling over the patio cobbles, as if she walked on eggshells and there was a look on her face that seemed to say she was in awe of her capable daughter, who rose head and shoulders above her and whose eyes had so often held disapproval. 'Don't you do that at Chestnut Close?' she repeated.

Looking down into the brown circled but still beautiful eyes of her mother, Zet shook her head. 'All box hedges and flowers standing like soldiers. I haven't altered it since we moved in.'

'Dig it up, start again. You're good at that, pet.'

'Dig it up...start again?' Zet repeated. She didn't say that she had no interest in the Essex semi. Instead, she said softly, 'I can come here and share this with you.'

200

The words sounded strange, heavy, loaded with unintended emotion. What had she ever shared before with this woman, her mother? How can parents become strangers? How can she stop it happening with her own children?

Zet?'

'Yes, mum.' 'Sophie told me.' 'About....'

Iris nodded, looking embarrassed. 'Your aunt can't keep a secret, didn't you know that? Has no life of her own, I suppose.'

Sophie had kept some secrets; Iris didn't know about Sophie's men. People had always talked about "poor Sophie", accepting the fact that she wasn't the type to attract men. "Devoted to her mother," they said with approval.

Zet forgot Sophie for as they went into the house, Iris, with a sideways glance, said, 'Jonty's a good man.'

Oh, sure, Jonty's a saint. Zet pulled in an irritated breath. 'Why are we discussing Jonty? It's your wonderful news we should be talking about.'

Iris nodded, looking pleased and, somehow, gracious, as if taking applause. The bed had been taken upstairs and Iris had her afternoon siestas, as she called them, on a comfortable, squashy sofa, where she now curled up. Zet settled in a wicker chair.

'Zet, can I just say one thing? A decent, boring man is the best thing since sliced bread. He's good to you, sticks at home, doesn't chase other women,' Iris said, with meaning. 'They're great fathers and don't let you down.'

As Iris talked, Zet found an interest in studying a cluttered shelf on which stood a doll she had made and dressed in Spanish costume.

'A good man, Zet, isn't troubled by impulses or lusts, won't catch you up in crazy things, won't ask you to dance wildly or make life sing, you won't live with fear he'll leave you.'

201

Iris studied Zet's face, searching for compassion, maybe, or understanding. 'I know what you're thinking, Zet. I gave that up. But you see, neither will he take risks, fly you to the moon; there's no excitement. No excitement - no sexual arousal, no passion.'

'Who wants a nice cup of tea?' Maurice, alarmingly awkward, was using the tray to push the door open.

Iris and Zet looked at each other. Ignoring the tea, Iris suddenly said, hands clasped in prayer mode, 'I'd like a party this Christmas. A really big party, with all our family and friends, the way we used to when I was young.'

Handing her a mug with a fond smile, Maurice warned, 'Careful, it's hot. As far as you're concerned, my love, you could have the moon if I could get it.'

Zet and Iris exchanged glances over their mugs. 'Can we have the party at your place, Zet?' Iris

pressed, 'There's more room, and I want it to be really a big party. Life's for living, I always say.'

Zet, swallowing weak tea, inwardly groaned. Christmas was a busy time, not only at the clinic but Rosetta dolls had become popular, some of the best hotels and shops around displayed them and sold them. She had orders to fulfil. But her throat tightened; she couldn't help remembering the times she had thrown cold water on her mother's fun.

Afterwards, Zet wondered what would have happened if she had been tempted to forget the party. For it was at the party that Gran dropped her bombshell.

Chapter Thirty-Six

Slamming the car door, Zet hurried into the house making a mental list of outstanding jobs.

The kitchen was a mess. Jonty turned with an anxious smile from the sink where he was having an uneasy relationship with potatoes. 'Thought I'd make a start.'

Oh, for God's sake! She nodded, eyes taking in the disruption and empty packets of frozen vegetables she only used in emergencies. 'Thanks,' she said stiffly.

Looking pleased with himself, he turned back to his work. 'I've taken the bodies out of the kiln as well.'

'Thanks.'

'How was your mother?'

'Great. Almost her old self.' Going over to the fridge, Zet removed the lamb she had marinated overnight, glistening with olive oil, smelling of garlic and rosemary. 'She's talking of buying clothes because she's lost weight. And dad's taking her to France for the day.' Covering the lamb with foil, she placed the dish in the oven. 'He's promised her a holiday in Spain, and they're going to a tea dance up West.'

'Sounds more like Iris,' he smiled over his shoulder. 'She said you called in yesterday.' Zet slammed the oven door and switched on. 'Yes. I forgot to tell you.'

'You're good to her. She adores you.'

He shrugged, dropped a potato into the bowl, muddy water splashed everywhere. 'It's mutual,' he said, fishing out the mutilated vegetable. 'She's warm and loveable and needs people.' He kept his back to her.

Moving around him, collecting empty soggy packets, Zet saw fresh vegetables in the rack and held back an irritated sigh. Dropping the packets in the bin, she slammed the lid and wiped the Formica top with a damp cloth.

'I'll go and prepare the dolls for tomorrow's lesson.' Pushing hair from her brow with a tired gesture, she left the room.

Going through to the garage they had turned into a workroom, she felt ridiculously tearful. It was Jonty's shoulder blades protruding from his blue striped shirt...the rounded shoulders...his face more finely drawn. Sometimes, she thought, with an ache in her heart, I hear myself running him down, I see his poor, hurt face and I hate myself because he's so kind and nice, but I have to tear away at the good piece of material he is and destroy it.

Guilt again. She smothered it. Because he did nothing, did he? Nothing to arouse her or thrill her or amuse her. But he loved her; he tried to please.

From the window she could see the nearby recreation ground. Darren and Alyson were somewhere amongst those bobbing figures she could glimpse on the swings and slides and roundabouts. They would be home soon. 'Home by six or confined to barracks,' were her no nonsense instructions. You can't have a nervous breakdown every time they go out, even if you feel like it with the things you read in the newspapers. She pushed away the mental picture of a village in the Yorkshire Dales where she had felt so safe.

Stop it, Zet. She turned to inspect the pink curvaceous dolls' limbs, spread on a trestle table. A leg was cracked. She picked it up and threw it into a bin, hearing the door open. She knew he would come into the room.

'I've done the potatoes, Zet.'

Wishing he wouldn't follow her around, she felt her nerves tighten. It was so irritating the way he informed her every time he did something. I don't go up to him every day and say, I've peeled the potatoes, I've made a doll, I've made a pie, do I? What is it with men that they want praise all the time?

204

'Oh, great,' she called over her shoulder, 'you've done the potatoes. What do you want, a medal?'

He walked away, leaving her feeling rotten, and guilty again. *The truth was, the irritating habits I lived with before Brad became unliveable with afterwards.*

She felt chilled. Hastily she forced her mind to concentrate upon her mother and this party she wanted. New Year's Eve seemed a good time. She shivered, remembering that Iris might not have been around to see the New Year. Needing her mother was new. *It must be a new beginning for Jonty and me, too. We're a family. You must try harder, Zet.*

Chapter Thirty-Seven

Iris made an entrance. Sweeping inside from cold darkness, dazzled by bright light, she paused just inside the warm house that smelled and sounded tipsy. Tinsel decorations danced a lively welcome, swirling and glittering in the frosty draught from the open door.

This was the old Iris, smiling, perky, in party mood, as Zet had, as a child, hated seeing her. But tonight, seeing Iris's beaming face, Zet relaxed, exchanging pleased glances with her father. *Life's for living*.

And, indeed, Iris out-sparkled it all. A taupe silk jump suit hid her thinness. Her short haircut and hollow cheeks made her eyes enormous and her face gamine. Cries of welcome rang out from Iris's brothers, Laurie and Albie, her sister Viv and their partners. Sophie had made a big thing of the fact that she had been invited to another party first and would come along later. Zet thought how strange it was that Iris being close to death had caused so many changes in the family.

Min and Albert sat uneasily among the exuberance of Jonty's friends and their wives. Of Maurice's brothers and sisters, only Dick, recently divorced, turned up alone and grateful. The others had moved too far away. Jonty's sister, Sue had declined; they couldn't get a baby sitter. Prominent on the sideboard stood a postcard from Austria, signed with a squiggle like a grin...Sarah.

Gran, smart in her best navy trouser suit and white blouse, feet squeezed into matching navy and white shoes, was holding court while warming her behind against the gas fire, although central heating made the rooms stifling.

Viv, Albie and Laurie had made hurried visits to see Iris on a few occasions, but there had been an awkward atmosphere between them. Not only that, her sense of humour had embarrassed them. They were uncertain how to treat the little sister who had been in the limelight when they were growing up.

Tonight, though, there was no awkwardness Zet saw, with relief. It was going to be a good party; she had planned for it and was determined to enjoy it. Furthermore, she had made a resolution, albeit it three hours too early.

She would make it up to Jonty; try harder to make their marriage work. She had made her decision; there was no going back. There's still time, you can do it, she told herself firmly, leaving the noisy room and making her way to the kitchen.

The artificial Christmas tree, loaded with tinsel, ribbons and fragile glass balls, had been moved into the hall to make more room in the sitting room. Min was out there, alone, staring with a wistful expression at the dazzling tree.

'You're a clever girl,' she said as Zet passed.

'It does look nice.' Zet smiled kindly. 'Comes down tomorrow, though.'

'That's what Albert said, not worth the trouble....' Min's voice trailed away.

Hurrying into the kitchen, Zet wondered if Min and Albert were having a good time. They were not mixers, but they cared for Iris, and Zet had made it clear that the party was for her mother. I'd better keep an eye on them; Jonty's friends seem to be avoiding them and Albert has hardly spoken to anyone, Zet realised, as she loaded a tray.

'We were all together the New Year's eve you met Zet,' Greg remarked to Jonty.

'That's why we invited you,' Jonty grinned before he took a gulp from a glass of rum and coke. 'And she's still up there on a pedestal.'

Greg looked concerned. 'You shouldn't put anyone on a pedestal, old mate.' He looked down into his beer. 'No one should be praised for just existing.'

Jonty smiled. 'I'm grateful she's stayed with me. I'm not much of a catch.'

Greg struck his head with the heel of his hand. 'Absolute, bloody rubbish,' he cried. But Jonty was looking, with a slightly beatific, sozzled smile, towards the door. Greg glanced round, knowing whom he would see.

Jonty watched her stand at the door, holding a tray, checking that everyone was being catered for. She looked capable, serene, slinky haired, sinuous bodied in a knitted angora wool dress with padded shoulders, in the grey of thunderous clouds. And private, self- enclosed, as no wife had a right to be.

He admired her long legs as she crossed the room, placed the tray on the table, talked to people, watchful, smiling, and perfect. Careful, somehow. She always seemed careful. She came their way and Greg said politely, 'Just saying. It's the anniversary of the night you two met.' With a formal smile, he moved away.

Jonty gulped the last of his drink. 'Fourteen years.' 'So it is.' She watched him wipe his mouth with the back of his hand. 'Is everything okay?' she asked, in a voice as crisp as a stick of celery.

As if I'm one of her guests, he thought. 'All my needs are catered for,' he told her. 'As always. Even if by remote control.' He watched her turn and walk away. Why do wives always smile that way whenever a chap's had a drink? It's the sort of smile they give to children. Makes you feel small.

'Remember?' Iris was saying to Maurice, as Zet joined them. 'That classy nightclub off Park Lane. The Mirabel. You could listen to music all night,' she explained, turning to Zet. 'This was before you were born, of course.'

'Sorry I spoiled your fun,' Zet joked, and Iris's face clouded.

'Oh, well… anyway, we saw Judy Garland at the Talk of the Town, went dancing at the Cafe de Paris; your father was a brilliant dancer.'

Maurice looked pleased. 'Remember our honeymoon at Clacton?'

Iris's face brightened. 'I had to wear a jumper, it was so cold. And you,' she reminded Maurice, 'wore a kiss-me-quick hat and you fell out of bed.' Turning to see Zet's brows rise, she added mischievously, 'They made a mistake at the camp; put us in a chalet with bunk beds'. She dug Maurice in the ribs. 'We made do, didn't we, pet?'

The evening laughed, danced, chatted and sang on, with Whitney Houston, Oasis, Chris de Burgh mixed up with the Birdie, Y.M.C.A. and Nat King Cole.

Iris drank vodka and played a tape of a new Spanish singer she had discovered. She called him Hoolio. She pulled Maurice to his feet and, pert and provocative, made him dance a slinky tango that Zet found embarrassing to watch.

'No Vera Lynn,' moaned Gran. 'Should have brought my own records.'

'Tough luck,' one of the youngsters joked. Everyone laughed.

Just before twelve, the doorbell pealed.

'Isn't a tall, dark handsome stranger supposed to come to the door?' Dick joked, going to let Sophie in.

'You've got to put up with me…short, fat and fair,' she defiantly answered back, pulling off her new black coat that smelled of cold outside air.

'You could do a lot more for yourself,' Gran greeted her, when she came into the room calling greetings. Sharp, critical eyes looked Sophie up and down. 'Why didn't you wear that blue dress I bought you?'

'Because I preferred this black one.' Sophie glanced at Maurice and went in the other direction towards Jonty who was with his friends. She gave him a smacking kiss that made him blush but look pleased.

'You look happy and peaceful,' she remarked fondly, at which he shook his head and waved his glass as if about to make an announcement.

'He whom Zet's oiled wheels pass over, loses forever any peace in life. We're all Zet propelled in this house.'

Amid awkward laughter, people squashed up on the settee so Sophie could sit down and Zet arrived with a glass of Dubonnet and lemonade with lemon and ice just as Sophie liked it and watching with amusement, Jonty waved his glass at his wife.

'A toast to Mrs. Stainless Steel.'

Twelve o'clock came and they sang Auld Lang Syne, kissed and hugged. Shivers ran up and down spines. Except for Zet, who couldn't believe that in the middle of such a good party, her mood had become heavy and dark with foreboding. Reaction, that's all. It had been a terrible year in many ways.

'Happy new year,' people said. She shivered. Hugging her laughing mother, touching her sparrow thin bones, smelling her scent, Zet felt her energy drain away, leaving her in the grip of exhaustion. Her heart began to pound. What on earth was happening?

Quickly, Zet left the room, climbing the stairs helped by the cool wood of the banister rail beneath her hand. The stairs seemed like mountains. What's happened to me? Going quietly into Darren's room, she sat on the edge of his bed, deep breathed and forced herself to relax. Must have been the heat downstairs, she felt better in this cool bedroom. Thank God, she thought, wondering what had caused it. There was a lot of flu about.

Moving between Darren and Alyson's rooms, she bent to give them light kisses. 'Happy new year,' she whispered.

210

Hearing a sound, Zet straightened up from Alyson's bed and turned to see her mother just inside the door, a watching shadow.

'I came up for the same thing,' she told Zet softly. Creeping into the room, wine glass in hand, she looked down at the pale hair spread over the pillow, the softly rising chest, and delicate features. They could hear Alyson's breathing.

'Grandchildren,' Iris whispered, 'fill you with so much love you don't know what to do with it.'

This shook Zet. From the light in the hall, she could see her mother's face, as she looked down at the bed. There was longing in it, and regret.

As they crept towards the door, Iris added softly, and unexpectedly...'I'd give up both my kidneys for my grandchildren without a second thought.'

'Oh, mum.'

Iris laughed softly. 'Not that my poor old kidneys would be of any use now.'

'Oh, mum.' Zet wanted to put her arms around her mother, but couldn't. She saw her mother's face...pale, thin, with swimming eyes.

'I wasn't a very good mother to you, Zet.'

'Of course, you were,' Zet said helplessly, but Iris shook her head.

'It wasn't that I didn't love you, but it was a crazy mixed up time, the sixties,' she confessed, as they left the room, closing the door gently. Zet went to go downstairs but her mother's hand came out, stopping her.

'Stay here with me a minute,' she pleaded, sitting down on the top stair. 'I had a miscarriage before I had you,' she said, in a low voice, as Zet sat beside her.

Faint moonlight came through the window at the top of the stairs, but Iris's face was a smudge, which maybe was how she wanted it.

211

'I didn't know.' Zet was wishing she didn't feel awkward, but they had never been ones for mother and daughter talks.

'No point.' The glass in her hand tilted and straightening it, Iris looked down. 'I was tired all the time, afterwards. I felt ugly; I wanted the good times back. I didn't want to go through pregnancy again; anyway I'd never been maternal. I thought of abortion, but ….' she hesitated and when she went on, her voice held appeal for understanding. 'Sophie talked me out of it, promised to help, even offered to have you live with her but your dad wouldn't let you go. And then,' she stopped, her voice was raw, and she sipped her drink. 'And then I had your brother.'

Tommy. Zet felt a ghost slip between them. Her little brother had died at five years old, and his name was never mentioned, as if he had never existed.

In a low voice, Iris said, 'I fell in love with my little boy. I always preferred little boys.' An ashamed look appeared on her face as she glanced at Zet.

'I know, mum. I know. I always felt,' she hesitated before going on. 'That for you, the wrong child died.' There were tears in her eyes.

Iris gasped. 'Zet. No. If I let you feel that….Oh, Zet,' her voice sounded choked, 'I'm sorry.'

'I understand, mum. It was an emotional time. You must have been nearly out of your mind when he died.'

'I was. Then there was your dad and me. I was rotten to him, Zet; I couldn't help it. He was having job problems, but you know him, he didn't say anything. He just soldiers on, doesn't he?'

Zet's clear voice was unusually husky. 'I think dad's always wanted to give you things, and when he couldn't, he probably just gave up.'

'I didn't see it like that, I just wanted to bring back the good times; I wanted to wipe out the hell of that time when Tommy…when he died,' Iris admitted softly. 'I wanted to pretend it hadn't happened.' She sniffed. Having no hankerchief, her bag was downstairs, she raised her hands and ran her fingers beneath her eyes, catching tears. 'Your dad,' she went on, shakily, didn't understand. He did more and more overtime, but it was forgetfulness I wanted.' Her voice rose. 'Life was so romantic with other men, I was utterly selfish, Zet.'

Zet remembered. The excitement, the romance, the feeling that your heart is splitting in two. Your children versus your lover. There was a minute or two's silence before Zet could bring herself to speak carefully, 'It seems to me that dad enjoys loving you and caring for you. I think some men are born, you could say, to be taken advantage of, they almost ask for it. But mum,' she asked, through a clotted throat... 'Why don't we love them for it?'

Iris studied Zet's shadowed face. 'Because being a mother,' she said pointedly, 'doesn't stop you from falling in love, any more than being a wife does. There's just more guilt.'

Her eyes gleamed in the dark, bright with tears, and she touched Zet's arm, 'Zet....'

Lights suddenly flashed on, flooding the upstairs landing. Both women blinked.

'Our coats are upstairs, Min.'

While her mother disappeared into the bathroom to repair her face, Zet went downstairs, passing Min on the way.

After Jonty's parents, Dick left, followed by friends. Returning to the sitting-room after seeing them off, Zet paused at the door, suddenly struck by something ominous in the atmosphere.

Gran looked around at those remaining, a secretive smile on her face. Don't they realise, the young, that when you get old you can read them like a book? I know more about you than you realise, she silently told them. All living a

213

lie. You never come and see me, as if I'm unimportant, as if I've nothing to say. Oh, yes, I know. You all think I haven't lived. I could stun the lot of you, right now. Take the smiles off your faces. Make you sit up and take notice.

Chapter Thirty-Eight

'Course,' Gran said aloud, 'I was on the stage when I was young.'

Faces turned her way. 'We know that.' Sophie, nibbling cheese straws, raised her brows at the others. Gran saw.

'If you're going to demonstrate your act, ' sniggered Laurie, 'I'm off.'

She fixed her gin filled eyes on him, her favourite. He was a Manager at Fords, wore smart clothes and a self satisfied expression, ran an expensive car, rattled around in a detached house with a detached wife who was having an affair with her boss at the bank, but Laurie didn't know.

Zet felt tension in the room. 'What about telling us one of the ghost stories you used to tell at our Christmas parties when I was little,' she suggested hurriedly.

Iris came back into the room, passing Jonty as he went to the kitchen for a fresh bottle of coke. Mary, Albie's hard faced, disapproving wife, who worked her fingers to the bone for the local church, was already pursing her lips and eyeing Gran, to whom she hardly spoke, with dislike.

Zet prayed the taxis would turn up soon. Too late. Gran made her announcement.

'Course, Laurie hasn't got the same dad as the rest of you.'

In the shocked silence, balloons hanging from the ceiling stirred and bounced angrily at the draught from the open door. The heating, as controlled as everything in the house, had been programmed to switch off at twelve and the house was beginning to cool down. Just outside the room, Jonty turned back.

Stunned eyes flew to examine Laurie as if he was a museum exhibit. His thin lips hung open, he had coloured to the roots of his coiffured hair.

Sharp, curious eyes switched back to Gran, who was balancing a glass half full of gin on her knees. 'Your dad,' she said importantly, gazing into the glass as if it were a crystal ball, 'was called David. He was a G.I. I met in the war.'

'Very original.' Viv threw her brother a spiteful look.

Bridget, Laurie's immaculate, distant wife, who had seemed politely indifferent most of the evening, suddenly sat up straight and exchanged interested glances with an astonished Zet, whose mouth had gone dry.

'We met at Cambridge,' Gran went on, looking around with pleasure, enjoying the attention, 'where the kids were evacuated with the Vicar. Poor little bleeders,' she chuckled. 'I only went to see them at Cambridge because the kids wrote that they were miserable. The kids said that the man of the house was interfering with Iris. A Vicar! I ask you. Just a blinkin' excuse to come 'ome, it was. Anyway, as things turned out, I met David, who was stationed there.'

'And?' Plump, easy-going Albie was twirling his glass in his hand, fair head tilted, eyes - he was a detective inspector - weighing things up.

Gran said, 'as you know, your dad was in the navy.' No one answered, and she went on, 'A year after I met David, I got a letter to say your dad was on his way 'ome.'

Zet found her voice. 'So you had to make a decision?'

Gran looked her straight in the eye. 'There was no decision to make, dear.' She tilted her head with that haughty look drink gave her. 'I sent David away and your uncle Laurie was born nine months later.'

'What happened to David?' Sophie asked weakly, wishing her mother hadn't said anything, but now it was out she was curious.

'I never forgot him, 'course not. And if things had been different....'

'We might have all been living in America.' Viv looked wistful. 'I might have married a millionaire,' she added, with an uninterested glance at her husband, Peter. Shrugging, he helped himself to a drink from bottles on the sideboard.

Above the clink of glass, Laurie asked, in a taut voice, 'How do you know...I mean about me? Dad...your husband...came home, and….'

The drink on Gran's knee tipped. She tried to reach it...missed. The drink soaked her trousers and Zet came to the rescue with a paper towel kept for just such an emergency. Gran hardly seemed to notice.

'His ship was hit in the Atlantic on the way 'ome. He never got 'ere.'

Her watery eyes turned to a thoughtful Iris. 'Just think...David wanted to take us to America, he had an uncle who was a Hollywood producer.'

'Come off it,' Sophie groaned.

'Tell me the old, old story,' Viv sneered.

'He might not have been lying,' Iris said flatly. 'Oh, mum.'

'What do you mean, Oh mum? He said he'd put you in the pictures.'

Zet raised her eyes to the ceiling.

'Leave her to her dreams,' Sophie announced, ignoring her mother's glare. And glancing at Iris, 'you're tired,' she said sharply. 'I'll drive you home.'

The sound of two taxis drawing up outside was a relief to them all. Only Laurie still sat, looking into his drink. Gran tried to struggle from the deep chair - couldn't - Peter heaved her up. She stood, not quite steadily, peering at them all.

'I wrote it all down in a book I got from Woolworth's, so that when I'm gone.... Didn't see any point in leaving you to read about it,' she announced belligerently. 'Besides, I wanted to see your faces.'

From the corner of the room the music they had all forgotten about played on.

The party's over...time to burst your balloons

217

Iris, swearing she wasn't tired, gazed up at the balloons as the open door set them swinging. She reached up, grabbed a red one and turned to Zet.

'Do you know, I'll never forget tonight.' She made an effort to smile, wanting Zet to know she was grateful. She flicked a glance filled with dislike at her mother.

'None of us will,' laughed Viv, pulling a glaring Laurie to his feet.

Thank you's were uncertainly said; promises to meet, uttered into the brittle night air, wafted away. Sophie squeezed Gran, none too gently, into the back of her Mini with Iris who said coldly, 'Well done, mum,' before she rested her head back and closed her eyes. Sophie lit a cigarette and started the car. Maurice, who had given up smoking when Iris became ill, wound down the window. Night came inside like icy disapproval, whisking the balloon from Iris's hand. She grabbed at it and dumped it on her mother's lap.

'You love bursting balloons,' she told her mother, who was sitting beside her cuddling her handbag to her chest defensively and looking out of the window. The old lady pushed the balloon away with a spiteful swipe, bit her lip, and said nothing. Iris caught the balloon and settled back again.

'You certainly went off with a big bang tonight.' She sounded deflated, almost as if she might cry, as the car followed the taxis like a funeral procession along the quietening avenues through which the old year had breathed its last.

Watching them go, Zet felt an ominous tug on her heart. Something told her that for this family - her family - life would never be the same again. The party's over.

Chapter Thirty-Nine

The sun, that summer, burned fiercely. Crow Street lay stifling beneath the faceless boredom of a killer. Pollution.

That was when Iris cried. The sun that she loved so much and had been waiting anxiously for was no longer her friend.

Coming inside from a brief spell in the garden, she reached out to support herself against a chair. 'I feel sick and giddy.' She looked dazed, as if she didn't know what had hit her.

Concerned, Zet saw hurt eyes, the eyes of a child who had been smacked and had done nothing wrong. As tears welled up and began to spill, Iris turned her head and wiped them away with her fingers. 'Oh, well. Never mind.'

She had padded outside so happily, wearing shorts and boob tube, shoeless, smelling of coconut, eyes shaded by a floppy sunhat, a Jilly Cooper novel in one hand, a chilled Sangria in the other.

'It's all the chemicals you've had,' Zet frowned, feeling for her, 'I'll bring you a cleansing diet sheet to get rid of the poisons in your body. Don't worry, everyone's feeling under the weather.' Don't panic, Zet.

The diet seemed to help and there was, thankfully, a cooler spell, during which Maurice and Iris drove to the coast, or the countryside, visiting places they had known when they were courting, or newly married.

'The car's more comfortable than that old motorbike of yours,' Iris pointed out and Maurice looked indignant.

'That was my Triumph,' he answered. But his eyes held fond memories. 'And I quite enjoyed having you cuddling into my back.'

'Mm.' Her face softened. 'You've never known that, Zet, have you.' Zet shook her head and her mother looked wistful, remembering.

'Riding pillion. The feel of a saddle between your legs, your arms around a man's waist, the smell and feel of his leather jacket against your face, the wind in your hair, the engine roar, the speed and freedom. Like flying.'

She didn't appear to hear Zet's sharp intake of breath and certainly couldn't read her mind. It's always something... a word, a tune, even television, Zet thought wistfully. Even on the weather map in the newspaper, my eyes are drawn right to the north, where the wild things are. She could be listening to the radio while cooking dinner, hearing the travel reports. The A66 across the Pennines was always mentioned. She was back there, driving to the Lakes and her skin shrank against her bones with the pain.

Then there was the children's interest in a television series ... All Creatures Great and Small, about a Yorkshire Vet. 'This was filmed where we used to live,' they kept telling her.

'Yes I know.'

'Come on, mum.' Darren particularly loved the series. 'It's starting.'

'I'm busy.'

The heat wave returned. Pollution levels in London reached danger level; traffic Police wore smog masks and cyclists were advised to do the same.

The sun burned hatefully. Barbecues sizzled; bare-bellied, tattooed drinkers spilled out of pubs; there was the stink of hot diesel from buses, even they seemed to have difficulty in breathing... gasping and retching along baking roads that glistened like melted candle wax. The air simmered with tension and resentments.

There were small communal grass areas now between new houses and flats, and these turned butterscotch brown, and sticky-skinned people lounged everywhere, like pigs on spits.

Iris pulled in deep breaths, her face suffused with relief. 'I love it out here in the garden when you've just hosed it down, pet.'

The pathos in her voice made Zet glance at her uncertainly as she hosed. Thirst quenching water, pure and lovely as diamante beads, glistened and dripped from leaves, and the thirsty earth sent up a warm, sweet scented thank you. The jaded flowers seemed weak and lifeless, but the Mediterranean geraniums were vibrant and blooming, happy looking, as if wondering what all the fuss was about.

The fountain's gurgle and splash had a cooling, calming sound and Iris admitted she had been sleeping in the garden room, as she called the lounge, on these hot nights, with the doors wide open, lulled by the running water.

'It sounds so alive,' she said in a small voice. Zet's stomach lurch with fear.

'Oh, mum.' *Sleeping with the door open!*

'What?' Iris looked puzzled into Zet's upset face... 'Nothing. It's nothing.'

Zet turned back to watch water gush from the hose.

She had never forgotten how safe she had felt in the Yorkshire village. She had never heard footsteps at night, only the slurp and whoosh of running water, or winds, hooting owls and muted howls of wildlife, the occasional car sliding quietly home.

Brad, oh, Brad. Iris is better now.... What am I thinking? That I could go off for a weekend, back to Yorkshire? I could say that I have a Course to attend. But no, after what Brad did? Even if he's still there, still free. Even if he would be pleased to see me? No. He tried to kill a man, for God's sake, Zet.

The stream of water from the hose pushed through the plants, bubbling around the roots, throwing glittering specks into the air, joyful and free.

221

The sun was a menacing white-hot face, cooking poison; it rose every day over London, burning the sky, sucking at skin and breath and covering the chemical laden city with an escape proof jacket. The suffocating sky, yellow, like pus, looked heavy enough to fall. At the end of each sweating day, tired, irritated people thankfully watched the sun slink like a hard, red boil into the Thames, leaving behind a breathless night stuffed with the sickly fumes of the day.

Gran was ill with a chest complaint and Zet persuaded her to close the cafe for two weeks and stay with her in Essex.

Sophie, plump, plum coloured and perspiring, went to B&Q and hauled back a sun umbrella, hoping it would enable Iris to spend more time in the garden.

'This is the life.' With a smile, Sophie collapsed back on a sun bed that almost filled the small patio. She wore shorts and a strapless silk top, from which her Factor fifteen Coppertone skin rolled with relief.

Iris sat at a table beneath the umbrella. Her face wore the absent expression of someone whose mind is far away. Sophie heard her speak as if to herself.

'Our moments dancing in the sun.' Turning her head, Iris saw her sister watching her and smiled. 'We have to enjoy them while we can, I think.'

Sophie drained her glass of iced tea. 'I intend to.' She placed the glass on the table with a clang. 'I'm going to Ibiza in September.'

As if she hadn't heard, Iris said softly, 'Maybe that's all there is, our dancing in the sun moments. The rest of the time we're shadow dancers, we think we're something we're not.'

'Some people more than others,' Sophie said slyly. 'By the way, can I borrow your leather flight bag?'

With a sudden indrawn breath, Iris pushed herself up from the chair as if she had come to a decision, and

222

padded inside. 'You can keep it,' she said, over her shoulder. 'I shan't need it.'

Jonty arranged for a photographer friend to blow up and frame some of Iris's photographs. And suddenly, Spain burned on the walls...brilliant, vibrant, amber and ochre, gaunt; sea like ink and sand like old parchment that Iris said she could almost feel, crumbling between her toes.

With them hung a gift from Min, a picture she had made herself from shells Iris had brought back from her Spanish beaches. And because Iris loved the look of terracotta, Alyson had the idea of placing old jam jars inside terracotta pots. Filled with flowers, eagerly supplied by Albert and Jonty's friends, who adored Iris, the pots looked unusual and lovely. With the little things that Darren and Alyson made, or bought with their pocket money, the room was filled with friends. And love.

Maurice bought her a new cassette by her favourite singer, Julio Englesias, or Hoolio, as she called him. 'The biggest gift of all,' Maurice told her, as he firmly pressed the "Play" button, and Iris's thin body began to sway with *Begin The Beguine*, is that you have your health back.'

'I'd like to see Tony again.' Iris looked apologetically at Maurice. 'Only to say...hello. He just seemed to disappear, you see.'

Since the good news about her health, there had been something almost frantic about her need to contact old friends and relatives she hadn't seen for some time; and she needed the company of people. It had surprised Zet how many friends her mother had. People just loved being with her and her illness hadn't deterred them as it had her brothers and sisters.

I love people,' Iris often said. 'And I have great friends. I've always preferred friends to family,' she added blithely.

If Maurice was disappointed that his own company wasn't enough for her, if he had hoped to keep her to himself, he was wise enough to keep silent.

'If that's what you want, my lady,' he said, with his kind smile. 'No problem.'

Tony had disappeared. Making enquiries, Maurice sensed caginess from the long distance haulage firm, Tony's employers. Ex employers, they told him tersely.

A few weeks later, they found out anyway, it was all over the newspapers. Tony had found fame, but not fortune, although he had tried.

Chapter Forty

The livid summer burned on as if it would go on forever.

Iris was resting in the garden room on the new divan Maurice had replaced the sofa with because she liked to sleep there. She was restless at night, she said, didn't want to disturb him. Not knowing, of course, that he lay awake upstairs listening in case she needed something.

The room was filled with light and scent and birdsong and the ceaseless gurgling of the fountain and the ticking of the clock that Albert had given her because she said she liked the sound of old ticking clocks.

She could see through the open doors, where the leafy garden and Zet, who was weeding, shimmered for a moment as if behind frosted glass. Panting in the heat, Iris thought of the active work of creation and moving consciousness that gardening must be. Like doll-making. Her glance searched a nearby shelf. She smiled wistfully when she saw the gipsy doll Zet had made. Her daughter's voice came back to her clearly. 'She's the image of you, mum.'

'Except for her long curls.'

Zet had not hidden her irritation. 'So? You're better, that's the important thing.' Still so vain, her tone said. They had both looked at each other and then laughed, recognizing something familiar in their relationship, and pleased with it.

'Anyway,' Zet had smiled, 'You look like Audrey Hepburn.'

'Do I really?'

Remembering that conversation, Iris raised her hand and touched her hair. Sensing him watching her, she looked into Maurice's kind, lined face and said, 'Zet works... too hard.' Hauling breath into her lungs, she added softly, 'Doesn't she know she's painting the darkness?'

***

He felt the hairs rise on the back of his neck. She held out her hand. Mutely, despairingly, taking it between both of his, he held on to the comfort she was offering. Silly old fool, he told himself, forcing back tears because it was like holding bones, her hand.

Searching her face, he found a luminous beauty, sharper curves, deeper hollows, but her beseeching, trusting eyes, from which hope had fled, emptied him. His body turned to ice as in the voice of a tired child, she told him

'The lodger's back. No more chemo, Maurice, I don't want it.'

He was aware of pigeons cooing outside, the thrusts of Zet's hoe breaking up the living earth, the beating of his heart and the clasp of her hot little hand, eyes searching his face. Trusting him.

He swallowed. 'Then you won't have it, lady,' said the broken-hearted man who would have given her the moon.

***

Iris developed serenity; people - friends, neighbours and, briefly, brothers, and sisters - sat around her as if she was a television, talking about each other as if she could help them, as if she was the Pope. She listened to them. Fighting for breath, she listened.

Zet was angry, she wanted her mother left alone. Why do they drain her, like vultures picking at the life she has left? What about when she gets better? Will they all come round then?

'Zet?'

'Yes?' Her mother was watching her from the bed, concern in her sunken eyes.

'Zet, I don't want anything done to keep me here, when the time comes, you know what I mean.'

A nod…a stomach lurch…no words. 'See Zet...you're strong.'

'Am I?'

'I've always admired your strength, Zet and...Zet, I love you.'

'Oh, mum.' Zet sat turned to stone. 'Oh, mum.' Looking away from Zet's bloodless face, Iris added,

'I always intended to go straight from life to death. Know what I mean? I've always dreaded hospitals, doctors, being messed about like meat on a slab. I don't want that,' she ended, and Zet nodded.

'Dad said he'll take you up West to Ronnie Scott's when you're better.'

Iris seemed to focus on the beautiful... her garden, television programmes like Come Dancing, nature and travel; she read poetry and there was music. All the time, music. Particularly hot, lively Spanish guitar, as well as her beloved Hoolio's throbbing voiced love songs. She hadn't lost her sense of humour, far from it. People also came to see her for a good time and a lot of laughter filled that room.

Appalled by her desperate fight to breathe, Jonty brought an electric fan to replace the useless Spanish one she waved in front of her face. As the poisonous cocktail poured inside, the angry fan pushed it back outside, the way the family began to close around her, pushing back the enemy. But still, her breath became more forced.

Zet, watching like someone detached, was chastened by it all. The importance of family was brought home to her. No matter that there were differences, incompatibilities; the way family closed around, hurt Zet the way something beautiful can hurt.

She explored every avenue of alternative medicine, fretted, fumed, not knowing that when she walked placidly into her mother's house, smiling, the remains of it lay on her face. Iris followed her with compassionate eyes

227

that reminded Zet of the television pictures of seals found washed up on a beach recently, struggling to breathe.

'Zet,' Iris asked, one day, when they were alone, 'Put your hand on my forehead.'

Zet did as she asked. Why do I feel embarrassed to touch my own mother?

'I always feel better when you touch me, Zet. I don't know why.'

Zet felt ashamed. Iris's forehead was damp and hot and felt like a stranger's.

'What are your first memories, Zet?' Iris removed Zet's hand from her forehead, but held it between her two thin hands.

Zet took a moment to think. What does she want to know? 'I was on a swing, dad pushing me; a park somewhere, I can remember a very strong smell of wallflowers. And at the pictures... I cried, I think.'

Iris repositioned herself, closed her eyes briefly, enjoying the relief of a cold hot water bottle against her back. Opening her eyes, she said with a smile, 'It was the Wizard of Oz. You had nightmares about the witch afterwards...I let you have a day off school...took you to the fair at Southend to help you forget it...remember?'

Zet didn't, but nodded and Iris looked relieved. 'You never liked the cinema... after that.'

Zet looked down as a sensation like a tingle flowed between their clasped hands, and collecting her thoughts, spoke slowly, 'there were more nightmares, though. I still have them. Always the same thing.'

Iris didn't have to ask.   She   knew   what   the nightmares were about.

An autumn day. A day that began like any other day, but ended in horror.

Chapter Forty-One

It had seemed an ordinary day to begin with. Windy, but other than that, there was no warning that this particular Monday morning was destined to be different from any other.

Zet had promised her mother to keep hold of Tommy until the bell rang but, once in the infants' playground, Tommy tore his hand from hers and ran off, taking the opportunity to meet friends before school started. Zet, who hated being teased by girls in her class about looking after her brother, didn't stop him. He was safely inside the school playground.

She let him go

The iron-tongued church clock next to the school started to chime. By the time it ran out of breath at nine, Mrs Hallam had rung her hand bell and begun forming the reluctant children into lines. Outside the playground, parents were clustered in chatty groups, waving and calling goodbyes through the railings. Zet's street had a rota system for the school run, and she waved to the neighbour whose turn it had been to escort her and her brother to school with her own children.

A biting wind cut across the Thames and the sports ground, stripping trees and carpeting the pavement with fiery leaves that crunched like spilled crisps. Parents stamped their feet, complaining that it was cold for October. Too sudden.

Zet's line of children was the first to move across the playground towards the open door of the school when a black car, crackling leaves beneath urgent tyres, swished into the kerb.

Something sounded different.

Something made people stir uneasily and look round. A latecomer maybe. Children get panicky if they're late.

The car door clicked open and the driver climbed out on to the road, a tall man wearing a navy windcheater and a pale, set expression. Even the car door slamming sounded different and would haunt these unsuspecting parents for a long time afterwards.

He had no child with him.

He stood, still and erect as a statue, looking over the roof of the car, eyes sifting intently through the crowd.

Huddling in knots, the parents - mothers all but one - hair, coats and skirts tossing in the wind - had got cold hanging about, now their voices sounded relieved, determinedly cheerful, waving encouraging goodbyes through shiny black spear shaped railings.

That important, reassuring last wave.

In a slow, determined way, the man walked round the car and on to the pavement. Leaves were hissing around his feet. Mothers pulled buggies and toddlers closer and a message rippled through the crowd like nerve gas, tightening necks and quivering in bellies.

He was holding a rifle.

Sleepy children, unaware, were slow, dragging their feet across the playground, towards the open door of the school.

In a cold, staccato voice, the impassive man called out a name. A young, shy-looking man, windswept and blond, turned, still waving at his daughter, even as the rifle was raised, finger already curling around the trigger. The sound was unexpectedly unimportant, a short sharp crack. The young man fell.

Zet was beside the railings, close enough to see it all. She was thinking that the rifle sounded quieter than those on the telly when she felt the shock of hands pushing her forward. Around her, children were tripping over each other, urged by terrified teachers; mothers were running into the playground, towards their children. He had the rifle raised as if about to fire again.

Passing close to him, Zet dropped her satchel on to the grey playground floor and bent to pick it up. Through the railings, she met the vengeful eyes of the pointing rifle.

230

It's me next.Something began gulping at her throat. Rooted to the spot, she became aware that the man's electrified gaze was fixed not on her but down at the ground. Looking down, she noticed what shiny black shoes he had. Her eyes moved along the ground to where Jody's nice dad lay amongst dirty leaves, his head oozing what looked like red jelly and ice cream.

She wanted to run, but felt bound in an iron grip and as if he knew, the man turned his head and looked straight at her.

'Move yourself Zet,' someone shouted, darting between her and the stare of the unnaturally still man beyond the railings. Hands pushing her, made her trip, hard hands, yanking her up and this is what made Zet cry. When they reached the door, teachers and mothers pushed the children inside as two more lines of children came from the other side of the playground to line up behind them. The sound of more shots. Screams. Children crying. Sirens.

Zet, eavesdropping from her usual place at the top of the stairs, heard, but didn't understand, that the man with the rifle, a soldier, was having an affair with Jody's mother. He had driven to the police station to give himself up. No one ever spoke to Zet about the murder. This was how it was done in those days. Bad things were not discussed with children. They had never happened.

All they told her was that her little brother had gone to heaven.

Chapter Forty-Two

'It's most strange,' Zet said. 'I began to think that the nightmares were a premonition. I was in a cage, unable to escape being shot and somehow, one day, it would happen again.' As a punishment, perhaps, for letting go of her brother's hand.

She kept silent about one thing. When Jonty was shot, she had felt as if her nightmare had come true. Looking back, she felt that only having the children to consider, the house move to organise, caring for her mother, as well as the depressed and resentful Jonty when he came out of hospital, had kept her sane. It had been an awful time.

The horror has been and gone, she reminded herself. She was free of it.

She could see that she had put herself in a cage and pointed a gun at herself. She had to be perfect or she would lose everything.

Another day, Zet asked, 'What about you, mum? Your first memories.'

Iris looked perturbed. 'Oh...men, pet. Men's laps, their rough chins, their hands all over me, a train journey, with Sophie....' Catching her breath, she admitted, 'Men meant sweets and presents and safety. The safety of a man's arms....' She looked at Zet, slightly shame-faced. 'Maybe it wasn't entirely that vicar's fault.'

'We're opposites, mum,' Iris told Gran who had squeezed herself into one of the wicker chairs and was easing her smart loafers from swollen feet.

Addressing Zet, Iris added, 'I laugh, mum cries.'

She turned to her mother. 'I had to get away from your constant crying. I wanted to be happy. It was almost as if unhappiness was contagious.'

Glancing at Gran's hurt face, Zet reminded her mother, 'You used to cry over films.'

'Oh, I know, pet, but films are different.'

Gran, flushed and hot, was breathing heavily, as if she had been running. Looking down at her swollen hands, she said, 'If only I hadn't made the wrong decisions, Iris.' Pulling a handkerchief from her shopping bag, she mopped her eyes. A strong scent of lily-of-the-valley filled the small room.

'I thought you hated me, I deserved it, I've never been a good mother....I tried, but everything I planned always went wrong.'

Iris gave a 'tch' of annoyance. 'Get off my deathbed; I don't want your tears. Your crying is probably the first thing I heard and it's not going to be my last.'

Watching and listening, Zet thought, she's enjoying this. It's spiteful. At the same time, Zet knew that these two women had never been matriarchs, never acted like mothers. I am, Zet found herself thinking, the first woman in the family to mother, which is why I put all my heart into it.

Zet also learned something else. That, as a child, you feel threatened by a mother who lives on the edge of a cliff. You want her at home, so you can feel safe. She suddenly felt compassion for the child she had been. In her imagination she was seeing herself when young. She remembered her misery when the house began to smell of L'aimant perfume and hairspray. She saw herself standing at the window of her mother's bedroom looking down at the street, watching her mother, dressed in her best clothes, going out for the evening. Zet remembered the click of her high heels, as she walked away, and how she watched until her mother turned the corner and was gone. She remembered her aunt Sophie arriving with her collection of games, and how they played Snakes and Ladders and ludo. And Happy Families, Zet's favourite.

'Balloons,' Iris said, 'When I go I want balloons... in the house...on the front door.'

Zet and Maurice looked at each other, stricken. From Sophie came a startled whisper, 'What will people say?'

'Since when have I cared for that?' Iris said weakly. 'If people disapprove you must be having fun.' There was a ghost of a grin.

Sophie felt helpless; resentful, too, in a way. As always, Iris, who, let's face it, had always been selfish, was getting all the attention. Take Zet, for instance, couldn't do enough for her mother. But who had been there when Zet needed someone? Sophie caught herself up. What an awful way to think. She loved Iris, faults and all. It was just that the flamboyance was too much. There were ways of doing things, weren't there? There was dignity, for a start. You should die with dignity.

Hearing Maurice's voice on the phone, Zet felt a shocked thud in her stomach.

It's in The News Of The World,' he said.

Zet flopped with relief that her father had not been ringing with the news she dreaded. 'Has she seen it, dad?'

'She's reading it now.'

'Alyson,' Zet called, putting the receiver down, 'Dash down to the newsagents for me, there's a good girl.'

'Oh, mum, just when....'

'I'll go,' offered Jonty, standing up from the breakfast table. 'What's up?'

'It's Tony.' Zet was standing at the kitchen door, washed and made up, not yet dressed, feeling exhausted. She had sat with her mother until late the previous night and then had kept waking up in bed thinking she could hear that tortuous breathing. 'Hurry up,' she cried, almost pushing Jonty out of the house.

British lorry driver in immigrant smuggling scandal, stated the headlines.

234

'Lorry drivers are getting twenty thousand pounds a trip for smuggling illegal immigrants into Western Europe. They work from a transport cafe in Bucharest and charge five hundred pounds a head to load stowaways into their trailers and drive them into Germany.'

Darren was listening wide-eyed. 'What's happened to Tony?'

Alyson looked upset. 'Will they shoot him?' She had passionately adored Tony.

'Of course not. He's on bail in Romania for smuggling desperate immigrants who have spent all their life savings on a dream.' Jonty looked meaningfully at the horrified Zet, obviously thinking, as she was....

....Iris had been so eager to travel with him on his long hauls, that she could quite easily have been caught with him and held over there.

Surprisingly, Iris took it philosophically. 'They can't hang him, anyway.' Her eyes met Zet's. 'He always did yearn for excitement. Now he's got it.' After a pause...'He got so jittery, lost interest in me, couldn't even...you know. I thought it was another woman. But it wasn't,' she ended, her head dropping back on the pillow. She smiled.

Iris's skin had lustre at first, and then it began to turn yellow, like an old doll. And then people began trying to breathe for her.

Zet fought against a sense of solitude, of deathly loneliness, of separation, the breaking of a human bond. There was still laughter, bright, luminous moments, as fragile as the Christmas baubles Iris loved, and there was a sense of hanging on...

'Breathe,' you wanted to keep urging her, 'Breathe

...breathe.' Her piteous eyes stared up at you and you felt cruel. Once she breathlessly snapped, 'What in the bloody hell do you think I'm trying to do?'

Breathe what? It was heartrending as her lungs tried to breathe the filthy remains of oxygen. It was impossible to keep these cramped houses cool and there was no sign of the heat wave ending.

'Breathe. Breathe, mum, breathe.' 'Come on, my Lady, you can do it.'

Painkillers lost their power, and you learned that when Iris was silent, the pain was at its worse. She was using all her pitiful energy to fight and the suffering in her haunted eyes tore you to pieces.

Jonty, who could hardly bear it, strode into the Crow Street house one day just as Zet was about to leave to collect the children from school.

'I've got her something.' His eyes, unusually sharp, dared Zet to argue.

Iris took the cannabis in tea and there was suddenly power in the room, they all felt it, as the pain floated away.

'It should be available on prescription,' Jonty argued, running fingers through his hair, his face lined with compassion.

'Oh, Jonty,' Iris said weakly, with laughter in her sunken, dark shadowed eyes, 'something illegal... is always so much more enjoyable. I did pot in the sixties, it's no big deal. Besides,' she added, a little mulishly, 'I'm entitled.' Seeing his face, she patted his hand. 'Now, don't worry,' she whispered tenderly, as if he was a child.

Zet didn't know what to think. She disapproved of drugs, but seeing her mother in pain was hell.

Zet was doing the ironing when the phone rang. She knew, as you do on these occasions.

Jonty blanched. 'Shall I answer it?' 'I'll go.' Her heart was pounding.

Maurice was at the hospice Zet had only left a couple of hours before. She heard him mumble as an old man does with his teeth out. 'She's gone, Zet. Lady's gone.'

Zet's legs gave way. She had to support herself with the telephone table. Oh, mum, it's over for you. Thank God. The tears ran, she swiped them away as you would irritating flies, the telephone was wet and she could hear his breathing.

After a moment, struggling to speak, he said, 'It was strange, Rosie. We were sitting quietly, she was in the armchair and…suddenly she looked at me, all bright-eyed, and said, "I feel so well, I could dance around the room."'

Voice breaking, he pulled in a calming breath. 'Rosie, even her voice was her normal voice, you know? She was smiling. She said, "Dance with me, Maurice." I didn't have any music….if only I'd thought. I held her in my arms and hummed, waltzed a bit, just slowly. And then she asked to lie on the bed, closed her eyes and died. And,' he said, beginning to sob, 'she wasn't there any more. Oh, love....' His voice failed him. Then …'you don't want to let someone go, do you? You just don't... you try to keep them back but you can't.' It was a cry from the heart.

Zet wept. She felt Jonty take the receiver, speak to her father, replace the receiver and take her gently in his arms. He wept too. That night they made love and she wanted it. It was the best she had known with Jonty. No raging passion, he treated her tenderly, like a child. They avoided each other's eyes in the morning like a couple of teenagers.

The safety of a man's arms, her mother had once said. Zet wondered...Should it be like that today?

At the house in Crow Street next morning, Maurice slipped his hand into a vase and removed the packet of balloons he had hidden. Zet had brought some from home, left over from Christmas. The vicar thought he had come to the wrong house, the neighbours whispered amongst themselves and Zet thought... mum, you've stuck your

237

fingers up at the ordinary people, you had your party and your masquerade ...well done.

'I forgot to tell her I loved her, dad.'

'She knew,' he said, looking at her with strained eyes. 'She took it for granted everyone loved her, it was the first thing she knew... adulation. Even when we split up, she knew I would always love her. She expected people to make sacrifices for her. Besides, you made her a garden,' he said simply. 'You made it for love, and she knew it. And Rosie?'

'Yes, dad?'

His eyes were glistening. 'I'm proud of you. Proud of the way you cared for your mum when she needed you.'

Zet felt a surge of grief mixed with release and the next moment she was crouched on the floor beside his chair, head resting on his lap and his gentle hands were stroking her hair while she cried as if she would never stop.

Zet went upstairs dreading the job she had to do, but she knew Maurice would hate it too. He would be feeling the way she did, disbelief that Iris was gone, that she wouldn't be singing around the house any more.

Oh, mum. Zet smiled and cried. Then she found a folded nightdress...

Iris had always tucked old scent bottles amongst her undies or nightclothes. Zet looked down at what lay in her hand. An old, half empty bottle of L'aimant. She pulled off the cap, held it to her nose, smelled the lingering trace of warm, rose based scent, and willed herself to feel her mother beside her, as she had done, all those years ago, when Iris had gone out for the evening smelling of L'aimant and Zet had stood at the window, watching her go, so afraid she would not come back.

If I tidy her room, she'll come back, I used to think. Oh, mum.

After the funeral service, Zet followed her father from the church. Passing down the aisle, he turned his head and said, 'She'll be seeing her rainbow by now, Zet.' He was trying to smile.

'Course she will, dad.' Reaching out, she gripped his hand and moved forward so that she was beside him, leaving Jonty and her children behind. She couldn't swallow. Count to ten. They walked awkwardly together, with clutched hands. The church doors opened, and she felt, in disbelief, cool, moist air rushing to meet them. It was raining. The heat wave had ended.

You could almost hear a small voice saying, 'Oh well, never mind.' And Zet turned her head, looking for the coffin, almost as if to say – look mum, it's raining.

The curtains had closed.

Chapter Forty-Three

To Frankie, Zet described her marriage as being like a well-behaved, controlled pet dog that would suddenly, for no reason, turn and snap. Closing the appointment book they had been discussing, Frankie's response was unexpectedly curt.

'You want to bring him to heel, you mean?' Zet's eyes opened wide and in a more even, neutral voice, Frankie said,' You can't expect everything to go your way.'

Defensively, Zet retorted, 'I don't.' 'Zet, come on...you do.'

'There's nothing wrong with wanting things right.' 'Right for whom?'

Zet tried to keep the irritation from her voice. 'Are you getting at me?'

'Getting into you would describe it better. I'm your friend. I hope,' she added, eyebrows flicking up comically, a way she had, which made Zet smile.

'Jonty's a good chap,' Frankie said, slipping from the desk and walking over to the window. Keeping her back to Zet, she added evenly, 'He's kind and gentle; all he wants in life is to be happy with you. He does all he can to please you.'

'That's just it,' Zet said, trying to hide her annoyance. Everyone seems to be on his side. I'm getting fed up with hearing how perfect he is. 'I'm responsible for his happiness,' she said, sitting forward and leaning her elbows on the desk, trying to get her point across. Frankie was apparently studying the street below the window and addressing her back, Zet said vehemently, ''No-one should be held responsible for another's happiness.'

Turning, Frankie studied Zet curiously. 'Have you never met anyone you've pinned your happiness on so much that you felt you had to try to please?'

When she received no answer, Frankie leaned forward, with her back to the window, stretching an arm each side of her on the sill. 'What about your Yorkshire man, Zet? Could you have left him because you were afraid that if you stayed you would depend upon him for your happiness and you didn't trust him? The impression I had of him is a man used to getting his own way, a man who loved women and left them. Not a man who would jump to your tune, Zet.'

Furious, Zet stared across the room. 'That's not fair. You know why I left. The family.' No one seemed to understand. 'You're a vulture, Frankie. You pick at bones.'

'Sorry, Zet, don't mean to.' Pushing herself away from the window, Frankie glanced at her watch. 'Hey, I must go.' With a wave, she hurried from the room, closing the door behind her, leaving Zet with the impression that Frankie had been glad to go.

Leaning back in her chair - there were two comfortable armchairs and a coffee table as well as a massage couch and the desk where Zet did her paperwork – she looked around.

The clinic had been converted from one of those large Victorian town houses, which meant all the rooms were like this one, spacious and serious, with high ceilings, and tall windows. The room, painted in relaxing cream and pink, felt airy and smelled fragrant. Through the window she could see the town hall, shopping precinct, the church.

She enjoyed the work. It wasn't just that the money helped at home, she found the act of massage therapeutic, with its smooth rhythmic movement. Her hands became instruments, soothing troubled minds and muscles, almost, at times, seeming to receive a message from the body, pinpointing trouble spots; there was a sense of achievement at the end of the day.

She could hear muted traffic sounds, teacups chinking somewhere, an occasional soft laugh, and voices murmuring from the waiting room from which taped relaxing music was audible. She thought of her

241

colleagues, all, of necessity, calm, professional, controlled people, who contributed to the pleasant atmosphere.

Unlike home. There, she searched in vain for the man she had married and found little she recognised among the scowls, the silences, the innuendos, and the self-deprecating humour, especially about his work. In trying to save her marriage, was she destroying him instead? But how? Why?

On the surface things were normal, with the usual outings, celebrations, barbecues in the summer, school concerts and sports days. Sophie and Maurice were around to help with the children during the holidays. Sometimes you wouldn't believe there was anything wrong. Maybe their marriage was what it isn't, rather than what it is. Surely it was a better marriage than a lot of people had. The children are luckier than most.

Yes, but their mother cannot bear their father's touch; their father uses business travel as escape; they are imprisoned by grief, guilt and by a love they can barely express. A great marriage!

In her dark nighttime ponderings, she suspected that her emotions and passions had been stretched too far for an ordinary marriage. And in her weaker moments she admitted ruefully, to Frankie, 'I have a vision of myself pulling the family the wrong way along the M25.'

On the evenings she had no doll-making classes, she sat opposite Jonty, when the children were in bed, sewing dolls' dresses or shoes, or cutting out patterns, and tried to work it all out.

I can't live with him, but I can't let go. She studied him as he read, watched television or listened to music, terrified by the prospect of divorce. Family life was the ultimate security, what she had planned for. And even as a child, what she had dreamed of. Hating life in her mother's home, she had escaped in dreams of a home and husband of her own. An ideal home. A perfect life.

242

Her head was like the London Underground, circling round and round in the dark. I thought after three years the pain would go away. But the grief and guilt are awful. Somehow the torment of my secret infidelity has come between us.

One evening, for longer than she knew, he had been watching her staring into space, hands lying still in her lap. Something troubled in her face moved him to frown. 'Is something wrong?' He saw her come to with a start.

'No. Nothing.'

Nothing, she silently added, but living on the edge of tragedy. Guilt, deceit, remorse, longing, in equal measure. And what she tried not to think of...Jonty could have died because of her infidelity. She would have been as responsible as Brad.

The vision of him, in his hospital bed after the shooting, and the way he looked across at her in the evenings, concerned, and the little things he did in an attempt to please, came back to her and she felt as if she was sinking beneath a weight of utter sorrow. Dear Jonty, what have I done to you?

She thought of the old Jonty, easy going and good tempered, and felt sad at the change in him. Yet despite the sullen moods and spiteful remarks, he still loved her that was the truth of it. It showed in the way he fussed over her sometimes, the looks of love, the sex they rarely shared when she felt like a mother, comforting him. It wasn't as easy as she had supposed to mend a relationship and carry on as if nothing had happened. But how do you force feelings that aren't there? How do you stop your hackles rising when he reaches for you in bed?

And Brad? How do you unlove?

You did the right thing, she told herself. All Jonty's needs were catered for. It was service with a smile and sex...an out of body experience for her. Yet the hunger in his eyes sometimes and his possessive love drove towards her like a battering ram. He injured her with his love and didn't know it.

She saw something of Jonty's possessiveness in her father, as he talked - a little too much - of his life with Iris, as if he wanted to expunge himself.

'I adored her, wanted her to myself, yet I stopped taking her out; I was a boring, lazy man,' he admitted, looking ashamed. 'I can remember when we first met; she used to say...'Let's go up West, Maurice.' And we'd go. She was young and lively; she wanted to fly. And maybe, looking back, I wanted to weigh her down to keep her.'

'You were just two different people, dad. It happens often in marriage, one is fast, the other slow, one's gregarious, the other a fire and slippers type. Frankie and I were only talking the other day about how people, when they meet someone they want, make themselves more attractive to that person by taking on that person's personality, submerging, even lying, about their own interests and needs. These are the lies and pretences of courtship. But then, of course, after marriage, real life takes over and people accuse their partner of changing. They haven't changed, they've just stopped acting, and that's when the trouble starts.' Zet sighed. 'Maybe it's true we're all playing parts.'

Maurice looked impressed. 'That's interesting, you know. I've always been a slow sort of person, I tired easily, but I certainly wasn't going to let on while we were courting that I was a drag.' Shamefaced, he admitted, 'in some ways I enjoyed having your mother to myself when she was ill. Awful, isn't it?'

'Human, dad.' But she saw how his possessiveness could have stifled Iris. Memory flashed back...herself as a child, crying because a balloon she was holding had been snatched away by the wind. Iris had watched it go...'Balloons don't like being held back; they need to be free. Once they feel the wind beneath them, they're away.'

244

Zet had felt the wind beneath her. She found herself envying those who were free, even her own daughter. Even aunt Sophie. Until the unexpected happened.

Chapter Forty-Four

Gran made a disapproving mouth and glared at Zet as if it was her fault. 'She's only moving that bloke in here.'

'It's Sophie's home,' Zet answered. 'And she hasn't had much of a life.'

'Not much of a life? With me waiting on her hand and foot?' Chins quivered with indignation. 'An old woman of eighty doing all the cooking and shopping?'

'We've asked you to leave it to Sophie, but you won't.'

'Don't want to be poisoned, do I?' was Gran's answer, face folded into stern lines, her eyes like moving ash, hot with spite. 'He won't last long; you see.'

Gran had a plan, and this was one plan she was determined would work.

Jack Crabbe and Sophie were two of a kind, or so Jack said in his loud, persuasive voice. The tall, portly Jack, sandy haired, with a large nose, skin reddened and toughened from his outdoor life of market stall and racecourses, liked the house, too

'Very nice,' he called out, rubbing his large hands as he came heavily downstairs from moving his belongings into Sophie's bedroom. 'Do us nicely, Lil luv; bit cramped though, we could do with the front bedroom really.'

Lily Garrity, he didn't like. 'Does she have to play her blinkin' music so loud?' he complained as he and Sophie lay in bed one night in the shabby room he had promised, one day, to decorate. 'What is it, anyway, it's bloody awful?'

'Band music actually. Mum's really taken to it, especially the Dam Busters March.' Sophie wondered why her mum no longer played her Vera Lynn or Bing Crosby records. The band was certainly loud... real wartime; planes roaring, the lot.

She giggled, feeling happy. It still seemed strange to sleep in bed with a man and to hear his voice come out of the dark beside her. Tonight he sounded fed up.

'S'not funny.'

She had just taken his mind off the music when there was a bang on the door.

'Sophie. Can't find them painkillers. Me rheumatism's driving me round the bend.'

'Wish it effing would,' Jack growled, rolling off Sophie's plump, accommodating body. She knew how to keep a man happy, Sofe did, as if she had made a career out of it. Pity about the old bag. He'd knife her one day, he really would.

His ex wife and kids had the house on the Isle of Dogs - not that it was worth much - leaving him living for the last twelve years in a grotty one bedroom Council flat off the Old Kent Road. Then he'd found Sofe. Looked after herself, Sofe did, had a bit of class, not to mention redundancy money in the bank, a part- time job and this little house in a back street, which was a haven after what he was used to. Tarted up a bit, it could be a little palace. People were snapping up these old places, renovating them and selling them at a profit and moving out somewhere decent. Epsom, maybe. And the old girl wouldn't live forever. Cost him nothing to live here, either, with all that food the old girl kept buying. Spent money like water. Though not on decorating or modernizing the house.

'Still be standing when I'm gone,' she said tartly. 'Life's for living now. And don't think I'm saving all my money to leave you lot, either. Mind you, I've paid for my funeral. I'll not leave you with debts. Not that I intend to pop off yet,' she would say, fixing him with a warring eye.

With the bit he had put by, and what he earned with his stall at East Street market and the stuff "off the back of a lorry", he and Sofe could have a good life. If it wasn't for the old bat.

The old bat became nocturnal. She decided, at last, to sell the cafe because she was feeling her age. And it appeared that someone her age had the right to wake in the night and call for help if she wasn't quite the ticket!

'Must look after meself,' she told Jack, smirking into his gritty smile and small eyes the colour of old pennies. He had a habit, as he was doing now, of jangling the change in his pocket, as if he knew it got on her nerves.

Zet heard both sides; the complaints came thick and fast when she made one of her flying visits after calling to see her father nearby.

But when all was said and done....'It's Gran's house, Sophie. There's nothing you can do,' she said, giving Jack a long cool look which always made his nose run and necessitated a hunt for an enormous purple handkerchief. 'Except, of course, move out and get your own place,' she added sweetly.

'Oh, no,' he said, busy wiping his nose and inspecting the hankie. 'That wouldn't do at all, would it Sofe?'

She looked coy. 'Wouldn't you rather we were on our own?'

He glowered. 'Where?' he demanded to know, tucking the hankie back in his pocket, 'underneath the arches?' With that, he left the room, and the house, slamming the front door so hard the house violently trembled.

Watching him pass the window, heading for the pub, Gran tried hard not to smile. 'I'll put the kettle on,' she said, in her dear old lady voice.

Sophie burst into tears and pounded upstairs. Gran carried in a tray of tea things and Zet jumped up from her chair to help. After pouring from a large brown pot, Gran went to the old-fashioned radiogram - which Jack said was worth a fortune now - and selected a record, and Bing Crosby began to sing *Love in Bloom*. But not too loud.

248

Not so loud that Zet couldn't hear laboured breathing as Gran made her way to her armchair making the old springs creak as she lowered herself into it. Zet looked around the room stuffed with souvenirs. All her life is here; only natural she doesn't want a stranger among her things, she was thinking when one of Gran's sudden announcements made Zet's cup crash down into her saucer.

'Our Laurie's gone to America to find his dad.'

'What? When? No one said.'

Gran shrugged and peered at Zet over her cup. 'Left Heathrow yesterday. He's spent all this time trying to find out his dad's address.'

'Oh, Gran.'

'What do you mean, oh Gran?' She put her cup down and scowled. 'It's his dad, he's got a right.'

'I just mean...I hope it works out for both of them. You never know. Is it what you want?'

Gran shrugged. 'I paid for the trip, pet. I got the money for the caff, see. It was for our Laurie's sake; doesn't affect me, my time of life. If I was younger...' She sighed. 'He was a bit of all right. That uniform, smiling blue eyes, lovely teeth. Like a film star, he was. It was so romantic, not like today.'

Not like today? Zet sipped her strong tea. The record ended, a new record dropped heavily on to the turntable, and scratchily began to play. *There's a small hotel...*

...the hotel by the lake, his lips hot on her skin...the togetherness, tenderness, laughter, their night together...she felt lightning flash through her loins. And then reality returned and she might have been in a plane that suddenly dropped a thousand feet.

Tensely, she looked across at Gran, needing to ask a question. The cup trembled; she put it down gently. 'Did you miss him when you broke up?'

'Course I did. What do you think?' Gran's faraway eyes held the story to the music that was playing. Maybe she had known a hotel room, too.

'Broken hearts were two-a-penny during the war,'

Gran said more softly. 'Couples who loved were torn away from each other - wicked it was - sometimes never to meet again.' After a pause, she added, 'But I do think....'

Zet leaned forward. 'What?' The grey eyes fixed on her were like watery mist.

'To have lived my life without it would've been worse.'

Zet felt as if she was clinging on to her grandmother for dear life. Yet they weren't touching. It was the knowledge and compassion in the old lady's remembering eyes; it was a woman's feelings. Zet felt her eyes fill.

Gran studied Zet's face with knowing eyes. 'Tell you what, pet. When you share a love like that, it's like walking in another country. Afterwards, you don't die, you get on with life, but you never walk again in that same country, you walk around it.'

In the silence that followed, Gran looked into Zet's absorbed face, sighed and perked up. 'It was a mixed up time, though, Zet. I couldn't get over how it happened and how different things could have been. I was mad with God, too, doing that to me. Getting your granddad killed after I'd sent the other one packing.'

Picking up the teapot, she said, sulkily, 'Yes, I was mad with God. I'd made the right decision and he did that to me. Another cuppa, darling?'

'What? Er...no thanks.'

Gran gave her a long look. After pouring her own tea, adding milk and sugar, she looked at Zet more intently. 'Piece of cake, then?' Gran believed cake cured everything.

'Er...I'll get it.'

Gran was already struggling to her feet. 'When I can't look after myself, she said tartly, wrinkled, reddened hands, gripping the back of the chair, 'I'll go.'

Zet looked up at her blankly. 'Go? Go where?' Gran pointed up to the sky. 'And when I get there,

I've a bone to pick with Him, no danger.' But Zet was still thinking of a love story that happened a long time ago.

Chapter Forty-Five

Sighing, Zet returned magazines neatly to a rack and, with an hour to spare before going off to do the weekend shopping, sat down and said, in a voice that meant business, 'Dad's getting too dependent upon Darren, you know.' Jonty looked up.

'What's wrong,' he asked tartly, 'with a boy going fishing with his grandfather? If his company helps the old man feel less lonely, Darren's the sort of chap who'd be pleased; some of us like to feel needed.'

Jonty always sounds as if he's accusing me of something, she thought, hiding another sigh.

'You have to read something into everything.' He looked irritated, resettling in his chair. 'You're like a neutralizing chemical that kills all known germs,' came unexpectedly from behind the magazine.

'Like Brobat?' she asked icily.

He turned a page. 'If you say so.' Watching him, Zet's lips tightened.

'Because I care about my family and want everything to be perfect for them?'

'Perfection can be a bit wearing, Zet.' He grimaced. 'I feel as if my penis is one of your brass candlesticks, dutifully polished once a week.'

She pulled in a shocked breath. At least he had the grace to look ashamed when he glanced over his magazine and saw the expression on her face. But he couldn't apologise. Something fought in him and stubbornness won. Taking a mint from the paper bag beside his chair, he unwrapped it and put it in his mouth, returning to his magazine. But he didn't turn the pages for a long time.

Feeling punched and winded, all she could hear was the click click of the sweet against his teeth. She could have screamed. Making an effort, she said, 'Jonty.'

252

Crunching, he looked up warily. 'Jonty, I think that was a rotten thing to say. I've always put your comfort first, kept the home nice....'

'Zet,' he interrupted, swallowing, sounding tired. 'You don't understand, do you?'

Raising her chin, she said, 'I think you're expecting a lot if you think things don't change in any marriage, sexually. You've had job problems....'

'I thought we'd come to that. I'm a failure, you mean, in bed as well. You've certainly made it clear that you're uninterested.'

'Be sensible Jonty. I've had years of worry with mum.' Her voice shook. 'What with that and .... well, I mean...you can't expect us to have the same relationship we had when we first met. At least we're still together, a lot of people we know aren't.'

He stood up, letting the magazine slip to the floor. 'But do we belong together? I get the impression that you're only visiting.'

She went very still. 'That's an odd thing to say.'

'I don't know what made me say it,' he admitted, running fingers through his hair. 'I only know that I wanted to give you everything.' His voice sounded young. 'I don't know where I went wrong.'

He sounded sorry for himself, as usual, and seeing his watery eyes, she wondered if he was in for a cold. He looked as if something inside him was eating him away. Must be a cold.

'I'm getting a drink,' he sighed, lumbering across the room in his slightly awkward way. 'Want one?'

She shook her head, could have said, you drink too much and it's only mid morning. But didn't. Just watched him pour whisky and soda and stare into it. But he didn't drink, just stared down into the glass.

'I gave you what you wanted, Zet. A house outside town, with a garden and your own tree. Remember?'

Zet could have wept. She was compelled by some inner honesty, to say...'Yes, but then I discovered the real wilderness.'

The room seemed to hold its breath.

With sudden pain in his eyes, he gulped down his drink. 'I've been invited on a camping trip. I assumed you wouldn't fancy it.'

'No way.'

'Thought you wouldn't.' 'How long for?'

'Just a week.'

'Who are you going with?'

'One of the old gang organised it. A sort of reunion. We don't see each other much now.'

She voiced her surprise. 'You're away so often on business. I'd have thought time at home with the children might be on the cards if you've time off.'

'They don't notice either of us is here lately.'

He sounded hurt. Alyson, in particular, had always adored him. Now she came indoors after school and brushed past him with scarcely a hello, making for her room which had "Adult Free Zone" written on the door. Out of school, she dressed in floppy shirts, trousers and boots and it was obvious his little girl had gone.

He looked so upset, Zet softened. 'Frankie said it will pass. Alyson just wants nothing to do with anyone over twenty-one. Part of being a young teen.'

'Oh, you've consulted the Oracle, have you?' He gulped down his drink. 'Frankie said....' he mimicked shrilly.

Sympathy gone, she stalked from the room. Within minutes she was leaving the house carrying a freezer bag and a neatly written list of meals for the next week. She liked to plan ahead. She liked an ordered, tidy life.

A week later, she was looking for a lipstick when the bedside phone rang. She picked up the receiver still rifling through the drawer with her free hand.

'Albert's dead.'

Chapter Forty-Six

It was the new spring colour, Forever Amber. Things didn't disappear in her house, maybe Alyson....

'What did you say, Min?'

'Albert. He was in his allotment, had a heart attack, I'm at the hospital and I can't get hold of Sue, they're out.' Min's quiet voice broke. 'Is my Jonathan there?'

Zet felt sick. 'Min, look, Jonty's away, but stay there, I'll come and get you. I'm sorry,' she said inadequately, hearing Min sniffing back tears. 'Wait there. I'll come.' She replaced the receiver, hand shaking.

Pulling herself together she slipped a red sweater over her blouse and jeans, took it off and changed it for a duller fawn, smoothed her hair with a brush. She had just arrived home from the clinic. Let me think...collect the children from school, go and see Gran. Give the children dinner; make sure they do their homework... doll-making class eight o'clock.

Re-arrange things. Ring Sophie. Contact Jonty. Where did he say the site was? Somewhere in the New Forest? Why hadn't he left an address? He had phoned a couple of times, though. Running down the stairs to where his leather jacket was hanging in the hall, she slipped her hands into the pockets, there might be a note of the camping site address there. No address. Just old receipts, and one not so old. Dated last Saturday. A receipt for Greek drachma.

Funny. She was sure he had said the New Forest.

By the time Jonty returned from his camping holiday, which he said dismissively, 'Wasn't up to much,' and 'I said it was a new site in a forest in Skiathos,' everything was organised. If he grieved, it was deep inside; he was quiet and remote.

Zet knew she would miss Albert. They had been friends, of a kind, ever since they had met, that day when

256

she had been so in awe of him. Maybe they had both had the same dreams for Jonty. He had seemed worried about his son, lately.

The funeral was stately and forlorn, on a mourning spring day when the rain hissed down irritably on to the gravestones in the cemetery where he had chosen to lie. The graves were neat and well tended. You can see the allotment from here, she thought illogically, standing beneath the black umbrella Jonty held.

The bad-tempered roar of the nearby motorway

seemed out of place. Looking over at Min, she was struck by her composure and dignity. Hope she isn't on Valium. Black suited her. She looked smarter than Zet had ever seen her.

No one, Zet saw, was crying, not even his kind-hearted but stern faced daughter, Sue, and she felt a surge of pity for Albert. He had been a good man, in his way. Autocratic, pedantic, but everything was done for the good of his family. The unfairness of life suddenly struck Zet. Albert had been typical of many... people who do no harm, do their duty, work hard, depend upon no-one, and yet their goodness seems to fence them in. What, Zet wondered, do people like that really want for themselves, deep inside? Do they have longings we know nothing about?

The family and two dutiful ex colleagues turned away from the grave, leaving him beneath polite, but not loving, flowers. Only the rain cried for Albert.

The front door opened. Jonty flung the car keys on the hall table and searched her out in the kitchen, looking shell-shocked. 'I don't believe it.'

He had been to see his mother. 'Mum's never coped alone,' he had told Zet, constantly, looking worried. 'She mustn't turn into a recluse; I mean, she's got no friends or hobbies.' This made Zet live in fear of him suggesting that

Min came to live with them. Looking at his face now, Zet's heart sank.

'What's happened?'

'I don't believe it. Spain! For three months. The place is up to here in travel brochures,' he said with an irritated sweep of his hand.

When she got over her surprise, Zet said, 'Good luck to her.' Who would ever have believed that Min's head had been filled with such dreams? Jonty ran a hand through his hair, staring at her with resentment.

'Mum said how much she admired strong women like you and your mother. She said your mother told her a thing or two about life.' He sounded wounded and disagreeable. Suddenly the easy-going Jonty had the ghost of his father about him, as he added, not very pleasantly, 'Of course, mum thinks you're wonderful.'

'Does she?' Zet said, surprised. 'It's sad, really,' she added thoughtfully.

'More like ridiculous, at her age.'

He looked quite put out. Zet hid a smile. 'I'm thinking of people whose longings are pushed aside by responsibilities or duty and as a result, end up having nothing lives.' There's a yellow brick road we all long to travel along perhaps, she thought silently, thinking of Iris, but few of us have the courage to set foot on it. Sometimes just because of fearing what people will say.

He was looking at her reproachfully. 'Mum had a good life. Dad did everything; she wanted for nothing.' But Zet insisted, 'Graveyards are full of women who longed to fly, but remained shackled. I'm forever grateful that I'm living in today's world,' she said with feeling, ignoring his sulky expression.

This seemed to be the last straw for Jonty. He flung himself out of the room. 'There was a time,' he called over his shoulder, 'when your home meant everything to you. I'm off to bed.'

Rinsing her mug, drying it and placing it on the mug tree, she sighed. He was acting very childishly. Besides, this most unexpected turn of events had surely solved a problem. She didn't want Min living with them; another reason for Jonty to resent me, she sighed, snapping out the light. Climbing the stairs, one of Gran's old sayings came to bother her head...trouble never comes singly.

Lying beside her, carefully not touching, Jonty was thinking of the tent amongst pine trees, chirping cicadas, pounding surf, lips tasting of ouzo, warm, soft sunburnt skin, dark teasing eyes, the welcoming plump body of a surprisingly sexy friend.

He felt a wave of irritation with himself; being unfaithful had not been comfortable, somehow. Sarah had known. She had shocked him by saying; 'Use me as an experiment laddie.' The shock was exciting. But not comfortable.

It was her Thursday afternoon off from the clinic and Zet was at her most contented.

Contentment was here, in the funny half-size room at the back of the house, tucked between the lounge and the garden, which she called her workroom. Here she was rarely disturbed and here, she spent her tranquil times.

If she thought of another place of contentment, her hidden garden in Yorkshire, she pushed it away. Instead, suburbia came through the open window...the waspish whine of a lawn mower, buses, lorries, cars, loud music, a barking dog; the sweet scent from lilies standing with cool faces beneath the window was mixed with curry.

Sunlight roamed pale walls, lighting up the painting, "Reflections" and a shelf of dolls, some proudly wearing blue ribbons where they had won competitions; there were brown phials of oils and scented candles. The room smelled faintly of calming geranium; in a bookcase, books on doll making, cookery and aromatherapy stood neatly with a book called Wuthering Heights.

He waited for her in dreams or sudden smells or certain songs, he waited, with eyes the colour of stone walls in the rain. And lying in his arms, she could feel the heat of the leaping fire on their sex damp skins as the scent of heather drifted through the open window. She longed not just for that but also for togetherness, tenderness, and companionship.

Today, her head was bent over her work. It was very delicate work painting a doll's rosebud mouth and then the phone shrilled....

....'Just ringing to let you know that Sophie's had a bit of bother and she's moving in with me.'

'She's what?'

'I'll explain when you come round,' her father said, in a mildly amused tone.

Chapter Forty-Seven

'It was mum's fault,' a woebegone Sophie explained when Zet arrived at her father's house as usual on Saturday afternoon. 'She made our lives a misery, and Jack blew his top. They had a row and she told him to go. No one,' she said fearfully, 'has said that to Jack before. He said it would be a relief to get away from her and I've not seen him since.'

Zet could only mutter platitudes that Sophie ignored, complaining, through trembling lips, 'Mum's always been the same; she can burst your balloon just like that. I've never heard a word of praise from her.'

'She's kind,' Zet murmured.

'Exactly. So you thank her for buying you clothes and food you don't want, afraid of hurting her feelings, which gives her permission to interfere and destroy your happiness.' Sophie looked at Zet piteously. 'I know it's sad because she's so caring, but she's a spoiler of life.'

Zet tried to be practical. 'You've probably done the right thing in leaving, then.'

Escaping as soon as she could, Zet drove to Gran's.

'What have you been up to, Gran,' Zet sighed. 'Nothing.' With a most un-gran-like demure expression, she sat with her swollen fingers clasped tightly in her lap, face crumpled and pink, and somehow, Zet saw, with a catch to her heart, how beautiful she had been.

Gran spoke in a defensive voice. 'When you get older, luv, you can read faces. I left school at fourteen but I've had an eighty-year Course on human behaviour. I wasn't daft enough to tell Sophie I was doing it for her own good. But ….' Looking down at her grasped hands, she couldn't hide the tremor in her voice. 'I knew that without this place, he wouldn't be so keen on her. He's a crook, Zet. I recognised it when I first saw him. Besides...'

261

Although they were alone, Gran lowered her voice. 'I met all sorts at the caff, police and crooks all came in; I still pop over there now and then to, you know, help out a bit, and I got a tip off. He only just escaped prison for GBH and his wife divorced him for knocking her about.' Gran's voice shook. 'I also know things about him that the police would love to know. I've friends in low places, you might say,' she added, trying to joke, despite the tears welling in her eyes.

Though taken aback, Zet was about to remind her that Sophie was a middle-aged woman, when she realised that Gran was crying. 'I believe you, Gran,' she said gently. And after a pause, 'Sophie will visit.'

Gran's head was bent, Zet had to lean forward to hear the mumbled,' She needs me to look after her.'

Not true, but... Zet pushed back the lump in her throat...Gran believes it. Crossing the room, she balanced herself on the old worn chair arm and, for the first time, took her grandmother in her arms. She smelled clean and warm, like a baby. Her body felt plump and cuddly and when Zet rested her chin on Gran's head and heard her weeping quietly, she just couldn't prevent her own tears, tears she seldom shed, from soaking the thinning, golden hair.

'It's three months since I've been with your dad,' Sophie said, looking shy and self-conscious. 'I don't know when I've been so happy. Look.' She held out her hands. 'I've stopped biting my nails.'

Her face changed. 'I didn't mean I don't miss Iris. We still call this room Iris's room. I feel close to her here,' she said sadly, looking through the patio doors into the garden where it was autumn again, just over a year since Iris died. She sounded apologetic. 'I never liked gardening much, but your dad does some.'

Zet sighed. The garden looked a bit like her, drab and uninteresting. The fence needed repainting too; it had faded to the colour of washed out old jeans. Maybe she should have offered to help but she felt it was too much of an effort, somehow. In a tired voice, she advised, 'Just be happy, take it as it comes. You never know.'

Sophie looked at her in dismay. 'What do you mean?'

'I don't know,' Zet answered honestly. 'It just came out.' She tried to smile. 'Don't look at me as if you think I'm psychic or something. It's merely that so many rotten things have happened. I feel life hasn't finished with me yet.'

Sophie's gentle eyes were concerned, 'I thought you had your life all organised.' When Zet didn't answer, she said, 'Anyway, cheer up. Life's for living, as Iris would say. And we're having a great time, Maurice and me. I've got him to go dancing and up West to the theatres and tenpin bowling. It's all go,' she laughed, putting a hand to her mouth in that self-conscious way she had.

Seeing the tender flush and the satisfaction on Sophie's face when Maurice came into the room, Zet brushed away a pang of anxiety; it was good that her father had started to live again and she said as much, adding, 'No wonder Darren said you fell asleep, dad, while you were fishing last week.'

Smilingly denying any such thing, he wandered into the garden and as Sophie asked about her beloved niece and nephew Zet watched him - a solitary looking, gentle man, putting nuts on the bird-table - and answered that Darren had seemed a bit put out at first when Maurice stopped coming round so often.

'But Darren has to work harder now he's at secondary school. I've told him I expect great things of him. It's Alyson who needs a push.'

'Darren hates change,' Sophie said. 'He likes life ordered. Alyson's the opposite, she'll flit about a bit before she decides what she wants to do.'

Sophie looked so much better, Zet noticed, as they talked. She no longer appeared harassed and the shorter, straight haircut suited her, even though Gran said it didn't, and she wore more fashionable clothes, not those Gran chose. Her face, being plump, showed hardly any lines as she said to Zet softly, 'I've come full circle. Back to my first love.' She sighed. 'Feels good.' She smiled at Zet. 'Remember our games?'

Zet nodded. 'When you came to sit with me while mum was out, you always brought the snakes and ladders with you, and the Happy Families cards.' She probably hadn't been very nice to her aunt. She wanted to tell Sophie that she hadn't meant it, that she really loved her.

'Thank you for what you did for me,' she said awkwardly. Sophie looked surprised, and Zet said, 'I was a cow to you sometimes; it was just…'

'It's all right,' Sophie reached out and touched Zet's hand. 'I understood.'

Zet swallowed. 'It was just…I hated her going out,

leaving me, when I was a kid. I don't know why.' Sophie gave Zet's hand a squeeze. 'Don't worry;

forget it. I loved babysitting you.' She hesitated, 'I always felt that you were partly mine. Besides,' she went on, 'I've got to a winning place. No more sliding down snakes.'

'Maybe you were too good at losing,' Zet said. 'Maybe you put other people first too often, didn't fight for yourself. Even with me, you used to let me win.'

Sophie laughed. 'You sulked if you didn't.' Her face fell into the anxious lines Zet remembered. 'How is it with you?'

'Business is booming at the clinic, and I can't keep up with the demand for my dolls,' Zet said brightly. '

'You know what I mean.'

Sighing, Zet admitted, 'I've a few more ladders to climb yet. I can't seem to throw a six, but I'll get there,' she added, with more confidence than she felt. As if she knew, as if she felt the tightening of the screw.

The telephone rang, like a scream, in the middle of the night.

Chapter Forty-Eight

Zet and Jonty drove to the hospital and were shown into a side room. Heart thudding, eyes adjusting to the dimly lit, one-bedded room, Zet reached the bed and came to an abrupt stop. Looking down, she felt the blood drain from her face. Helplessly, she turned to Jonty, who was standing behind her, his face white.

They were looking down on something, grotesque. Zet's hand went to her mouth, stopping a scream and the room began to spin.

Gran. Oh, Gran. Fighting nausea, she saw thin, distressed hair spread over the pillow... half closed eyes in a puffy face; hands, Gran's red, work raw hands, on the bedcover, naked without the gold wedding ring. Her nose was broken, her skin a red pulp; livid bruises showed on her arms, neck and the part of her chest exposed by the gaping white gown.

You break up, Zet silently groaned, closing her eyes for a second. You just break up inside, you feel helpless, and you don't know what to do with such agony and you want to pretend it hasn't happened. And the love you feel...it spurts out like a wound.

The split lips moved. 'Sophie?'

Zet whispered, 'She's on the way', and reaching out, touched Gran's hand gently. Her own hand was shaking. She felt as cold as ice. That anyone could do this to a defenceless old lady. She stifled a sob. 'You'll be fine, Gran.' With tears in her eyes, she was gabbling anything that came into her head. 'What would we do without you, Gran?' Those bruised lips tried so hard to smile.

Nick Peters gazed through the office window into the ward. 'She's great, isn't she?'

With a grin at the young constable, the doctor admitted, 'She's already driving us round the bend.'

266

Standing with them, Zet found nothing to joke about and asked tartly, 'She's going to be all right?'

The doctor reassured her kindly, 'I told you.'

Addressing Nick Peters, Zet's icy voice slapped the smile from his face, 'what are you going to do? You can't let old people be beaten up in their homes like that.'

Nick shuffled his feet. He heard the same thing all the time. You can't let it happen...but you do. 'I know it was five hundred pounds, but if she'd let him take it, Mrs. Bestwellen, maybe....'

Zet snapped, 'Gran wouldn't do that.' Feeling angry with everyone, she blinked back tears. 'There was her wedding ring too, and bits of jewellery. And I find that statement pathetic. You're saying we should let burglars steal our possessions because it would make your job easier? Her voice became shrill. 'Should we supply a bag for them to carry the stolen goods out in?'

Her insides were raging with violence that was foreign to her, but he regarded her steadily and she calmed herself, listening to what he had to say.

'She couldn't give us a description, but maybe when she's over the shock...or perhaps you can find out more.' He frowned. He had seen a look in the old lady's eyes...fear, and something else he couldn't put a finger on. She looked evasive.

They were around her bed in the main ward: Zet, Jonty, a grim-faced Maurice and Sophie, her face blotchy and swollen. 'If I'd been there it wouldn't have happened.'

'You've a right to a life, pet,' Gran muttered pathetically. 'At least,' her slit eyes moved to Maurice, 'You've got a good bloke now.' He tried to smile.

Concerned, Zet thought he was looking pale; he seemed to have aged ten years but, after all, he'd been through a lot. She thought with hatred of the burglar.

It's not only the victim who is affected; it's the whole family. My family.

267

Taking a comb from the bedside cabinet, she gently combed Gran's hair, unable to join in as everyone joked about all the visitors she'd had, family, neighbours, friends, old customers from the cafe, and how nice she looked.

'Oh, yes, bloody marvellous,' Gran muttered. 'Fancy, a face-lift at my age.' She tried to smile; across the puckered skin, stitches moved like spider legs. 'My face looks like a laced up old boot.' Lifting her hand, she gingerly felt her nose. 'Always wanted a nose job. Here's that handsome copper again. Hello sweetheart.'

'Remember anything yet, Lily?' Annoyed to feel himself blushing, he looked around hopefully. They gazed back at him, exasperation written clearly upon their faces. They wanted him to have the answers. He and the doctor had chatted for a while. 'We have one thing in common,' the doctor had sighed. 'People expect us to work miracles.'

The beautiful blonde, the granddaughter, had her blue, cut-glass eyes on him; she made him feel like a criminal. Her face was stony. He had a vision of her lying beneath him; he thought of bringing that slim, perfect body to life.

Clearing his throat, he asked, 'Sure there wasn't anything about the bloke that stood out, Lily? Any reason why he chose you, do you think?'

Embarrassed, he saw by their faces that they knew what he was thinking. Gran's house was the only one in the area that hadn't been modernised; to be truthful it was shabby, not the house where a burglar would expect to find much of value.

The old lady's bruised lips parted, as if she was about to speak. Everyone stared at her, waiting to hear what she had to say. She made a sound in her throat, as if words were stuck there. She moved her head on the pillow so that she was looking at her daughter, Sophie, sitting beside her eating grapes.

There was a lengthy fraught silence.

The daughter stopped eating and stared back at her mother without speaking. She looked terrible; her hair was a mess; her face was red and shiny because she never stopped crying.

'I've no posh things,' Gran said in a weak, unsteady voice. 'It was just money he wanted,' she muttered. Her poor, puffed eyes remained on Sophie as she added, 'We thought it would be safe inside the radiogram, didn't we?'

Seeing that Sophie was crying again and couldn't speak, Nick asked gently, 'did he make you tell him where it was, Lily? Is that why he...?'

Gran turned to him, eyes confused. 'He didn't ask?'

Something clicked. From where he stood at the foot of the bed, Nick recalled that surprisingly little had been disturbed in the house. A porcelain doll had been smashed and some old gramophone records, but not much else. The burglar hadn't searched; hadn't asked. 'It was someone you know, then?'

There was a skin-prickling silence. Nick ran a finger around the inside of his collar. It was hot in the ward. 'Did he threaten you, or someone in your family?' The daughter closed her eyes as if about to faint.

'Don't remember,' whispered Gran. And closed her own frightened old eyes as if to say she'd had enough of life for a while.

'Flippin' marvellous,' Gran complained to Zet. 'Just my luck. I'd have given anything to have my picture in the paper when I was young and beautiful. Fame at last.'

Zet had arrived just as the journalist from a National newspaper had gone. There had already been one from the local paper and the B.B.C. team, who were doing a series of programmes on crime, were due to arrive any minute.

'You'll steal the show,' the drawn-faced doctor said, coming up to perch with a tired sigh on the bed.

'Don't use that flippin' word, *steal*.'

269

'Sorry.' He hesitated. 'Were you really a stripper?'
'Who told you that, luv?'

The doctor smiled. 'You talk in your sleep.'

'It was fan dancing.' Gran looked pleased. 'Different from stripping,' she explained haughtily, adding a sharp, 'Have you heard of Phyllis Dixey?'

He shook his head and with a wink at Zet, took a chocolate from the box of Black Magic she offered.

'Phyllis was a famous fan dancer, luv. In those days you couldn't show anything, you had to make the audience think you was going to, though. The law said you had to keep your fans up. Mind you,' Gran told the doctor who was enjoying the break, 'I always was a clumsy clot; I was banned twice.' She chuckled. 'But so was Phyllis.'

Zet returned the doctor's smile. He looked as pleased as she was to hear Gran's chuckle. It's odd, thought Zet. Now Gran really has something to cry about, she's been brave and cheerful instead. Embarrassing though, how she had treated the poor woman Counsellor who had called to see her. The nurse had told Zet all about it.

'How do you think we got on in the war?' Gran had raged. 'Cried on someone's shoulder every time a bleeding bomb dropped? Sod off.'

Laurie arrived at the hospital in a panic about his mother, but with exciting news.

'Come off it,' Gran snorted, mopping her bruised eyes with a tissue after listening avidly to his story. She was looking down at the photographs spread over the bed cover. 'How can I see David, looking like the back of a bus?' she moaned.

'He's not coming until summer, that's six months away,' Laurie explained eagerly. 'You'll be your old beautiful self then.'

'You always did have a touch of the blarney, young Laurie.' David had Irish blood in him, she remembered. Studying her son, she noticed something different. The tan

270

maybe...looked peculiar when from her ward on the fourth floor she could see great spinning snowflakes settling on the roofs of the town. But it was more than that, his manner was relaxed, he looked happier and held himself with more confidence. Some marriages, she sighed to herself... don't have any patience with all these divorces, mind...but some marriages squash people the way those car breakers turn cars into a lump of dead metal.

After he left, she lay back and closed her eyes. What would her marriage have been like if Wally hadn't been killed? Funny in them days...she hadn't for a moment considered leaving her husband, it just wasn't done. But she had been tempted. God almighty she had been tempted. To this day, she thought, I don't know where I found the strength to send David away.

'Something wrong Lily?'

She opened her eyes. It was that new young nurse with the lovely lilting voice. 'No. I'm just....'

'Missing your family?' the nurse, who had left her family in Ireland, asked sympathetically, and Lily nodded. The nurse patted her hand and walked away. Lily's eyes followed her. Young, pretty, lovely figure. Just as she had been once. If only....

It's my youth I'm missing, nurse. I'm frightened. I'm frightened because inside this rumpled old bag that I've become, I'm still me. I feel the same as I did then. I'm me but no one seems to see it. Will David?

Chapter Forty-Nine

One day the phone rang and she puffed into the hall, moaning, picked up the receiver, put it to her ear….

'Hi, Lily! How ya doin'?'

She started to shake. Surely it couldn't be fifty years since she heard that low, spine-tingling drawl!

Getting to know each other again over the telephone first was a good idea; he couldn't see what a state she was in. Besides, she had shopping to do before he arrived…new clothes, curtains, and things to brighten the place up. And she had paid a neighbour's unemployed son to paint the house.

They spoke across the Atlantic many times, and soon he would be with her again, the man she had, brokenheartedly, said goodbye to forever. David. The name she could now speak aloud.

What a strange shy, yet deeply emotional reunion it was. She couldn't face going to Heathrow. Laurie had met David, driven him to the East End, dropped him off outside the house and driven away. He didn't notice eyes watching him from behind curtains. Lily did, as she waited, shaking like a leaf, at the open door, hoping she wouldn't bawl her eyes out.

'You know something?' David said, those bright blue remembered eyes fixed on her, although his hair was white, but just as thick. 'You never left my mind, Lily.'

'I can't believe we're together again,' she said, feeling her eyes shining. 'Remember that Vera Lynn song? *Don't know where, don't know when?*'

He broke into song and she joined him....'*but I know we'll meet again some sunny day.*' Then they burst into laughter for rain was belting down beyond the new pink velvet curtains.

Remembered laughter. It was all so wonderful as the years rolled back. How could they have laughed when there was death all around them, and each time he left the air base in his bomber plane might have been his last day on earth?

'I not only remember the song, but we're sure as hell gonna dance to it again,' he promised, with a grin that showed white teeth a man of eighty had no right to.

'You G.I.'s,' she teased, 'think you can have everything you want.' Recalling his passionate response to that private joke in those days, she added a more prosaic; 'It's all that disco stuff now, anyway.'

'You'll see.' He was always one for surprises. That hadn't changed either.

Somehow he discovered that the Waldorf Hotel in London held tea dances. She felt so glamorous wearing one of her new dresses - it was the colour of milky coffee, lace on satin - with her hair done, softer, over her face to hide her scars. Scars that had brought tears to those crinkled sun-gazing eyes of his. 'We fought for a better, safer world, Lily.' His voice broke, as if he was afraid to say more.

But nothing dreary was going to stop them from enjoying their blissful reunion. She was fatter; he was stiffer with a bit of a paunch. That's what anyone else saw.

They were David and Lily, lithe, young, beautiful and so much in love, dancing to a proper band over a glossy dance floor, with death and destruction a heartbeat away. Still was. But forget it, live for today. Again. And yes, the band, after a request from David, played *We'll Meet Again*.

Re-living their once-in-a-lifetime romance brought back, as if it were yesterday, the throbbing, thrilling, fearful, all encompassing passion of it, the intense body clinging longing, and she saw by the glow in his eyes that he felt it too.

'Gee, you're still the smartest, most beautiful woman here.' They were dancing as he spoke. And when they stopped for sandwiches and tea, he added, 'And the same

273

wisecracking gal, with a lot of nerve, who can laugh and cry at the same time.'

'You're still the same David, too.' Except that she noticed he was more self-confident. Still tanned, fit, with a wide grin, a furrowed, thoughtful forehead, but less of the daredevil gleam, and less innocence in his blue eyes.

He showed her photographs of his home in California, his wife who had died three years ago, his three daughters, grandchildren, and dog.

'C'mon back with me?' he asked, as he had then. 'No,' she said regretfully, as she had then. 'There's my family, you see.'

He sighed. 'Sure. Still your folks, eh, Lily?' But he smiled his charming, brilliant smile and insisted, 'But you must visit.'

She thought about it. Wondered at the world she was living in where you could hop on a plane to America as if you were getting on a bus to East Ham. Money was no problem; she had enough for the trip. But an aeroplane at her age? She'd been frightened to go over the Thames on the Woolwich ferry at one time. 'Come on, Gran,' Zet insisted, 'you can do it'. She liked David. He was retired now, but as she remarked to an unimpressed Jonty, 'David looks every inch the successful man who started as an Insurance Agent and ended up running the Company, doesn't he?'

He had told her that he had never regretted his decision not to join his uncle's film studio. It had eventually been taken over by a television company, anyway.

'Hey, thanks for your support, Zet,' David laughed. 'But if she won't come, I'll fly back to see her next year. If we're both here,' he joked. Death had always hung over their shoulders. Even then. Even now.

Laurie drove them to their old haunts in Cambridge; they visited the silent, white stoned American cemetery where men David had never forgotten lay. 'Hey, you guys,' he said softly, eyes glistening, 'I'm back to see ya.'

274

They rode a red bus to London, an ambition of David's, and another day, sitting on her new sofa, browsing through photograph albums and old theatre programmes, she told him a secret she had kept from him. His bushy white brows shot up.

'I thought you were a dancer.' 'I was. A fan dancer.'

'It will be the regret of my life that I missed your performances,' he joked, not at all shocked, and Gran looked amused.

'Go along with you.'

When pressed, she told him, 'I started in the big pubs, then the local Empire, it's the Odeon now; after that I was at the New Cross Empire, the Woolwich Empire, and my favourite, Wood Green, which had a sliding roof. When it was rolled back, you could see the stars,' she said, eyes softly reminiscent.

'You always were a star to me.' Looking at her, his face was full of tenderness. 'I adored you. I never regretted it, only the pain I felt when you turned me down.'

'I thought you went away hating me, David.'

He shook his head. 'I walked away the only way I knew how, I guess. When I sobered up I knew deep down you were right. I thought of a guy coming home from war and finding his wife gone. Hell, I didn't wanna be responsible for that.'

They saw in each other's faces the pain of parting, felt the desolation as if time circled around them and returned them to yesterday.

'I'm sincerely sorry about your husband,' he said soberly, 'I guess if I'd known I'd have come back. And my son....' he shook his head, eyes misting. 'You don't know what it meant to me to have my boy come and find me like that. And I never knew.' He was silent for a bit, then....'I loved my wife, we had a good marriage. But you gave me moments to live for. And we needed them in those days,' he said huskily.

275

'An affair of the moment,' she nodded, eyes wet.

'Might have been a flippin' lifetime if things had been different.'

He smiled lovingly at her. 'I guess affairs are like flowers, they last just a season. Marriages, children and mortgages are built in concrete. Or they were then.'

'But our flower will never die,' she reminded him softly. They stared down at the album she had put together with such care for him, filled with photographs of Laurie's childhood. Laurie had always been special, she realised. David, she thought silently, I tried to forget you, but I never really did. When he left, her old heart twisted as he asked again, 'Please come over, Lily.' There was pleading in his eyes, as there had been then.

'Oh, David.' She had to look away. In a low, trembling voice, she told him her final decision. 'Sophie needs me.'

She heard the car door slam. Laurie's car was pulling away from the kerb and she raised a hand, waved. She saw his dear face watching her through the window; he waved when the car reached the corner. He was gone. Again. As far away as he could possibly be. Oh, David.

Chapter Fifty

'Sophie is only a couple of streets away,' Maurice answered when Zet asked him if he was lonely. 'At our age, we don't have to live in each other's pockets. It's only right for Sophie to move back to Gran's.' He had been asked to live at Gran's too, but had declined.

'I lived on my own for a long time,' he reminded her. 'Just me and the dust,' he joked. 'Besides, Sophie's concerned about Gran, she's getting forgetful.'

It's you I'm worried about, Zet thought, studying him with concern. He looked tired; his skin had a yellow tinge she didn't like. Yet he still insisted upon taking Sophie out and about. Their family had never been the touchy feely sort yet today she reached out, laid a hand on his arm, wanting to touch him. Feeling edgy, she said tersely, 'Go and see your doctor.'

'Don't start fussing over me, bossy boots. I'm not used to it.'

But Zet wasn't put off. 'I want dad to have a check up,' she told Sophie.

'Can't a man get any peace?' he grumbled, after they had ganged up on him. And Zet looked at him with love, this man who asked for so little in life.

When she phoned him after his tests, he was infuriatingly vague. 'I think you're a witch,' he teased.

Dad....' she warned, exasperated. 'Okay. They suspect gallstones.'

Zet was cheerful when she drove him to the hospital where he had to stay for tests. 'Gallstones are easily dealt with these days, dad.'

Two days later, Sophie and Zet went to see the hospital specialist together.

The tall, moustached, serious looking man who greeted them, wore the virtuous expression of one who believes in straight talking. Coming round his desk, he perched on the edge and regarded the scared women seated before him. 'We haven't completed all the tests yet, but what I wanted to see you about is that we've discovered a faulty heart valve.'

Exchanging glances, Sophie and Zet spoke almost together. 'What happens now?' Zet asked sharply. In a trembling voice, Sophie said, 'He's never been ill.'

The specialist addressed Zet, who looked as if she blamed him, cautiously. 'We have to carry out more tests.' And turning with a reassuring smile to Sophie, explained, 'it often goes undetected; he might have appeared slower and tired more easily than others, that's all. He was probably born with it.'

'What happens now?' Zet repeated. 'We'll carry out those tests this afternoon.'

'That's quick,' exclaimed Zet, suddenly terrified.

Maurice had a crowd around his bed when Zet was asked to go and see the Specialist. Darren and Alyson were there, and Sophie. Gran was reading aloud a letter she had received from David saying Laurie, who had left his wife and gone to live in America, had arrived safely.

Zet had to walk, on legs which seemed to have disappeared, back to the ward, stand at the door and watch her father laughing at Darren, holding Alyson close to him as she perched on the bed, letting Sophie fuss around him. Zet had to stand there, push back tears, ignore her breaking heart and walk towards the bed. They all looked round.

She met her father's eyes across the turned heads and fell into a black hole. I can't bear it. This is too much for me to take.

Zet talked to him alone, asking the others to wait downstairs.

Tears started to his eyes. 'I'm sorry, Rosie.'

'You've nothing to be sorry for, dad.' The Specialist's voice rang in her ears. The cancer has attacked his liver.

278

She shook her head at her father. 'No,' she protested in a hard, cold voice. 'I'm not having it.' Spreading her hands, still shaking her head...'I don't care how much it costs, we'll get the best treatment....'

He smiled weakly. 'You always did expect life to go your way. You can't plan everything, Rosie.'

'You'll get better, dad. People do. You have to be positive.' You have to be here for me.

'Rosie.' His face creased. 'I want you to promise me something.'

'What?' she said, like her child self, sulky, rejected. 'I'm not like your mother, not as brave. Could never stand pain.'

'What are you asking?' she frowned.

'Don't let me hang on,' he pleaded urgently. 'Please. I've never asked anything of you but that.'

Cold fingers jerked her insides, but she nodded. And heard a clear, authoritative voice that she supposed was her own, say, 'But you won't die. I won't let you.'

He let his head fall back on the pillow. 'You're strong, Rosie.' And gazing at her stubborn face as if he wanted to imprint it on his mind....'You'll know what to do.'

Zet tried everything, went everywhere. She consulted specialist after specialist, even in America, with David's help. But there was nothing they could do for him there that they couldn't do in England. Zet's days were a mixture of dread and hope; nights left her raw and bleeding. She refused to give in.

Until the day when he said wearily, 'Leave it, Rosie, my love. No more, eh?'

There was a gentle garden surrounding the hospice where he had asked to go. She spent a lot of time there with him when he was able to make it.

The rest of the time she grieved terribly. Grief - a flesh eating monster that left no room to breathe or live. She

279

loved her kind, gentle father so much. Why in the hell had she wasted so much time? Wherever she was, whatever she was doing, if she wasn't with him his drawn face, with the patient, loving smile, was before her. There was the soft touch of his hand on her hair when she bent towards him, a thin hand that trembled. Nothing else mattered but her father.

She had wanted him to spend his last weeks at her home, she wanted to look after him, but he refused.

Zet liked to get her own way. She took over a lot of the care of him, asked to be shown what to do to help him, washed him, fed him, massaged him with soothing oils, and learned to use the morphine he needed to kill the pain. Once that started, he could hardly talk any more.

Watching over him, she saw how the bedclothes hardly rose across his drug filled body - he was merely, she mourned, a capsule - she worried that she had let him down, there was so little she could do to help him.

She gave up her work at the clinic and ended her doll-making classes. A tanned, young looking Min fussed over Jonty as if she had only just discovered him, moved into the house and helped look after things there; Frankie was a constant visitor.

Jonty was understanding, co-operative, worried for her, treated her as if she was one of her porcelain dolls. He worried because she lost weight. He visited Maurice but seldom stayed long, leaving with barely disguised relief.

Sophie came, which seemed to make Maurice anxious; he felt he had to comfort her, as if he was responsible for the tearful state she was in. Gran just sent her love, she said it was too much like a farewell line-up, for family he hadn't seen for years turned up, said hello, and embarrassed, scattered again, afraid to say goodbye. It was just..."see you."

The children visited, but not too often, Zet wouldn't allow it. There was a calm atmosphere, nothing

280

frightening about the hospice; laughter was strangely often heard, even fear was absent, but it wasn't a part of this world, more a satellite, gently flowing in a stream that led away from the main river of life. The children belonged in the main stream; their lives were just beginning. Her father's was ending. She was going to lose her father. Again. Yet something extraordinary began to happen.

She began to share with him a sensation of calm, the confusing world retreated and peace bound them together. The scattered ends of her life came together, and it seemed, in a strange way, that this time with him was a gift from him to her.

One autumn day the sun flamed as if making a last effort, filling the hushed room with moving reflections as birds flitted past the window and trees made dancing patterns on the cream walls. The scent of newly cut grass and languishing bonfires drifted inside through the open window, the birdsong sounded emotionally sweet.

He tried to speak. She leaned closer, so that his dear breath lightly, so lightly, fanned her pale cheek. Sounded like...'How long...?'

Eyes, enormous and sunken, eyes without hope, stared up at her, the struggle to pass a message showed quite clearly. The morphine no longer had the power to help him as it had. Every stifled groan was a knife tearing the skin from her body. In his agonized eyes, the stark message said...come on... you're hard...you know the way.

His lips moved....'Time to hit the road... proud
...love....'

The screaming steel teeth of a shredder grabbed her body. He was too good for this. This man who had never deliberately hurt anyone, was being forced to suffer. They, all of them, were responsible for this torture, for putting him through hell when surely heaven - if there was such a place - was waiting for him. A terrible shudder went through her. Her icy lips touched his hot, dry skin, felt the

281

sharpness of his cheekbones and she wondered why...why do you leave it so late to kiss someone you love? Oh, dad. She sat up and put her arms around herself, rocked herself in anguish.

She saw his eyes pleading with her. She saw the drip attached to his frail arm, lashing him to the rack....

Watching him drift off to sleep, she felt herself stretched upon a rack of mental pain such as she had never known as if his suffering moved into her own body through the dear hand - that dear hand wet with her tears - that she held until its grip loosened.

The white-haired, calm-faced Irish nurse came to find her in the garden, to tell her that her father had gone.

Zet was crouched, cuddling herself, on the seat in the rose arbour, his favourite place, and turned dazedly to meet eyes full of compassion and understanding.

Side by side, they walked back across dry, crackling leaves. The brick walls of the Elizabethan house were tinted pink and above the roof the sun was floating away like a red balloon. Zet felt herself shrink as they crossed the terrace and the door came towards her. Her steps faltered, the nurse paused too.

Taking Zet's face between her two gentle hands, the nurse said softly, 'To be sure, darlin', isn't it the finest gift you can give, to assume another's pain so that a loved one can rest?'

A long moment later, they passed out of the dying day into the calm place and the sun went gently into the dark night.

Chapter Fifty-One

The house clearance people came to remove what was left of a life. After they had gone, Zet wandered through the house in Crow Street, in the company of ghosts and herself, when young.

As her mind rummaged through the past for reasons and asked questions, the sound and scent of the past returned... perfume in the dust, echoing voices, happy footsteps; she heard her mother's laughter, music...but no answers. Through the window she saw the dead patch of garden, the silent fountain, and the rain drenched Spanish cobbles where her mother had walked barefoot.

God, the aching loneliness of hollow-sounding floorboards, empty rooms, the silence that makes you listen to your own heartbeat. She had never felt so bereft and adrift or - her heart thudded - on the edge of insanity.

Lock up, Zet. And go. She did. And left the house for the last time.

The rain had stopped. Taking the car keys from her handbag, she was about to open the car door when a familiar call made her heart sink. Shoving the key in the lock, she pulled open the door.

'Sorry about your dad,' said Audrey, behind her. 'They were a lovely couple, your mum and dad.'

Reluctantly turning round, Zet nodded, before slipping into the driver's seat. Pushing grey hair from her eyes, Audrey looked embarrassed.

'I'd better be off,' Zet said, feeling detached, unreal, reaching for the door handle.

Audrey seemed to make up her mind. 'Remember that dolls' house?'

Zet frowned. Her fingers curled around the keys in her hand.

'You remember,' Audrey pressed. 'The one your dad made you.'

'That was years ago; yes, I....'

Audrey bit her lip. 'I pinched it off the skip, for my kids.'

Zet turned and slid the key into the ignition. Rude she knew, but she had to go. 'So? It had been thrown,' she said impatiently, and Audrey nodded.

'Wait.' Audrey said anxiously, 'Thought I'd tell you, it's in our loft here.' She studied Zet's face uncertainly. 'But I've got to get rid of it. We're moving, y' see.' She gave a pleased giggle. 'Just thought I'd tell you. The furniture in the doll's house is broken, careless little bleeders, mine were. Shall I chuck it?'

Zet could have cried. 'I…no, I mean yes, I would like it back,' she said, swallowing hard. 'For the family, you know.' Every time she saw the dolls' house she would imagine the clever hands and the loving heart that had fashioned it.

'Right you are. How's your Gran?' Audrey asked, dropping her voice and looking secretive. 'You know.'

'Sophie's worried about her,' Zet frowned, 'but....' 'Not surprisin', is it? You've got a problem there.'

No more. Zet had had enough. She reached towards the ignition. 'Can I come back for the dolls' house another day?' she asked, in a jerky voice that made Audrey look down at her oddly.

''Course. You've had a rotten day. You're soakin' wet. Want a cuppa?' She looked concerned and kind.

Zet shook her head. 'Must go.' *Go.* She pulled the door closed, started the engine and the wipers, because the rain had started again and Crow Street was a blur.

The whole journey had been a blur. It was frightening. Here she was, sitting in the Happy Eater beside the noisy A1, with no idea where she was going, thinking things like… I'm an orphan; eternity has gone...time has started. Where am I going, not only now but also in life?

Somewhere within the grief-stricken shell-like structure that she was, she was grieving not only for her

284

father but for her own failures. Where had she gone wrong? Death was obviously both painful and revealing, an end and a beginning. She felt a need to reassess her life. Frankie had said something similar recently ...

'Being in the wrong place, feeling trapped, can bring about ill health if you do nothing about it. Hanging on is very commendable but sometimes it's the worse thing you can do. At the very least, I think you need to get away, reassess things.' Zet wished Frankie were here.

In the sleepless nights, she had confronted her own mortality. 'There's no one between me and death,' she told Jonty, needing someone to understand. 'You have to grow up when your last parent dies. You think you're grown up, but you're not...until then. There's no one left to pick you up when you fall.'

'Don't be silly,' was his way of cheering her up. Jonty didn't understand what she was going through.

But who did?

Sophie? Sophie had taken to her bed. Gran lived in the past. David had phoned and she felt she could have talked to him had he been here. For there was no one else, grief hadn't brought her family together; rather it had given rise to spite. Recent arguments came back to her.

'I wish you'd shut up about exams, mum,' Alyson snapped.

'Don't speak to me like that.'

Alyson tossed her hair. 'How many 'A' levels did you get?'

'Enough,' Zet snapped, after only the barest pause. Adding, 'There are things I could have done if I'd wanted to but I put my home and my family first.'

'What did you ever give up for us?'

Zet felt dreadful. Not sorry for herself but sorry that she had been misunderstood. It was unfair; she had never neglected the house or the children. She said quietly, 'All I can say is that I've tried.' She felt an ache in her throat,

285

overwhelmingly alone in her helplessness. Had it all been for nothing?

Now here she was in a busy roadside café, surrounded by cheerful families, a long way from home, with no idea where she was going. Finishing her coffee, she paid her bill and headed for the car. Changing her mind, she returned inside to the telephone kiosk.

'But you only went to the shops, mum.' 'Where's Darren?'

'Helping at the pet shop, as usual. He practically lives there.'

Zet spoke about needing to get away. Alyson complained about jeans she needed ironed for tonight and anyway...what about dinner?

Zet said there were meals already prepared in the freezer. 'Take three out now. Your dad will be home from Sweden tonight.'

Alyson's voice brightened. 'He's home already. I'll go and get him.'

Zet replaced the receiver.

Outside, feeling cool air hit her after the stuffy restaurant, hearing the sea-like swish of passing cars, she thought: they're all going somewhere. And me? *On the road to anywhere.*

Slamming the car door she started the engine and nosed back into the traffic, picking up speed, forty... fifty... sixty...seventy...

A1. To the North screamed the signs.

Chapter Fifty-Two

Welcome to North Yorkshire.

Passing the sign, she opened the window. The wind from the moors, which was battering the car and even making great lorries shudder, whooshed the scent of peat inside, tumbling her hair and she felt an answering wildness.

'Face things,' Frankie had advised. 'And remember that sometimes you have to learn to let go.'

'Let go of what?' Zet had asked.

Frankie had hesitated. 'I can't answer that for you. Sometimes an obsession is like a distant view, not so beautiful when you reach it. But you have to reach it to know that.' The words were familiar; Zet couldn't remember where or when she had heard them before.

Leeming. Bedale. Leaving the raging A1 behind... turning left into a winding, placid lane and her whole being slipping into a pool of quietness. Feeling unreal. At the petrol station...'Come far, luv?'

'About six years.'

'You've not been back 'ere for a long time then?' 'I never left Yorkshire. I just lived in Essex.' 'Oh, ay!'

She parked in Bedale high street and, like a sleepwalker, stretched her legs, bought things in the chemist, floated in the familiar steady pace of life, the airy feel of the wide street, and breathed and breathed.

She drove across wild, empty moors, following the switchback road that wound through sheep bleating land, and on to Reeth. Not far from there she recalled a small village squeezed between hills.

Bed and Breakfast. Vacancies. As she drew up outside the vine-covered inn, the sign creaked in the wind.

'I don't really know how long,' she said hesitantly. 'I'm touring.'

'No problem, luv,' beamed the landlady at the reception desk, handing her a key. 'Not this time of year.'

287

In her cosy room, kneeling on the padded window-seat, leaning from the open lattice window close to the creaking floor, she sniffed damp heather, peat and chimney smoke, listened to the river tumbling by, and felt she was moving through a film, watching herself, with no idea what would happen next.

What did happen was a sudden and crushing weight of tiredness, as if a hammer was trying to knock her out. She gasped. Clutching the thick chintz curtain, she closed her aching eyes until this silly, really silly tired thing had passed. Zet was never, usually tired. When she opened her eyes, the sinking sun had broken through cloud and the leaping river below was glinting like silver foil. She took a deep breath. She knew where the river had come from...a village up in the hills, on the edge of the moors.

She parked the car in the village and walked past the church and the pub, vaguely remembering she'd had nothing to eat since... when? She was feeling a sense of letting go, letting life take her where it would.

She could be intruding.   He had said he was too much of a vagabond to marry again, but people change.

I certainly have, she sighed, passing the small green and the reedy pond with its bent willow. She saw the beginning of the housing estate and across the road....

Her heart leapt when she saw the house. Solid, stony-faced, drenched in evening sunshine. Smoke was twirling from the chimney and her pulse began to race.

I was in the area, thought I'd look you up.

Couldn't pass by without calling to find out how you are.

Hi. Remember me?

Is your husband in? My husband and I are old friends of his.

Just called to say hello.

Hello. How's the flying going?

Mary?

288

Above her head a curlew soared into the sky with its cry like wild laughter.

There was no knocker, no doorbell because once, he had told her, people around here used to just tap on the door and walk in. But there were few strangers then.

She raised her hand and rapped with her knuckles.

After a long wait, footsteps hurried along the passage. Not heavy enough for Brad. The door swung open. The breath she was holding in flew out in a gasp of dismay.

Chapter Fifty-Three

He was about her height, early thirties maybe, pale faced and dark haired, slim with the look of someone who had recently lost weight. Jeans and cream sweater expensive, dark eyes behind black-rimmed glasses, not welcoming. He spoke with the suggestion of a northern accent and barely hidden venom.

'Viewing is by appointment only. Didn't the Estate Agents tell you?'

'Er, no.'

'The new girl forgot, I suppose.' Disagreeable eyes swept over her and he appeared to come to a decision. With obvious reluctance he held the door open wider, 'You might as well come and look as you're here.'

Speechless, Zet walked inside. Feeling decidedly uncomfortable, not to mention unwelcome, her eyes swept the hall for signs of Brad and with a sick sensation, saw the familiar gun rack. It was empty. Wishing she hadn't come, she followed him into the sitting room and came to an abrupt, stunned halt. It was like a time warp.

The sofa, the piano, the doll on the sideboard... she closed her eyes against the sharp pain of remembrance. This was the room she had loved in and arrived at like a homing pigeon. When she opened her eyes, he was watching her suspiciously.

Folding his arms, he propped himself by the door, as if blocking her escape. He studied his feet, raised his head and scrutinized her with a deliberate leer that was meant to suggest she was as welcome as bed bugs.

'You're not here about the house, are you?'

She shook her head, feeling the beginning of a flush, and he scowled. 'Bloody snooping reporter, I suppose.'

What is he talking about? Still dazed from the strangeness of being here, she shook her head. Try the truth, Zet. 'I came hoping to still the clamour in my head.

That's why I came to Yorkshire, I mean. While I was here, I thought I'd look up an old friend, Brad Hardstone.'

His unblinking stare unnerved her; she took a deep breath. 'He used to live here.'

His face softened, but his voice was still sharp and unfriendly as he shocked her twice. First, by saying, 'I'm his son, Danny.'

And secondly, 'My father had a heart attack.'

She felt the blood drain from her face. Frowning, he moved from his place at the door and came towards her. 'As you're not from the papers,' he said, indicating an armchair, 'you can sit down.'

He watched her perch on the edge of the chair before he answered her unspoken question. 'He's fine now.'

The shock of relief left her dazed. Not seeming to notice, he crossed the room in a graceful and self-important movement; a small man who seemed far from home.

'He's apparently a very fit man, has a healthy life style; it was a mild attack,' he told her, perching on the sofa. *She couldn't take her eyes from that sofa, the memories*….'He's selling up here and buying something smaller,' she heard him say. Crossing his legs, he sat back. Not comfortably. Not, somehow, belonging.

She moistened her lips and nearly blurted out, *He loved this house*. 'He's not here, then?' she asked instead, and he shook his head.

'My father's away in the States.' With a wry smile, he added, 'Mary went with him.'

He leaned forward, studying her. 'You look all in,' he frowned, adding in a begrudging voice, 'can I get you something?'

She tried to swallow, shook her head, decided she ought to go only found her limbs were trembling. As if he sensed her struggle, he jumped up and left the room, returning a moment later with a glass quarter filled with brandy. 'I've put the kettle on.' He looked curious. 'In case you fancy coffee.'

Pulling herself together, she took the glass, smiled a bit to say thank you, and gulped the burning liquid down. He took the glass from her with a keen glance. 'I shocked you. I'd have told you differently if I'd known....'

She raised her chin. 'Known what?'

He smiled at her defensive tone. 'If I'd known how close you were to my father.'

It wasn't a pleasant smile, and irritation stirred in her warming veins. 'I didn't know him long,' she explained. 'Long enough, obviously', he returned, snapping the glass down on a small table. He smirked. 'But don't worry, he has many years ahead of him yet, the doctors say.'

He doesn't like Brad much, was the thought that surprisingly came to her. And she didn't like Danny, she realised. There was something too slick, artificial and hard about him. Brad, by contrast, was himself, nothing artificial. What you saw was what he was, take him or leave him, he used to say. Her empty stomach was burning with the brandy. And then he had done that dreadful thing to Jonty that hadn't seemed in character at all. Or had it? Her first impression of Brad had been of someone ruthless.

'I'll get the coffee,' Danny said, with a sharp look at her face. Reaching for her empty glass, he left the room with obvious relief, leaving her to gaze around.

How she remembered this room. My God, how she remembered it. The sofa, where they had curled up together in front of the fire. She turned to look into the hissing, spitting flames as at an old friend, remembering the sensation of heat against her bare skin. She bent and ran her hand across the silky fireside rug...remembering. Deliberately remembering, for it was obvious that what had driven her here was the need to get him out of her system.

She had only ever seen him as the man she loved; she had never looked into the face of a potential killer. It would surely have made a difference.

Over there, on the sideboard, stood the doll she had made him for his birthday. It was called "The Carpenter", an old man wearing a cap, sitting at a bench, holding a piece of carved wood in his hand. He wore a check shirt and a tiny hammer poked from a pocket in his leather apron; he had rosy cheeks, a roguish smile and a white beard to match his sheep's' wool hair.

She remembered the day they had collected the sheep's wool from the moors. Even now, excitement pumped her heart as she felt again the wind whipping her cheeks, snatching at their laughter and companionable talk as they pulled clumps of wool from tough grass, stone walls and fences, so that she could make wigs from it.

Jumping up, she wandered across the room; the pads of her fingers glided across the silky, gleaming dark wood of the piano lid; she only had to glance at his tapes and CD's, and his voice was throbbing in her head. The remembered click of the old-fashioned latch of the door made her spin round guiltily.

As she returned to her chair, Danny placed a tray on the table, plopped himself down on the sofa and indicated she should help herself to the mug of coffee, and whatever she wanted in it.

He had coffee, black with no sugar, on the table in front of him and watched her impassively as she ignored the sugar, poured milk, and sat back nursing her mug feeling, and probably looking, uncomfortable.

'Drink up,' he ordered smugly as he sipped his own steaming drink, 'You look as if you've seen a ghost.'

Surprisingly, she did drink up what she discovered was very good ground coffee which took away the taste of brandy she didn't much like. And astonished, she saw him grin. He could have been a different person, his whole face lit up - the word elfin came to mind - and she found herself smiling weakly back and thinking he was younger than she had supposed.

'That's better,' he said, with a bossy air of triumph.

'Now we're friends, tell me what you're running from.' 'What?'

He smiled at her shocked expression. 'If you don't tell me,' he said, gulping the cooler coffee, 'I'll make you sit here and listen to my jokes.' He snapped the mug down on the table.

She did the same with her own mug and raised her brows. 'I don't laugh at jokes.'

He clapped a hand to his brow. 'I don't believe it. Woman,' he said dramatically, 'who sent you to ruin me?'

'No one sent me,' she said seriously to this madman. 'I didn't know I was coming. I just drove and found myself here.'

'But angel, you've told the famous Danny Stone that you don't laugh at jokes.'

She froze. Danny Stone? Her mouth dropped. 'Aren't you that comedian?' she said in astonishment, and heard him groan.

'You're so good for my morale, darling.'

'Sorry. I never watch comedians. I....'

'I know,' he nodded. 'You never laugh at jokes.' Another faint smile tugged her lips. 'Brad's son?

You? I can't believe it.'

He nodded. 'He doesn't laugh much, does he?' A pause, and, looking down, running a finger around the rim of the mug...'He didn't tell you about me, then?'

A catch in his voice made her pause before saying, 'not much.' She frowned, sensing some deep-rooted pain, but had no energy for it; she flopped back in the chair.

Stretching out and relaxing, he said, with slick cheerfulness, 'Now. Talk to me. About you.'

Unnaturally obedient, she did. She talked of her childhood, her family, her marriage, right up to her father's funeral and how she had emptied her father's

294

house, driven away and just kept on driving with no conscious plan. There was just the most compelling urge to escape her present life.

'It wasn't until I was halfway up the A1 and saw the Bedale turn off that I knew some force was driving me to the Dales.'

As she talked, hardly recognising her tired, flat voice, a pulse ticked in her neck. She was aware that everything she did was with effort… breathing, talking, acting normal. Danny's voice was sounding far away. It was a frightening sensation.

'And it was only when I was in my room at the inn that I knew I had to come and see Brad, if he still lived here.'

And then she was too tired to talk or think any more. She had trouble breathing, as she often had lately. She couldn't take a full breath; trying to pull air into her lungs sent her heart palpitating, drenching her in sweat. Exhaustion claimed her like death.

Afterwards, when she tried to recall what happened next, she could only remember that tiredness took her over with vicious intent, leaving her helpless in its grip. She might have been a child.

She vaguely recalled that he drove her back to the inn in her car, saying she wasn't fit to drive. He called the sympathetic landlady Avril, told her Zet had been ill and needed complete rest. He asked for soup to be sent up to her room, which Zet barely drank and it started again, the inability to swallow, the gasping for breath.

A doctor came, just when she really felt she was going to die. In a nightmare, she thought she heard the doctor ask Danny for a paper bag. Danny hurried downstairs and returned with a handful. The doctor took one, twisted its neck and thrust it towards her mouth.

'Now breathe into it,' he ordered, supporting her with an arm around her back.

Gradually, as she breathed, she felt better. 'You're hyperventilating,' the doctor told her. Resting her gently back on the pillow, he felt her pulse and kept his hand covering hers; she liked the feel of his hand.

Danny sat on the bed, listening as the doctor told them, 'Over breathing, in other words, caused by exhaustion, strain or overwork, anxiety perhaps. You breathe too much, take in too much oxygen and expend too much carbon dioxide, which makes you short of breath. You try to breathe in more and you end up fainting. I expect you've been yawning a lot lately?' Zet nodded.

'When you breathe into the bag,' he said, watching her carefully, still holding her hand, 'you get carbon dioxide.'

Trying to concentrate on the doctor's precise, faintly accented voice, Zet looked with silent apology at Danny. 'Is that all it is? I thought I was dying. I feel a fraud.'

'Looked pretty terrifying to me.' He sounded so kind the tears came to her eyes, blurring her sight of the doctor as he stood up to go.

'I'd say that over a long period you've been full of worry and anxiety. Your nerves are shattered.' He gave her a sedative which she swallowed with sips of water and when he said goodbye she looked up into his face, registered something interesting in his high cheekbones and unusual long slanting eyes, and fought against this dreadful "ill-type" tiredness to whisper, 'Thank you.'

Afterwards, she vaguely recalled the two men pausing at the door to talk, noted a fondness in Danny's expression, before she passed into a state of oblivion.

She slept. Arousing only for trips to the bathroom, to sip soup, milk or glucose drinks. Obedient as a child, she swallowed pills. Her eyes refused to stay open. Sleep ate her up. Oblivion. Escape. Danny, she found out afterwards, hardly left her.

In the oddest experience of her life, she, of all people, allowed herself to be tended like a baby.

'I'm hungry.' Gingerly pushing herself up in the bed, she looked across the room and saw Danny sitting on the window-seat, reading a script.

He looked up. The scent of chips, scampi, all sorts of things, was wafting through the open window from the kitchen below. Her eyes were wide, alert, fixed on him. Then realisation dawned; flushing, she tugged on the bedclothes, pulling them around her.

'I've been such a nuisance. I don't know what happened. I just collapsed. I'm not even sure how long....'

'Four days, but don't worry about it,' he said with a smile, putting the script down on the windowsill. 'You're back with us. How do you feel?'

'Washed out,' she said weakly, watching him cross the room. 'But new.'

'Good,' he smiled, coming up to the bed.

'But I'm so embarrassed.' She glanced down at the revealing top of a strange white cotton nightdress; she was hot and sticky in the central heated room, with no memory of having washed herself. Her smell rose from the bedclothes ...scented soap and baby powder. Danny? What else had he done?

'Forget it,' he ordered, reading her flush. 'I started out as a nurse, years ago. And,' he paused, 'I nursed a friend recently, who....' Breaking off, he placed a smile over some remembered hell. 'It was because of Dick...Dick Kortas.' She looked blank. 'The doctor,' he added.

'Oh, right.' Her memory of the doctor was hazy, but she nodded.

'Dick's an old friend, I grew up wanting to become a doctor just like him.'

Saying nothing, Zet just let him carry on. She knew all about aims and ambitions, she thought sadly, with that dreadful thump of disbelief in her stomach.

'I wasn't clever enough,' Danny admitted in a rueful voice, 'so I took up nursing instead.' He paused, looking away from the understanding in her face to the glorious darkening view through the window. 'Dick's had a hard life. He's Polish; he was shut up in the Salt Mines during the war. But,' he sighed, 'he's retiring next year; it will be a great loss to the people around here. Anyway, this won't do,' he said more cheerfully, turning to look searchingly at her.

'Do you feel up to taking me to dinner?' he asked, checking his watch. 'Five o'clock, just gone. Clean yourself up,' he suggested firmly, with his elfin grin. 'See you downstairs about six-thirty.'

She stared at him. What else was there? There was no order, no planning; exhaustion had swept like an incoming tide into her life and left her stranded. She nodded. He looked pleased.

She had nothing to wear except the jeans and cream sweater she had arrived in but her underwear was newly washed; she felt touched, humbled and embarrassed. Not that she could feel embarrassed for long, everyone was so kind and Avril fussed around her like a mother hen. Another new experience for Zet.

Brad, she discovered, as they ate, wouldn't return from his holiday for a month yet. He and Mary were staying with his daughter in Florida.

'No, they're not married,' Danny said, merely picking at his steak and salad. 'He always said no one could replace my mother. Just as well.'

She looked at him curiously, only just noticing the pallor of his skin, the stubble on his chin, and the shadows beneath his eyes. 'Why do you say that?'

'He's the sort who wants to dominate, bend a woman to his will.' Pushing his half eaten dinner away, he added, 'Same goes for sons.'

'People change as they get older, you know,' Zet said, filling her fork with sole and delicious lemon sauce.

'Maybe.' He was silent for a moment, as she ate,

then he asked, 'Do you know how my mother died?' She answered gently, 'Yes, I do.'

'We were there, you know, all of us.' He frowned. 'My grandfather played cricket for Yorkshire and we were all watching except for mother; she had gone up with her instructor; she had ten more hours flying to do to get her certificate. She collided with another light aircraft and came down in the field next to the cricket pitch. The other plane lost a wing but managed to land safely. Because,' he added grimly,' the pilot was very experienced.'

She stared at him, stirred with pity, imagining the scene as he spoke. It was so horrible...what can you say?

He hadn't finished. 'At the funeral, I heard my grandmother say to father..."I don't know what my daughter was doing up in the air. She was always afraid of heights."' Behind the glasses, Danny's eyes hardened. 'Everyone said he killed her.'

'Women do things for love.' Zet tried not to think of how she longed to see Brad and yet dreaded it, in case she hated him. 'I don't think your father could be held responsible.' And yet...what he had done to Jonty surely showed that Brad had a temper, if thwarted. She sighed, laying her knife and fork down on her empty plate. Danny shrugged, as if her defence of his father irritated him. 'Let's take our coffee into the bar,' he suggested, standing up and tossing aside his napkin.

Following him, Zet pushed the thought of Brad away. Tonight she wanted to let all the complications of life pass by. She heard a click, as someone dropped a coin in a slot and pressed a button to choose a record.

Help me make it through the night, sang Gladys Knight, with her usual heart stirring, shivers-down-the spine emotion. Lost briefly in the music, Zet suddenly realised he was eyeing her with concern.

'Are you all right, Zet?'

'I'm fine.' Making conversation she asked, 'Have you been here with me all the time?'

'Yes, in your room. In the other bed.'

299

She studied him over the rim of her cup. 'You're a most amazing man.'

'You're an amazing woman,' he said, watching her closely. 'I've not met anyone quite like you before.'

'God,' she sighed, looking into the blazing log fire. 'I should hope not.' Something slipped around her, something cold and lonely. She felt remote from the world outside, didn't want to face it. She looked across the small table at Danny, not knowing her appeal showed.

His eyes behind the glasses were large, dark, and intense. 'Will you be all right tonight?' he asked, and she trembled. In and out of the laughter, conversation, tinkle of glasses, through an atmosphere of fun, friendship, life, threaded the music. *Let the devil take tomorrow - for tonight I need a friend.*

'No,' she said.

She stayed for a week. A week, during which they walked, talked, dined and slept together. But not in the same bed. Neither did he show any inclination to be in hers. She thought with distaste how she had let herself go, who would fancy her? Besides, he was younger than she was.

Chapter Fifty-Four

The doctor returned to check her over and as the weather was mild, they walked together in the garden. She looked at him properly for the first time, studying the high cheekbones, long eyes, and narrow-bridged nose. He was as slight as an iron chain is. He showed off the barely discernible paunch that had come with age, with pride, as if it was a badge. He walked as if he pulled behind him, a ball and chain invisible to others.

His eyes were unusual, between green and yellow like the khaki of a soldier's uniform; at the moment they were fixed on the Dales with a soft, telling expression as they stopped to lean on a stone wall.

Remembering what Danny had told her, she felt her heart twist. It wasn't only his past; something about this doctor touched a chord in her. He wasn't, she realised, unlike her father in looks; small, modest looking, quiet, with an inner sadness.

Impulsively, she said, 'you love this place, don't you?'

'Not just this place, but England,' he said, turning from the view with his gentle smile. My wife, Berta and I, we are grateful to England. Berta runs our farm. I intended to farm,' he added, leaning against the wall, 'but I found it was people who interested me. I studied hard to repay what England gave us.'

Looking searchingly into her face, his eyes were tired but with a piercing light that she found, with an odd tingling in her bones, she couldn't turn away from.

'My parents were farmers; but they...my brothers and sisters also... didn't survive the holocaust. I,' he paused, 'well, that's enough of that. What about you?'

Before she could answer, he took her hands in his, and somehow she relaxed, feeling a warm glow and a sense of well being such as she hadn't felt for a long time. He began to speak, telling her about herself, and she jokingly

301

asked, 'Are you psychic or something?' He didn't smile back.

'Doesn't go together, does it,' he answered seriously, 'a doctor who's a spiritual healer.'

Zet felt an inner quiver, a stirring as if something began to uncurl, as he went on: 'you're a healer, too, Zet.' His voice was matter-of-fact, but he startled her. Afterwards, she was to describe it as like coming face to face with a speeding train. There was a sensation like rushing wind, and then the air seemed to stand still. She had a jumble of thoughts... impossible... me?

He was watching her carefully. 'How do you know?' she asked, resting back against the wall. She could feel hard knobs of stone pressing into her lower spine. She clasped her hands, prayer-like, in front of her.

His smile was rueful. 'I know, believe me. Now, tell me about your work.'

She told him. At the end, he said, 'Many of your clients felt themselves cured by coming to you.'

It was a statement, more than a question. She nodded, remembering them, the grateful ones, those who told her they felt their symptoms, their aches and pains improved; those whom she had recommended to go to a doctor because she felt something was wrong. Instinct, she had believed.

'You have healing hands,' he said. 'With the aromatherapy?'

He stirred, and thrusting his hands into his trouser pockets, said, 'aromatherapy is part of it.' Looking round the garden, he added, 'Calms the mind, relaxes. Aroma is around us everywhere. Here, smelling flowers and herbs, heather in the air, it's all therapy. But the cures are in your hands, my love.'

Her insides jerked. Her father's endearement...*my love*.

He went on to describe holistic treatment, or hands on healing as some called it. He talked of types of holistic treatments, like reiki, watching her reaction carefully. He ended by explaining self-help. 'This occurs during the process of creating something with your own hands. Look how therapeutic you find your doll making and cooking.'

'Oh.'

'What is it?'

'Just,' she swallowed, 'someone I used to know, who said something similar to me. He was a farmer, businessman, singer, yet he was also a craftsman; he made beautiful furniture. He said people need to work with their hands.' *He also killed.*

'My father was hypercritical,' Danny said. They were sitting on the swing seat in the sloping back garden that seemed to be cut into the side of a hill overlooking the scenery she had once called "Scenic wallpaper". The moors, dotted with sheep, rose above their heads one way, and down towards the river the other. It was a comfortably mild, drowsy, lemon coloured day until she remembered.

'Mum,' Darren had once asked. 'Why don't the sheep fall off that steep hill?' My children, she thought in sudden panic, went right out of my mind. I forgot them. As if forgetting them meant they didn't exist.

Danny moved his foot so that the chair swung gently, with a soporific effect and, without guilt, she let the children go, hearing him add, 'With a hypercritical parent, you tend, as a child, to cope by acting, because you're afraid of your real self, of whom you have a low opinion, being found out. You distance yourself from real feelings to create a buffer against self hatred.'

Head resting back, enjoying the rocking motion, she looked at him sideways. 'But you're so successful.'

He grinned at the envy in her voice. 'Driven by fear of inadequacy and unpopularity, darling.' Grimacing, he added, 'I don't usually talk like this....'

'What were you like as a child, Danny?'

'Shy, awkward, grew up to think I wasn't sexually eligible. No oil painting, more an oil slick.'

303

'You're enjoying this, running yourself down,' she argued, feeling annoyed. 'You shouldn't do it and I refuse to laugh.'

'Why? Take the serious things in life trivially and the trivial things seriously, as Oscar Wilde said. Acting is the best way to be true.'

She let the slickness that had first got her back up pass her by. 'Your father must be proud of you,' she pressed.

He shook his head and looked into the distance. 'I think that everything I've done has been to get back at him...drugs, and drink and....' He hesitated before going on.

'There's confidence and self love in a bottle. It was seeing a friend die recently....' Turning to her, he stopped, unable to go on and she reached for his hand. With a grateful glance, he said, 'I've got a lot of sorting out to do; I've come back here to find myself.'

But only while your father wasn't here, she thought, saying aloud, 'you and me both. Funny we met like this.' She was sorry to leave; she had enjoyed his company. Maybe she had nothing to prove and neither did Danny. 'I feel more relaxed than I've done for a long time,' she told him as they said goodbye outside the inn. 'I know now what I have to do.'

He said softly, 'Ours has been a very special friendship.'

Her voice was husky. 'It was unique for me, and very wonderful.'

'Why are we talking in the past? Come down to London.'

'I might come,' she said, with a smile. 'When I've got myself sorted. But I'll never forget you.'

He smiled. 'I feel as if I've been caged up inside myself. You came along and turned a key, left a door open. Made me think.'

'Me too,' she said quietly. 'I'm not blaming anyone else; I caged myself up working for perfection. I was looking at the open door not sure whether to go out or not. Not sure where courage lay; in staying or leaving.' He nodded. 'You made me think of things like love, family loyalty, struggling to live a life that's wrong for you and having the courage to break away. It seems to me you put up a tremendous fight, Zet. Don't belittle yourself.'

Blinking away tears, she gently retrieved her hand and pulled open the car door. Hesitated. Without looking round, she said, 'Do something for me?'

'Anything.'

'Talk to your father. That's how you'll find yourself, Danny, trust me.' She swung round, facing him. 'Once, I wondered why I didn't love my family, then I found all the love hidden beneath a load of everyday things; you know… resentments, differences, and misunderstandings. It's your power, Danny; to know that whatever you do, they're always there, even if they disapprove, is tremendously freeing. You can be what you want to be.' She faltered. 'The odd thing is, that even when they've gone, you still feel them there, behind you.'

Driving away, she saw him, through the wing mirror, standing so still, watching her go. She had got to know him well over the last week. But one thing she didn't know…what could be trapped inside such a successful man?

'You're away, then,' Dick said. 'Fit and well, raring to go.'

'I wouldn't say that; God, no.' she said. She still had to face going home.

They were sitting in his surgery. Glancing around, she saw a couch partly hidden behind a screen, a washbasin in one corner and a glass cabinet stacked with books in another; children's drawings fixed to a wall; pictures of Berta, a wedding photograph and grandchildren on his desk. A shelf showed off pottery vases and dishes that he made himself, in what spare time he had.

Sunlight was flitting around the walls; there was the sharp shriek of birds outside, the musky smell of bonfires and cut grass came through the opened window. She was reminded of a silent room where a man lay dying, and her heart twisted.

'Why didn't I know, Dick? About my parents, I mean.'

He waited a moment before he spoke, smoothing a pen between his fingers. 'You possibly did, but when it's someone you love, you tend to deny it to yourself. You wouldn't have accepted it, Zet.' She nodded, her mind going back.

Seeing her hurt face, he said gently, 'healers don't always cure, you know; but give comfort, especially to the dying.'

'Maybe I did. A little.'

He pulled in a sigh. 'The saddest of all sadnesses, 'he told her, 'is what we see and cannot tell. You must never take to heart your failures. You are not God. Remember that,' he warned.

He was watching her with concern. 'I believe our path is mapped out for us. If we try to change that, and fight it, then we become ill. We can't always see it, but life, which seems to do odd, uncomfortable or cruel things to us, is leading us in the right direction after all. Enlightenment is when you recognise it, turn from the path you wanted to take and go on to the one that has been planned for you. Stop fighting it.'

With a fond smile, he handed her a sheaf of leaflets. 'Information about healing training courses,' he told her. 'Holistic medicine might be the way forward for you.'

She felt as if a load had lifted. No, not a flash of light, just a sense that she had been dressed in uncomfortable borrowed clothes and they had fallen away was the only way she could describe it.

Chapter Fifty-Five

'Zet, I've a confession to make.'

'Yes, I saw the burger cartons in the bin.' It was her first night back from the north. The children were in bed, dinner had been cleared away and, facing him across the kitchen table, she tried to joke.

'You didn't have to eat takeaways and junk food, the freezer was....'

'I like junk food,' he interrupted, sulkily. 'We all do. Always have.'

She was stunned. Yet she hadn't said her piece yet, hadn't told him about the decision she had made. Before she could speak, he told her something that froze her to the core.

'Moving back from Yorkshire was my idea, not the firm's.'

For a minute, she couldn't take this in. Frowning, she put a hand to her forehead, collecting her thoughts. Watching her uncertainly, he nodded, picked up a raffia tablemat and studied it, flicking it over and over in his hands. 'I couldn't cope with what I knew about you and that singer.'

He sounded desperately sad. 'Oh, Jonty.' Her eyes filled. 'I'm so sorry,' she whispered, full of remorse. Such inadequate words, when she bled for him.

Without looking at her, he admitted, 'I couldn't face you with it, in case you left. When you chose to come back with me, I tried to turn a blind eye, but I didn't cope very well there, either.'

'Jonty, I made the decision because of you, not just for mum.' Huskily, she said, 'you were kind and good, everything I wanted, and,' her voice choked with tears, 'I did that to you.'

He looked up. The mat fell from his fingers. 'I thought that to have you would be enough. But I couldn't cope with thinking of you and him. He was an invisible presence every time we were together. Might have been in my mind, not yours,' he shrugged, 'but I couldn't help it.' After a pause, he added, 'I always expected to lose you.'

'I wanted to keep our marriage going, I really did,' she said honestly, 'but I've changed you, made you something you're not.'

'You've had it tough, too, Zet.' He looked up. 'What with your parents and everything.' After a pause, he said, in the saddest voice she had ever heard. 'It's a bit of a pig, you know, not to be able to comfort someone. Especially when that someone is your wife.'

They stared at each other, husband and wife, strangers. She broke the long silence by asking, through stiff lips, 'How did you know about Brad?'

He blew out his lips, ran fingers through his hair and sat back more restfully on the hard chair. 'Remember old Jack, the northern manager before I took over his job?' When she nodded, he said, 'The firm received a letter from his wife about your affair.'

He heard her sharp intake of breath followed by a shocked exclamation. 'She was the one who sent the postcards then.' In a strained voice, she went on to explain.

He listened and nodded. 'The Personnel Manager felt bound to speak to me about it, but his view was that my marriage was none of the firm's business.' He swallowed before going on. 'But it wasn't only that. I phoned Dick one day and Margaret answered. She asked if your car had broken down as it had been in the station car park for three days. It was that time you said you drove to the Lakes.'

When she said nothing, he added, 'even over at the shop…I went there for burgers when you were away, there were women talking…'

'And?'

'Zet,' he said heavily, 'do you think a red car was a sensible choice for someone wanting to be invisible?'

Oh, God, she thought, feeling herself shrinking… guilty, devious, deceitful, lying…words that described her wonderful love affair. How we can kid ourselves.

Breaking into her thoughts, he said miserably, 'I thought you were too good for me.' He sat up straight and picked up the mat, twisting it in his fingers. 'You were way up there on a pedestal and I guessed someone else would come and take you away.'

She was astonished. 'But I admired you. Your brains, your exam passes, your nice home and family. There was no reason for you to feel that way.'

He shrugged. 'Well, I did.'

'Oh, Jonty. Reminds me of something Frankie said.' She looked at him warily, expecting a sarcastic remark, but he said nothing and she went on, 'you pretended to be what you thought I wanted. I never got to know you.'

'I saw you and I wanted you,' he said simply.

'We should have talked more, Jonty. We were so busy at the beginning, and it was so exciting, you getting promotion, aiming for the top, getting a home together. We lived for success, didn't we?'

He shook his head. 'You did.' He sounded aggrieved. 'I rode along with it because that's what you wanted.'

'What about you and Sarah? I just wondered.'

He dropped the tablemat on the floor, bent over, picked it up, and took a deep breath. 'Sarah is just Sarah, someone I don't have to pretend with.'

'What are we going to do?' she asked, feeling that she had never respected him so much. She had overpowered him was the startling realisation that came to her. But it wasn't too late. She hadn't had a chance yet to tell him what she had decided to do. He had taken the wind out of her sails. I'll tell him now, she thought, that I've found work that I really want to do and that I want us to start again, really trying this time.

'It's got to be a split,' he said.

309

'What?' Stunned, she hardly recognized the firm, decisive note in his voice as he said, 'we're tearing each other to pieces; I don't like what it's done to us. And there's me.'

'You?'

'Yes. I've given up myself to you. I need to find myself again.'

Her brows rose. He wasn't usually one for introspection, but then, according to him she had smothered the real Jonty. She swallowed, confused. 'I see. And the children?'

'We'll make sure they're okay. What were you going to tell me, by the way?'

'Nothing much. Nothing at all, really.

Zet stared at her daughter, wondering if she had heard correctly. 'What?'

'I just said, about time,' Alyson repeated, shrugging. 'You and dad haven't been getting on for ages, we know that, don't we Darren?'

He scowled. 'S'pose.'

Tossing her hair back, Alyson asked, 'you weren't staying together just for us, were you?'

'That, Alyson...and other things.'

Alyson sighed heavily. 'You shouldn't have. I wouldn't stay with a husband I didn't get on with just for the kids.'

'You wouldn't?' Zet asked faintly.

Shaking her head, Alyson said, 'we've got to fly the nest, mum. Then you'll be alone, you and dad.'

'Well, not quite yet....'

'Besides,' Alyson said heatedly, 'Do you realise just how unimportant your marriage is?'

Taken aback, Zet glanced at Darren, who was miserably looking anywhere but at her, and turned back to Alyson. 'No, I don't, actually.'

'Be real. There are people starving; people with no roof over their heads, no food, no hospitals, their sick die in the gutters, and you're worried about which house we're going to live in.' Alyson flung her arms in the air.

'Oh, Alyson,' Zet said with a strangled laugh. 'Are you crying, mum?'

Yes I'm crying, laughing, bemused and put in my place by this daughter who is much more mature and worldly than I was at the same age. She sees the world; I saw only my own selfish part of it and I was obsessed with one dream.

Alyson bit her lip. 'Mum? You don't usually cry.'

'No.' Zet looked at Darren, saw his lips were trembling, and forcing a smile, said, 'Alyson's right. We're so lucky. Remember that. Remember how loved you are. Two homes or one, does it make any difference, as long as they have love in them?'

They stared at each other, Zet and her son. 'You know you're loved, don't you?' she pressed, feeling her heart wrench.

'Leave off, mum,' he shrugged. But his lips twisted into a begrudging smile. 'Can we have a dog?'

Alyson interrupted, 'I'm going away next year, anyway.' Tossing her hair, she added, 'To India.'

Zet's heart sank. 'Next year's a long way off....'

Alyson shook her head. 'I've made up my mind. All you grown-ups think about is what's going on in your own heads and bodies. It would stick in my throat to massage over indulged bodies or hypnotize someone to stop them overeating, for money that would keep a starving family for a year. A year?' Her eyes were wide.

While Zet struggled to find something to say, Alyson added, 'Frankie brought me some information.' Her face clouded. 'When you were at the hospice, with...granddad; Frankie was brilliant, for a grown-up. She has a friend who arranges relief trips to Romania, she's going to see if I can help.'

311

She didn't discuss this with me. Zet felt a rush of pain. Sharply, she said, 'you're a little young yet.'

Alyson tossed her hair. 'Frankie said....'

The divorce was going smoothly. Jonty was living with his mother. Zet was in the process of selling her father's house and would be able to buy another home when the heavily mortgaged Essex house was sold. It would need to be a more modest house. She didn't plan to rush. Life, however, had other ideas, and events began to move quickly, and, in Gran's case, tragically.

Chapter Fifty-Six

'I found her tights in the fridge,' Sophie whispered tearfully. 'She forgets things, even which day of the week it is. And she comes in with bags of food she can hardly carry, looks at you the way a child does, as if she knows she's done wrong but hopes you won't tell her off, because I do, now.' She looked anguished.

Resting an elbow on the kitchen table, she lowered her head on to her hand. Her voice was muffled as she went on....'She's spending money as if there's no tomorrow. I can't bear hurting her; you break up inside just looking at her. I don't know what to do.'

Zet glanced around. Her heart sank. Cans were stacked on the kitchen tops because the cupboards were full. Packets were piled ceiling high. The fridge was jammed, as was the freezer.

'I've got enough towels and jumpers upstairs, and skirts, to open a shop,' Sophie whispered, pushing wisps of untidy hair from her face. Zet could have cried. Especially heartbreaking were the lists.

'Look,' Sophie said tearfully, pointing at the scribbled notes on the table. In barely decipherable writing, Gran had scribbled...My telephone number; my address; children's names. Zet's house is at...

Only a few weeks before, Gran had arranged to come and see Zet but had got lost, although she had been there many times, and, fortunately had been helped by a kind stranger to find her way home.

'What can I do?' Sophie looked at Zet with stricken eyes. 'I can't stop her going out.' She ended in an anguished wail. 'Poor mum.'

In the front room, Zet cuddled Gran, stroked her hair, broke up inside because Gran didn't use hair dye any more; it was mostly grey; blinking back tears, Zet's throat ached. She could see by the vacant expression in Gran's eyes that she wasn't living in this world at all. She talked to you, but what she said had no connection with the conversation. She's gone, Zet thought bleakly, and we didn't say goodbye.

Zet cried. Holding the familiar plump body close, she cried. Not wanting to let go. Oh, Gran.

'What are we doing about Christmas?' Sophie asked unexpectedly and forlornly.

Zet had hardly given Christmas a thought. 'The children are going to Jonty and his mother Christmas Eve and coming home Christmas morning. You and Gran come over for Christmas lunch.'

Forcing enthusiasm into her voice, she said, 'we'll give Gran a good time...bring her old records and....' Zet's voice dried up. She couldn't go on.

Christmas Eve morning, the children had just left with Jonty, and the phone rang.

Gran? Heart banging against her ribs, Zet lifted the receiver.

Not Gran; instead, the voice in her ear was clipped and efficient. 'The divorce is through. You're a free woman,' Karen, her solicitor said. 'Happy Christmas, Zet.'

Shaking, Zet replaced the receiver. She must have thanked Karen, she supposed. She didn't remember. All she knew was that she found herself sitting on the stairs tasting bitterness and failure in her soul. Giving in. Giving up. Giving herself hell.

After a while, she became aware that she had been staring at, but not seeing, the hall table. There was a secret about the beautiful hall table. Brad had made it especially for her, and she had taken it home, saying she had bought it. Tears came to her eyes. So many lies.

On the table, blurred like an unfocused photograph, stood the dolls' house her father had made. Two gifts, made with love. Her throat ached, forcing back tears, but why? There was no one to see. Her head went down on her knees. the fight went out of her, and wrapping her arms around herself...she sobbed.

It was Christmas morning. Zet had slept badly and consequently rose late. What did it matter, she asked herself, splashing her face with cold water? Everything was organised - table laid for lunch - shining glasses and cutlery - green crackers, red candles, even beautifully wrapped parcels stacked on the floor beneath the small, artificial Christmas tree. Odd the way you carry on automatically, without feeling, without heart, sort of remote control, really.

The kitchen, when she walked in, was cool and sterile. She had peeled the vegetables last night, made the stuffing. There was nothing to do but drink the sherry she had bought for Gran and wait for Jonty and the children to arrive.

Oh, and put the turkey in the oven. She had removed it from the freezer last night, hadn't she? She had been wrapping parcels.... drinking sherry, listening to carols from York Minster on the radio, which had brought back memories.... She and Brad gazing in awe at the Minster's stained glass windows, exploring York's narrow streets, riding in a horse and carriage, herself riding a carousel in the park, like a child.... the carousel had been playing *Somewhere my love*.

She didn't hear the key turn in the lock, or the children's excited voices as they swooped into the sitting room. When Jonty came to find her she was in the kitchen, crouched on the floor beside the freezer, holding the body of an incredibly solid turkey, crying her heart out.

For an astonished moment, he could only stand there. Then he shot across the room, pulled her up and into his arms and held her as she sobbed and his shoulder felt quite comforting, actually.

315

He had never seen Zet helpless before. Sad, frightened, but not helpless, there had always been that steely determination there ready to cope with any problem. Now she was crying as if her heart was broken.

She grabbed kitchen roll for her eyes and nose, and was dabbing and explaining and trying to smile when a woman called from the doorway.

'Am I interrupting?'

Zet and Jonty turned. His arms fell away, leaving her alone and isolated. But seeing who was standing in the doorway, Zet's tear-streaked face relaxed into relief. The one person she could talk to was here, like a miracle.

'Frankie,' she gulped, relieved. 'I've been a fool.' 'Oh?' Frankie frowned. Avoiding Zet's eyes, she surveyed the silent, chilly kitchen as if she had never been there before.

Zet tried to laugh. 'I forgot to take the turkey out of the freezer. Isn't that...?'

Something made her pause. Frankie was looking down at her feet now, mumbling 'I'm sorry,' as if she couldn't care less and as if the pattern of the floor tiles was more interesting.

Zet sniffed back the last of the tears. Frankie was uninterested in Christmas, of course. But why was she so stern and unfriendly? Zet didn't like to admit it to herself, but today she needed a friend.

Looking from Frankie to Jonty, her voice shook and sounded surprisingly formal and uncertain. 'This is a surprise visit, Frankie?'

The silence was uncomfortable. Jonty's face moved from embarrassment to guilt to blushing. 'Will you manage?' he asked, addressing the turkey.

'I'm perfectly all right, now.' Zet was bending to pick up the bird, keeping her face blank, putting two and two together but it didn't add up. She rose, face flushed. 'I'll cope.' The bird landed with a crash on the kitchen top. Everyone jumped.

316

Frankie sounded matter-of-fact, so sensible, so soothing. 'Jonty needed someone to talk to. You know how it is.'

'That's right.' Jonty hesitated. Running a hand through his floppy hair he stared uncertainly from Zet to Frankie for a long time, then he made a move.

Crossing the room, he reached the door and Frankie checked his face, slipped a hand into his and they exchanged a long glance during which Frankie seemed to be silently telling him something.

Turning to Zet, who felt as if she was just coming round after an anaesthetic, he cleared his throat as if about to make a prepared speech. He sounded pompous. He looked flabby; she hadn't noticed how much weight he had put on.

'Er, Zet. Frankie made me realise I've always been afraid of you and I had to make the break.' He cleared his throat. 'She made me see that being second best had become a way of life to me and that I no longer had to accept it. It started when I was a child.' A pause. 'You know what I mean,' he said in a self-pitying voice. 'Feeling left out, trying to be what others wanted in order to get love and attention.'

'Oh, please.' Zet's face felt stiff from dried tears, but she managed a withering look. 'Frankie helped you to find yourself,' she said, not hiding sarcasm. 'She probably said...."there comes a time in life when you have to learn to let go."'

Frankie flushed an unbecoming red.

Zet just thought of something. Her suspicious gaze crossed the room to Frankie in the doorway. 'Was it you told Jonty about Brad?' she asked accusingly. Frankie went to speak, but Jonty jumped to her defence. 'I told you how I knew, Zet.' He hesitated.

'Frankie just confirmed it that's all.' 'I bet she did.' There was silence.

'Oh, well, never mind,' said Zet at last. 'I've got some sausages.'

No sooner had Frankie and Jonty gone than Alyson came into the kitchen. Told about the turkey, she retorted scathingly, 'some people today won't have any food at all.'

'Leave it off, Al,' grumbled Darren from the doorway. 'It's Christmas,' he mumbled with a full mouth and chocolate stained teeth. Hearing footsteps outside on the path, he glanced through the window. 'Here comes Aunt Sophie. I bet she's brought us a game.'

Everyone laughed. Christmassy laughs. 'I'd rather have a dog,' he grumbled.

'We can have the Xmas dinner tomorrow,' Zet said with forced brightness.

Alyson grimaced. 'We're going to dad's the day after. He's taken a week off work 'specially. You'll have a lot of turkey to get through by yourself.'

Zet looked at her, feeling as if a hand had grabbed the back of her neck. A lot of turkey to get through suddenly sounded the loneliest words there are.

Chapter Fifty-Seven

Gran looked happy and serene when they left her at the Home just after Christmas. Only Sophie was in tears and Zet, as she crashed the gears starting the car, was finding it difficult not to join her.

'It seems a nice place. Comfortable. The staff really care, Sophie.' She heard Sophie's sobs beside her.

'I feel like a murderer.'

Zet turned out of the Home's car park on to the road. 'You couldn't cope with it. I've got to earn a living, so I couldn't give her twenty-four hour care, and her kids are busy, too.' Waiting for a gap in the traffic, Zet knew it sounded wrong. They loved Gran, why had they no time to care for her? Reasonably, she supposed that it was women's change of circumstances; they were no longer stay at home housewives with time to support elderly relatives. Guiltily, she pressed her aunt's hand. 'She's not safe to leave for a moment.' It was true, but still....

There was a sniffing silence as they both mourned the deterioration of Gran... the sour, soiled smell when she had always been so sweet...the way she sometimes didn't recognise her own feet...the way she bumped into doors. But worst of all was the undressing... stripping off her clothes in front of anyone. Left alone, she was likely to wander into the street naked.

'Wasn't it awful telling David?' Sophie gulped as the car moved off. 'He couldn't make out why she didn't know him on the phone.'

They were stopping and starting along the busy Saturday high street; shops ransacked before Christmas were displaying sale signs, people were queuing at Woolworth's for lottery tickets. Gran's favourite place, the shops. Zet, heart aching, could almost see her, bobbing about in the crowds, laden with bags of goodies mostly bought for others. And now....

Zet felt stabbed in the heart. Stuck behind a Safeway's lorry, the car slid to a halt outside the great stone Odeon, and with a pang, Zet saw them, for a moment she was sure she saw them...the ghosts of two lovers, Iris and Maurice, on the steps. It was a bingo club now. Once it had been a cinema, before that a variety hall where Gran had lost her reputation.

'She has her radiogram, Sophie.'

Sophie blew her nose. 'But she doesn't know how to put the records on.'

'They have concerts and singsongs around a piano. Gran will like that.'

Sophie sounded brighter. 'She will, won't she?' ''Course she will.' The car lurched on and Zet, feeling sick, turned her mind to David. She had told him how Gran often smiled. 'I think that in her mind she's somewhere nice, David. She sings a song, over and over. Something about...*We'll meet again*. You gave her a wonderful time when you came over. Hang on to that.'

He made no plans to return to England and Zet wondered how you could feel the loss of someone you hardly know. 'We'll visit Gran often, Sophie. We can do that.'

Everyone else seemed to be making plans; for the first time in her life, Zet had none.

Alyson had begun working on Saturdays helping to organise the Romanian trips and was collecting information for her trip to India. Not only that, she informed Zet she would no longer eat meat. She didn't expect Zet to have two lots of meals to prepare, in future she would look after herself, she said, nose stuck in a vegetarian cookery book.

Darren talked about eventually going to Durham University. 'Why Durham?' Zet asked, feeling ripped apart.

320

'I liked it in the north,' he explained. She recognised concern for her, in his eyes but also the longing to have something back that had been good. He hesitated. 'Anyway,' he added gruffly, 'my mate's older brother goes there and he says it's brill and if I do get to be a vet Yorkshire would be a great place to work.'

He sounded as if his mind was made up. He was the sort who made a plan and stuck to it. He was also kind, and was becoming protective; she must make sure that he didn't take responsibility for her. He had his own life.

'You'll make it, Darren.' Her warm smile showed, she hoped, that she would be fine and that she was proud of him. Looking relieved, he smiled back.

Jonty came round to discuss taking the children abroad to get some winter sun. 'Something I always wanted to do,' he told the pale skinned Zet. For some reason, she felt crushed.

While he was there, he sat in his old chair, crossed his legs, his ankle bobbed so she knew he had something uncomfortable to say. It sounded, when it came, like a confession.

'I'm leaving the firm.' Before she could ask, he told her, 'I'm joining Shelter.'

'Shelter? You won't make money there.'

'Hope you're wrong.' He looked at her with his familiar wrinkled brow. 'They're expecting me, with my experience, to do just that. But not for me, for the homeless.'

Zet couldn't believe what was happening. She still felt bewildered by it all when, in an attempt to comfort Sophie, who had the distressing job of clearing out Gran's clutter, Zet took her up West. Danny had sent two tickets for his show at the Palladium, and Zet thought a good laugh would do Sophie good. It did more than that.

321

Going backstage afterwards, Zet was amused to see how Sophie became animated with Danny and his friends, especially one, a short, grey-haired, kind-but- shrewd-eyed man who was introduced as Gerry, nick- named Pinkie, semi retired theatrical agent; he seemed to find Sophie comfortable to be with.

'Married but not living with,' Sophie explained cheerfully two days later when Zet was going through Gran's things with her. 'Fancy me, up West, mixing with the stars, going to that posh Italian restaurant in Soho.' There was a pause. 'Wouldn't Iris be envious.'

'Watch yourself,' Zet warned.

'What do you mean? I'm fine. Thank God for HRT. It's you I'm worried about.'

'I'm a bit under the weather. It's quiet here, with Darren and Alyson in Tenerife with Jonty and...er... Frankie. I thought of going away for a few days.'

'But Danny invited us up West to a party. He particularly wanted you to come. He said he has a surprise for you.'

Zet's face softened, but she shook her head. 'Give him my love, Sophie.' She wondered why her aunt looked so distressed, her lips were moving the way they did when she had something to say. Zet stared at her and Sophie gave in to temptation.

'I'm not supposed to say,' she said in a rush, 'But your Brad will be there.'

Zet remained calm. 'He's not my Brad any more. Neither do I want him to be.' Her over-romantic aunt looked disappointed. 'That's all water under the bridge,' Zet told her. 'We're strangers now; maybe,' she sighed, 'we always were.'

Sophie was looking at her curiously. With a pang, Zet recognised that her fascination for Brad had drained away. How ironic. So she stuck to her decision. 'I need to be away from here, alone, to think. By the way, don't tell anyone where I'm going.'

Sophie looked indignant. 'I can keep a secret, you know.' She opened a black plastic bag and put her hand inside. 'Look what I found while I was clearing out.'

She pulled them from the bag, one by one…colourful battered boxes; there was ludo, snakes and ladders, and a worn pack of Happy Family cards, among others.

'Oh, Sophie.' With a lump in her throat, Zet said, 'chuck them away. You and your games.'

Sophie sighed too. 'Yes, me and my games.' She looked rueful. 'We are what we are,' she said, throwing the boxes without ceremony into the bag and twisting the top closed.

Chapter Fifty-Eight

It was still there, the lonely wind-bashed Tan Hill inn, standing as if waiting for her, in frozen solitude, with the rest of the world falling away at its feet. Chimney smoke rose to mingle with grey clouds. Zet had ten thousand acres to herself. Not silent, though, what with the scream of raw winter wind cutting through the heather and the indignant rage of birds.

Icy rain started to lash down; wind pushed the hood from her head and tugged at her hair. Battling her way to the inn, her red anorak filled out like a balloon.

She was sitting in the deserted bar when she heard a car draw up. A moment later hurried footsteps tapped on the stone floor of the outer porch. The heavy oak door swung open. The bored landlord looked up from reading the newspaper and grinned. 'Happy New Year, Mr. 'Ardstone.'

'Happy new year,' came the curt answer, restless dark eyes sweeping the room until they alighted upon the startled, rain soaked waif beside the big grate.

Disturbed by the draught, the fire leapt, sparks burst from its heart and flames reddened the drawn pallor of her face, accentuated the purple shadows beneath eyes that looked as if they had seen a ghost. He pushed the door closed and the fire quietened. With the sea roar of the wind and the screech of curlews shut out behind thick, safe walls, Brad walked towards her.

'I went to Danny's party yesterday. Your aunt told me you were here.'

'You've had a long journey.' Six years long.'

'You look tired, Brad. Come and sit by the fire.' 'Sorry about Iris,' he said, sitting down. 'I liked her.'

In answer to her unspoken question... 'Sophie told me.' His tone said that Sophie had talked a lot.

Brad gulped down the hot coffee the landlord brought him. 'You were supposed to be at the party.'

'I knew about Danny's surprise. I mean, that you were it.'

He looked impassive. 'Not just me,' he told her. 'Danny wanted you to meet someone. He wanted to tell you he's happy now.' Zet heard his voice change. 'The person who makes him happy is called Sean.'

Hearing his sigh, Zet understood a lot of things. 'I'm glad for Danny.'

His thick brows drew together. 'You didn't want to meet me again?'

She swallowed her wine. 'I thought I did, a while ago. I thought that if I faced you, I would accept that you were violent enough to kill, and see you as you really are,' she said coldly.

She saw him move back as if she had hit him. 'I don't understand.'

Zet shivered. 'Jonty almost died.'

'I know. I felt guilty in a way.' She stared at him, not hiding her disgust, especially as he relaxed back in his chair and looked innocently sheepish.

'Zet, I'm ashamed to admit it, but....'

He actually smiled. 'Forget it,' she snapped. But she had been right. She felt sick.

Staring into her face, he clinked his cup down into the saucer. 'Listen.' He sounded so urgent that she did. 'After you nagged me about killing things, I sold my guns. I didn't tell you.' He shrugged and looked away. 'I felt like a wimp. But I knew you hated the thought of me killing things.'

'Brad. I'm talking about people,' she emphasized, pushing the images away, 'not birds and animals.'

'I'm not with you.'

Her voice hated him. 'Shooting at Jonty.'

He recoiled. 'You mean you thought it was me?' There was no doubting the shock on his face. She looked down into her blood red wine, feeling the first stirring of doubt.

'I see.' His voice was bitter. He took a moment to pull himself together. 'I don't know why you were never informed by the police, but I suppose you'd already left the area when....'

She glanced up at him, alert. 'When what?'

His mouth tightened. 'Some poor bugger from a mental hospital had been sent out to live in the community. He couldn't cope. He took pot shots at cars; he was caught when he killed a local farmer bringing his kids home from school.'

Hearing her gasp of horror, he added, 'the kids were unharmed, but....'

She closed her eyes; one hand went up to shield her face. He was appalled at how white she had gone. Her hand was shaking and he reached out, brought it down and held it between his two hands. 'Come on, Zet. It's okay.'

With her free hand, she lifted her glass and gulped down the wine. 'That poor family.' There was a stunned look on her face; she looked so dreadful, he went to the bar and ordered two brandies.

When he returned with the drinks to the fireside table, he pushed her drink towards her, taking a sip of his own. 'So you've hated me all this time?'

'I tried.' As they sipped their drinks, Zet felt herself return to normal. It was as if the passion had never been. It was like meeting each other again as strangers. It was a time for being honest. She forced a smile. 'Then there were all your women.'

'No more than any normal unattached man,' he said with a taut smile. 'They'd make good journalists around 'ere. If they don't know, they make it up.

They'll all be curious now why I've taken the house off the market.'

'You're not moving then?' she asked, and he shook his head.

'I was going to stay with Danny for a bit, in that flashy docklands penthouse.'

'You won't like it.' She hesitated. 'Mary might like it.'

His brows rose. 'Mary? She's in America, got a job over there. I went with her to introduce her to my daughter, show her around. You're right about London, though. I had to come back.'

She felt a settling sensation. A man and a woman talking in a pub. Ordinary and normal and she mentally thanked God for it.

She sighed. 'Me too. It calls me, this place. It always has, I think.'

He studied her with friendly interest. 'What do you plan to do?'

'Nothing planned at the moment.' She looked down at her empty glass. 'I've been there…all those plans. I just want....'

When she hesitated, he gently finished for her....'To see which way the wind blows.'

'Yes. Obviously I need to make a home for the children to come back to during their holidays and....' She looked at him, wondering whether to say anything.

'And?'

'I do have just one thing planned, actually. It's a new discovery. Something....'

'Good?' he asked, when she hesitated.

She nodded. 'It won't interest you, though.' 'Try me.'

'I want to open my own holistic clinic.' She explained about hands on healing, the Healing training courses she would take, the sort of people she would work with.

He looked as surprised as she had expected him to, but he recovered quickly, and the disappointment in his eyes drew her to place her hand over his.

'It's a gift I have, I'm grateful for it and can't waste it.'

He nodded. 'I remember how you could soothe. I felt better with you,' he said, and there was a wealth of meaning in his voice.

She felt his skin beneath her hand. 'Yes, but I understand that you're fully recovered now, Brad?' He looked at her intently.

'From the heart attack, yes.' There was an expectant silence.

Gently she removed her hand. 'For the moment, I'll just wait and....'

'See which way the wind blows?' He nodded. Sighed. 'Right.'

Hearing the wind bashing against the windows, she faintly smiled. Helping her on with her jacket, he said, 'As an old friend, am I allowed to pass on to you a lesson I learned the hard way?'

They called goodbye to the publican and walked to the door. 'You can try.' She pushed the door open and walked into the lobby. He was close behind her.

'We're all entitled to our dreams, Rosetta. Sometimes our dreams are for others, we get carried away.' She saw his eyes were dark and sad as he checked her face. What he saw there made him go on, 'But each of us must dream for ourselves. Dreaming for others not only risks ruining lives but steals their dreams, and this,' he said, as if his throat hurt, 'we have no right to do.'

She felt the stirring of compassion. Staring into his face she saw the lines there, lines of guilt, and knew this was a load he would always carry.

He read the questions in her eyes. Nodded. 'I had a dream, after I fell in love with you. But you had a dream, too. Our dreams were different. I had no intention of taking anything from you that you didn't offer.' He paused.

'I couldn't offer,' she cried. 'There was the family.'

He nodded. 'My son told me more about you than I knew myself.'

328

A long, probing stare passed between them. The wind pounded against the door as if trying to come in. Turning, she pulled the door open, walked outside. The rain had stopped. The wintry day glowed like the whites of smiling eyes. The force of the wind nearly took her breath away. Her 'goodbye' was whisked into the air to join the cry of the curlews that always sounded like laughter.

The moorland road twisted, rose and fell, like a snakes and ladders board, shiny from the recent rain. She followed his car, driving past remote stone villages and across moorland as far as the crossroads, where they would drive away in different directions, he to his house on the moors, she to the southbound motorway, a new life and her children, whom she would support in their own dreams and plans.

A weak sun appeared. She could see him ahead, slowing down at the crossroads; his arm came through the open car window. He waved goodbye. This would be the last goodbye. She knew she would never see him again. She would have no reason to return.

She saw that the signpost that once stood erect in the middle of the road was missing.

The signpost had always swung round in the wind, confusing tourists, but today it had been blown down; she saw part of it lying in a ditch. It was suddenly rather exciting, a rather free and wild thing.

She could just go the way the wind blows.

His house stood square and firm, like a welcoming friend. Smoke from the chimney was dancing in the wind, as if it didn't know which way to go. She turned on the doorstep before going inside, and pointed into the sky. It was a rainbow, faint and watery, as if the colours had run...but still a rainbow.

And here we'll stay, until it's time for me to go.

329